THE GLYN DŴR LEGACY

Also by Bill Bailey:

A Ha'porth of God Help

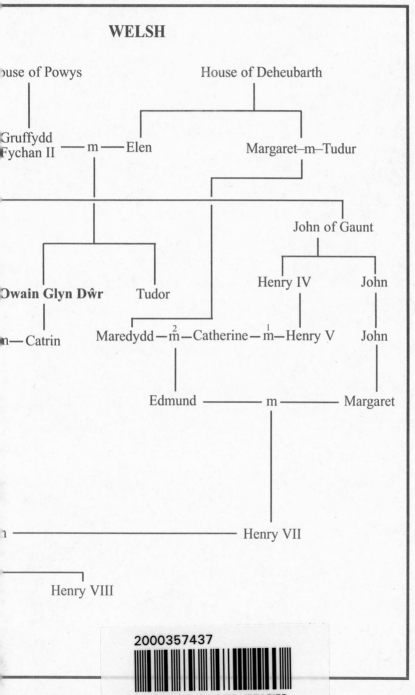

WELSH

the Glyn Dŵr Legacy

Bill Bailey

UNITED WRITERS
Cornwall

UNITED WRITERS PUBLICATIONS LTD
Ailsa, Castle Gate, Penzance, Cornwall.

British Library Cataloguing in Publication Data:
A catalogue record for this book is
available from the British Library.

ISBN 1 85200 098 8

Printed in Great Britain by
United Writers Publications Ltd
Cornwall.

To Jean, for her patience and encouragement.
My thanks too, to the National Library of Wales
whose Owain Glyn Dŵr exhibition provided
the inspiration.

Glendower Three times hath Henry Bolingbroke made head
Against my power; thrice from the banks of Wye
And sandy-bottomed Severn have I sent him
Bootless and weather beaten back.

Henry IV. Act III Sc i

Map of Wales

Chapter One

It was late spring in the year of our lord 1400 and a cool evening breeze ruffled the waters of the moat as a sturdy young man strode with the confidence of youth past meadows and orchards towards Sycharth Manor. The longbow he carried and the quiver on his back proclaimed him an archer, but his plain leather jerkin and helmet bore the arms of no lord and the set of his shoulders, the thrust of his chin, implied he held no man to be his master.

The man paused and leant on his longbow to look at the fortified manor on its motte within the moat. Gazing thoughtfully at its wooden palisade he was not unduly impressed and wondered whether its lord could afford much of a retinue. He sighed, as though almost regretting the impulse that had led him into leaving the service of Lord Mortimer, the Earl of March, at Ludlow Castle on the completion of his indenture there.

True it would be good to serve a Welsh noble and speak his native tongue again, but then most of the Mortimers' archers had been Welsh. With a shrug he cast the thought aside, it was only chance that had brought him here. If he could not find service with Owain Glyn Dŵr at Sycharth, the castle of Lord Grey of Ruthin was not much more than a few day's march away and the marcher lords always had room for a good Welsh archer.

With a wry smile Idris the Archer braced himself and, slinging his bow over his shoulder, set out towards the castle, thinking that at least he'd get a bed for the night there and, with luck, a meal and a pot of ale as well. As he approached the drawbridge a dark-visaged young man of about his own age came through the imposing gate-house to stand on the drawbridge as though to bar his way. No archer or man at arms this, his blue high necked tunic was of good Welsh cloth, his belt held by a golden clasp and he

9

stood there arrogantly, hand resting on his sword hilt, watching Idris approach. As Idris drew near the young man's lip curled and his nose twitched as though in distaste at Idris's travel worn appearance. Holding his hand up to halt Idris, he asked contemptuously, 'What do you seek here fellow, we want no vagrants here!'

Idris flushed and, shoulders back, chin thrust out, retorted, 'I come to seek service with Lord Owain Glyn Dŵr, not to listen to his minstrel whine!'

His face contorted, the young man stepped toward Idris, drawing his sword as he did so, and said angrily, 'No minstrel I, but Gruffydd ab Owain . . .'

Gruffydd had not finished speaking nor taken a full pace forward though before Idris's right hand flashed to his shoulder to instinctively draw an arrow from his quiver and stand menacing Gruffydd with his readied bow.

'Aye, no doubt,' he replied calmly, 'and a dead Gruffydd, lest you sheath that pig sticker of yours!'

Gruffydd's face paled, Idris was only a few paces away and that arrow would pierce mail at a hundred yards, let alone cloth at twenty! Obviously torn between prudence and loss of face, he hesitated, whilst Idris stood there unflinching as though awaiting a charge of French cavalry. Then, sullen faced and backing slowly along the drawbridge, Gruffydd sheathed his sword muttering as he did so, 'Service? You'll find no service here, wretch, unless it be as a swineherd!'

Idris gave a tight grin as he thought, that's right, my young lord, and a hungry bed by a hedge tonight for me as well, if only I can get safely away from here! His heart sank then, although his longbow remained unwavering, as he saw two men at arms come out of the gate-house. His concern was caused not by the sudden appearance of the men at arms, but by the presence of the man who led them. Dark complexioned and of powerful, stocky build, his grey, fur trimmed cloak served to emphasise broad shoulders. A single gold medallion spoke of wealth and authority. It was the sheer intensity of the eyes though, that transfixed Idris. Dark and deep set under heavy brows they took in the scene at the bridge in one glance.

There could be no doubt that this was Owain Glyn Dŵr, for here was a leader of men. Idris had long known that he was a man esteemed, indeed loved, by many amongst the Welsh. Respected too by the English if distrusted, for whilst all knew that he was as learned in law as he was an able soldier, it was known that he little liked the English governance of Wales.

As Owain Glyn Dŵr approached, Idris lowered his bow for he knew full well that whilst he could kill the two men at arms before they could rest a hand on him, it would be a death sentence for himself. Lord Owain paused by Gruffydd, sarcasm giving an edge to a voice that though clearly accustomed to giving orders could as easily coax success from those more powerful than he.

'Very wise, Gruffydd! Drawing your sword twenty paces from an archer is apt to get you skewered!' He turned to Idris with a droll, 'And you, archer! Would you lay siege to my manor alone? Put your weapon away and tell me what you seek here!'

Somewhat abashed, Idris replaced the arrow in its quiver and held his bow loosely at his side whilst wondering how long it would be before he found himself viewing the manor from one of its dungeons. The great man betrayed no emotion but Idris sighed to himself thinking that no doubt Lord Owain would remain just as unperturbed whilst ordering his execution. When at last he spoke though, he showed none of these fears as, head held high, he looked the Lord of the manor of Sycharth in the eye.

'No siege, my lord,' he said firmly. 'I sought only to protect myself, as any archer would, when this,' he hesitated, seeking a description of Gruffydd that would not offend, 'esquire drew his sword on me, when I came only to seek service with your lordship.'

Lord Owain had been watching him intently as he spoke and now, frowning, turned to look at Gruffydd for a moment before, without speaking, turning back to Idris. Stroking his black beard, his brown eyes piercing into Idris's very soul, he asked quietly, 'What do they call you, archer, and where do you hail from?'

'Idris, my lord, and some weeks past I served my Lord Mortimer at Ludlow Castle.'

Lord Owain nodded thoughtfully and turning to the men at arms, muttered something that Idris could not hear, before turning again to Idris to say, 'One of Lord Mortimer's archers, eh, and seeking service with me now? Well, my impetuous Idris, go with these men, they will show you to your lodging for the night, time enough to talk about service on the morrow!'

11

So saying he turned to rest his hand on Gruffydd's shoulder and lead him away through the gate-house and into the shadows beyond.

Idris looked warily at the two men at arms as they approached him, dungeon it was for him now, he was sure. He braced himself and brought his bow to his front, his right hand raised to his shoulder ready to draw an arrow from its quiver. The two of them he could take, there was little to lose now! As they came towards him one of them, hand casually resting on the dagger at his side said calmly, 'Come on now, Idris bach, Dafydd I am and it's not trouble we're looking for, not after you taking young Gruffydd down a peg or two like that. No, just a pot of ale tonight with us and service with our Lord Owain the morrow it is for you!'

As if to show his good intent, he took his right hand from his dagger and smiling, held it out in friendship towards Idris. Reluctantly at first, Idris loosed his grip on the arrow and cautiously stepped towards the man at arms. Reaching out to take the man's hand he found his own taken in a grip of steel and the dagger at his stomach. Triumphantly now, Dafydd said between clenched teeth, 'Now Idris bach, gently it is, or I'll have your guts to feed the crows!'

The other man, at Idris's side by now, took him by his other arm and, relieving him of his bow and quiver, said as he did so, 'You'll not need these where you're going!'

As Idris was led, struggling, through the gate-house and into the courtyard, he saw Lord Owain and Gruffydd walking towards the great hall. At that moment Gruffydd turned to look over his shoulder at Idris before, with a contemptuous sneer, turning away again. Seething with anger and frustration now, Idris's struggles became even more violent until Dafydd put the dagger to his throat.

'Enough!' he snarled. 'Lord Owain said for us to do you no harm, but you try my patience, archer!'

Then, with the dagger still at his throat, Idris was hustled through a doorway and down some stone steps before being thrust into a dank, windowless room with an earthen floor. The heavy oaken door shut behind him, the bolt slammed home and he heard the echoing laughter of Dafydd and his companion as their footsteps receded into the distance.

It took a few moments for his eyes to become accustomed to

the dim light afforded by the small barred opening in the door. What eventually he saw gave him little encouragement: the cell was about eight paces by twelve and the only furnishing was a scattering of straw of somewhat doubtful cleanliness against the far wall. Whether it was emanating from the straw or the growth of fungus on that wall, a damp, sour smell began to catch at the back of his throat and he coughed involuntarily.

Dejected, Idris sat down on the earth floor, his back against the wall to the side of the door, head flung back, eyes closed, arms hanging loose by his side. So much for service with Owain Glyn Dŵr he thought bitterly, happy enough I was serving my Lord Mortimer, why did I have to come here and meet that bastard Gruffydd? It was only chance that had led him there, chance and perhaps a little curiosity about Owain Glyn Dŵr, foremost amongst the Welsh gentry. Now it seemed that curiosity could well be satisfied at a high price.

His empty belly rumbled and he folded his arms across his stomach. He'd last eaten when he had broken his fast and at first sight of the manor he'd seen only a pot of ale, a hunk of bread and piece of cheese. Until he'd met that bastard Gruffydd that was! The long day's journey and the tensions of his arrival at Sycharth had taken its toll, his head drooped on his chest and gradually his thoughts became disjointed, as Idris the archer fell into an exhausted sleep.

Owain Glyn Dŵr stood with his back to the log fire smouldering in the hearth, hands clasped behind his back as he looked thoughtfully at Gruffydd. To Gruffydd, standing there apprehensively waiting for his father to speak, Lord Owain's stocky figure seemed to dominate the great hall of Sycharth manor. He did not know why it was so, but in his father's presence he always felt dwarfed and, fearing the expected rebuke, resentment rose like gall in his throat as he thought of his confrontation with the archer.

There was an ominous glint in Owain's brown eyes and those dark eyebrows drew together as he asked thoughtfully, 'What did you say to provoke the archer, Gruffydd?'

Gruffydd frowned as if hurt at the accusation. 'Why, nothing Father! I just asked him what business he had here and he answered me churlishly then threatened me with his bow! You saw the rest!'

'Aye, I saw the rest and had I not, your mother might now have been grieving for her son! Watch your tongue in future Gruffydd, no archer seeking service here threatens you so without some cause.'

Gruffydd flushed crimson. 'But Father . . .' he began, before Owain interrupted him.

'Enough! This night he'll cool his heels below, as a warning. On the morrow though, he'll enter service here,' he smiled now, but his eyes flashed warningly, 'and do not provoke our impetuous new archer, Gruffydd, I have a feeling you'll cross him at your peril!'

With a nod in emphasis, Owain turned away and strode off to his chamber leaving a furious Gruffydd glaring at his back.

The rattle of bolts being withdrawn brought Idris to wakefulness slowly, painfully, his whole body aching as a damp chill reached through to his very bones. As he rubbed his eyes the foetid air caught at his throat again and he almost retched. It was only that which made him realise where he was, for the faint glimmer of light from the barred opening in the door hardly enabled him to see the opposite wall of his cell. The door creaked open unwillingly and Dafydd entered the cell briskly and kicked Idris's outstretched feet.

'On your feet, archer! My Lord Owain would have words with you,' he paused then added, 'before he has you hanged no doubt!'

Idris, remembering the stratagem by which he'd been brought to the cell by Dafydd, glared up at him resentfully and, without stirring, muttered, 'I trust it is many words then!'

Dafydd merely replied irritably, 'Come on, my Lord Owain is not a patient man!'

Idris's only movement was to raise his eyes to Dafydd. 'Nor I impatient to meet my gallows!'

Surprised that his hands were not being bound and that Dafydd appeared to be alone, he reluctantly got to his feet. Resting his hand on Idris's shoulder familiarly, Dafydd led him out of the cell and up into the courtyard where the early morning spring sunlight almost blinded Idris after the gloom of his cell. He stood there blinking for a moment until the pressure of Dafydd's hand on his shoulder urged him on across the courtyard and into the kinder light of the great hall.

Entering the hall, Idris paused as he saw Owain Glyn Dŵr seated in a high backed chair at the far end of the hall, with a scowling Gruffydd standing by his side. Owain was not scowling though, just sitting there, hands resting on the carved arms of the chair, gazing calmly at Idris, as though his judgment had already been given.

Dafydd silently urged him on again, then his hand fell away to rest on the hilt of his sword as they walked towards Owain. Idris, conscious of the dirt on his face, the sleep in his eyes, nervously brushed back the russet hood of the short scalloped cape that covered his shoulders and ran his hand through his black hair.

Gruffydd stood there glaring arrogantly at Idris, a hand resting on his father's chair, a heavy gold chain around the high neck of his brown surcoat, his short, black hair uncovered. There could be no doubt that Owain was his father. Despite the difference in age one could see they were from the same mould. They both had black hair, brown eyes, the same nose, the same imperious thrust of the chin. No, there was no doubting Gruffydd's claim to be ab Owain!

As Idris drew near, Owain Glyn Dŵr raised his hand gently without taking his forearm off the arm of the chair and Dafydd tugged quietly, needlessly, at Idris's jerkin and they both stopped. No longer nervous, Idris frowned, wondering why both Owain and his son seemed so familiar as though he had known them both somewhere, sometime, before. Involuntarily he shrugged and almost smiled as he thought that if so, it was not an acquaintance that was likely to be renewed for long.

Behind Owain Glyn Dŵr, dust glistened in the light from a great stained glass window at the end of the hall as he sat there for a moment, looking at Idris without speaking before glancing quickly at Gruffydd, almost as if comparing the two young men. Idris imagined he saw Owain give an imperceptible shake of his head before turning again and saying gruffly, 'So, Idris the archer, you came here seeking service with me! After a night as my guest, is that still your wish?'

Idris could hardly believe his ears. No gibbet for him after all, it seemed! His eyes brightened at the thought and his chin lifted.

'I've not eaten since I broke my fast yester-morn, my lord. For a meal and a pot of ale, I'd raise my bow for the devil himself.'

Owain Glyn Dŵr frowned, fingers drumming the arms of his chair for a moment, then he glanced from Idris to Gruffydd and back again before he spoke, his words all the more menacing because of the softness of his voice, 'And you raise your bow, or any weapon, to one of mine again you'll find yourself truly serving with the legions of hell, and happy enough to be there after I've done with you! Now get you to your quarters and cleanse yourself, you smell as though you've been quartered in a cesspit!'

With an indignant frown, Idris opened his mouth to speak, but before he could do so, Dafydd took him by the arm and hustled him out of the great hall. As they got out into the courtyard, Dafydd shook his head as if in despair.

'What's up with you, Idris,' he asked, 'do you want to get yourself hanged? There's Owain Glyn Dŵr taking you into service after you threatening his son like that, an' all you want to do is stand there an' argue with him!'

'It was him!' blurted Idris. 'Telling me I smelt like a cesspit when it was because I'd spent the night in his bloody filthy dungeon!'

'Aye,' nodded Dafydd, 'an' my lord's mercy that was, letting you cool off so you could save your neck!'

His nose wrinkled then and stepping back from Idris his head fell back and, pointing at Idris, he guffawed, 'Right he was though Idris, smell just like a cesspit you do! Follow me, I'll show you where you can get some water,' and he laughed again as he added, 'but keep your distance, mind!'

Chapter Two

As the door of the great hall closed behind Idris, Gruffydd shook his head angrily and strode over to the hearth, to stand before it, arms folded, lips compressed, eyes blazing more fiercely than the logs on the fire. His head on one side, Owain watched him for a moment with an amused smile, before saying quizzically, 'You do not seem to approve of the archer being taken into service, Gruffydd?'

Glowering, Gruffydd remained silent as though not daring to speak, then exhaled a long held breath before saying tersely, 'No, Father! He should have had a good whipping for his insolence, then been sent on his way and lucky he'd have been at that!'

Owain laughed. 'What! Would you whip a man for following his trade, Gruffydd? Short on grace he is, I grant you, but mettle enough to hold his ground despite the hazard! He'll hold no grudge though . . .' he paused, ' . . . and I would that you held none either!'

Gruffydd remained silent for a moment whilst looking at the fire truculently, then turning to his father muttered with evident reluctance, 'As it pleases you, Father!'

Owain tossed his head in evident exasperation. 'Come now, Gruffydd, just two young bulls meeting head on and neither wanting to give way, that's all it was! Nothing to make a blood feud over! Like enough you are in age and temper, I think,' he paused and, frowning, added, 'aye and like enough in looks too.'

Mouth open and eyebrows raised in astonishment, Gruffydd looked at him in horror. 'What? That . . . that smelly, filthy wretch . . . like me?'

Owain threw his head back, roared with laughter and rising, went over to Gruffydd and slapped him on the back. 'Offended

17

you, have I? If you'd spent the night in our guest room below, you'd not be smelling like your mother's rosewater either! Now away with you, I leave for Glyndyfrdwy in an hour.'

Somewhat mollified now, Gruffydd gave a weak smile and there was almost a note of apology in his voice as he replied, 'No, Father, I suppose not, but what takes you to Glyndyfrdwy?

Owain frowned, his face darkened. 'I see the Lord Grey of Ruthin two days hence about my common land at Croesau which he has seized.' His voice rose in sudden anger, 'That land has been in our family for generations, I'll see him in hell before he takes it from me! Be he English marcher lord or no, I'll keep what's mine!'

It was Gruffydd's turn to be the pacifier now. 'Of course you will, Father, you have just title, I'm sure he'll see that.'

Owain snorted angrily, 'Just title! Little heed he's paid to that thus far. I'll not be robbed by some English thief though! I did not misspend my time at the Inns of Law in London, I know the laws of England as well as I know the code of Hywel Dda and I'll not be cheated! I'll take my plea to King Henry himself if needs I must!' Pursing his lips, he shook his head and added thoughtfully, 'I'd rather it was King Richard to whom I took my plea though, I served him well in his Scottish wars and he favoured the Welsh more than does this Lancastrian usurper!'

'Usurper or not, Father, Henry now wears the English crown! He'd not favour your plea if you addressed him as usurper rather than majesty, or liege lord!'

Owain glanced sideways at his son and smiled. 'Think you so? Well, fear not, tongue in cheek, I'd kneel to the prince of darkness himself and call him majesty if it would secure my land from that thief Ruthin!'

Gruffydd replied thoughtfully, 'King Henry is but like yourself, Father, he was aggrieved over land! When his father, John of Gaunt died, Richard dispossessed him of his inheritance and exiled him to boot! Little wonder that he took advantage of Richard's campaign in Ireland to regain his land and then, because of Richard's weakness, to seize the throne. Anyway, John of Gaunt was Richard's uncle, so Henry Bolingbroke was in line of succession to the English crown, howsoever remotely.' He laughed. 'What matters it to us, one Englishman or another on the throne, an Englishman will still be Prince of Wales and has been

18

ever since Llewellyn!'

Owain smiled indulgently. 'True enough Gruffydd, with Llewellyn killed in battle and the deaths of his brothers Dafydd and Rhhodri afterwards, Welsh independence suffered a blow from which it never recovered. We've had English Princes ever since, for a house divided is ever weak and the Welsh gentry are indeed divided, owing what little they have to their English sovereign.'

He paused and stroked his beard meditatively. 'It is beyond doubt though, that Edward's grandson, Richard, was the true successor to the English throne and English or no, Gruffydd, he was thought well enough of by our Welsh gentry.' He gave a wry smile. 'Better the devil you know, perhaps it was, but we'd all come to terms with . . .' he shook his head and paused, seeking the right word, ' . . . reality I suppose. None of us trusted each other any more than we trusted the English and Richard was liked well enough, for an English King. A house divided: that's always been our trouble in Wales, Gruffydd! Only Llewellyn was ever strong enough to unite the Welsh gentry and he had traitors enough within! So we all gained what we could and held what we gained, be it from an English King or a Welsh Prince as our liege lord.'

Gruffydd looked at his father indignantly, as though Owain had committed an act of betrayal. 'But, Father, surely one day we'll have our own Welsh Prince again?'

Owain shook his head slowly. 'Not in our lifetime, I fear, Gruffydd: not with the wealth and size of England and the way they've strategically placed castles across Wales. Owain Lawgoch, from the princely house of Aberffraw, was the last hope of that. A brilliant soldier he was, who'd served the King of France. He had French support when he set out to take Wales from the English Crown, but he only got as far as Guernsey before French enthusiasm for the campaign waned.

'Twenty-two years ago now it is since the English had him murdered . . . well, so it is said, although a Scot it was who did the deed. Owain Lawgoch was the last of the House of Aberffraw . . . and the last Welshman who sought to be Prince of Wales, there is not likely to be another now. No, Gruffydd, we must make what peace we can with our old adversaries, gain what we can, hold what we can. If we thus deceive them, it is no deceit to deceive deceivers and Henry would deceive us that he is king.'

Whilst Owain was speaking, Gruffydd had been growing increasingly impatient and when at last Owain paused, said angrily, 'But, Father! You are descended from all the Princely Houses of Wales, from Hywel Dda and Llewellyn the Great, even from Caradoc of ancient fame! If anyone should be Prince of Wales, it is you! What has compromise gained you and all the rest of the Welsh gentry? A minor castle here, a manor there with some poor hillside grazing land! The great castles in Wales are all English held and only the English have rights of citizenship in the towns around them. The best land along the marches is farmed by English farmers for English lords. And that is *compromise*, gaining what we can? We only hold what crumbs fall from the English table, so be damned with compromise!'

Owain laughed. 'If you would have me be Prince of Wales, Gruffydd, turn not too many archers away from my door whilst I am away, mayhap I'll have need of them!' Laughing now, he patted Gruffydd on the shoulder. 'But lest there's any more such talk of treason, I'd best be off to Glyndyfrdwy, for I am content with a castle here and a manor there, however small you may feel that inheritance to be!'

Gruffydd flushed, shook his head in denial and said quietly, 'I'm sorry, Father, I meant not that . . .'

Owain smiled and punched him on the arm. 'I know you meant no ill, Gruffydd, but have a care when you speak so of the English: most of the Welsh gentry, including us, have some English blood in their veins! You know well, too, that Sir John L'Estrange was my father's ward. I am esquire to the King himself and hold my land, the land of our ancestors, from the English Crown.' He winked and with a proud nod, added, 'And few enough of the Welsh gentry can say that! Their land has been fragmented at each generation through the gwelau, our Welsh laws of succession. One day when you inherit the lordships of Cynllaith Owain, Glyndyfrdwy and my manors in Cardiganshire, you will have good cause to be pleased that English law applied.'

Gruffydd frowned and his eyes clouded as he replied, 'I pray that day may be long distant, Father.'

Owain smiled reassuringly. 'Aye, I know that! Now, you've delayed me long enough: we can talk more on these things when I return from Ruthin, eh?

*   *   *   *

Gruffydd and Catrin, his younger sister, stood by their mother's side in the courtyard to watch Owain, accompanied by a small mounted escort, set out for Glyndyfrdwy. Lady Marged seemed concerned as she turned to Gruffydd.

'I worry, Gruffydd, lest your father reins not his temper as well he does his horse when he meets Lord Grey.'

Gruffydd smiled. 'Have no fear, Mother,' he said reassuringly. 'Father will guard his tongue and rely on his knowledge of the law rather than choler to settle the dispute.'

Marged favoured him with a wry smile. 'You know him less well than I thought you did then, Gruffydd! He'd sooner throw down the gauntlet to Lord Grey over this dispute than fence with him over the niceties of English law!'

Turning, she smiled as if she had not a care in the world or a thought in her head and waved farewell to her lord with her kerchief. Looking at her as she did so, Gruffydd thought how well her rich, green silk dress became her. Emphasising as it did her full figure, it was almost in itself a statement of her rank as the lady of a minor marcher lord. He glanced at the slight figure of Catrin and smiled fondly at her. Barely sixteen, she was his favourite despite, perhaps even because of, her waywardness.

His smile vanished and he frowned, no doubt Catrin was waving to their father, but why was her smile directed at the nearest of the archers? His face hardened into a scowl as he saw that it was Idris who was smiling broadly in return. Annoyed that the archer was already so well favoured as to be chosen as one of Owain's escorts on this important mission, Gruffydd hissed, 'Catrin! Stop smirking at that archer fellow!'

Catrin and her mother turned towards him in unison and Catrin said innocently, 'I was but bidding farewell to Father, Gruffydd!'

Her mother just smiled indulgently, before saying mockingly, 'Your father not through the gateway yet, Gruffydd and you're lord of the household already!'

Gruffydd flushed indignantly. 'Catrin is young, Mother, but old enough to know that she is a lady and should not be familiar with Father's soldiery!'

Lady Marged's eyebrows arched and, with a mischievous smile on her lips, replied, 'Quite true, Gruffydd, and you are wise

21

beyond your two years advantage to tell her so . . .' Her jocular tone changed to one of urgency, 'But your father salutes, Gruffydd!'

He turned and looked towards the gate-house just as his father turned in his saddle and Gruffydd raised his hand in salute. Then, with a clatter of hooves and accoutrements, Owain and his escort were across the drawbridge and setting off at a swift canter down the gentle slope beyond to begin the long journey to Glyndyfrdwy.

Gruffydd walked out onto the drawbridge to see them on their way and stood there until they were lost to sight as they turned onto the track leading northwards. Turning, he walked back pensively into the courtyard, still seeing in his mind's eye Idris the archer smiling back at Catrin. The insolence of the man galled him and he was furious with Catrin for encouraging the archer . . . and there was no doubt in his mind that she had done so. Determining that he would have a quiet word with Catrin, preferably not in the presence of his mother, he walked across the courtyard and into the great hall.

Catrin was standing there talking animatedly to Iolo Goch, the poet minstrel, but she turned as Gruffydd entered and blushed. With a nod to Gruffydd, Iolo walked over to his harp in the far corner of the hall and began to play softly, smiling at Catrin as he did so.

She was smiling too as Gruffydd approached.

'I thought you wanted to go to Glyndyfrdwy with Father, Gruffydd?'

They were not the most placating words she could have chosen, for he had been hurt when Owain had rejected his request. Under Welsh law it was four years now since he had come of age at fourteen and he had seen it as his right that he should be involved in such matters. His father had thought otherwise though.

'No Gruffydd,' he had said when asked. 'One of us must stay and watch the hen-house lest the fox steals the chickens whilst we are away!'

Annoyed, Gruffydd had replied tersely, 'There have been no border raids these few years since, Father, and you'll be keeping an eye on Lord Grey!'

Owain had grimaced and said quietly, 'It is after long periods of peace that the unwary are slain in their beds, Gruffydd!' He smiled to soften the blow. 'You'll be my seneschal whilst I'm away, eh?'

Gruffydd frowned at the memory and his voice had an edge as he answered Catrin sharply, 'No, but that's not what I wanted to talk to you about, Catrin!'

His sister, unlike her English mother, had surprisingly blue eyes and as she looked at him now, her eyebrows raised in surprise, there was anger in her voice: 'Why do you speak to me so, Gruffydd, am I your servant now, you my lord?' She paused there and, her anger melting, she began to giggle. 'I know! You're still angry about that archer!' Shaking her head dismissively, she continued, 'Don't be silly, Gruffydd, I only smiled at him because he smiled at me . . . and because when he did he looked like you, at least when you smile!'

This was the second time he had been told that the archer looked like him and he liked it even less now than he had the first time. His lips creased into a thin line and his eyes smouldered. 'I speak to you like this rather than it be our father who speaks to you, Catrin!' he began angrily, to add with his lip curling: 'Ladies of our household do not ogle archers like some camp follower. It is neither good for their honour nor for the discipline of our Father's soldiery.'

Eyes wide in astonishment, her face flushing redly, Catrin snapped, 'I wager a smile from me will not debauch our Father's soldiery beyond his limits of control, although I have no doubt it would yours! As for my honour, brother, if a smile from me is seen as besmirching that, then that is no problem for me albeit, it seems, for you!'

With that, Catrin picked up her skirts and flounced out of the great hall, leaving a speechless Gruffydd standing there, less confident now in his temporary role of seneschal and head of the household than he had been at the commencement of the conversation.

Chapter Three

Owain and his escort set out from Glyndyfrdwy at first light but it was noon before the party arrived in sight of Ruthin Castle and the small town that huddled below it for protection. The castle's squat bulk seemed to glower at them menacingly now as they approached, its keep towering above the square curtain walls. The round towers that stood like sentinels at the corners and either side of the gate-house were reflected in the wide moat surrounding the castle that glistened calmly in the spring sunshine. To Idris's surprise the drawbridge was being raised even as they drew near and Dafydd turned to Owain and exclaimed in his gruff voice, 'It seems we are not welcome here, my lord!' He grinned. 'What now, do we set up camp and lay siege?'

Idris thought this attempt at humour somewhat misplaced and indeed, it seemed only to have irritated Owain Glyn Dŵr who responded with a scowl, 'Save your breath, Dafydd, to hail the castle and gain entrance for me!'

Thus rebuked, the burly man at arms raised a massive hand to his mouth and threw back his head, to call in a voice fit to raise the dead, 'Hey there, within the castle! My Lord Owain Glyn Dŵr seeks entry to speak with your lord!'

The only sign of life they had seen thus far had been the creaking of the drawbridge as it was being raised and there was no movement from within now, nor was there any response to Dafydd's hail.

Idris watched Owain, who red-faced with choler, sat rigid on his mount, slapping the reins irritably against his left hand. His mouth was set in a thin line, his lips almost bloodless in their compression. At last Owain snapped, 'Hail them again, man! And this time put some body in it, don't whisper like some bloody nun in a convent!'

To Idris's amusement Dafydd, face as red as Owain's now, bawled again at the blank walls of the castle. It seemed for a minute or so that his efforts were to be of no more effect this time either. Then at last a helmeted head and mailed shoulders appeared on the tower to the right of the gate and, after surveying Owain's party for a moment, called down, 'Lord Ruthin grants audience to Owain Glyn Dŵr, but only he shall enter!'

The head and shoulders disappeared below the ramparts to be replaced by archers now on both towers of the gate-house and, as if at a signal, the drawbridge was lowered. Without command, Idris and his fellow archer leapt from their mounts to stand behind them, bows readied. Smiling, Owain raised his hand to them, palm outwards. 'What, would you give your lives so readily for your threepence a day? Put up your weapons men, I'll see the English bastard on my own, have no fear. "Grants audience" indeed! I'll stuff the words back down his throat and choke him!'

Dafydd sidled his horse up to Owain's and put his hand on his lord's arm with the familiarity of one who had shared his campaigns.

'Is that wise, my lord? Knowing them, it could as well be a trap as not!'

Owain grinned. 'Think you so, Dafydd? If I do not ride out of there in an hour, you have my permission to come in and get me, eh!'

With that, he flicked the reins against his mount's neck and set off at a canter across the lowered drawbridge and through the castle gate. Dafydd, the old campaigner, watched him go for a moment then, turning to the others, said sharply, 'We'll take cover in that copse where we can rest the horses.' As he led the way he looked over his shoulder at Idris. 'As well we watered the horses before we tasted the hospitality of Ruthin Castle!'

Laughing, Idris tapped the flask at his belt and replied, 'No doubt our lord will be met with wine and meat, but water it is for us, eh, Dafydd?'

Dafydd shook his head. 'No meat or wine he'll get there, nor want it! Lord Grey wouldn't give him water if he was dying of thirst and if he did, Lord Owain would throw it back in his face!'

Arriving at the shelter of the copse they dismounted and, as

b

they tethered their horses, Dafydd looked anxiously at the castle.

'I trust we'll not have long to wait, I'll not be content until Lord Owain is safely out of that thieves' den.'

Rhys, the man at arms who'd been with Dafydd the previous night, was standing by his horse, drinking some water from a flask whilst looking at the archers still manning the twin towers of the gate-house. Taking the flask from his lips he asked, 'What, not relishing earning your pay by going in after Lord Owain if he overstays his welcome, Dafydd?' He paused, mouth open, pointing at the castle with the flask and cried out urgently, 'Look, there's Lord Owain now!'

One look at Owain Glyn Dŵr galloping madly across the drawbridge as though the fiends were following and, without a word, they were hastily untethering the horses, mounting and racing towards their lord. Fast though he had galloped, Owain barely cleared the drawbridge before it was being raised, but still he had not reached safety, for all around him fell the steely fingered arrows from the archers on the gate-house towers.

Idris and Iestyn, his fellow archer, were now within range of the towers though, and dismounting, quickly replied to the assault on their lord. Without even pausing to glance at them, Dafydd and the other men at arms raced on. As well they did, for even as they came up with Lord Owain, a shaft from the towers felled his horse from under him and he lay there, his leg pinned beneath his dying mount. With arrows flying all around them, Dafydd and Rhys struggled to free Owain, whilst the other two men at arms futilely shook their fists at their assailants in the gate-house towers.

At last when Idris was almost despairing of Dafydd and Rhys freeing Lord Owain, there was a cry of pain from Owain and he was dragged free. Clutching with both hands the leg that had been under the horse, he was helped onto Rhys's mount and then, with Rhys up behind Dafydd, they were galloping towards the relative safety of the copse again.

Idris was still loosing arrows at the towers as Owain and the men at arms galloped past them. Notching another arrow, he said to Iestyn, 'One more and then back to the copse, eh, Iestyn?'

Idris watched the flight of his arrow as, straight and true, it winged its way to the tower and grimaced as he saw one of the archers there clap his hands to his face, then fall across the battlements. Idris turned to Iestyn but even as he opened his mouth to speak, Iestyn gasped and clutched at the arrow buried deep in his chest before, eyes glazing, he fell to his knees and slowly toppled sideways to the ground.

Idris hesitated for a moment, realising that Iestyn was dead, wondering what he should do, but knowing that he could not leave him lying there. Taking a deep breath he bent his knees and taking Iestyn in his arms, lifted him, to place him gently across the saddle of his horse before, with a last venomous look at Ruthin Castle, setting off to join the others.

It was a solemn group who made their way back to Glyndyfrdwy that afternoon, with Idris leading Iestyn's mount laden with the corpse of the dead archer. They rode in silence after Dafydd's first enquiry of Lord Owain as to what had happened in the castle to lead to his hasty departure.

'A trap was it, my lord?' he had asked. Then, as white-faced, Owain glanced at him without reply, Dafydd shook his head before continuing, 'I knew you should not have trusted them, should have sought safe conduct before you entered there!'

Lord Owain rubbed his right thigh before replying and when he did, Idris could see that his face was pale with fury rather than pain, his voice stiff with suppressed anger, 'God save me from your bloody preaching, Dafydd! When next I call upon Ruthin it shall be with main force and to linger long enough to leave my mark upon it!' He glanced at Idris. 'But now it's to Glyndyfrdwy for us and bury poor Iestyn there.'

He did not speak again, nor did they pause upon the way, until they reached the manor at Glyndyfrdwy, where they wearily dismounted, yearning only for food, drink and respite from the grim silence of their lord. As a stable lad took his horse, Owain glanced at Idris and said quietly, 'You did well today, young Idris and earned your pay.' His gaze now encompassing them all and smiling for the first time since he had entered Ruthin Castle, he added, 'You all did, and you shall be in the van when we call there again!' With that he turned and limped away to the great hall of the manor house.

Idris stood there for a moment and watched him go with mixed emotions: pleasure at his lord's praise and guilt . . . guilt over the death of Iestyn. He could still hear himself saying to his comrade, 'One more and then back to the copse, eh, Iestyn?' If only he'd

27

left well alone, Iestyn would be here now. He turned to look at Iestyn, to see that a small group had gathered, with Dafydd telling them of the day's venture. Hands were carefully lifting Iestyn off the horse now and Idris shook his head as he watched them carry the body away, I earned my pay today right enough, he thought, but no pay for Iestyn, is there?

At Sycharth the following day, Marged, called from her tapestry work, came into the great hall with Catrin from the far end as Owain Glyn Dŵr limped in from the entrance hall, his sword's scabbard slapping against his thigh. Frowning, her blue eyes anxious, she hurried over to him and rested a hand on his forearm.

'What ails you, Owain, what happened?'

He glanced at her ruefully before averting his eyes as he answered, 'My horse fell! I suffered no worse than a few bruises though and a leg that'll be stiff for a week or two!'

There was disbelief in Marged's eyes as she turned to Catrin. 'Wine for your father, Catrin and hasten, I think he needs salve for more than just bruises!' She was smiling as she turned back to Owain. 'And how came your horse to fall, Owain, did your friend Lord Grey have ought to do with that?'

He gave her an amused smile. 'Will you let a man have no peace after a hard day's ride, woman?' But, as she continued to gaze at him, eyebrows raised quizzically, he laughed. 'Aye, you could say that Grey did, one of his archers killed my horse from under me and one of my archers to boot!' They both turned in surprise at a sudden noise to see Catrin standing, blue eyes wide in alarm, hand to mouth, a tray hanging limply by her side. The pitcher and goblet she had brought lay shattered on the slate floor, the wine glistening around the fragments in a widening pool. Marged frowned, but Owain was the first to speak, saying with a laugh, ' 'Twas meant for me to drink, Catrin, but cry not over it, 'tis but a broken pitcher, not the crack of doom!'

It was as if she had not heard him. She still stood there with furrowed brow, her face pale in the dark frame of her hair and asked, her eyes pleading as if dreading his reply, 'You said one of your archers was killed at Ruthin, Father?'

Owain smiled understandingly and nodded slowly. 'Aye lass, that's right, he followed his trade and earned his pay as all such men must, one day.'

Catherine looked at him in horror, then, her voice high pitched with shock, she cried, 'Oh, Father . . !' and letting the wooden tray fall amongst the shattered fragments of the pitcher she turned and ran from the hall.

Owain turned to Marged, mouth open, his brown eyes wide in amazement. 'What on earth's the matter with the lass, Marged?'

She looked sideways at him for a moment before saying, with a touch of irony, 'Perhaps she did not think of an archer earning his pay just quite like that, Owain!'

Owain sighed, then smiling again, he shook his head in exasperation, as though realising that women, particularly young women, still did not understand the realities of life in the Welsh marches. Stroking his beard, he glanced at Marged.

'No, perhaps not, my love, perhaps not!' He grinned. 'But I'd still relish a goblet of wine after my journey!'

Blindly, Catrin rushed out of the great hall into the courtyard, still hardly able to believe that her father could be so callous over the death of the archer. She could still remember how the archer had smiled at her as he had rode out of this very courtyard with her father, but he had not come limping back like her father, he had not come back at all! Tears sprang to her eyes as she thought that he was only a boy, not much older than her and now he was dead!

Looking listlessly around the courtyard she started as, over in the far corner of the courtyard, she saw the archer unsaddling his horse. Catrin stared unbelievingly at him for a moment and then, almost as though he had felt her staring at him, he looked up and his face lit up with that same boyish smile he had given her as he had ridden out over the drawbridge. Her heart came to her throat and, without thinking she picked up her skirts and ran over to him, to look up into his eyes, reach out and touch him on the arm.

'Oh, you're safe,' she murmured. 'My father said . . . I thought . . .'

She lowered her eyes, her hand fell away from his arm and she stepped back a pace, unable to continue. He reached out and patted her upper arm, his brown eyes softening in understanding.

'It's all right, my lady, it's all right. I'm Idris. The archer who died back there was Iestyn, but it was kind of you to sorrow so, whoever fell.'

Catrin blushed crimson. 'I'm sorry, Idris . . .' she whispered, ' . . . I'm sorry for your friend!'

Turning, she hurried back whence she had come, leaving Idris gazing thoughtfully after her.

Idris, still standing there holding his saddle, was so lost in thought as he watched Catrin hurrying over to the hall, that he had not noticed Gruffydd striding purposefully towards him.

Not until Gruffydd was at his elbow and saying with a sneer, 'Tend to your horse archer and keep your eyes off my lady sister, or you'll yet have the whipping you earned the day you came here!'

Surprised, Idris turned his head quickly, his mouth opening to respond angrily, just in time though he saw the calculating look in Gruffydd's eyes and checked himself. Looking his lord's son calmly in the eye, he merely said quietly, 'I was but thinking it kind of your lady sister to say she sorrowed that Iestyn was killed at Ruthin, few such ladies would grieve an archer's loss in their lord's service!'

Gruffydd hesitated for a moment, lips pursed, eyes thoughtful now, as though unsure whether to believe Idris. Then, lips curled, he said with a sneer, 'Yes, just so! We could ill afford to lose Iestyn!' Turning away, he started to walk towards the hall, before glancing over his shoulder at Idris to add with a malicious smile, 'Now you though, that would be no loss!'

Idris gritted his teeth, holding back the angry retort that was on his lips, knowing that Gruffydd was deliberately trying to provoke him. He sighed, thinking that were he not now indentured to Lord Owain, he'd saddle up again and, horse thief or no, he'd be over that drawbridge and away! Shaking his head, he looked at Gruffydd's retreating back and mouthed a silent curse but then he saw that Catrin had reached the door to the great hall where she turned to smile at him.

With no thought of Gruffydd's warning now, he smiled too and raised his hand eagerly in acknowledgement, only to let it fall quickly as he saw Gruffydd stop in mid-stride, head turning quickly towards him. Idris, whistling innocently, began leading his horse away to the stables and Gruffydd turned back towards

Catrin, but she had disappeared inside. Idris glanced cautiously towards Gruffydd to see him hesitate and then, with an angry shrug, follow Catrin into the great hall. Idris smiled to himself, thinking I'll wager he has a word with my lady Catrin when he gets inside. The smile turned to a frown though as he thought of how it seemed that he had made an enemy of Gruffydd. He was still frowning as he led the horse into the stables. As he came out he met Dafydd and Rhys, who were grinning broadly at him, and Dafydd asked, 'Crossing swords with young Gruffydd again were you, Idris?' Nudging Rhys he added, 'I can see me and Rhys taking you down below again if you're not careful! What was it this time, you making eyes at the young maid, Catrin?'

Idris flushed and snapped, 'I'd not make eyes at the lord's daughter! She came over to me and said she was sorry about Iestyn, and Gruffydd . . . well, he was just trying to get me into trouble!'

Dafydd roared with laughter and turned to Rhys. 'Well, I suppose the last bit's true enough, Rhys, but the rest of it . . . well young Catrin wasn't smiling at her father when we left for Ruthin, was she, Rhys?' He winked at Idris. 'I reckon she's taken a fancy to you, boy, but you'd better watch your back though, or that Gruffydd will slip a knife in it while you're making eyes at his sister!' He slapped Idris on the back. 'Never mind, I know where there's a pitcher of mead, come along with us and we'll drink to Iestyn, God rest his soul!'

Chapter Four

There was great commotion in the courtyard of Sycharth manor: toing and froing of ostlers saddling horses and leading them towards the gate-house, dogs barking, a servant waiting with a stirrup cup for Lord Owain, and his family gathering to bid him farewell. Dafydd, Rhys and Idris, already mounted and waiting to escort Owain Glyn Dŵr, were chatting amongst themselves about the forthcoming journey. They were only to accompany him as far as Shrewsbury, for there he was to join with the Earl of Arundel's retinue for the remainder of the way to London.

Gruffydd was standing importantly by his younger brother, Maredudd, obviously conscious of the fact that, for the next two weeks at least, to all intents he would be the lord of the manor. Idris glanced at him as he stood there arrogantly, hand on sword hilt, stiff necked, for all the world as though he were the Prince of Wales' constable of Caernarvon Castle, rather than the temporary custodian of the fortified manor of Sycharth.

Idris hid his amusement, satisfied that at least for this day he would not be there to be at Gruffydd's beck and call, for no doubt there would have been many calls and few of them pleasant! He was looking forward to the journey too, he'd got to quite like Dafydd and Rhys and they would be amiable companions for the journey to and from Shrewsbury. He glanced at Dafydd who was helmeted, shoulders and throat encased in chain mail, his upper lip hidden by his drooping moustache, a wart prominent on his left cheek. Dafydd caught his glance, nodded and said with a wink, 'There she is now look, Idris, come to say goodbye to you she has!'

Idris looked in the direction of Dafydd's nod, to see the Lady Marged followed by Catrin and her sister Alice walking out of the great hall with Owain Glyn Dŵr. Lord Owain took a goblet from a servant and was drinking the wine chatting the while with Lady Marged. He looked a martial figure: like Dafydd, he too was helmeted and wore chain mail, with his sword in its worn leather scabbard at his side. No fancy court sword this, but one he had worn and used in battle against the Scots for King Richard.

Giving the goblet back to the servant Lord Owain smiled at Lady Marged and touching Catrin lightly on the arm, walked with them towards the gate-house and the ostler holding his horse. Pausing by Gruffydd and Maredudd, he stood there for a moment as though giving his sons some last minute instructions before, slapping Gruffydd on the shoulder, he mounted his horse and led his small retinue out of the gate-house. Turning in his saddle, he waved farewell and, as he did so, Idris also turned, to see Catrin and her lady mother smiling, their kerchiefs fluttering in the breeze in response.

Idris turned away, but as they rode across the drawbridge he smiled to himself, sure in his own mind that Catrin's smile had been only for him. The thought stayed with him as they made their way past the church and the mill by Afon Cynllaith then onto the track that led southwards towards the high road to Shrewsbury.

The track was narrow and they rode two by two, so Lord Owain and Dafydd led the way with Rhys and Idris following. Lord Owain was cheerful, his talk to Dafydd full of his coming journey to London with the Earl of Arundel and of making his plea to Parliament against Lord Grey of Ruthin's seizure of his common. It sounded to Idris almost as though Lord Owain were already returning in triumph to Sycharth, with his common restored to him and Lord Grey roundly rebuked.

'No, Dafydd,' Lord Owain said at last, 'I'll not have to take to arms against him to get my land back, border raiding's a thing of the past, the law is the way now – using the English law to get my Welsh land back off the English,' he laughed. 'It's not only cheaper, it pleases my humour!'

Dafydd gave him a sideways glance and snorted, 'Cheaper maybe, my lord, but I bear arms not for my few pence a day but for the spoils of war: little enough there was of that in Scotland and none since then!'

Idris and Rhys looked at one another, nodding their agreement:

after the little affray at Ruthin Castle and Iestyn safely buried they'd all half hoped for a punitive raid on Ruthin town and the chance of some booty.

Lord Owain laughed. 'This is the year of our Lord 1400 not 1300 Dafydd! The rule of law is with us now and we must live at peace with our neighbour, be he English or Welsh! For the loss of your "spoils of war" you'll reach old age to tell your grandchildren of battles long since fought and won!'

Dafydd was not to be appeased though.

'What, should I be a peasant then, my lord, to die at forty of short commons and hard toil? Nay, a soldier I since but a lad and sooner that than till the soil!'

Idris and Rhys both nodded again in their agreement. Neither caring for the villein's lot whether in Wales or England. Even though the shortage of labour since the great plagues had changed the relationships between lord and villein, the peasant who lived much beyond forty was a rarity and many died before then, worn down by hard labour and starvation diet. Neither Idris or Rhys had any hankering for that way of life.

Lord Owain glanced at Dafydd's robust, even portly, figure alongside him and grinned. 'I warrant that after short commons for a week or two, Dafydd, you'd wield your spear or sword with less weight but more agility!'

Dafydd grunted, 'A bit of weight behind the thrust never did anyone any harm, my lord!'

He looked around, frowning at Idris and Rhys who were both chuckling, and turned back to Lord Owain as he too joined in the merriment. At last Lord Owain, wiping his eyes, said 'Do you think not, Dafydd? I fear your weight will be the death of someone yet!'

Dafydd turned angrily on Idris and Rhys as they started to laugh again. As if it were a signal, they both rubbed the back of a hand across their face as though to wipe the smile off their faces and he turned away, still unsure of what was amiss.

After that Dafydd fell into a gloomy silence, whether at the laughter at his expense, or at the awful thought of peace on the Welsh marches, none knew. Lord Owain humouring him, they rode on in silence until they sighted the massive tower of the Church of St. Michael at Alberbury. They were well into England now and but a little more than an hours' hard riding to

Shrewsbury, so Lord Owain ordered a halt there to rest and water the horses whilst he went to pray in the Loton Chapel for the success of his mission.

It wanted two hours to noon when Lord Owain came out of the church unsmiling, to stride silently to his horse and mount up. All three of his retinue were aware that his erstwhile cheerfulness and joviality seemed to have been left behind him in the church, as though instead of strength or peace he had found there only a foreboding of mischance. They rode on in silence after that, Lord Owain's solemn mood seeming to have cast a cloud over all of them.

Entering Shrewsbury through the Westgate they made their way to the marketplace, where the Earl of Arundel's retinue had already arrived and were tending to their horses after their journey, the earl himself being then entertained by the burgesses. Lord Owain seemed to cast aside his gloomy mien as he dismounted for, to Idris's surprise, he was smiling as he handed his reins to Dafydd. Striding over to a grey-haired man attired in a fur trimmed travelling cloak and with a cross on a silver chain around his neck, Lord Owain held out his hand familiarly in greeting. 'Simon, the years treat you kindly!' His eyebrows rose then, his brown eyes puzzled, 'But I knew not that you were making the journey too?'

The older man gave a wry smile. 'My old bones would wish it were not so, but my lord the Earl desired my counsel on your plea whilst we journeyed, to better aid your cause.' As Owain frowned in his concern, Simon laid his hand on his arm. 'My old bones will bear it well, Owain, and I would see Lord Grey yield to you, so I journey gladly!'

As Idris watched, Lord Owain thanked the elderly cleric before turning to Dafydd to say, 'Return to Sycharth now, Dafydd, and make haste to see you get there ere nightfall!'

Idris smiled as he saw Dafydd's long face, no carousing in the stews of Shrewsbury for them if they were to reach Sycharth before dark! But Owain was smiling now, too, as he opened a pouch and threw a coin, to be deftly caught by Dafydd. Raising a warning finger to Dafydd, he said sternly, 'A pot of ale and a bite to eat for you all and then to Sycharth . . . tonight!

Dafydd touched his helmet with a finger and straight-faced replied, 'Tonight it is, my lord,' and handed the reins of Owain's horse to him. Then, with a wave of his hand, he led the others along a way obviously well known to him. As they walked their horses along the narrow street, Idris turned in his saddle, to see Lord Owain talking earnestly with the Earl's chaplain who was nodding slowly in reply. Idris smiled, it seemed Lord Owain was losing no time in rehearsing his plea!

Minutes later the three were dismounting in the courtyard of a small inn with gabled windows and bulging walls. A cheerful Dafydd led the way into the inn and Idris instinctively hunched his shoulders as he entered, fearing for his skull against the oak beams of the low ceiling despite his helmet. After the bright sunlight outside, it took some time for Idris's eyes to accustom to the dim interior of the inn, but Dafydd seemed to have no such difficulty, for he was already calling out for ale and meat.

Seating themselves on a bench by a heavy wooden table and easing themselves of their helmets, they stretched and yawned, relishing their leisure after the morning's hard ride. A surly potman appeared now and slovenly pushed three pots on the table, spilling ale on the table as he did so.

Short, potbellied and stubble chinned, he had a greasy apron around his waist, his soiled shirt open at the neck. He looked at them with open hostility.

'Welsh, are you?' he asked. And then, as though needing no reply to his question, 'There's no meat, just bread . . .' he dropped his eyes as Dafydd glared at him, ' . . . and cheese,' he added reluctantly.

Idris could see Dafydd's choler rising to match the reddening of his face, his hand knuckle-white as it rested on the knife at his belt, and breathed a sigh of relief as Dafydd asked, quietly, 'Where's Annie?'

There was a malicious light in the potman's eyes now as he answered tersely with something akin to pleasure, 'Dead!' and turned to go. With surprising lightfootedness for such a heavy man, Dafydd was on his feet and around the table to spin the potman around, saying, as his knife pricked the man's throat, 'You'll speak with some respect when you talk of Annie . . . ' a bead of blood rose on the man's throat as the knife pricked harder, ' . . . or my friend here will give you another mouth to smile with! Now fetch us meat and more ale!' White-faced now, the potman turned to go, but swivelled his head around as Dafydd tapped him on the shoulder with the knife to say, 'And when you come back, smile, potman . . . or . . . ' and with an evil grin, Dafydd just waved the knife warningly.

Idris glimpsed the fear in the potman's eyes before the man fled to the inner recesses of the inn, whilst Dafydd just stood there for a moment calmly putting his knife back in its sheath before sitting down again. Picking up his pot of ale, Dafydd nodded and smiled reassuringly at the other two, before saying confidently, 'I think we shall have meat after all, boys!'

There was a changed atmosphere at Sycharth, with Lord Owain's confident, relaxed, leadership replaced now by the strutting arrogance of Gruffydd, who was seemingly intent upon showing that, for these few days at least, he was lord of the manor. Three days after returning from Shrewsbury, Idris, weary of the oppressive atmosphere brooding over the manor, set up a target butt on a meadow by the church alongside Afon Cynllaith to practise his archery.

It was a fine afternoon, the clear sky marked only with white puffs of cumulus, the surface of the river rippling in the light breeze as Idris took his stance some seventy yards from the butt. Notching an arrow, he drew the bowstring back until, with his left arm fully outstretched, his right thumb was tucked into his cheekbone. He was about to let fly the arrow when, from the corner of his eye he saw a wisp of blue almost come into his view, making him turn his head quickly in that direction. With an exasperated sigh, he relaxed the tension on his bow, lowering it as he did so.

Nearly alongside the butt now, her black hair ruffled in the breeze, the blue of her dress matching the sky, the young Lady Catrin waved happily and called to him, 'Hello, Idris!'

Idris, his brow furrowed, sighed again: in relief this time, as he thought how close she had walked to death which, no doubt, would have cost him his own as well! Replacing the arrow in its quiver he walked towards her, his bow held loosely at his side.

'My lady,' he exclaimed his voice harsh in his relief, 'it is not wise to walk to an archer's butt as you did then. Relaxed now, he added quietly, 'Not lest you wish to be pinned to it like a butterfly!'

With a dismissive wave of her hand she replied, 'I called to you, but you did not heed me! How should I know you were playing with your bow and arrow?'

Idris looked at her, his eyes wide in his astonishment. 'Me, playing . . . with my bow and arrow, my lady? I practise my archery each day and needs I must, for 'tis my life, my trade . . .' Looking at her standing there, hand on hip, defiant of his rebuke, he could not help but smile and added lamely, ' . . . 'tis what your father pays me for, my lady!'

It was her turn to look abashed now, her hand dropped from her hip and her eyes softened as she replied quietly, 'You mean, like your friend, Iestyn?'

Idris shook his head slowly. 'Well, he wasn't my friend really, I'd only known him a few days, but he was a comrade in arms.'

He hadn't answered her question though and she persisted, 'But that is what my father pays you for?'

He looked at her thoughtfully for a moment, not knowing what to say, then, 'No, not really, my lady. Your father pays me to help protect his land, his manors, and family . . . ' looking into her eyes then, he hesitated, thinking yes, like Iestyn, too, if needs must.

Catherine's solemn moment was past though and she laughed happily. 'That's good then,' she said. 'You can put your old bow and arrows down and protect me whilst I walk along the river bank!'

Idris looked at her smiling cheekily up at him, saw the laughter in the blue eyes and thought why not? Then, remembering Gruffydd scowling at him, warning him, murmured, 'Oh, I can't my lady! My practice, you see . . . I must complete my practice!'

He could tell whose daughter she was then: the laughter left her eyes, her chin came up imperiously.

'You said my father paid you to protect his family. So, protect me!'

He looked around him, but there was no aid in sight. He was not even sure that he was looking for aid, but rather seeing if Gruffydd was in view. There was neither and he turned his gaze back to Catrin, the prudent half of him hoping she had changed her mind, the other half just hoping. One look told him that Catrin had not changed her mind but was standing there amused at his indecision. Prudence giving way to hope, he said, his voice tinged with resignation, 'As it pleases you, my lady!'

Catrin softened, her blue eyes all innocence now. 'It pleases me, Idris, but call me Catrin . . . you need only call my mother "my lady".'

With that she turned and tripped off towards the river bank and Idris, his bow over his shoulder now, followed, half wondering where this path would lead.

Chapter Five

Idris walked up to the plaited straw butt, looked at the arrows with which it was pierced and shook his head disconsolately. An hour before noon Catrin had said and now it was nigh on noon and still there was no sign of her. For three days now, he had practised his archery desultorily as he waited hopefully for sight of her. Each day she had come along the path to the mill by Avon Cynllaith waving happily to him, as if catching sight of him by chance, but not today.

As he stood there irresolutely twisting the arrows out of the butt, Idris was not thinking of his marksmanship, but of walking side by side with Catrin along the river bank these last few days. Of the formality between them slipping away as gently as the river flowed, of Catrin edging a little closer to him each day until it seemed to him as though they were not lord's daughter and paid retainer, but an archer and his maid.

He pulled the last arrow out of the butt viciously and thrust it back into its quiver, thinking as he did so that that was the problem: he was an archer and she was but a young maid. It had humoured her to pass the time with him for an hour or two and now she had found some other toy to play with! With a philosophical shrug of his shoulders, Idris thought that perhaps it were better so, sooner or later Gruffydd would have learnt of their walks together and would not have been amused.

Whilst he had been engrossed with his thoughts of Catrin, it had clouded over and a wind was gusting across the meadow. With an anxious look at the now threatening sky, he set out for the manor, hoping to reach its shelter before it rained. He had only just passed the church and was approaching the manor's tall, stone built dovecote however, when suddenly the rain came and he ran for the shelter of the dovecote.

Closing the small oak door behind him he heard a gasp and felt, rather than saw, movement in the dim interior of the dovecote. Peering into the gloom, his right hand went involuntarily to the knife at his belt and there was a sharp edge to his voice as he asked, 'Who's there?'

There was definitely something, someone, moving towards him now, but he relaxed and sheepishly let his hand drop from his knife as he heard Catrin's soft voice:

'Oh, you frightened me so, Idris, rushing in like that!'

His eyes more accustomed to the gloom now, he could see her as she put a basket containing a few eggs onto the earth floor then, frowning, she placed her hand on his arm.

'What brought you here anyway, Idris?' Then, as he hesitated, her head on one side, she gave an impish smile and asked 'Did you know I was here?'

Idris's heart beat a little faster as he felt the warmth of her hand on his arm, the nearness of her body, and he smiled as he shook his head. 'No, my lady, I was on my way back to the manor when the rain came and I hurried to take shelter, I'm sorry if I startled you.'

Her hand still on his arm, Catrin giggled and moving closer to him, looked up into his eyes.

'Yesterday it was "Catrin", now it's all "my lady"! I wager you'd be blushing if I could but see you properly!'

Her soft body was touching his now, her lips parted, as she peered up to him as if seeking to confirm her wager. Looking down into her eyes, Idris shook his head as he rested his hands on her shoulders.

'Nay, I'm not blushing, Catrin!'

Then his arms were around her, holding her close, the dim interior and the musty smell of the dovecote all forgotten as they kissed. An age later it seemed, they drew apart and Idris was frowning, shaking his head, as he murmured, 'I'm sorry, Catrin, I didn't mean to . . . '

He stopped and shook his head helplessly, his eyes closing in horror at the thought of what young Gruffydd would have had to say if he had come upon them in such close embrace! Opening his eyes, he found himself looking down into hers, his arms still around her. Catrin, no wit abashed, was looking up at him, smiling, her eyes all innocence. Without saying a word, she

41

snuggled up to him again and, reaching a hand behind his neck, pulled his lips to hers once more.

It had stopped raining when at last Idris tentatively put his head out of the dovecote and looked anxiously around. Seeing no one, he stepped boldly out onto the dirt pathway and a demure Catrin followed him daintily through the doorway to pause there and hold out her basket for him to carry. Idris looked askance at her for a moment but Catrin had that imperious look about her again, so hitching his bow more comfortably over his shoulder, he took the basket, before walking beside her along the path to the manor.

As they arrived at the drawbridge, Dafydd and Rhys came through the gate-house, only to stop and step aside at sight of them. Idris wished them both at Ruthin, Shrewsbury, anywhere but there, but they, it seemed, were happy to be present to watch his discomfiture. As they passed, Dafydd, obviously striving to keep a straight face, muttered, 'Been to market, then, have you, Idris?'

Cringing inwardly, Idris walked on, with a demure Catrin beside him and the subdued laughter of Dafydd and Rhys ringing in his ears.

Not without some feelings of guilt, Idris avoided the meadow by the mill for the next few days, conscious of the fact that it could as easily have been Gruffydd, rather than Dafydd and Rhys, who had greeted him on his return to the manor with Catrin that day. He knew, too, that Gruffydd would not readily have put such an innocent interpretation on their return together. So, anxious to avoid a confrontation with Gruffydd in Lord Owain's absence, he abandoned his customary archery practice.

That first day there was only a sarcastic comment from Dafydd about an archer not practising his archery, only an occasional glance by Idris towards the gate-house to see if, perchance, Catrin was leaving the manor. The second day found Idris watching anxiously for a glimpse of her and after breaking his fast on the third day he decided that surely by now it was safe for him to spend an hour at his target butt and, if Catrin happened to pass that way, well, what harm in that?

The dew was still glistening on the meadow, a hint of mist lying over the Afon Cynllaith, as Idris paced out his distance from

42

the target butt, took his stance and let fly his first shaft. Hours later the sun was high in the clear spring sky as he leant on his bow and, gazing contemplatively at the arrow still quivering in the target, decided that Catrin would not be appearing. He was still trying to console himself that it was for the best and wondering why that was never what one yearned for, when a sharp voice behind him roused him from his reverie.

'You ply your trade well, at a target, archer!'

He turned his head quickly to see Gruffydd standing there with big Dafydd at his heels.

Mortified he had been so engrossed thinking about Catrin that they had been able to come upon him unawares, he flushed, sensing Gruffydd's remark as derogatory rather than complimentary, and snapped, 'Aye, your honour, and I ply it as well with ought else before me!'

Perhaps it was the memory of that day when he had stood on the drawbridge, with Idris's bowstring taut, the notched arrow pointing at his heart, that made Gruffydd redden with anger. His mouth open as if about to make an angry retort, he suddenly paused as though in mid-stride and, frowning, was looking beyond Idris now, towards the mill. Idris turned his head and sighed as he saw Catrin walking towards them. Behind Gruffydd, Dafydd raised his eyebrows expressively at Idris and raised a forefinger to his lips in silent warning.

Gruffydd was not heeding either of them now, instead he was striding purposefully over towards Catrin. As they drew together, Idris heard Gruffydd snap, 'And what, pray, brings you here, sister?'

Without a glance at Idris, Catrin answered innocently.

'Why, Mother sent me, Gruffydd, to tell you that your meal is ready!'

Gruffydd grunted something in reply, then with a cold stare at Idris and a nod as if to say they would continue their conversation another day, he turned on his heel and brother and sister walked off towards the manor. They had only gone a few paces before Catrin gave a surreptitious glance over her shoulder at Idris and he could have sworn that she actually winked at him before quickly turning her head away again. Idris turned, to see Dafydd frowning in obvious exasperation.

'I've told you before young Idris,' said the big man despairingly.

'You'd best look for your pleasures elsewhere! If Gruffydd finds out you've been making eyes at each other there'll be a motte of trouble in store for you!'

A hail from the gate-house, warning of a rider approaching, made Dafydd and Idris pause for a moment before continuing into the great hall for their midday meal. A single rider did not constitute a threat, rather would he be welcomed with a meal and mead or wine according to his station. A few minutes later, Idris was dipping his bread into a steaming bowl of cawl when there was a commotion at the door and, bread poised between bowl and lips, he turned his head. To his surprise, Lord Owain his face like thunder, was striding into the hall, a grey riding cloak flung back over his shoulder, sword scabbard slapping against his leg.

Idris looked at Dafydd in consternation: they were supposed to have ridden to Shrewsbury on the morrow to meet Lord Owain, but Dafydd, wide-eyed, was shaking his head and seemed just as mystified at their lord's sudden arrival. At the top of the table, the Lady Marged, Gruffydd, Catrin and Maredudd had risen to their feet to meet Lord Owain, whilst the younger children just sat there, their chatter hushed. Lord Owain had reached the top of the table by now and was unclasping his cloak to fling it aside as Lady Marged, smiling in welcome, laid a hand on his arm.

'We did not expect you until the morrow, my lord. Your escort . . . '

Alongside her Gruffydd was frowning, nodding in agreement, obviously fearing his father's wrath. Owain though, waved his hand, as though brushing aside their concern.

'No matter, but some wine, for God's sake! Would you have a man die of thirst in his own hall?'

Gruffydd rushed to the table to pour a goblet of wine and nervously handed it to Owain, who drank it greedily as he stood there. Then, wiping his lips with the back of his hand he smiled at Marged.

'That's better! I've not stopped save to water the horse all morning!'

Then, taking her arm, he walked her back to the table and sat down beside her at its head. This caused some confusion amongst the children, for before Owain's arrival Gruffydd had been seated there and all the others had moved up a place. Idris grinned at Dafydd as Gruffydd eventually ousted Maredudd, who only reluctantly gave way.

Meanwhile a servant was hurrying to Lord Owain with a platter of meat and the Lady Marged was refilling his goblet as she asked anxiously, 'And your plea fared well with my lords in Parliament, Owain?'

There was silence in the great hall, as all those present waited for his answer. Dafydd and Idris leaned forward looking up the table at Lord Owain, anxious not to miss a word, their food unheeded before them. Owain, a capon leg raised to his lips, looked at Marged for a moment blank-eyed, then put the chicken back on his platter and pushed it aside as though he had lost the appetite for it. With a disgusted snort, he picked up the goblet and drank from it before slamming it down on the table. Frowning now, Lady Marged was shaking her head slowly, her eyes clouded, as though fearing the answer that she now had no need for him to give.

'Fared well! What should I have expected to hear from that band of English thieves? Lord Grey is a baron of Parliament, would they humble one of their own before me?'

He reached for his goblet again which Gruffydd, his eyes now strangely bright, hastened to fill. Owain, a distant look in his eyes, drank from it as if unaware of Gruffydd's presence then after wiping his lips he continued, 'John Trefor, the Bishop of St. Asaph, spoke up for me, but Arundel, despite all his promises of support on the journey to London, lost the stomach for it on the day, told me afterwards that he could not speak for me as my good lord, since I was the King's esquire! That would not have stopped his father, the old Earl, from speaking his mind! No, it fared not well for me in Parliament, Marged. When Lord Grey spoke, it was "my lord this" and "my lord that", but when I was on my feet, it was "that barefooted Welsh clown"!'

He reached for his platter again now and picked up the capon leg once more; raising it to his mouth he bit into it hungrily then chewed thoughtfully for a moment before turning his head to her and saying quietly, 'They'll rue the day they ever said that to Owain Glyn Dŵr and find a barefoot Welshman can bring down many an armoured English lord!' He pointed the stripped capon leg menacingly at Gruffydd. 'And you, my son, you ride

tomorrow to my cousins in Ynys Mon to call them to council . . .
and waste no time on your journey!'

Lady Marged, her face full of concern now, held her hand out
as if to detain him. 'Owain, give thought before you act, my love,
what matters a piece of common land to us? Peace and content
we've had here at Sycharth to watch our children grow, and it can
continue so, whether or no Lord Grey holds the common at
Croesau.'

'Think you so, Marged? If I stand idly by and let him steal my
land at Croesau, what next? Shall he take the manor at
Glyndyfrdwy or the meadows here whilst I touch a forelock to
him?'

'But the King, Owain . . . take your plea to the King, and abide
by his ruling on the common!'

Dafydd and Idris all agog at the far end of the table, conscious
of the fact that what was being talked about at the top of the table
could bring them booty or burial, were straining to hear what was
being said. They saw Lord Owain shaking his head slowly, heard
him say, 'John Trefor had audience with the king on my behalf,
to be told that Henry could not intervene in a petty dispute
between a marcher magnate and a King's esquire!' His lip curled,
his disgust evident in his face. 'Any other esquire's lord would
defend him in his need, but not my liege king! A usurper, he feels
his hold on the crown too precarious to jeopardise it for me!'

Dafydd nudged Idris. ' 'Tis as well you've practised your archery
young Idris, I wager we'll lay siege to Ruthin Castle itself before
the month is out!'

Idris though, was paying him no heed, but watching the drama
playing itself out at the top of the table and heard Lady Marged,
her eyebrows raised in horror, say quietly to her husband, 'Hush
my lord, if you were misheard, it could be held to be treason that
you uttered!'

Taking another draught from his goblet, Lord Owain looked
around him and said defiantly, 'My liege lord or no, usurper he is
and so I'll say! Richard would never have treated me thus,
perhaps we should see him on his throne again!'

Marged frowned in her surprise. 'Think you he is still alive
then, my lord?'

Owain, looked sideways at her. 'Alive? Of course he's alive,
madam! Henry has stomach enough to sit on his borrowed throne,

46

but I wager not enough for regicide!'

At that a murmur went around the hall and heads craned forward, the better to see, to hear, what was to follow. They did not have long to wait for with a gesture, Owain commanded the servants to clear away the tables. Sighing, Lady Marged gathered her daughters and younger children around her and left for her chambers, leaving Gruffydd and his fourteen-year-old brother Maredudd at the table with their father.

Whilst all this had been going on, Dafydd and Idris, ears cocked, had lingered on over their pots of ale, as though they had not noticed anything amiss and Owain called to them now, 'Here, you two! There'll be something for idle hands to do here!'

Rising they both walked to the head of the table, to stand there awaiting his instructions whilst Owain spoke to his sons: 'You are to go to Ynys Mon and my cousins, Gruffydd, calling them to council at Glyndyfrdwy. Tell them to bring their retinues of lances and archers with them and to come not hungry, but well supplied. You, Maredudd, to your Uncle Tudor with the same errand. Tell him too, to send word to your mother's kin, Philip and Gruffydd Hanmer, to join us here with their retinues.'

He leant back in his chair, stroked his beard and looked thoughtfully at Dafydd and Idris, saying at last, 'Well Dafydd Mawr, you wanted booty and it seems as though you yet may have to earn it ere the month be out! In the meantime you can go with Idris here to array all lances, archers and every fencible man from my manors in Cardigan and bring them to our aid here with all haste.' He shook his finger warningly. 'And let any such man tarry there at your peril and his! For years they've nursed their cattle, tilled the soil and harvested, 'tis time they paid their feudal due!'

With a hint of a smile now, he nodded to them, saying in dismissal, 'Now off you go and bring my men of Cardigan here before August month is out!'

Grinning, Dafydd touched a finger to his forehead and, in a voice reminiscent in volume of that with which he'd hailed Ruthin Castle, said eagerly, 'Aye, my lord!'

Touching Idris on the arm, Dafydd turned to go and Idris was about to follow him when Owain said quietly, almost regretfully, 'It seems you'll have your chance to claim Iestyn's due from Ruthin, archer!'

47

Before Idris had chance to answer, Gruffydd, sitting back in his chair, looked at him cold eyed and said in a voice which revealed little of his feelings, 'I'm sure he will, Father, he does well enough at the butts!'

Idris quickly flushed and made a half step back towards the table, but before he could go further or say a word Dafydd tugged warningly at his sleeve and with just a glance at Lord Owain and a quiet, 'Aye, my lord,' Idris turned away again.

In that brief moment though he had glimpsed the inquisitive glance Lord Owain had given Gruffydd, had seen the appraising look he had been given also, as though Lord Owain were trying to place where they had met before. Then turning away he walked quickly out of the hall and into the summer sunshine of the courtyard with Dafydd, who rubbing his hands, said enthusiastically, 'No border raid this, Idris, mark my words! Lord Owain is preparing for a real campaign, though with winter not far away it can't last for long, that is . . .' he rubbed his chin, then tugged at his drooping moustache thoughtfully, ' . . . not unless he's thinking of rebellion!'

Startled, Idris turned on him quickly. 'What do you mean?' he asked. 'Rebellion, against who?'

Dafydd gave a bellow of a laugh. 'Why, the King, the English, who else?' he asked, and grinned as he slapped Idris on the back, 'What does it matter, there'll be booty in it for us . . . an' we live that long!'

With that he strode off, leaving Idris looking thoughtfully after him. Rebellion it is for sure, he thought and heard Lady Marged's quiet voice as she had told her husband, 'it could be held to be treason!' He smiled wryly, no doubt it could! Hanged and quartered rebels they did and he winced at the mere thought, but what could he do but as his lord bid?

Chapter Six

Owain toyed with the goblet of wine as he watched the two retainers leave the great hall then looked at his two sons thoughtfully. Once these four left on their errands, he would be committed, there could be no turning back then, not ever. Gruffydd was leaning forward, bright-eyed, taut as a bowstring, eager to begin his journey whilst Maredudd, smooth cheeked, a straying lock of black hair over the forehead, brown eyed, was gazing trustingly back at his father.

Maredudd's just a child really, he thought, but, at fourteen, a man under Welsh law, as old as Llewellyn was when he set out to regain Gwynedd. Looking at him, Owain hesitated, for himself he had no fears of the coming conflict, but could he place Marged, Maredudd or any of the children in such jeopardy? He sighed and shook his head, there never was any turning back, he realised that now, not from the moment Lord Grey set foot on Croesau and even that was but the trigger.

Ever since Llewellyn's death the Welsh nobility, with the blood of Princes in their veins, had been treated like country squires, fit only for minor office or perhaps to captain a band of lances or archers in some English war. Seldom, if ever, were any rewarded with a knighthood!

If King Richard really is alive, he thought, as all the rumours would have it, to unseat Henry and restore Richard to the throne, could gain the support of half the English magnates!

The Mortimers almost certainly, for the young Edmund, Earl of March, now a ward of Henry's, had greater claim to the throne than the King. Rumour had it too that the Percies, who held the Scottish marches, felt ungenerously treated by the usurper, so mayhap they'd see advantage in a turn of coat! And if Richard

c

were to regain the throne with such aid from Wales . . . his roaming thoughts were interrupted abruptly by Gruffydd.

'What now then, Father, what plans have you for this council and the forces you'd have us bring to Gwynedd? Is all this but for a raid on Ruthin or to regain Croesau? I doubt your cousins in Ynys Mon would favour such hazard for so little gain!'

Never before had Gruffydd so apparently doubted his judgement and Owain looked up sharply, his hand raised as if to strike. Thinking though that there must be no dissension at the start of this enterprise, he just wagged a forefinger and spoke quietly as if to cool his son's ardour, 'The council first, Gruffydd, is to consider our position here at Sycharth, in Gwynedd and indeed, the principality as a whole. All that in relation not only to the English marcher lords, like Grey, but to the English Crown and to our heavy burden of taxation. To discuss why it is the Welsh have no citizenship rights in the towns around the English held castles in the principality. To consider, too, the legitimacy of Henry's claim to the throne and, if he has none, whether his son can indeed be the Prince of Wales! As to the forces we array here, that is but to give some substance to the words we utter!'

As Owain spoke both his sons' eyes widened in amazement, but Gruffydd replied first.

'Then it's not just about a strike at Ruthin then, Father . . . it's rebellion?'

Owain remained silent as he reached for the pitcher of wine and poured some into his goblet. Raising it to his lips he sipped at it, almost as though taking communion, before saying quietly, 'Aye, if it is indeed rebellion to reclaim our own and the council wills, it could well be so.' Seeing Gruffydd's eyes light up, he added, 'Be not too eager for such conflict, Gruffydd, before it ever succeeds, you could be too old a man to wear a princely coronet . . . or a dead one!' Rising, he sighed, 'But you must go to make preparations for your journeys tomorrow and I, too, have some preparing to do!'

The two brothers rose to go and Owain smiled, thinking how different they were: Gruffydd, shoulders squared back, chin out-thrusting, hand on sword hilt, the very picture of a fighting cock. Maredudd, hand on chin, quietly thoughtful as though assessing what might lay ahead. As usual it was Gruffydd who spoke, when perhaps there was little to be said, 'I'm glad you see it now,

Father . . . ' and as Owain, black eyebrows arched, looked at him inquiringly, he added portentously, ' . . . that it is time to claim your true inheritance, Caradoc's throne!'

Owain gave a wry smile. ' 'Tis only "Time" will tell, Gruffydd, whether I seek it before my time or no, and many a man will pay his due in blood before we find the answer! God save you be not one.'

Gruffydd hesitated, his face clouding at the rebuke, before turning and hurrying out of the hall followed by Maredudd. As they got to the door, Maredudd turned to smile at his father and half raised his hand, either in farewell or salute. Owain watched them go for a moment, then looked around the hall with stained glass window at the far end, the great wooden pillars holding up the minstrels' gallery and the lofts where the minstrels slept, the oaken beams supporting the slated roof.

He shivered despite the sunlight streaming in through the windows, the fire in the hearth. For suddenly, instead of the familiar hall, he was alone on the motte of Sycharth, around him only the charred remains of the timbered hall, before him only a scene of desolation, a ruined church and Afon Cynllaith running red.

An air of expectation hung over Sycharth now whilst all there awaited the return of Owain's emissaries. It was an atmosphere of mixed emotions too: amongst the older ones there was tight lipped determination at the thought of war, with memories of previous border raids and sieges to counter the enthusiasm and excitement of the youngsters, whose only talk was of adventure and victory over the English. The prudent kept silent and bent their heads as they honed their weapons and greased forgotten bits of mail back to suppleness.

No one, however, awaited the return more anxiously than Owain for on that depended whether his enterprise was to become a rising of the whole of Gwynedd and Ynys Mon, the granary of North Wales, or just another border raid. Pacing up and down the great hall he struggled with his conscience. Was he about to kindle a flame that would light a path to the restoration of the ancient princedom of Gwynedd, perhaps even that of Llewellyn's united Wales? Or was it all just the response of an aggrieved child, hurt because his father had unfairly favoured an older, bigger son.

He gave a wry smile as he thought of Gruffydd's derisive comment about hazard and scant reward. Whether his cause be one of national pride or merely personal spite, the butcher's bill would be dear enough, the reward more elusive than the payment exacted. Henry's England could call on far greater resources than that of all Wales, let alone the puny force that Owain might raise by calling on the support of family, even were it to be given. This was the wager on which he was about to stake everything, not only his manors here at Sycharth and Glyndyfrdwy, but those of Iscoed Uch Hiren and Gwynionydd in Cardigan as well.

Not only was he probably the richest of the Welsh gentry, his five hundred pounds a year income comparing well with most of the English gentry and . . . Light footsteps interrupted his chain of thought and Marged came up to him wearing that green silk dress which favoured her so well. Strange how he always thought of her as Marged rather than her English name of Margaret as she liked to be called, he thought. Just as Marged always called their eldest daughter Catherine, who preferred being called Catrin. He smiled at Marged now as she came up to him, and asked, 'Why so solemn, Marged?'

Frowning, she gasped in her astonishment, before snapping, 'Why solemn? You about to bring all Gwynedd to war, aye, and the rest of Wales too perchance, and you ask me why so solemn! Are you out of your mind, my lord, placing your few retainers against the might of England?' She waved her jewelled hand around the hall. 'Why dream of princedom, when your many manors provide so well! Prince you may not be, yet undoubted principal you are amongst your Welsh uchel . . . ' Owain laughed as she struggled with the pronunciation, but tight lipped she persisted, ' . . . uchelwyr, and a marcher lord as well!'

Straight-faced, as though tutoring a child, Owain carefully mouthed the correct pronunciation then with a smile, trying not to patronise, 'Gentry might be easier for you to say, Marged . . . nobility perhaps, if you want to flatter.' There was a touch of irony in his voice as he continued, 'For nobles in our own land we were . . . before the English came.'

Her face flushed under her fair hair and her blue eyes flashed indignantly.

52

'Your memory serves you ill, my lord, if you forget that I am *English*, your mother *English*, and thus your children more English than ever they are Welsh!'

Almost mocking now, he waved a finger at her. 'Ah, there you are mistaken, Marged dear, our children are all full Welsh. 'Tis only the Jew whose ancestry is taken from the mother's side, here in Christian Wales, it is determined by the father!' He shrugged. 'Of course, I know not what obtains in England, so few there are there who can swear to a father at all!'

She shook her head and, with a gesture, waved his words aside.

'You do but distract me from my argument, sir! I ask again, why do you want, even need, to make war over such a trivial matter? Glyndyfrdwy is less favoured land than here at Sycharth, Croesau common the . . . ' she stumbled seeking the right words, ' . . . the least loved part of Glyndyfrdwy!'

Owain remained silent as he looked at her thoughtfully, for she was asking the question to which there was no logical answer. He knew that Croesau was not worth war, not even a border raid for a few cattle. It all had to be more than that, much more than that, if he were to convince the Council he had called to risk their all in the fortune of war. But the die was cast and if they dared not, then he was alone, for he could not turn back, not now!

Marged put her hand on his arm, her face close to his, eyes pleading. 'Stop now, Owain, while there be still time. The mere muster of your force will likely deter Lord Grey from any more incursions on your land . . . .'

She stopped and they both turned towards the door as it was flung open and Rhys, breathless from a dash across the courtyard, rushed in to stop, panting, in front of them. Owain, relieved at not now having to answer Marged, grinned at him.

'What, have you run from Ynys Mon to bring us tidings, Rhys, that you pant like a lapdog at my knee?'

Taking one last deep breath, Rhys, shook his head and said urgently, 'No, I ran but from the gate-house, my lord! A rider approaches, a messenger from Lord Grey of Ruthin by the arms he bears!'

Owain raised his eyebrows and turned to Marged. 'What news can our friend at Ruthin have for me, I wonder? Nought good, I fear!' He turned to Rhys. 'Go greet the messenger, Rhys and treat him civilly, have the servants bring him wine or ale, he's not the maker of his master's misdeeds! Then bring him here to me so he may complete his errand.'

As Rhys hurried out of the hall Owain turned to Marged, but before he could say a word, she raised a finger to him admonishingly.

'That was good advice you gave Rhys, Owain, may you treat the master's message as civilly as the messenger!'

Owain raised his eyes to the rafters, peering as though seeking for signs of worm, before lowering them to her face again, his own a picture of exasperation.

'Indeed I shall, Marged, if it but be good news!'

It was her turn to be exasperated now and it was evident in the sharpness of her tongue. 'How many times do I have to tell you Owain that my name is Margaret! "Marged" makes it sound as though a pitcher of wine had passed your lips!'

Owain grinned. 'Aye, lass, you're right enough. Marged has a gentler touch to it than Margaret, for that has a shrewish sound!'

She was about to make a rejoinder when the door opened and Rhys entered, leading the messenger from Ruthin who was bearing a rolled letter. Bowing, the messenger said formally, 'My Lord Grey of Ruthin, who has but yesterday returned from London, presents his compliments to you, my lord. He has sent me with all haste bearing this letter for you from His Majesty, King Henry.' He paused as he offered the letter to Owain, then added, 'I was told, my lord, to wait at your command.'

Taking the scroll, Owain glanced at Marged before breaking its seal and scanning the letter anxiously, hopefully, and moved out of earshot of the messenger. As he read though, his face darkened with anger, his hand dropped to his side and he looked at Marged, speechless.

Frowning, her mouth open, eyes questioning, she hesitated a moment before asking, 'What is it, Owain, what does it say?'

Owain snorted, 'Fool that I am, I thought for a moment that perhaps Henry had changed his mind, had interceded on my behalf, but no . . . ' he paused, then with a bitter smile he waved the letter in front of him: ' . . . No! It's but a trap, a devil's snare!'

Exasperated now, Marged reached out to him as if to take the letter, to read for herself what it contained. 'For goodness' sake, Owain! Tell me what it is the King says!'

Owain glanced at the letter again before looking up at her and, controlling his anger, said quietly, 'It is a letter of array, Marged! Henry is calling me to service, to fight 'gainst Robert of Scotland!' Holding the letter up to the light now, he began to read aloud:

' "To Owain Glyn Dŵr, Esquire,

' "By these letters patent you are required and commanded to cease every excuse and hasten to draw towards the town of St. Albans with all the forces at your command, every man being furnished and arrayed as his estate demands, to arrive at the said town no later than the twenty-first day of August in this year of our Lord 1400. . ." ' He raised his eyes to Marged. 'And so it goes on, I'm to be at St. Albans in three day's time for his campaign against Robert of Scotland. Three days! If I were to set out this minute without a single man to accompany me, I'd not be there in time and well he knows it!' He waved the letter again. 'Lord Grey must have been well pleased to be his errand boy on such a mission!'

Marged clutched his arm now, frowning, her eyes appealing.

'But it is a King's array, Owain and you a King's esquire! You must go! If you don't . . . '

'I know!' he interrupted sharply, 'I know, Marged! It says it all in this damned letter, "Under pain of forfeiting all fees, wages, annuities or estates held for the Crown!" As I said, it's a trap, a devil's snare, I must be there three days hence or pay the penalty and I can't, it's just not possible! If I arrive late, or without my main force, my lands may still be forfeit!' His eyes took on a distant, questioning look, as he asked sarcastically, 'And if that were so, I wonder who would be granted my manor of Glyndyfrdwy by His English Majesty? Lord Grey of Ruthin, no doubt!'

There was anguish now in Marged's voice. 'But you must go, Owain! Go now,' she pleaded. Then, with a guarded glance at the Ruthin messenger who stood there waiting, as though oblivious to all going on before him, she added, 'I will send Dafydd to follow you as soon as he arrives with . . . with his companions.'

Owain smiled as he took her arm and led her over to a window overlooking the courtyard, then letting her arm go he said quietly, 'That was tactfully put, Marged! But no, I cannot go, not now, 'tis a plot I'm sure! Were I to do so, I fear it's not a march to Scotland

I'd take, but to the King's tower in London! No I must abide here and wait the outcome of the council. If all must now be forfeit, I'd sooner fight to hold it a free man here than a prisoner in the Tower, my knowledge of the English law would serve me little there, for many go in, but fewer out!'

Patting her gently on the arm, he turned and walking over to the messenger, said quietly, 'Rhys here, will show you to a meal, messenger, whilst I pen a letter which no doubt your lord will convey to His Majesty the King on my behalf.'

The messenger bowed and saying, 'My thanks, my lord,' turned towards Rhys, who led him towards the door and out of the great hall. Glancing at Marged, Owain said with a wry grin, 'All I have to do now, my love, is to write a careful letter to my liege lord, the King!'

Marged shook her head now, as if in despair.

'What are you going to say to him, Owain?'

He shrugged and grimaced. 'To tell you truly Marged, I do not know! All I know as yet is that I must buy me some time and thus prevent Lord Ruthin come storming Sycharth.' In answer to her questioning look he waved the letter. 'I doubt not that he has the King's command to enforce this warrant of array, or make me pay my forfeit and I'd as lief not give him lawful cause. Yet what to say, is yet another matter! Surely it will take all the skills I once learned in the Inns of Law!'

With that he turned and, head bowed thoughtfully, walked slowly off to his chamber. As if it were a signal, there was the melodious sound of a harp from the minstrels gallery and Marged looked up to see Iolo there, his fingers gently plying his harp and gazing soulfully into the distance as he quietly sang a lament for Llewellyn's death in battle. Tears sprang to Marged's eyes and turning away quickly, she hurried out of the hall.

Chapter Seven

It did not take long for the import of the letter brought by Lord Ruthin's messenger to spread around the manor. Tongues wagged and heads nodded as the word was spread from servant to stableboy, from stable to cottage and cottage to distant holding within the manor's demesne. Lord Owain, the word said, had been called to the King's service as was his due and had refused. All knew what that meant!

There were fearful glances towards the northeast, whence Lord Grey of Ruthin's force would come, for come it surely would, they all knew. Cattle were herded away from open fields and the unwilling brutes hidden amongst glades in woods. Sheep were driven to the high lands, grain hidden and valuables, such as ever they were, hurriedly buried for the time being, although sometimes the very haste of their interment gave cause for scratched heads! Where it was possible, young maids were sent away to relatives in the west, some as far away as Ynys Mon. Those who, perforce were to stay behind, dressed in rags and slattern looked, this being not the time for a maid to catch a man's eye.

Around the manor men kept watch around the clock lest they be taken unawares, water was stocked in barrels around the wooden palisade, food and water for the people stored, as was fodder for the animals. In the courtyard, the grindstones constantly turned as men put an edge on weapons, or tools that served as both. In every man's mind there was the question whether the forces Lord Owain had called to his aid would arrive in time. There were those too, who marvelled at his prescience that he had called that aid before ever the threat was known!

On the morning three days after the Ruthin messenger had

departed from Sycharth, Lord Owain came out of the great hall into the courtyard and bit his lip as he looked around him. He turned as he heard movement behind him, to see Marged and Catrin walking towards him. Marged was looking worried and Owain thought she seemed to have aged in the three short days since the arrival of the letter of array. As she came up to him, she asked, 'There's no word from Ruthin yet then, Owain?'

Owain smiled. 'If by word you mean is Lord Grey's main force on the horizon yet, the answer is no, my dear, but ask me tomorrow and we may well have heard from Ruthin!'

Catrin was holding tightly onto her mother's arm, her face pale, her eyes frightened, as Marged said quietly, 'Oh, Owain! I did not want you to go, but you should have gone, my lord. The King will make you pay your forfeit and what will happen to us all then?'

Owen glowered and answered sharply, 'Between them, he and Lord Grey would have made me pay that forfeit at all events, madam, but whilst I'm here 'twill cost them dear to take their due! My letter will have bought some time and in but a few days now my men of Cardigan, my brother Tudor and my cousins from Mon will all be here. Perhaps Henry and his Ruthin lapdog will find it all a meal too salty for their taste!'

Marged, her face strained, her lips almost bloodless, whispered, 'And if they do not come to your aid, my lord, what then?'

Going over to her, he took her in his arms and looking into her eyes, gave that mischievous smile that had tugged at her heart all those years ago when first they met.

'Why then, my love, the wager's placed and lost!'

She looked around at the activity taking place in the courtyard. 'Then what of all this, Owain?' she asked. 'Why do they sharpen swords, hoard the grain and wet the palisade if not for a siege?'

Owain threw back his head and laughed. 'A siege, my love, a siege?' He leaned towards her, and almost whispered, 'Had I all the men and all the weapons I could ask for, I could hold this place for two, perhaps three, days against such forces and siege weapons as the king or Ruthin could bring! It is a manor, not a castle. I do but make such preparations as I can and in so doing, keep the people occupied . . . 'tis better so for their spirit,' he smiled again, 'and for mine too, I dare say!

'Never fear though, no harm will come to you or the children. If the aid I called comes not before Ruthin does, I'll call truce and give the manor up, 'tis no stain to yield to force majeure and they'll not harm you then.'

Seeing her face fall, the tears begin to well, he drew her to him and said gently, 'Come now, my lady of Sycharth! These next few days our people will be looking to us for courage and we'll not fail them, shall we?'

Looking up at him, she held back the tears and she shook her head as she said, 'No, Owain! We'll not fail them!'

Owain slept fully dressed in the gate-house that night, ready for any alarm. Even so it was a disturbed sleep and in a wakeful moment he rose and went to join the watchman in the tower.

'All quiet?' he asked needlessly and the watchman nodded. Breathing deeply of the mild night air Owain gazed around at the moonlit scene, the church etched sharp, its windows lit with reflected light, the shadows black. Suddenly, there was a flash of light on the river and they both tensed, heads craned forward, listening, watching. As no movement followed they slowly relaxed and the watchman sighed in relief.

'Our friend the moon caught a fish jumping!' laughed Owain. 'The men of Ruthin have no need to wet their feet to pay us a visit . . . ' he paused, then added the warning, 'but if it were me, I'd likely come that way!'

With a last look around, he turned to the watchman, then said, 'I'll go below, but if you are in doubt do not fear to call me, I'd rather be here and not needed, than below when I am!'

Stepping lightly down the wooden staircase he laid down on the straw mattress that had been placed there in the gate-house for him, wondering for a moment whether relief would come in time; surely Tudor would be on his way by now, the cousins from Ynys Mon too! He shrugged, there was little he could do now but wait and, with a premonition that there would be no alarm that night, was quickly asleep.

Light filtering through the archer's slit of the little room slanted across Owain's face and he brushed it aside with his hand, but it persisted and slowly his eyes opened. Glancing around he struggled to orientate himself for a moment, then was quickly awake and on his feet. Looking out of the slit, he could see that the approach to the manor was undisturbed, but turning, went up the stairs to the tower. The watch had changed and Rhys was there to greet him.

'Good morrow, my lord, a fine bright day and peaceful as a Sabbath day should be!'

Owain gave a thin smile. 'You're bright enough, Rhys, I trust your eyes are as sharp as your tongue?'

Rhys grinned as he replied, 'Oh, aye my lord, fear lends great distance to the sight and keeps a man awake whilst others sleep!' The grin faded and he added quietly, 'Do you think that Dafydd will be back today? I never thought I'd miss his company, but with so few of us around, it makes me feel quite naked!'

Hiding his concern, Owain pursed his lips and nodded, his look as confident as his voice, and more so than his thoughts. 'Aye, today, tomorrow at the latest I would think, Rhys. My brother and my cousins too should be within hailing distance soon.' He gave Rhys a sideways glance. 'That will bring some comfort, eh?'

'Indeed, my lord,' said Rhys, 'the more the merrier! I'm not one to grieve over sharing what Lord Grey's men may hurl at us from across the ditch.'

Owain looked down at the moat, not wide enough by half, he thought, it would not cause an experienced soldier to more than pause in his stride. He brushed the thought aside, and winked at Rhys.

'And you watch my back for me, Rhys, I'll lead you across the moat at Ruthin,' he said cheerfully, 'before ever they set foot inside this courtyard. There'll be enough for you to share with Dafydd then!'

Without waiting for Rhys to reply, he turned away and made his way down into the courtyard, thinking, that'll give Rhys something to tell his cronies, the prospect of a raid rather than defending Sycharth ought to cheer them up.

The warning shout from the gate-house tower that afternoon of a lone rider approaching, signalled the return of Maredudd. Minutes later he rode across the drawbridge at a gallop to rein up almost outside the great hall as Owain hurried out of its doorway quickly followed by Marged and Catrin. Marged had been worrying particularly about Maredudd despite Owain's telling her that he would be all right. Saying, 'He's still just a boy, Owain,' she refused to be reassured when told firmly that Maredudd was fourteen and had come of age! Leaping from his horse now, Maredudd, face flushed, hair in disarray, ran up to Owain bright eyed and all smiles.

'They're coming, Father,' he said triumphantly. 'Uncle Tudor and his men are but half a day's march behind me. Two hundred of them, Uncle Tudor said, archers and lances too!'

Owain breathed a sigh of relief and clapped young Maredudd on the shoulder.

'Well done, my . . . ' He stopped and corrected the unspoken word, 'Well done son, a soldier's work you've done these last few days! I'm proud of you!' He turned to include Marged. 'Aren't we?'

He could see that Marged was restraining herself from going over to Maredudd and hugging him, instead she only smiled, though whether at Maredudd's safe return or at the news he brought, Owain could not tell. Her eyes shining, or perhaps just glistening with unshed tears, she said quietly, 'Yes Maredudd, very proud!'

His arm around Maredudd's shoulder now, Owain led the way back into the great hall, so they could all hear the story of Maredudd's adventure.

A few hours later Tudor and his two captains rode into the courtyard to be greeted at the gate-house by Owain, with Maredudd standing proudly alongside. Tudor, mailed and armed, was grimed from his journey, but beneath all that it was plain to see he and Owain were brothers for they were alike as two peas in a pod. Broad shouldered and of medium stature, they were both powerful men who stood there in all the confidence and pride, indeed the arrogance, of their nobility. Both men were bearded, black haired, brown eyed and with the same hawk like family nose: it might have been one man looking at a picture of himself as he had been just two years earlier when armed for war. Except that is, for the wart above Owain's right eye.

Tudor grinned as he shook Owain firmly by the hand. 'I see I'm in time then, Owain!' he said. 'From what young Maredudd told me I thought your need was greater than just a meeting of our council! I expected Sycharth to be but glowing embers by the time I got here, your friend Lord Grey in full possession of what was left!' He spread his hands. 'And now all this! Why, 'tis as though Sycharth has declared a holiday!'

Owain laughed. 'Not so, Tudor, I am well glad to see you . . . and even more, that you have not come alone, for I believe we shall have need of all who'll join our banner before the week is out.'

Stepping out onto the drawbridge Owain looked down towards the church and Afon Cynllaith where all was activity as Tudor's retinue made camp on the meadow by the church. There was all the usual bustle and noise of a small army establishing a base after a long march, with tents being erected, fires lit, horses being led to water or settled for the night. There was a stream of people from Sycharth too, making their way towards the encampment carrying casks of ale, bread and haunches of meat, for these were welcome visitors! A few there were who carried no food, women loitering around the edges of the camp giggling amongst themselves, talking boldly with any soldier who'd pause in his labour.

Smiling, Owain turned to Tudor, satisfied his men would fare well enough that night and nodding towards the hall, said, 'Let's go in, a meal and a pitcher of wine waits your attention. I'm sure you'll do justice to both!'

With that he led the way into the great hall with Tudor, his captains and Maredudd following. As they went in, they found Marged waiting for them and she greeted Tudor warmly, 'It is always good to see you Tudor, now more than ever! How is Olwen? She is well I trust, and the children . . . '

Laughing, Owain interrupted, 'Peace, Marged! Let them get to a goblet of wine, they've ridden hard to get here and must be dying of thirst!'

With Tudor's presence the tension that had existed prior to his arrival eased. His reinforcements ensured that it would require more than a raiding party from Ruthin to take Sycharth, or arrest Lord Owain for his failure to answer his array by the King. The tension eased, but the threat was still there so it was a great relief to the inhabitants of Sycharth, not least its lord, Owain, as over the next few days further reinforcements arrived.

Their arrival was eagerly awaited by all and there were many who gazed longingly from the parapets or, if privileged enough, the gate-house tower. Strangely, amongst these latter was Catrin who, until now, had seldom shown any great interest in climbing to the lookout position. Now, however, she was seldom away from there except for meals and, whenever Rhys kept watch, was forever asking him when Dafydd would return with the men of Cardigan.

It seemed that Rhys knew well that it was neither the men of Cardigan nor Dafydd in whom her interest lay, for often he teased her. 'Oh months, my lady!' he'd respond. 'Cardigan is a great distance away, with hills and rivers for the men to cross!' Then he'd go on to explain at length that it was not all the men of Cardigan who'd come, but only those of her father's manors there until, all out of patience with him, she'd flounce away, down from the tower.

Nor was it the Cardigan men who came first, but Owain's cousins from Ynys Mon, or Anglesey as the English called it. A rich island it was too, for more than half the grain for North Wales came from there and that was evident in the apparel of Owain's cousins when they arrived. Unlike his brother Tudor they came not armoured but as gentlemen attending court, escorted by men at arms, their captains.

Their retinue was a pleasing sight for Owain's eyes: full five hundred well armed men, almost half of whom were mounted on their small, sturdy Welsh horses! Now Sycharth was secure, for nearly a thousand men stood to arms there, few marcher lords could readily raise a greater force than that!

He and Tudor barely had time to greet their cousins, Rhys and Ednyfed Tudur, in the courtyard when there was a cry from the watchman to announce Dafydd's return.

'Well met, cousins,' Owain said shaking them by the hand. 'With my men from Cardigan just arrived we have a force assembled here that will ensure no marcher lord will put a foot across the border willingly!' He laughed and slapped Ednyfed on the shoulder. 'Henry himself on his march to Scotland will pause and wonder whether he should yet head north, eh?'

With much laughter and jesting Owain led the party into the great hall, saying, 'Tonight, we feast and make merry, tomorrow we ride to Glyndyfrdwy . . . '

Ednyfed stopped, then glanced at his brother, Rhys, as if surprised, before saying, 'Glyndyfrdwy, cousin, I thought . . . '

Owain smiled reassuringly. 'The council meets at Glyndyfrdwy cousin, for the immediate threat was here at Sycharth and here the need for your retinues. We meet in quiet, privily, at Glyndyfrdwy tomorrow noon, to discuss matters of great import, I believe, to our lands here in Gwynedd, Powys and indeed the whole of Wales!

Chapter Eight

As Idris rode up to the drawbridge of Sycharth with Dafydd and Talwyn, one of Lord Owain's captains from Cardigan, he breathed a sigh of relief that at last the long, hot, journey was over. He was hungry and thirsty and the main topic of conversation between them for the last hour was of a long drink and a hot meal when they got to Sycharth but even that had ceased as they drew near to the manor.

The horses' hooves rang hollow now as they cantered onto the drawbridge and Idris, looking up at the gate-house tower thought, or perhaps imagined, that he glimpsed Catrin there. If she was there at all, she quickly disappeared and he smiled to himself, thinking that he had indeed missed Catrin whilst he'd been in Cardigan. He was surprised at himself too, as he realised how much he looked forward to seeing her again.

They were through the gate and into the courtyard when he saw her and it was no illusion now, it was Catrin. She stood by the door to the gate-house tower. It had been her up there after all, but now it was as though she had not noticed their arrival and Idris felt a twinge of disappointment, of hurt.

Her head turned then and when she glanced at them it was apparent their arrival was expected.

'Hello Dafydd,' she said, 'Lord Owain is in the great hall.'

Idris's heart gave a little leap and his face flushed red beneath the grime of a long day's ride, for although she appeared to be speaking to Dafydd her eyes held his in a steady gaze.

Dafydd seemed to be having difficulty in keeping his voice suitably respectful as he replied, 'Aye my lady, we'll just stable the horses, then I'll make my report to him.'

So saying Dafydd was about to lead the way to the stables,

65

when Catrin exclaimed urgently, 'Oh no, Dafydd! My father said that you and Captain Talwyn,' she looked at the other rider, eyebrows arched and, as he nodded, continued, 'should report to him immediately you arrived.'

Dafydd looked from her to the horses before, with a nod to Idris, handing him the reins, saying, 'Oh well, Idris bach, you've drawn the short straw!'

Catrin though, pointing at two men walking across the courtyard, said all innocence, 'Look, there's someone coming for your horses now.'

Dafydd smiled knowingly, saying, 'Come on, Tal, Idris can see the horses settled for the night,' and taking him by the arm headed towards the great hall. He had only taken a few steps, however, before glancing back at Idris, he winked, then quickly turned his head away again.

As the two captains departed, Idris thought longingly of the pots of ale they would undoubtedly have in their big hands in a few moments. As he looked at Catrin though, standing close to him now, her blue eyes gazing up at him, all he could think of was that day in the dovecote and of kissing her there.

Catrin was moistening her lips with the tip of her tongue, putting her hand on his arm.

'You've been away a long time, Idris,' she said softly. 'I was afraid that you would not come back in time!'

Perplexed, Idris frowned, and asked her, 'Come back in time? In time for what Catrin?'

Her hand tugged on his sleeve now as she whispered, 'Come in the gate-house and I'll tell you all about it!'

Idris looked at her then, his heart beating a little faster, looked around the courtyard, but it was deserted. The people of the manor were either in the great hall or greeting the newly arrived men from Cardigan and Ynys Mon. Catrin was smiling now as she pulled harder at his sleeve and not unwillingly, he followed her into the gate-house.

Minutes later Idris smiled as, still holding her in his arms, he said, 'You still haven't told me why you were frightened, Catrin, what happened?'

She told him then as she snuggled up close to him: about the letter of array that came too late, of her fears that Lord Grey would attack Sycharth. Initially that gave him a warm protective

66

feeling, but gradually the import of her words sunk in. Suddenly the gate-house chilled and he shivered. Catrin, leaning back, her hands on his chest, asked, 'What's the matter, Idris, does holding me make you cold?'

Laughing, he shook his head. 'No Catrin, never that! 'Tis but a ghost walked by, these walls are old enough!'

If the ghost had passed by though, the chill was still in his bones, for he realised that not only Lord Owain, but he too, was a rebel now, should he raise his bow against any who came to arrest Lord Owain. He saw Catrin still looking up at him, the blue eyes thoughtful, but her moist lips, the warmth of her body close to his, pushed all thought of rebels and the dread fate that awaited them, aside. With a grim smile he thought, an' I follow my trade is it likely I'd live forever? Bending his head to hers he kissed her again thinking now, not if Gruffydd finds us here!

The next day the servants had cleared the meal, but the wine and fruit were still on the table in the hall at Glyndyfrdwy, for this was more a family council of war rather than a parliament. Well fed they sat back in their chairs and waited for Lord Owain, their accepted leader, to begin.

He sat there at the head of the table with his brother Tudor on his right, his oldest son, Gruffydd on his left as though they were but three pictures of the man at different stages of his life, so much alike they looked.

His brothers in law, Philip and Gruffydd Hanmer, his cousins Rhys and Ednyfyd Tudur faced each other across the table. The English Hanmers fair haired, their fresh complexions making them seem younger than they were, as they looked across unsmiling at the ginger haired, blue eyed, Tudurs.

The dean of St Asaph, Hywel Cyffin, hands clasped in front of him as if in prayer, his clerical robes and serious mien setting him apart from the members of the family, sat facing Lord Owain. Alongside the dean was the bard, Crach Finnant, whose wise counsel Lord Owain often sought, not entirely to the approval of Hywel Cyffin, for Crach was known to be a seer, a prophet. Lord Owain spread his hands, as if to embrace them all.

'Brothers, cousins, I thank you for so readily coming to this council.' He smiled. 'And with such welcome strength!' He bowed his head to the end of the table. 'And you too, learned gentlemen, for you both know how much I value your wise counsel.

'When first I sent word to you all it was because of a very real and present danger to us here at Sycharth . . . '

Lord Owain paused and stroked his beard, thinking that that was perhaps a bending of the truth. As he looked around the table though heads were nodding sagely and some leant forward as though not to miss a word. At the end of the table Crach Finnant's saturnine countenance remained impassive and his eyes had a far away look as though he were with, but not of them. Owain shook his head, then continued: 'Much has happened since my messengers left Sycharth on their urgent errand such that, when I have told my tale, strong men may feel the stakes too high, the hazard greater than the prize. Yet, if you but hear me out, you well may feel a century of ills, a confluence of circumstances, have led us to an opportunity which may never come to Wales again.'

He took a draught of wine, ran his tongue over his lips and, his eyes bright with fervour, hwyl, continued, 'Wales, our land, once ruled by Welsh Princes: Powys, Gwynedd, Deheubarth, is ringed by English Castles not to protect, but to subdue. The taxes which burden all our people are raised not for their benefit, but to pay for the castles that keep them all in servitude. How must the English nobility laugh at us, the slaves paying for their own shackles!

'Around those castles, towns have grown, towns we never felt the need of 'til the English castles came.' He smiled and waved a hand. 'But that is progress, so I'm told! Is it indeed progress though, when English people are brought to inhabit those towns?' Glancing at the Hanmers, he waved his hands again. 'Ordinary, decent English people, I have no doubt, but is it right that only they have rights of citizenship in the towns? Is it right that no Welshman has rights of citizenship in the towns in their own land?

'We are all but lieges of the English King, or English lords, yet round this table sit descendants of all the princely houses of Wales and there are others throughout Wales. How many of our fellow Welsh gentry sit in the English Parliament and contribute to our governance . . . too few to count you well may say!

'You may say too, that Llewellyn's reign as Prince of Wales, was but a short one, that he held the Principality with the English King as his liege lord and that was all six score years ago. All that is true, if you have the stomach to accept we are a subject race. But . . . ' he held his index finger up as if in warning, 'was not Llewellyn's liege lord then, the legitimate, the undoubted, king of England?'

There were gasps around the table and some sat back in their chairs and looked at him in surprise, but Gruffydd sat there smiling, eyes bright, looking at his father as though it should be a halo rather than a coronet on his head.

It was his brother Tudor who spoke first, to answer a question with a blunt question. 'Say you then, brother, that Henry is a usurper to whom we owe no allegiance?'

Lord Owain looked him in the eye steadily for a moment before answering, but when he did his quiet voice seemed to penetrate to every corner of the hall.

'Are there any here who doubt that Richard, the second of that name, lives? And if he lives, can Henry indeed be the rightful King? If he be dead, as few believe, should not the rightful king, be Edmund Mortimer, Earl of March? So! Either a live Richard is king or, if he be dead, then Edmund should be king.' He shook his head as though breaking bad news to the bereaved. 'In neither case, can Henry Bolingbroke be king by right!'

Frowning now, as though that had triggered another thought in his mind, he continued: 'That leads me to another point! If Henry is king, yet should not be, it also follows that his son the Prince, who some call Hal, cannot be the rightful Prince of Wales, for if the father is not king, surely the son cannot be prince!'

The silence that followed was broken by Philip Hanmer saying with a wry smile, 'Perhaps I, an "ordinary, decent Englishman" may speak on what may seem to be but Welsh affairs. Yet what transpires here may well affect my sister and her brood and so affect me too. There may be truth in much of what you say Owain, but one thing you cannot gainsay: that Henry is the anointed king of England, by Holy Church approved. As such, it is to him that I and my brother here, owe our allegiance.'

Pursing his lips, Lord Owain nodded before replying, 'All here may speak, every voice has equal weight and you, my kin by marriage no less than any other. 'Tis true that Henry was anointed by the Church, I wonder though whether that was by duress, or mere recognition that by force of arms he was de facto king.' He nodded shrewdly and raised that finger again. 'De facto note, but not de jure!' Looking at the Dean of St Asaph now, he asked, 'If not de jure, is that anointment any more legitimate than the false crown he wears?

Hywel Cyffin pondered the question for a moment, hands pressed together and raised to his lips, then shook his head. 'I do not know, Lord Owain, whether duress was present when Henry was anointed. Nor can I say his anointment was in recognition of de facto kingship, though if as you suggest, King Richard, who was of undoubted lineage, lives, then he must still take precedence. 'Tis also true that Edmund, Earl of March, whose grandsire was Lionel, the Duke of Clarence, takes precedence over Henry Bolingbroke, whose father, John of Gaunt was younger brother to Lionel.'

Heads around the table shook or nodded dependent, perhaps, upon whether they had followed the cleric's explanation. The silence that followed was broken at last by Owain's cousin, Ednyfed Tudur, whose gruff voice matched his square, heavily built frame. Frowning he scratched his ginger beard with spatulate fingers. 'All this talk of lineage of English kings bemuses me, cousin! It matters not to me which English bastard sits upon their throne,' Dean Hywel winced and the Hanmer brothers stared at him stony-faced, but ignoring them, he continued, 'I came here to take up your quarrel with Grey of Ruthin,' then, as if it were an afterthought, 'and perhaps, just perhaps mark you, in hope of some little gain in doing so! Yet in my camp at Sycharth, all the talk is of you refusing Henry's array and this you have not mentioned!'

Lord Owain shrugged and tossed his head dismissively. 'I have spoken thus far, cousin, of the disease that ails our country, not of the symptoms and it is a symptom of which you speak! It is a *symptom* that Lord Grey could seize my land, and I gain no redress by English law, in which I am well learned! It is a *symptom* that Henry could send me a letter of array with notice impossible to meet, yet hold all my lands forfeit should I not obey! It is a *disease* that an English king and even more, a usurper English King, holds such governance over us!

' 'Tis by such a one, that I am now named rebel, traitor, my lands forfeit, my person fit for any who dares to arrest and deliver me to that *king*! My wager's placed, my die is cast, I fight to hold that which is mine by right, by heritage, a Wales free from the English yoke! I ask no man to follow, hold no man false who has no stomach for so great a hazard. Yet what better time to dare such an enterprise? A false king on England's throne, that king embroiled in war with the Scots, our Celtic cousins who, like us Welsh, are descended from Brut!'

Dean Hywel frowned, being not enamoured of such mythology, but he did not, could not interrupt Lord Owain's flow.

'Not only is Henry now marching on the Scots, but he has quarrels too with France their ancient ally. Across our western sea, Ireland, like us, rests unhappily under English governance and struggles against its chains. Edmund, the Earl of March, Henry holds as ward or rather, I should say, as hostage for the conduct of the Earl's uncle, Edmund Mortimer the elder. Nor can the Percies be enamoured at his reign: they supported him when he wrested the throne from Richard, with but scant reward it seems! Other magnates there are who also look askance at Henry's claim to sovereignty. Was there ever a king who had so weak a grasp on England's realm? What reward would Richard give were we to aid him to his throne again? What better time to wrest the sceptre from a king who never was!'

He reached to take some wine, but before he could put the goblet to his lips, his brother Tudor rose to his feet and raising his goblet called out, 'I am for Lord Owain!'

Around the table there was a shuffling of feet as others began to stand, but before anyone could say a word, Owain's son, Gruffydd ab Owain, raised his goblet and, his voice exultant, cried, 'I am for *Prince* Owain!'

All the others were on their feet now and none abstained as they raised their glasses to toast their Prince, thus vouchsafing their allegiance. As they lowered their glasses, Prince Owain stood, sipped his wine and said quietly, 'I drink to you, my brothers, for now are we all brothers in arms, brothers in a righteous enterprise. Know you all this: once we put our hand to this plough there is no turning for the furrow, but straight it must go to the very end of the field, for we are then committed, whatever our destiny may hold. I say again, if any man has secret doubt, leave now!'

He looked around the table, but there was no movement, no

shuffling of feet, just steadfast looks from grim, committed faces. Owain sighed in relief and nodded to Hywel Cyffin.

'Will you, Reverend Dean, seek a blessing on this endeavour so that, with God's help, we may prevail?'

He closed his eyes, half listening to Hywel intone his prayer and wondering the while exactly to what destiny he had committed them all. When the Dean finished praying, there was a muttered 'Amen' from those around the table and Prince Owain opened his eyes to proclaim, in a voice no longer quiet, 'Brothers, when you leave here, tell all who'll heed that I, Owain Glyn Dŵr, cry defiance to the usurper, Henry Bolingbroke and welcome to my proud banner all those who would be free of him and his adherents!'

With shouts of acclaim those assembled rose, to break up into groups of twos and threes to talk excitedly about the outcome of the council. Seeing Crach Finnant standing alone at the end of the table, thoughtfully gazing into space, Prince Owain walked over to him and took him by the arm.

'Crach, my old friend, why so silent when now, if ever, I need your counsel?'

Crach shook his head, his solemn face cracked into a sad smile. 'What could I say, Owain, that you would heed? I can but prophesy, not change the course of history!'

Owain smiled understandingly. 'I know, old friend and yet I feel it in my bones that if you cannot change, you can foretell, events. So humour me, for now I yearn to share your vision of the future, so I may be as well prepared to meet my destiny as ever man may be!'

Crach Finnant rested a frail hand on Owain's arm as he shook his head sorrowfully and almost whispered in reply, 'I cannot share that which I cannot see. But deep in my heart, Owain, I have a dreadful fear that you have come a hundred years too soon!'

As he looked into the seer's pale eyes a chill came over Owain and he shivered, but shrugging the feeling aside, he smiled with a confidence he did not now possess and touched the old man's fragile arm lightly.

'Ah Crach, you cheer me that you had no fearful vision of my cause. For your heart's ease, I may tell you that many a man across the whole of Wales will soon be saying that I came a hundred years too late!'

Crach Finnant smiled politely, but Owain sensed a distance between them now as the old man replied, 'I pray it may be so, Prince Owain, but now, if it pleases you, I must go and rest my old bones.'

Watching him go, Prince Owain's eyes clouded and he shivered again at the thought of the old man's prophecy.

d

Chapter Nine

Whilst Marged's brothers, the Hanmers, went straight from Glyndyfrdwy to marshal their forces at their estates, the others, whose forces were already encamped around Sycharth, returned there to plan for war. On their arrival they were met at the gate-house by their captains who, warned of their approach, were anxiously assembled there to glean the results of the council.

Idris standing beside Dafydd and Talwyn took one look at the grim face of their lord, the banner proudly borne by his son Gruffydd and turned to Dafydd.

'What is it to be then, do you think, Dafydd?' he asked. 'A raid on Ruthin, a siege of Lord Grey's castle there, or what?'

Dafydd shook his head. 'We are more than enough for a raid on Ruthin, Idris, but a siege of Ruthin Castle? No, I think not, we have no siege weapons, no mangonel, no catapults, without them it would be too long a siege. We shall have to strike hard and quickly, before the other marcher lords come to Ruthin's aid, as sure enough they would. Our main force would look small indeed by comparison then.' He nodded towards the newly arrived group of lords, who were halted now at the approach to the gate-house. 'But hush, I think we'll not wait long to know what apprehends!'

Lord Owain turned now towards the assembled captains, his brother Tudor on his right, Gruffydd holding his banner aloft, on his left, all flanked by his cousins Ednyfyd and Rhys. There was complete silence as Lord Owain, still mounted, looked at the group of captains as though looking each man directly in the eye, then, pointing to his banner as it fluttered in the breeze.

'Captains all, that banner proclaims me Prince, appointed so by the grace of God and by my lords in full council assembled! We stand united, in that we hold no other man to be Prince in

Wales and here declare we owe no fealty to any king or prince who falsely reigns over our neighbour, England!'

He paused and a tremor went through the silent crowd as though the earth had shaken, for no such words had been spoken there or in any part of Wales for over a century. Then a murmuring began that swelled into a roar, a rattle as swords were drawn, raised above heads and excitedly waved. One man shouted, 'Prince Owain!' quickly joined by the others as they all hailed, 'A Prince! A Prince! Prince Owain for Wales!'

Prince Owain smiled proudly, confidently, at them and, flanked by his grinning kin, he also drew his sword to point it towards the encampments below.

'Go tell your men to prepare for war! Tell them we are not alone! My emissaries already ride to call all Welshmen to my banner and then we march on England!'

To loud huzzas, a smiling Prince Owain waved his sword triumphantly and turning, was led into the courtyard by Gruffydd bearing his banner as though it were the Holy Grail, as indeed, perhaps for Gruffydd, it was.

As the excited group of captains left to spread the word amongst their men, Idris and Dafydd stood there for a discreet few minutes before going into the manor themselves. Sober faced, Dafydd turned to Idris.

'So then, Idris bach,' he said. 'A raid on Ruthin, a siege of Ruthin Castle? No, my boy, we're laying siege to all of bloody England!'

Prince Owain, following the bannerman Gruffydd, entered the courtyard smiling, to be met by Marged her face set, cold, gazing at him not in welcome but as though he were a stranger. Alongside Marged, a pale-faced Catrin curtseyed as he rode up to them and dismounted, whilst a thoughtful looking Maredudd bowed his head as much in sorrow, it seemed, as in allegiance.

His smile somewhat strained now, Owain went over and embraced Marged warmly, but she was stiff, unresponsive as he held her and gave no answering kiss on his cheek. Still holding her, he stepped back half a pace and frowned. 'No welcome for your returning lord then, Marged?' he asked as he waved his hand at the blue sky. 'Why so chill at Sycharth, when all around 'tis summer still?'

Pulling away from him, Marged shook her head and said bitterly, 'Summer Owain? Rebellion knows only bleak winter, widow's weeds and orphaned children!' A gesture of her hand embraced the manor, the courtyard and the children grouped around her. 'Would you hazard all this, all of us, for sake of pride, for pique, for mere title? I care not who rules in England or even in Wales, whilst we dwell safely, happily, here at Sycharth. Nor do I care for any title you may gain. An esquire, one Owain Glyn Dŵr, I married and I am well content with that, my lord!'

Tears began to well in her eyes and turning hurriedly away, she shepherded the younger children back towards the great hall, leaving only Maredudd and Catrin standing there as though they knew not where to look. For a moment Owain was not sure himself either, then, not daring to look at his grinning kinsmen, said to Maredudd, 'You heard my call to arms out there Maredudd?' And as his son nodded, he smiled confidently and nodded towards the banner-bearing Gruffydd. 'What think you then, will you follow my banner, or . . . ' Owain glanced at the retreating Marged, 'take the woman's view?'

Maredudd looked at him steadily for a moment as though considering his reply: 'Of course I'd follow you, Father . . . '

Owain's face darkened as Maredudd paused, shocked that his son might have any hesitation over the answer. 'Of course I would,' Maredudd continued. 'Were I but privy to the argument. Yet I was not present at the Glyndyfrdwy council so, unlike Gruffydd there, I am ignorant as to why such remedy for so little apparent cause!'

Owain stepped back as though he had been struck and looked around him at the now serious faces of his brother, his cousins; at Gruffydd, whose face held not seriousness but scorn, contempt. Gritting his teeth, he shook his head angrily. 'Maredudd . . . ' he began, but his brother, Tudor, touched him on the arm and, smiling understandingly, said with a toss of the head.

'Maredudd's right, Owain, he was not there. You'd not have any man follow without knowing the cause and least of all, your son!'

Owain, lips pursed, nodded slowly in agreement, as he looked at Maredudd. It is nothing about the cause, he thought, it is all about: why was Gruffydd there and not Maredudd! Aloud though his voice was calm, understanding as he said to Maredudd, 'Your Uncle Tudor speaks with the voice of reason . . . as you did too my son. One should not ask any man to follow blindly, or only knowing half the story, so you and I will speak, when freely you can then decide.'

As Maredudd nodded in response, Owain turned to speak to Catrin hoping for some unqualified welcome, but she seemed to have slipped away so, turning to the other men, he smiled. 'It seems there's more debate on our return than at our council! I trust we fare better at the table: wine I can promise but, from our cool reception here today, I fear we'll feast on but short commons!'

Catrin was torn between running after her mother, to try and comfort her, or trying to find Idris and seek comfort herself, for she was frightened. She did not know why she was frightened really, but her mother clearly feared this . . . this rebellion of Father's, perhaps with cause, for she had more knowledge of border raiding than Catrin. For years now there had been comparative peace along the marches, except for petty border squabbles . . . like Father's quarrel with Lord Grey.

After hesitating for a moment, Catrin saw that her father was getting cross with Maredudd who she knew was sulking because he had not been allowed to go to Glyndyfrdwy with all the men. Quietly she sidled out of her father's line of vision and slipped away from the group, unsure where to go to find Idris, sure only that she wanted the comfort of his arms around her.

She knew that he would not be in the encampments down in the valley by the church and in any event, her mother did not like her going down there, not now that all the soldiery were there, but where could she find him? Disconsolately walking around the courtyard beneath the parapet she came upon the fletcher working at his trade, truing arrow shafts with a blade of sorts. Beside him was a man bent before a stack of finished arrows, complaining as he examined one after another, 'Where do you find such crooked shafts, Emrys, I've not found one that's true amongst a score or more!'

The fletcher winced as though in anguish at such a slur upon his craftsmanship.

'My arrows not true, Idris? As true as the Lord's cross, each one, I tell you, show me one that's not and you're a liar.' He sniffed. 'Aye, and probably an English one at that!'

With that final insult he turned away to hold the arrow shaft end on to his eye before rotating it with his finger. Smiling in satisfaction, he nodded at the bent figure of Idris. 'And there's another for you! True as can be!' He glanced around at Catrin standing there and, flustered now, lowered the arrow to his side saying, 'I crave pardon, my lady, I saw you not . . . '

His words tailed off, perhaps because she was not looking at him, but at Idris the archer, who was standing now and, to the fletcher's obvious amazement, actually smiling familiarly at the Lady Catrin. He seemed even more amazed when Catrin said to Idris, 'My father wants you archer, come with me!' Idris just dropped the arrow that he had been examining on the ground and, still smiling, followed her not towards the great hall which Lord Owain and all the other gentry were just entering, but in the direction of the gate-house.

As Catrin and Idris walked away, she turned her head to see Emrys the fletcher pick up the arrow Idris had discarded and examine it before, wiping it carefully, replacing it with the others in his racks. Laughing, Catrin turned to Idris. 'Do you always choose your arrows so carefully, Idris? Old Emrys seemed aggrieved you fussed so over them!'

Idris glanced sideways. 'True enough, Catrin, but then he labours safely at his workbench, but I perforce must use them sometimes other than for sport at the target butt.'

Catrin frowned and her face suddenly serious she put her hand on his arm. 'Oh, I know Idris, I fear for you, for all of us: my father said . . . '

Idris stepped back a little from her and as her hand fell from his arm, looked anxiously around the courtyard, before continuing towards the gate-house.

'I know,' he replied. 'I was with Dafydd when Prince Owain returned!'

Moving closer to him again Catrin almost whispered, 'Is my father really a Prince now, Idris?'

Idris laughed. 'I am but an indentured archer, Catrin, indentured to your father. If he tells me he is a lord, then so he is. If other lords then call him 'Prince,' why, so do I, for I know not what it is that makes one man prince, another king, unless it be his father!'

Catrin frowned again, as she tried to unravel his reply, but they were at the door to the gate-house now and opening it, she went in. Idris, with one last look around the courtyard, followed.

Both within the manor and down in the encampment below, all was activity in the few days that followed, as all the men prepared for a campaign. It was clear to all, from seasoned captain to mere boy, that this was to be no quick foray across the nearby border with England followed by a hasty return with a few stolen cattle.

Certainly Idris had no doubts: each moment he spent with Catrin, each confidence she whispered as they clung together, confirmed to him that this would be no short campaign, but war. Every instinct told him that now was the time to flee, now, in the confusion of all others' preparations. Two days' march and he would be clear of this madness, might even profit from his knowledge!

Yet each time he held Catrin in his arms, her warm breath on his cheek as she whispered to him of her fear and that she loved him so, he weakened and vowed he loved her too, that he'd protect her! Now though, as he waited for her in the shadows by the dovecote, looking anxiously towards the moonlit manor, starting at the slightest sound or at the sudden movement of a bat silently flitting by, he was resolved. And all of Wales should rise, he thought, yet so would England too. Not for love of Henry or any other king, but for their ancient enmity! How then can Owain win against such overwhelming force. He shook his head, thinking, no, there is no reason in it, it is time to go!

He saw her then, or thought he did, a shadow flitting over the drawbridge on silent feet, her pale dress fluttering like a moth around a lantern as she was caught by the moon before it hid behind a cloud. Then she was running to him and crying breathlessly, 'Oh, Idris, I couldn't get away . . . ' and he was holding her close to him, smoothing her hair, laughing, soothing:

'Hush, Catrin, 'tis all right, I'm here!'

As she looked up at him, her arms around his neck, the moonlight revealing the frightened look her eyes held, he felt himself weakening again but steeling himself, he held her away from him.

'Catrin,' he began, 'I am . . . '

He paused as Catrin, nodding her head, interrupted him.

'I am too,' she said in apparent agreement and shivered as she added, ' 'tis chill out here!'

Turning, she reached out to open the door to the dovecote, gently pulling him inside with her, Idris shook his head as he followed, wondering why it was he could so easily be trapped. Moments later, lying there with Catrin in his arms he no longer felt ensnared, for as his manhood grew he bravely knew he'd follow Owain on this new crusade.

Chapter Ten

'It is not that I'm worried about Lord Grey, Owain,' Tudor said, frowning, 'we've more than enough men here already to lay siege to Ruthin. If we could interdict his castle undisturbed, time would be our friend and perforce, in time, he'd ask for quarter. Yet you, as well as I, know that time is but an English ally here, for it would bring, fast foot, marcher lords to relieve him from our interdict. Men we have enough and more will come, I have no doubt, but what we lack are siege weapons, without these we cannot quickly bring such castles down!'

As Tudor sat back, bluff Ednyfed, shaking his head, laughed. 'Lay siege to Ruthin, cousin Tudor, what need is there of that? Long sieges, and that I grant you it would be, are costly affairs: sapping of the besieger's spirit as those inside wait out for winter, if nothing else, to lift the siege. That is not for such a force as ours! What we must do is strike at the English purse: raid, burn their crops, sack their towns,' he grinned. 'Aye, rob them of their cattle, sheep and women too . . . ' He gave a gruff laugh again. 'We can always let them have their women back!'

Prince Owain suppressed a smile at his kinsfolk: his brother Tudor, the careful, thoughtful, strategist, Ednyfed, no pitched battle for him either but rather the eternal border raider: a bloody nose for the enemy, a quick profit for himself and a carousing on a safe return!

Yet each in his own way was right. Their main force had not the time or siege weapons to bring the great castles of the English down quickly. Striking at the 'English purse' made sense! His force was mobile, their enemy entrenched with long lines of communication and support, especially those castles on the West coast: Caernarvon, Aberystwyth, Harlech, which could only really be supplied by sea if interdicted.

Smiling broadly, he spread his hands and announced, 'You are both right! That must be our strategy!'

As they looked at him, amazed it seemed, that he should consider such diverse views agreement, he continued, 'We must, at all costs, avoid the pitched battle with a superior English force! We must strike hard at the 'English purse', their towns, cattle, crops;. extract high ransom, too, for their captured nobility and so finance our war, for war, mark you, it is! Harass their supply routes, aye and stretch their resources too, by striking as hard, as often and far apart as may be; by seeking support from elsewhere too: Robert of Scotland, Charles of France and the rebellious Irish. Suborn whichever English magnates we might wean away from Henry and to the cause of Richard, who yet may live.'

Ednyfed's brother, Rhys Tudur, grinned and nodded at Ednyfed and his cousin Tudor. 'I never thought that such views as theirs, Owain, could ever be married and thought that we would be here till crack of doom for such matters to be resolved. Yet through your magic tongue, not only have they been married, but given birth to such children as will yet see us march to victory!'

By the vigorous nodding of their heads, the other two obviously gave their approval to the broad strategy Owain had announced and he smiled. 'And we are agreed on that, let us also be agreed on this: whoever strikes for us, wherever they might strike, fight under one banner, that all may see we are united and that it might better confuse the enemy!'

Again there was a nodding of heads and he continued, 'Marged's kin will presently join us with their men and others too will come, brought by my missives to the gentry and the clergy . . . '

Rhys Tudor, eyebrows arched, interrupted, 'Think you the Hanmers will return then, Owain? Quickly enough they fled from Glyndyfrdwy!' He laughed now. 'And the clergy, why write to them? What will they bring to our aid?'

Owain sighed. 'Thomas you should be called, not Rhys, Doubting Thomas! The Hanmers will be back, beyond doubt, I warrant. As to the clergy and why I wrote to them: are they any less disadvantaged by English governance than us? Does a Welsh Archbishop hold the see of Canterbury or York? How many of the Welsh clergy carry a bishop's crook or hold high office in the church? Do you think that ambition is but a secular vice?' He shook his head as though shocked he should even think it, then smiled. 'Of course it is: even though the clergy may only want preferment within the church that they may better use their wisdom . . . but want it nevertheless! The clergy, I tell you cousin Rhys, are embittered by their lack of preferment and by the pretensions of their English superiors. Who better then than they to preach the justice of our cause, to give their blessing to all who join our banner?'

Rhys grinned. 'No doubting Thomas I, cousin, I only make the Devil's case, but you're more politic than I gave you credit for! So then, do we await the strengthening of our force? If so, I fear for the temper of our men, brought here with such urgency and then allowed to sit encamped with nought to do!'

Owain looked around the great hall, but, apart from the four of them, it was empty. Raising his goblet he sipped at the wine, whilst the others looked at him expectantly. At last he spoke, his voice low, confidential:

'No, Rhys, we must not let their keenness lose its edge! This is what we shall do . . . '

He told them then, how it would all begin, how they would make their first strike against England, how their lives would change . . . forever!

Dafydd gave Idris a sour look. 'I've never got used to it, you know, Idris, never!'

Idris looked at him in surprise. 'What's that, Dafydd?'

Almost as though he hadn't heard, Dafydd didn't answer Idris directly, but just stood there for a moment, looking out over the bustling encampment on the meadows by the church below them. They were on the gate-house tower waiting, as they had been for days now, for it all to begin. Dafydd turned to Idris.

'You'd have thought I would have by now, but I never have. I think sometimes that it's what war is all about: waiting! Waiting for this, waiting for that, but mostly waiting for someone to make a decision and when they do, it's usually too bloody late.'

Idris grinned. 'A few months now Dafydd and you can relax again, for winter will be on us and there won't be much campaigning then!'

That only got him a sardonic look from Dafydd. 'It's all very well for you, young Idris, you've got things other than war on your mind at the moment.'

Idris turned quickly on Dafydd. 'No, I've not,' he flustered. 'I'm anxious for it all to begin, earn my pay!'

Dafydd leered as he mimicked, ' "Anxious to begin I am, earn my pay!" That's what you were doing in the dovecote last night then, was it Idris, earning your pay?'

Idris flushed crimson and furious now, snapped, 'Is that how you spend your nights then Dafydd? Snooping around corners like an old woman, hoping to glean something to gossip about!

Dafydd's chest puffed out indignantly. 'Me, snooping, gossip? My nightly rounds I did, as ever! As well for you, I think, I was alone and came upon the dovecote without young Gruffydd by my side! More than one red face I would have seen, I fear. An alarm there would have been that would ensure you'd not see the end of this or any other war!' He wagged a finger at Idris warningly. 'Have a care young Idris, some there are who'd not soft foot away, as I did then!'

Idris snorted, but had no reply to that so, with an angry glance at Dafydd turned and stomped down from the tower. As he reached the small room below, the door to the courtyard opened and in tripped a smiling Catrin, her eyes brightening as she saw him.

'Oh, Idris,' she exclaimed, 'I thought I saw you on the tower!'

He put a finger to his lips, then pointed upwards and whispered, 'I was with Dafydd!'

Her lips formed a silent, 'Oh,' before she said aloud: 'Yes, Idris, my father wants you!' Her voice dropped to a whisper, 'And I do too, my love!'

Idris frowned, desperately wondering what he could say, what he should do, but a smiling Catrin solved his problem as she said in a loud voice, 'What, would you keep my father waiting, archer?'

Half way across the courtyard, Idris glanced back, to see Dafydd still there on the tower, watching their progress now rather than gazing at the encampment. As Dafydd shook his head in apparent sorrow, Idris quickly turned his head away and followed Catrin, not caring greatly where she led, as long as it was out of sight of Dafydd.

Into the great hall she led him, empty now for it was mid-morning, then up a narrow flight of stairs to one of the minstrels' lofts, not where they played, but where they bedded for the night. This small, narrow, loft was seldom used it seemed, for it was empty save for a wooden seat and cobwebs that took the place of curtains there. Idris barely had time to look around the loft before there was the sound of footsteps in the great hall below.

Going to the balcony, he looked down furtively into the great hall, but breathed a sigh of relief as he saw that it was only Iolo Goch going to his harp by the hearth.

'What is it, Idris?' asked Catrin as she came alongside him to also peer into the hall.

He turned to her, and putting his arm around her, pulled her to him, whispering, 'It is only Iolo!'

They watched in silence as Iolo began plucking at the strings as though tuning his harp, before the apparently disjointed sounds merged into a tune whose soft, warm tones seemed to fill the great hall and enveloped them as they stood there watching. Catrin turned towards Idris in his arms.

'Iolo plays his harp so beautifully, Idris!' she whispered. 'It is so peaceful, I cannot believe that it will ever change!'

Idris pulled her gently back into the shadows of the loft, and whispering too, told her, 'It will not change, my love, not for you, not here at Sycharth!'

Even as he said it, he knew it could not be so, for he knew that everything had changed, for all of them, when Owain was proclaimed Prince. As he lay there with Catrin in his arms, with the strains of Iolo's sad melody all around them, he did not want to think of that, indeed of anything that could part them now. So he told her again as he stroked her hair, 'Nothing will change for you, Catrin, not ever!'

As the long column snaked its way along the dusty, moonlit, tracks Idris, riding, alongside Dafydd, was thinking of Catrin. His eyes pricked as he remembered what he'd told her. 'Nothing will change', he'd said and he gave a rueful laugh at the memory, everything had changed! Dafydd turned his head, to say in a sibilant whisper, 'Hush, we make enough noise without you braying like a donkey!' Still in a whisper, he asked, 'What makes you laugh anyway, thinking of a fat merchant's purse weighing down your belt?'

Somewhat unconvincingly, Idris lied, 'No! I was thinking of us all tripping over each other in the dark, when we could have made our way by day!'

Dafydd snorted, 'Dark? Why it could as well be day, so light it is! Now, when I was in Scotland with Prince Owain . . .'

Idris raised his eyes skywards in exasperation, Dafydd never seemed to tire of relating his exploits in the Scottish campaign nor run short of words in the telling either! Waiting for an opportunity, Idris broke into Dafydd's monologue at last.

'That must indeed have been a campaign, Dafydd, not like our little foray here! Why must we lose our sleep to march at night though?'

Idris's acknowledgement of his past deeds seemed to have put Dafydd in good humour. 'I wager it is not the loss of sleep you fret over, young Idris! Yet you are safer here than with your dalliance back at Sycharth.' He chuckled. 'And any profit here will be in gold, not maiden's kisses!'

Idris tossed his head irritably, wishing he'd let Dafydd ramble on about his Scottish exploits. 'You'd not tell the difference twixt man and maid in Scotland, Dafydd. I'm told that in that wild land the men all wear skirts!'

'Ah, Idris bach, there you're wrong!' said Dafydd in all seriousness. 'Hairy they are as their own Scots cattle, and powerfully wield their claymore. Now there's a weapon for you . . .'

Idris closed is eyes . . . and ears, almost wishing he'd not baited Dafydd.

The moon retreated as dawn broke and shadowy shapes gave way to mounted men at arms and archers whilst spearmen trotted alongside the riders. Ahead Idris could see the white tabard Prince Owain wore over his armour and chain mail, alongside Owain was his brother Tudor and Gruffydd ab Owain. Looking at them now, Idris thought of the departure from Sycharth.

The courtyard there had been bright with sunlight, the manor mellow with age that well became it, bright too, the women's dresses as they waited there to bid the men farewell. There had not been many men in the courtyard: the Prince, his kin and Dafydd with half a dozen retainers. All others had been formed up outside the manor, ready for the march.

Idris, mounted, was waiting alongside Dafydd and Rhys whilst Prince Owain and the others bade their farewells. Lady Marged stood there straight-faced, hands clasped in front of her, bowing her head as Prince Owain smiled at her, as if in acquiescence rather than approval of his venture. Solemn young Maredudd, stood beside her, his sword belted like a man, which of course he was. Idris wondered whether Maredudd scowled so because he too disapproved or because he was left behind to hold the manor. All of Prince Owain's other children were lined up there too, all eight of them, as if the Lady Marged were trying to remind Prince Owain of something. Idris had looked at Catrin then and he had tried to tell her with his eyes, that which he could not say aloud. He sighed at the memory, thinking now, as he had wanted to tell her then, I'll come back, my love, I'll come back.

Whilst Idris had been lost in thought the column was passing through a wood, but suddenly they broke through into a clear area to see before them Ruthin town, nestling below the castle standing four square on its motte. Prince Owain raised his right hand and the column came to a reluctant halt, as those behind who had not seen or heard any command jostled the ones in front. Idris watched as Dafydd, called forward by Prince Owain, quickly returned to spread the word. They were to disperse amongst the shelter of the woods and so, unobserved, wait upon Prince Owain's command to fall upon the town.

They sat together, all three, Dafydd, Rhys and Idris, breakfasting on water from their flasks and crusts of bread, watching from their vantage point as the town began to wake.

'It's market day,' said Dafydd cheerfully munching at what seemed to Idris half a loaf, 'look at all the wagons going through the town gate!'

Idris looked, but it was not just carts piled high with produce that made their way through the gate, but merchants leading laden wagons, shepherds driving sheep, cattle lowing, children darting hither and thither. It seemed as though all the world was happily making its way into Ruthin town and all this was but half a mile away. Above the town, grim Castle Ruthin slept on, unaware it seemed of the threat that lay in wait, like a tiger about to pounce!

There was a rustle of movement now and Idris turned his head and seeing Prince Owain mount up, he said quietly to Dafydd,

' 'Tis time, Dafydd!' then they were mounting too, the blood hot coursing in their veins at the thought of the coming fray.

Prince Owain's sword was drawn now as he turned toward them, waving his sword once above his head he pointed it at the waking town and shouted, 'Dewi Sant am Cymru!' Then, spurring his horse, he was off at a gallop toward Ruthin, heedless it seemed, whether any followed. He had no need to look behind for they all followed, galloping, running, screaming, shouting, as though to raise the devil himself and chill the heart of any who dwelt within the walls of Ruthin town.

Before any had time to shut the gate, the Welsh army were pouring through it and into the market square to fall upon the merchants, farmers and their wives and gaping citizens, like wolves on a sleeping camp. Suddenly all was mayhem as stalls uptipped, women screamed, chickens squawked, cattle lowed and sheep ran helter skelter as arrows flew, lances stabbed and swords struck out.

It was all exciting at first for Idris as he rode around the market place waving his sword enough to frighten the devil himself yet drawing no blood. He sickened of it all though as he saw a spearman prick a shepherd who tried to drive his sheep to safety, then, as the frightened shepherd turned, the spearman thrust again and blood spurted like a fountain as the shepherd fell. Eyes bright, the spearman tugged at his weapon to withdraw and ran on to thrust again at any who came his way.

Idris glimpsed Dafydd, dismounted now, holding a knife to a merchant's throat, the merchant pleading, thrusting a purse at Dafydd, the knife slashing and the merchant falling, a hand to his throat hopelessly, uselessly. Dafydd saw him then and with an evil grin, put the purse in a pouch at his belt. The noise was almost deafening with shouts of fear or defiance as men tried to defend themselves against the onslaught with tools or staves. High pitched screams as women saw their menfolk killed and here and there as a woman was dragged, screaming, into a nearby house.

It was not long though before it was all over and a deathly quiet came over Ruthin market day, a bloody market day that those who lived would long remember. A day for which none there would forgive the Welsh. Idris watched as Prince Owain, sitting astride his horse, gazed on Ruthin's ruined market square.

From Owain's stern visage Idris could see that Owain cared little whether any forgave this day, so long as all remembered and remembered well the day that Owain Glyn Dŵr came to market there!

Afterwards whilst some of Prince Owain's men drove cattle and sheep through the town gate, the others put Ruthin to the torch before trooping out of the gate themselves. Idris looked back to see a man at arms come hurrying out of a house followed by a weeping woman screaming abuse after him. As she got to the door she spat at the man at arms, who turning, leered as he bawled, 'Sorry love, I can't stay, but I'll come back!'

Sickened, Idris turned away for he'd seen, not the unknown Englishwoman there, but Catrin, sobbing in her despair.

Minutes later they were back in the woods from which they had erupted on Ruthin and they all turned, to see a pall of smoke hanging over the town, flames licking the roofs of the houses. Above all though, Ruthin Castle still brooded silently, unmoved it seemed by what had gone on below. The English shackles still held as firm as ever.

Idris turned to Dafydd but, thinking of the merchant who had uselessly surrendered his purse, couldn't bring himself to speak to him, so turned to Rhys. 'There's brave they are in their castle, Rhys, but they couldn't sally out to save their town!'

It was Dafydd who answered though, 'Quite right too! A hundred there are there at the most, had they sallied out, we'd all have been across their drawbridge like a ferret down a rabbit's hole and where would they have been then? No, they played according to the rules of war, Idris.' He paused and with a knowing look added, 'And you don't like those rules lad, you'd better stick to chasing maidens!'

Chapter Eleven

With a last look at the sacked and burning Ruthin, the jubilant band of raiders turned their backs on the scene of their victory and began the march to Glyndyfrdwy from where Owain, it was said, intended to make further forays. At the rear a few drovers herded some of the stolen sheep and cattle, food now for Owain's army. The rest of the livestock, accompanied by pack horses and wagons laden with the spoils of war, headed westwards into Wales, to be sold to fill Owain's war chest. Some of this booty would, no doubt, find its way to the English held towns and thus, unwittingly, would the English help to finance Owain's war.

Idris was moodily riding alongside Rhys, trying to avoid Dafydd after the rebuke about the rules of war. Rhys however seemed to have no concern about the day's work and happily whistled away before turning to Idris. 'What do you think of these then, Idris?' he asked slapping a pair of leather boots hanging from his saddle: 'Fine, aren't they?'

Idris regarded him sullenly. 'Whose throat did you cut for those then, Rhys?'

Rhys laughed. 'Don't let Dafydd hear you, Idris bach, sensitive he is, see!' He grinned. 'I had to cut no throat though, hanging from a stall they were and I took them as I rode past. I hope they fit!'

Idris had to smile, despite himself, at Rhys, amidst the scene of carnage, pilfering a pair of boots and hoping they would fit! He grinned, as he looked at the boots: 'You picked them big enough, Rhys, I doubt they'll pinch!' He thought of Dafydd then though, and he said bitterly, 'And you think that Dafydd's sensitive, you've not seen him at his work!'

Rhys was silent for a moment before saying with a sideways

glance, 'Oft enough I've done that, Idris, and long enough has Dafydd plied his trade to do what he is told!'

Idris looked at him askance. 'Told? Was Dafydd told to . . . '

Rhys interrupted him sharply, 'Dafydd was told the plan, Idris!' He waved his hand at the line of march. 'Do you think it took all of us to sack a town the size of Ruthin?' he turned his head and spat emphatically: 'Dafydd could have done it with fifty spearmen! Did you not see that Gruffydd hung back there in the wood, with nigh on a hundred men?'

Frowning, Idris tried to remember seeing Gruffydd in the town, but couldn't picture him there. Then, thinking back to when Prince Owain mounted to lead the attack on Ruthin, he recalled Gruffydd riding to the rear of the column. Nodding slowly, he replied, 'I just thought that we all rode into Ruthin!'

'We went to Ruthin, Idris to strike the fear of God into all there, that the terror of those we left might have wings and make our future attacks the easier! Such noise and havoc we created there the castle garrison could not remain asleep! If they had sallied out, then Gruffydd's force would storm the castle whilst we made sure the sally force would not return. Dafydd spoke truly Idris, 'tis not a game we lightly play!'

As he listened to Rhys, Idris had a sinking feeling and now, shaking his head, he said quietly, 'I think I have no stomach for some of what I saw at Ruthin and that's God's truth!'

Rhys smiled. 'Each man must ply his trade as he sees fit, Idris! If you would be an archer and fight in the centre van of serried ranks of lances, then do not seek your reward with forces such as ours! Prince Owain will forever fight against 'force majeure' as the Frenchies have it and hence will have to fight and run away. Nip at King Henry's heels as a hound would cattle, take their castles like a thief in the night, not by lengthy siege, strike and run, yet see no indignity in that!' Rhys paused and gave Idris a sly look. 'I fear that's not the comfort you sought from me, Idris bach, but me, I only ply my trade, do what I'm told and what I must and stomach what I have to. If you would seek honour, lad, or to keep your hands clean as a maiden's in my lord's parlour, then seek it all elsewhere!' He winked at Idris. 'But I fear me that you'll stay and end up in my lord's parlour with my lady Catrin if God so wills . . . or in the dungeon if he doesn't!'

Idris sat back in his saddle and said in a voice laden with the

91

exasperation he felt, 'Dafydd must have a mouth even bigger than his hands!'

If Rhys's tone had been avuncular, it was derisory now. 'Think you I have need for Dafydd to whisper tales to me? The manor is a community, Idris, just like an English village! Nothing goes on there that someone does not know of, and knowing, whispers to a friend . . . and all are friends! It's common gossip that you are sweet on the young Catrin and she on you and that young Gruffydd knows but cannot prove. Wagers have been taken as to how long it is before Prince Owain knows and whether he'll make you knight or grace you with the favour of his dungeon!'

In the days that followed there was little time for Idris to brood over the warnings of Rhys and Dafydd and, although yearning to return to Sycharth, he had scant opportunity to pine for Catrin. All through the remaining days of September, Prince Owain's army marched on towns throughout north eastern Wales and beyond the border in England.

His main force, swollen now by those of his brothers-in-law, the Hanmers, fell upon the towns of Denbigh, Rhuddlan, Flint, like locusts and, like locusts, left only desolation behind them. If Prince Owain's intention was to pillage and strike terror into the hearts of the English inhabitants, then Idris felt he had succeeded well. Unlike Ruthin, these towns were well inside the Welsh border and the attackers had more leisure to strip them bare without fear themselves of being taken unawares by relieving forces.

Strip them bare we did, thought Idris, as he rode alongside Dafydd from the smoking ruins of Flint. Hours it had taken them just to organise the train of wagons and pack horses to carry the booty away and much wailing there had been by those cowed citizens who remained. Who remained . . . he brushed the thought aside, if they hadn't resisted, tried to save their chattels, more would have remained. He turned to Dafydd.

'Success again then, Dafydd!'

Dafydd nodded, his brow furrowed. 'Aye to some degree, Idris! The custodian of the castle, though, knew his business well . . . too well to poke his nose out of the castle gate against such a force as ours!' He grinned and pointed with a thumb over his shoulder at the heavily laden pack train that followed slowly behind them. 'It will be some time though before they hold a fair day in Flint again!'

With a sly sideways look at Idris he added, 'That's a fine chain you have around your neck! Worth many a week's pay for any archer, I warrant!' He raised an eyebrow. 'A gift, perhaps?'

Unblinking, Idris looked him in the eye. 'Aye, Dafydd, a kind of gift I'd say. Fair return for clemency sought . . . ' he paused before adding '. . . and given!'

Unabashed, Dafydd just grinned. 'I told you that you were soft! But you're learning, Idris bach! Now you've got your hands dirty there'll be no stopping you!'

Idris turned his head quickly, to stare at Dafydd, feeling stifled as though the thin gold chain around his neck was choking him, but before he could say a word, Dafydd was saying quietly, seriously, 'But flaunt it not, Idris, put it away lest others envy,' he winked, 'nor give it to your lady Catrin, either, or our Prince up ahead there will have it for his war chest. Some things a man must hold for his old age, not for the common good!'

With that he spurred his horse and cantered away on some errand of his own, leaving Idris staring after him, thinking of the man from whom he had taken the gold chain. An old man he'd been, as old as the Prince, forty-five at least and fat, his chins wobbling with fear, his face ashen as he tore at the chain around his neck with fat fingers.

'Please,' he had pleaded, 'take this chain . . . it's gold, pure gold, but spare me, for God's sake spare me!' He'd babbled on then, tears on his fat cheeks, 'My wife, my children . . .' but, his chin flecked with frothy spittle, he had fallen silent. Dropping to his knees then, his hands clasped together as though in prayer, as indeed they were, he had raised his eyes to Idris in silent entreaty.

Idris flinched as he remembered holding out his hand, waiting there until the merchant had offered the chain with a palsied hand. Idris shuddered as he thought, too, of not only taking the chain from the man's trembling hand, but pointing to the rings on his fingers and saying, 'Those too!'

He remembered Dafydd's words and there was the taste of bile in his mouth as he thought, yes, you're learning, Idris lad, the pity is that you can take such little pride in the progress that you make!

*   *   *   *

Two days later Prince Owain left the main body of his army, which seemed to grow every day as men flocked to his banner either having heard of his call to arms or lured by the tales of his successful pillaging. With some fifty men he rode to Sycharth, leaving Tudor in command of half his army, already over three thousand strong, together with his cousins from Mon. The remainder of the army he put under the command of Maredudd, supported by his uncles, the Hanmers, with orders to follow him to Sycharth.

Amongst those Prince Owain took with him to Sycharth was Dafydd, who he increasingly used now as the captain of his personal guard together with Rhys and Idris. It appeared that Prince Owain had not forgotten what he had told them after that first abortive visit to Ruthin, and now seemed to keep the three friends close to him.

As they followed Prince Owain, Idris asked Dafydd quietly, 'Why has the Prince split our forces, Dafydd? Why are we going on ahead?'

Dafydd shook his head in exasperation. 'You'll never make a foot soldier, Idris, you're always wanting to know why! Yet why you ask me I know not, for I'm not privy to the Prince's thoughts.'

Rhys grinned. 'True enough Dafydd, but I wager that you'll have guessed the reason for this stratagem!'

Dafydd gave a superior sort of smile and tapped his nose with a forefinger. 'I might and then, I might not, have so discovered! All I can tell you though . . . ' Idris and Rhys turned their heads and leaned towards him the better to hear his words, 'that I noticed that the Prince's brother, Tudor, bestrides a mount that must be sibling to his own!' He paused now for effect but they just gazed at him open mouthed so, with a nod for emphasis, he continued, 'Not only that, but the Prince and Lord Tudor's armour, chain mail, helmet and tabard all are look-alikes one for the other! Now that is all I know, so think on that, for that should tell you all!'

Idris looked from Dafydd to Rhys, but he seemed just as mystified as Idris as he sat astride his mount open mouthed, scratching his chin. Turning back to Dafydd, Idris began, 'But

Dafydd . . . '

Dafydd shook his head. 'No more questions! I've said enough for you to solve the puzzle, devise the strategy, if you would be a captain, not just an archer fit for bending bows!'

His pride assailed, Idris opened his mouth to reply, but Dafydd was already riding off to the rear of the small column and shouting at some laggards there. Idris looked at Rhys, but saw no help there, for the man at arms, apparently no longer struggling with thoughts of strategy, was gazing stolidly ahead. Still worrying about those leather boots, is Rhys, thought Idris, they're too big, but he won't part with them!

It was the last day of September when they came to Sycharth again and a blustery shower swept across the meadows where Owain's army had encamped. At the head of their band Prince Owain's tabard clung wetly to his mail and Idris's metal studded leather jerkin was sodden, heavy and held its foetid smell close about him.

He wiped the back of his hand across his mouth and peered at the manor, looking strangely hostile now as it sat on its motte, silhouetted against the overcast sky, the drawbridge raised as though against unwelcome visitors. The manor appeared strangely deserted too, for all was silent, nor was there any sign of life: it was as if they had come upon a deserted cottage in a woodland clearing. Idris's heart came to his throat as he thought of Lord Grey falling upon Sycharth in revenge for the sacking of Ruthin; he thought of Catrin . . . and of the woman in Ruthin town screaming at the man at arms. He felt sick at the very thought, but it could not be, the manor still stood! Lord Grey would have razed it to the ground in his anger!

Idris saw Prince Owain raise his hand and the weary band came to a halt just out of arrow shot from the manor's palisade. Dafydd, alongside Prince Owain, called out now in his stentorian roar, 'Ho there, within! Lower the drawbridge for Prince Owain!'

A helmeted head cautiously appeared on the gate-house tower. a pair of eyes below the helmet scrutinising them for an eternity before disappearing. Minutes passed it seemed without any response to Dafydd's hail and, a hand on his sword hilt, Rhys glanced at Idris. Grimacing, he said quietly, 'No welcome home for us, it seems, Idris!'

Idris, thinking that there might be real archer's work to do, just nodded grimly as he loosened his bow on his shoulder and fingered an arrow's feather in his quiver. They all heard it then, a creaking as the drawbridge began to lower, a thump as it rested on its bed. There was no other sound though, no hail, no friendly greeting and Prince Owain just sat there for a moment as though pondering what he should do. Then, with a wave of his hand, he moved them on and they all walked their horses towards the drawbridge. Every man's eyes were alert, his hand upon his weapon and Idris felt the blood pounding in his veins, knowing not what they would find when they crossed the drawbridge, or who they might meet.

It was not until Owain, with Dafydd at his side, followed by Rhys and Idris, were half way across the drawbridge that the manor's iron studded oaken gates suddenly swung open. There, facing them, was a phalanx of spearmen. As they entered they found they were flanked on either side by a dozen archers, arrows notched in the bows drawn back to the full extent of the archers' arms.

Prince Owain halted, Dafydd, Rhys and Idris around him now, weapons drawn. Owain was holding the reins loosely, his head bowed and Idris heard him exhale a long held breath in a great sigh before, raising his head again, he roared, 'Gruffydd!'

The archers either side of the gateway lowered their bows whilst others, posted on the walkway of the palisade, rested on theirs and, shuffling uncomfortably, the spearmen lowered their lances, looking everywhere but at their Prince. Faces appeared now at the windows of the manor that overlooked the courtyard and Idris glimpsed a pale faced Catrin looking down on them before she quickly disappeared.

From the rear of the spearmen, a somewhat abashed Gruffydd came forward to greet his father with a low bow. As he raised his head again, Prince Owain said dryly, 'There was no great need, Gruffydd, for such an honour guard! A glass of wine, some dry clothes and a good fire in the hearth would suffice!'

Gruffydd was helmeted and arrayed in chain mail, but looked more ready to do penance than go to war as, shamefaced, he looked up at his father.

'I am sorry Father, 'twas that we received intelligence that

Lord Grey was marching on Sycharth with full two hundred lances!' He gestured with a hand towards the armed men gathered in the courtyard. 'So we prepared thus at your approach lest it be but a stratagem of Grey's.'

Prince Owain stared at his son for a moment before saying, in a resigned voice, 'I would have thought that perhaps you might have recognised your own father a little sooner, Gruffydd . . . ' he paused before, shaking his head in exasperation, he added, 'but then, 'tis a wise man who knows his own father!'

Perhaps it was only in Idris's imagination, but he could have sworn that Prince Owain was looking at him not Gruffydd as he spoke.

e

Chapter Twelve

For Idris the stay at Sycharth was all too short, as four days later they were on the march again. The fourteen hundred men at arms, spearmen and archers led by Maredudd and his uncles, who all arrived two days after Prince Owain, barely had time to set up camp in the meadows below the manor, before it was all being dismantled and the army was heading eastwards. For this time they were marching into England. There would be no confusion there as to who was friend or who foe, for every man's hand would be against them, every man the enemy.

Prince Owain had reined up on the drawbridge at Sycharth. He had smiled grimly at them for a moment without speaking, his tabard ruffling in the gusty October breeze. Then, raising a mailed fist, he said in a voice loud and clear as a trumpet call, 'Men! fellow Welshmen! We have but two enemies! First amongst these is the English king, who falsely rules over England, who would unjustly rule us too and have his son, an English whelp, be Prince of our ancient Principality! The second is any man, who calls himself Welsh and who supinely lies, content with such false governance. Today, we march on the first of these our enemies, Henry Bolingbroke of England . . . but hear you well! Tell all you meet, that Owain Glyn Dŵr calls traitor, any Cymru who does not answer the call to free ourselves from English dominance! And now, for Dewi Sant am Cymru, we march . . . on England!'

The air around Sycharth manor had resounded then with loud cries of 'Dewi Sant am Cymru,' from the assembled army, but above all were the cries of 'Prince Owain am Cymru,' . . . 'Prince Owain for Wales!' the man who many there saw as a saint indeed, a new saviour for Wales.

Foremost amongst those were the three friends, Dafydd, Rhys

and Idris, but whilst he hailed Owain, Idris's eyes had been upon Catrin, who stood demurely beside her mother Marged at the gate to the manor, behind Prince Owain. If the Lady Marged was as enthused as his army by Prince Owain's oration, she was showing great restraint, for her face was solemn, her hands clasped in front of her, forefingers together, as though in prayer. Idris hoped that she was praying, for he knew that they needed help as they embarked on this assault.

'A toe in the water,' Dafydd had said it would be, but Idris could not help but feel that they were invading England, all fifteen hundred or so of them! Dafydd had said that they would be joined by another fifteen hundred led by the Prince's brother Tudor, but Idris still had doubts that even such a force could prevail against England's might, however false a King Henry Bolingbroke might be.

As he looked at Catrin though, he knew that he was not kept there by Prince Owain's denouncement as traitors those who did not fight against King Henry; nor even that that meant a sentence of death if apprehended by the King's men. No, for that was double jeopardy, hanged by Owain for not fighting for him or hanged by Henry for doing so! His lot had been cast when first he'd marched on Ruthin with Owain. What kept him there was Catrin and the few days he'd been back at Sycharth had shown him that he could do no other, he was bound to her and thus to Owain, by stronger ties.

To the sound of cheering Owain had spurred his horse then and cantered to the head of the column, followed by the three who were now seen by most as his personal bodyguards.

Dafydd had winked at Idris.

'What did I tell you, Idris, laying siege to all of England we are now!'

Idris had not really heard him but answered, 'That's right, Dafydd!' without even looking at him. Instead, Idris was looking back at the Lady Marged and Catrin, but seeing only Catrin there as she stood forlornly by her mother's side.

That was only a few hours ago and already they had crossed Offa's dyke. Before them lay the walls of Oswestry, the grey slate rooves of its houses glistening from the rain that had fallen that morning with no sun since to dry them out. It seemed ominously quiet as they approached the town, with no man working in the fields, no cart trundling through the town gates and, indeed, with all such closed, it seemed as though one looked at a sightless man.

Idris turned to Dafydd. 'It seems that no one's home, Dafydd, or that we are unwelcome visitors. It's as quiet there as any Sabbath day. Do we pass by? This Oswestry is hardly yet the heart of Henry's England?'

Dafydd looked soberly at Idris. 'No, we'll not pass by, Idris, though some may wish we had! The burgesses there must have had word that we marched this way and so have put the shutters up, but those walls will not hold us out, nor yet those gates! We'll wave a flag and blow our trumpets and they'll all fall down! Shortly now, you and Rhys will come with me to take a closer look at Oswestry, unless my instinct's wrong!'

Barely had Dafydd finished speaking before he was spurring his horse forward in answer to Prince Owain's signal. With a questioning glance at each other, Rhys and Idris quickly followed to rein up just within earshot as the Prince issued his instructions to Dafydd. At last Dafydd touched a forefinger to his helmet in acknowledgement and, turning, took in his beefy hand as though it were a twig, the Prince's banner that Gruffydd offered. As he nodded to them, Idris and Rhys spurred their horses to ride up on either side of him and, proudly bearing Prince Owain's banner, he led the way towards the town gate.

They did not hurry, but allowed their horses to walk sedately, the better to keep the townsmen waiting for the Prince's message. Although conscious that it was unlikely that any of the few men on the town's ramparts would bend a bow at such obvious emissaries, Idris felt a pricking at the back of his neck as they slowly approached the town gate, but the air was more threatening of rain than arrows. They were at the gate now, the approach worn and rutted with the passage of many feet and carts, yet all was still, silent.

Riding up to the wooden gate, Dafydd firmly thumped it with the stave of his banner, then stepping his horse back he raised his head and roared, 'Burgesses of Oswestry! Prince Owain Glyn Dŵr demands surrender of your town to his just governance, when all persons therein, be they Welsh or English, will receive his clemency!'

The town it seemed was deaf as well as blind, for there was no response to Dafydd's hail, just silence and even the helmeted heads on the parapet had disappeared. Oswestry, it appeared, was a deserted town. Dafydd looked grimly at Idris, then back at the gate, as though willing it to open then, after a few moments, he called to the blank face of the town again, 'In the name of Prince Owain Glyn Dŵr, I demand surrender of your town. Resist his lawful demand at your peril!'

After a moment there was a rattle of chains, of bars being withdrawn and slowly, fearfully it seemed, the gate was opened a crack, sufficient only for a man to squeeze through and one by one, three men appeared, all dressed alike in dark green cloaks, fur trimmed around the collar, and wearing flat crowned, wide brimmed, velvet hats. Once out of the gate, they arrayed themselves in a line, in the centre of which was a man as alike the merchant in Flint from whom Idris had taken the gold chain as could be his brother. Broad of girth and double chinned, he fingered with spatulate fingers the chain around his neck as though it were a talisman. He started to speak, his voice high pitched, 'I . . . .'

Dafydd gruffly interrupted him. 'Who are you? Why do you speak for Oswestry?'

The man rubbed away a bead of sweat from his upper lip, before looking from one to the other of his companions, sharing the blame.

'I am a burgess of Oswestry! . . . ' he looked at his companions again, then head up, his chin stuck out defiantly: 'By what right does this . . . this Owain Glyn Dŵr, demand surrender of our town, a town whose charter we hold from Henry, King of England, himself!'

Dafydd favoured all three burgesses with a cool smile.

'*Prince* Owain Glyn Dŵr!' he corrected the speaker, adding dryly after a pause, 'As to what right he has to your town why,' he pointed with a thumb over his shoulder at the army now ranged in a body facing the town, 'there's right enough for you, I wager!'

The man on the first speaker's right spoke now; a tall man, thinner than the first, his nose had an arrogant tilt to it, his lip a supercilious curl. His lips hardly seemed to move as he spoke and his voice had a nasal tone, as though it were beneath him to speak to such as Dafydd.

'We shall not surrender our town to some band of barefoot robbers! We are King Henry's men and owe allegiance to no other!'

The fat man turned to him, put a hand on his arm and, sweat running down his cheeks now although the day was cool, said soothingly, almost pleading, 'Quite right, of course, Alan! All that is true, well, except I'm sure, they are no barefoot robbers! Perhaps though, just perhaps I say, we should hear this . . . this captain fully out, lest what he has to say . . . requests that is, is not contrary to what we owe to our liege lord, the king.'

It seemed that the three burgesses had not resolved what they should say before they came to meet Dafydd, for the third one interrupted now. All of forty, Idris guessed that he might be, of middle stature and sturdily built, with the confident mien of one who'd seen a campaign, a siege or two and outlived them all. Looking Dafydd in the eye, as one soldier to another, the man's voice was as firm as his message: 'These walls are thick enough to hold you off, lest you have catapults, and men enough we have inside 'til the relief we've called upon, comes to our aid!' He grinned confidently. 'Why should we give that which you cannot take?'

Dafydd answered him in like vein, equals talking the same language and thumbed over his shoulder again. 'That is but part of our main force, yet that would be enough as I and you, I think, should know. Nor do we fear any relief that comes, for it'll not come in time to be of aid. When we break through,' he winked at the man now, 'as we both know we shall, that will be retribution day! Great shall be Prince Owain's wrath that any needlessly died this day and, in his fury, none shall be saved of all your citizens, nor any stick nor stone be left upright of your fair town. "Oswestry" it shall then be called no more, but "Desolation"!'

The fat man blanched, his eyes rolled upwards till only the whites could be seen and wringing his hands, he gulped before speaking again, his high pitched voice quavering, 'Gentlemen, please, there's no need of such direful talk!' And reaching a hand out towards Dafydd he said anxiously, 'Please Captain, allow us time . . . a little time, to talk amongst ourselves that we may then return and talk with you of peace, not . . . ' he visibly shuddered now, 'not Armageddon!'

Dafydd hesitated for a moment, then nodded. 'Agreed, but do not, in your talk of time, let your thoughts wander to hopes of redemption in this world! In one quarter of an hour hence one word only I wish to hear, "Surrender!" If I do not, you'll wish Hell's legions fell upon your town and not those of Prince Owain Glyn Dŵr!'

All three burgesses nodded, but it was only the third man, the one so obviously a soldier, who held Dafydd's eyes as though he had no fear of crossing swords with Dafydd or any other man. Then turning the three went back into the town, the gate quickly slammed shut behind them and the whole town seemed to turn its blank gaze on Owain Glyn Dŵr's army once again.

With a tug on the reins Dafydd turned his horse around and spurring, galloped back towards Prince Owain, banner flying, with Idris and Rhys racing to keep up with him.

Prince Owain, still mounted, looked at Dafydd thoughtfully. 'Well,' he asked quietly, 'will they open the gates, or did they ask for terms?'

'The fat one would open up and bless you as you entered,' replied Dafydd grinning. 'I'd swear I saw a puddle at his feet! He's asked for time to parley with the others. Of the other two, one's of bastard nobility I'd say, anxious to gain honour at whatever cost, the third's a one time man at arms who knew his trade. He's the one to watch, for if he counsels surrender, he's man enough to sway or force the tall one to his view, however reluctant the bastard might be. If he counsels fight, then 'tis two to one and the fat one will find a chapel where he might sweat and pray! I told them a quarter of the hour and I'll be back and if they'd not surrender then, there'd be no quarter!'

Idris noticed that Prince Owain merely nodded abstractedly as though he'd heard Dafydd, but that it was something not worth mentioning. Idris's heart sank as he sat on his mount praying that Oswestry would open its gates and listened as the others talked quietly of how they'd take the town if the burgesses did not surrender. Idris listened and took all in though, that he might learn the art of war, not just the craft of archery. At last, with a nod from Owain, Dafydd tugged at his reins, turned his horse towards the town and set off with Rhys and Idris to meet the burgesses again.

Their approach must have been seen, for Dafydd had no need to hail, the town gate opening as they arrived. Only one burgess came out this time though, the one of middle height, the soldier. He wore no cloak or velvet hat now, but was accoutred in attire more suited to his mien. A man at arms, in mail, he stood before

103

them hand on sword, his grey eyes steely, unyielding as the the mail he wore.

As Idris watched, Dafydd took one look then smiled, a grim, humourless smile.

'We have your answer then, you will not yield?'

'No! I command here now! On behalf of Henry, King of England, I will accept your surrender and pledge his pardon to you all excepting only the traitor, Owain Glyn Dŵr!'

Dafydd grinned. 'Attack was ever better than defence and that I grant, but you promise that not yours to give even were it warranted!' He pointed to the town. 'Yet many there will never pardon you for what you bring down upon them this day. Pray God we meet not, within those gates!'

As he finished speaking, Dafydd turned his head towards Owain's army, raising a hand as though in benediction as he did so. Idris, following his every action, saw Prince Owain raise his hand also, in acknowledgement and the whole army seemed to advance, but foremost in the centre, was a group of archers, racing towards the gate.

Every movement then seemed to blur as the town burgess or town captain, retreated quickly within the gates, Dafydd and his companions spurred their horses towards the advancing army and archers from the town parapets showered arrows like hail all around them. Idris, knowing better than most the fearsomeness of such weapons, cringed on his saddle as they fell, wishing he were the pedlar not the buyer there. The air was thick with arrows now but slowly Idris realised that fewer were aimed at him. Then they were through Prince Owain's advancing army and reined up to take stock of their fortune. It took no more than a blackbird's count to realise that all three had safely escaped the deluge of arrows from the town walls and Dafydd and Idris grinned at each other as Rhys complained.

'Another rule of war that was, no doubt, Dafydd! Make a target of us, to let our army advance unscathed.'

Dafydd though was not listening to his complaint, but had turned his horse, so he could better watch the town. Idris had turned too and was amazed to see the sky appeared dark with arrows aimed at the town's parapets, where wisely, not a figure stirred.

Moving towards the gate, beneath this sheltering umbrella,

was what at first seemed to Idris, to be a many legged, giant lizard. Yet it was not, for its every leg was a stalwart man, its body the trunk of a once massive tree. Ponderously it moved towards the gate . . . it was there now, where but short minutes ago he had stood and heard the town's defiance.

Even as he watched, the ram began to swing, was crashing with the sound of thunder against the solid town gate. Afterwards he could not recall how long he watched, he only knew that all the while the sky was dark as arrows flew; that on the parapet no one moved and over and over there was a crash as the great ram knocked upon the gate for entrance.

There was a constant toing and froing as in ones and twos men relieved those on the ram and gradually there was movement too, however slow, as the seemingly immovable gates began at first to creak, to splinter and then, suddenly to swing wide open. To cheers and yells, the whole army surged forward to pour, like a flooding river, into the town.

Facing them as they entered was a motley assembly of spearmen and archers, townsmen bearing unfamiliar pikes, villeins from nearby farms armed with fearsome looking, but unwieldy, farming tools. All gathered behind a makeshift barrier, they stood to meet Owain Glyn Dŵr's advancing army, some looking as though they'd met it all before and some, not wanting to meet it ever again.

In the brief moments before the opposing forces met, arrows fell amongst them as here and there attacker or defender fell unheeded as an arrow reached its mark. But soon, too soon for many, they were at each others' throats like fighting dogs and there was little room for an archer to ply his trade without danger to his friend. Men swore at each other, hacked with sword or thrust with spear, fought with hands and feet, or any weapon that came to hand. They grappled, gouged and fought with tooth and nail, nor were there any who asked for quarter for all knew none would be given.

Gradually the defenders gave ground to the surging tide of Owain's army, step by step they were beaten back, bodies left lying at every step like ripples on the sand, until at last they were overwhelmed and the tide swept into the town as would the incoming sea a beach. Merciless as the sea it was too, as it engulfed the town, destroying all in its path, all that could not be taken away, all that was of no value . . . and life had the least of value that day.

The sky was darkening when at last quiet began to descend upon the town, but for Idris it seemed as though it were not the peaceful silence he had sometimes found at Sycharth, but as though night came silently, ashamed of what the day had seen. It was then that he saw Dafydd for the first time since they entered the town and the fierce fighting within the gates.

With Rhys and a few other men at arms, Dafydd was herding three men in halters towards where Prince Owain Glyn Dŵr stood with Gruffydd. As they came nearer, Idris could see they were the three burgesses who had met them that morning. The one in mail still held his shoulders erect, as he stood facing Prince Owain defiantly, although his hands were bound, his head bloody. The oldest of the three, the fat man, had to be supported by two men at arms, he was so reduced by abject fear. The tall arrogant one held himself stiffly and seemed to ignore them all, but Idris thought that that might be because his eyes were glazed and he did not see them.

Prince Owain turned from Gruffydd, to ask Dafydd, 'You found them all, then Dafydd?'

'Yes, these are the three we met this morning at the gate,' replied Dafydd. He pointed to the soldier. 'He earned his pay, whatever that might be and gave no ground to any man . . . 'til he met me!'

The soldier glanced sideways at him and his bloody lips grimaced in what might have been a smile, but he said nothing.

Prince Owain asked, 'And these others?'

'I found them in the cellars of a house nearby, my lord, debating, so they said on thoughts of surrendering the town to you!'

The fat man, eyes downcast was nodding vigorously, but appeared too terrified to say a word. Ashen faced, the tall man just gazed beyond Prince Owain, but stayed silent, as though disdaining to speak to any such as he.

Prince Owain stroked his beard and shook his head, then said softly, so softly that Idris had to strain to hear the Prince from where he stood, 'This morning you three men could have saved your town this desolation. All within it could have been spared the wrath they faced, but you,' and here he pointed to the soldier, 'in your o'erweaning pride, thought you could withstand a force whose strength you had not then assessed.' He nodded to the tall, haughty one and said in a voice resonant with contempt, 'Like your friend, your arrogance would not allow you to surrender your town and yet your honour was too fragile a thing it seems, for you to defend it with your sword, as he did.' Turning to the fat man, he sighed, 'and you, no doubt, loved the esteem of your good citizens, took pride in such power your wealth afforded and yet had not the strength it seems to make these two proud men bow to your wiser counsels to save your town.'

He paused, then in a firm, unwavering voice he announced, 'For your three sins, Pride, Arrogance, Weakness, you three shall hang!'

Idris gulped as the three men were hustled away by Dafydd. The soldier still erect, his hair, such as was not matted with blood, blowing in the wind; the fat man carried to his fate as he had been carried to Prince Owain; the tall one in a world of his own, unseeing and unknowing, it seemed to Idris, of what was about to befall him.

Not long after that, as the evening shadows fell on the silent town, Prince Owain's men put Oswestry to the torch. As they left, Idris turned to look back on the town square where the three burgesses stayed. Silhouetted against the burning buildings, they hung there watching, with unseeing eyes, the desolation that Dafydd had prophesied.

Chapter Thirteen

After leaving Oswestry in flames behind them, Prince Owain's army swept northwards to join up with his brother Tudor's forces which had been ravaging the marcher towns of North Wales. As Prince Owain's men went through the small town of Holt like a swarm of locusts a rider, his horse flecked with lather, rode up to where Prince Owain watched the sacking of the town with Gruffydd, his brothers-in-law, the Hanmers and a small retinue.

Idris, standing with Dafydd apart from the nobles, was surprised to see that it was the Prince's other son, Maredudd, riding up to the group with a broad grin on his face. Idris's surprise was due to the fact that it seemed Maredudd had ridden alone through hostile country to meet his father, but here he was, unharmed after what had obviously been a speedy ride. The explanation was not long forthcoming as a breathless Maredudd greeted his father, 'Father, I bring news from my Uncle Tudor! His forces were leaving Harwarden when one of his men took a captive who said your forces were attacking Holt. I rode on to tell you that he will join you here.'

Prince Owain smiled. ' 'Tis good to see you safely here, son, though I might have wished to see you come with an escort! What business had your Uncle Tudor with the town of Harwarden?'

Maredudd glanced at the pillage of Holt taking place before him, catching his breath the while, then, turning back to Prince Owain, he said quietly, 'Much the same as yours here at Holt, Father, but he bade me tell you that he has a bigger prize in view, of which he will advise when you both meet.'

Prince Owain said nothing, merely nodded his acknowledgement but his eyebrows rose a little as though surprised at the tone of his brother's message. Then he smiled again as though brushing aside his annoyance and, including the Hanmers now, he replied, 'Good! It's time we all held our council, when we can all debate our plan of war . . . and I can then decide upon the plan! It will be good to see my brother Tudor and my cousins from Ynys Mon.' He turned to Gruffydd. 'Give orders to set up our camp near here, Gruffydd, but make it to the West a little, lest the smoke from Holt offends our nostrils with its pungency!'

Gruffydd glanced at the town and, following his gaze, Idris saw that parts of the town were already alight. The pillaging was almost complete it seemed and the town, like so many before it, was being put to the torch.

Idris had no camp to set up that night for Dafydd had found an empty cottage, whose owner had either fled at their approach or had earlier sought an illusory refuge in the town of Holt. Whatever the reason, it was empty now, not only empty but bare, its two rooms stripped of anything that was moveable and there was little enough else. Empty too, was the byre that adjoined, although it was so malodorous, that its aroma seemed to seep through the very walls into the living rooms alongside.

The rooms were warm and dry, however, and for Idris and his companions, that was luxury enough for the night, especially since any discomfort was alleviated by ale and meat 'borrowed' from the town of Holt. They even had a candlestick and a candle that Rhys had also borrowed. It was companion to one with which he'd lit a torch that helped illuminate the night sky above Holt, but Idris did not wish to think of that. Sufficient for Idris tonight was the fact that he was well fed, that he had shelter, light and coins in his pouch to add to the growing hoard he had accumulated. Their consciences untroubled by the day's exertions, Dafydd and Rhys were soon asleep, but Idris lay awake, his mind going over the events of the day then retracing his steps back through the towns they had sacked and made desolate. The more his mind wandered over these events, the more confused he became, unable to understand how destroying those towns would make Wales the freer or King Henry's hold on his throne the weaker.

At last despairing of sleep, he rose and went outside the cottage to stand by its doorway looking at the night sky. The clouds scudded past the half moon from which the light seemed pale compared to the harsh red glow that still hung over Holt. There was no escape for him, it seemed, from the harsh reality of this rebellion. He shook his head, wishing he could accept it all as philosophically as Dafydd and Rhys and turning, walked slowly along the track away from the cottage.

It was all so quiet he found it hard to believe that an army slept nearby, where sentries kept their watch and, as he walked, wondered whether there were any uneasy consciences like his amongst those gathered there. The track led past a small copse now and, hearing a sound as of a branch brushed by, he stopped and instinctively his hand went to the knife at his belt. He waited a moment, poised to strike, but there was neither sound nor movement and he breathed a sigh of relief.

He was about to walk on when there was a sound as of a stifled cry and drawing his knife he crouched and stepped cautiously into the copse. The layer of leaves underfoot softened his footsteps, but the trees still had enough leaves to make the moonlight patchy within the copse. Alert now, his left hand out before him, the knife held low in his right, he took one step at a time further into the copse but still he heard nothing. An owl hooting made him start, then relax again, sure now that it had all been in his imagination, there was nothing, no one, there. Straightening he began to retrace his footsteps to the track, but he had only taken a few paces before he heard that stifled cry again, almost alongside him.

Idris stopped abruptly, his heart pounding, his knife firmly grasped in his fist. Looking around him, he saw her then, a woman crouching in the undergrowth holding a bundle in her arms. The hand holding the knife dropped limply to his side and with a sigh of relief he said quietly, 'Come on, stand up, there's no need to be afraid, I'll not harm you!'

A head turned up towards him, large, frightened eyes gazing at him, but she still crouched there as though frozen, unable to move.

'Come on,' he repeated, I won't hurt you!'

Slowly, her eyes watching him as she would an adder, she rose to her feet, stepping back from him as she did so, still holding the bundle close to her chest.

Idris could see now though that it wasn't a bundle, but a baby and the mother was a young girl, not much older than Catrin. He held his left hand out, palm towards her whilst he quietly slid his knife into its sheath and, smiling, asked her, 'What is your name?

110

Where are you from?'

Cowering there and still silent, she seemed to shrink away from him whilst the baby clutched to her breast began to cry again, this time though, the mother made no attempt to stifle the cry. Idris did not know what to do, he thought of Owain's army camped nearby, of the Prince's brother's army now camped to the north of Holt. Still smiling reassuringly, he took a step forward, hand outstretched as though to take her by the arm. Immediately, she retreated from him, holding the baby closer to her and turning her head away as though seeking a path of escape. Then, as though realising there was no escape, she turned back towards him with drooping shoulders, a look of despair on her face. Idris frowned. 'Don't be frightened,' he said softly, 'I'll not harm you.'

Seeing her cowering there, the pleading look in her eyes, Idris thought of Sycharth being sacked, burning, and Catrin hiding there, in fear for her life. He held both hands up and backed away slowly.

'All right, I'll go, but I want to help you! Where do you want to go?'

Frowning, she opened her mouth as if to speak, but closed it again and stood there irresolutely for a moment. Then, taking a deep breath she said something, hesitantly, but so softly that Idris had to ask her again.

Pointing eastwards, she almost whispered, 'Broxton.'

Not knowing where that was, Idris smiled, thinking that at least he could see her safely on the road, a mile or two should see her safely past the camp of Lord Tudor's men, at least until they sent out foraging parties on the morrow. Where, or how far, they might go then no one could tell. He held out his hand to her.

'Come on,' he said quietly, 'I'd best get you away from here.'

She hesitated a moment before, trying to hold the baby upright, she bent down seeking awkwardly to pick up a bulging canvas bag. As she struggled with it, Idris reached out and, reluctantly at first she let him take it from her. Then, with a wondering look from the girl, the strange trio set off for Broxton, wherever that is, thought Idris.

They walked in silence along the track towards the cottage for a few minutes then the girl began to drag her feet until, as the cottage came in sight, she stopped. Her face pale in the moonlight she clutched her baby to her and cringed from him. Shaking her head, she said fiercely, 'No! I'm not going in there!'

Idris just looked at the girl and, holding a finger to his lips, whispered, 'Quiet! There are people there you wouldn't want to meet!'

Then with an exaggerated display of tip-toeing past the cottage, he walked on. Looking back after a few paces, he was relieved to see that she was following again, almost crouching, making herself small, as she did so. Idris grimaced, thinking that he did not want to meet Dafydd or Rhys just now, either. They would never believe what he was doing, much less understand!

After a while, the girl seemed to relax and as she gained confidence, began to respond to his attempts to talk with her. It seemed that she had fled from Holt when she heard of Owain's army advancing on the town. Her husband was evidently an older man who kept shop there, but she didn't know where he might be, for he had refused to leave with her. Idris turned his head away as she told him that, for he could hazard a guess that her husband no longer kept shop in Holt. She told him that she had an older sister at Broxton, nodding her head positively as she said that and going on to tell him that she'd be safe there, with her sister.

Glancing sideways at her, Idris saw that she was looking at him, her eyes pleading again and he nodded reassuringly. He could not bring himself to tell her that she would be safe though, for until the winter came, there'd be no such place.

After half an hour's trudging Idris thought that they were sure to be past any danger from Lord Tudor's encampment and turned to the girl, whose name he had discovered was Rose, intending to leave her and return to the cottage. One look at her though and he could see that the terror of the day had taken its toll and she was almost exhausted. Calling a halt, he led her to a bank at the side of the track where gratefully she sank down beside him and they sat in silence. Soon he was aware that, still holding the child, her head had dropped on his shoulder and, putting his arm around her protectively, he let her sleep. How long he sat like that he did not know, but after a while there was a stirring beside him and he saw her looking up at him.

For a moment there was a flash of alarm in her eyes, but slowly it faded and she smiled up at him as though content that she and the child were safe there with him. He felt a strange sense of satisfaction in that smile and, touching her gently on the cheek, said softly, 'We must go now . . . I must be back ere dawn.'

As he stood up she braced her shoulders, sighed and with a nod held out her hand to him. Taking it, he helped her as she rose unsteadily to her feet before picking up her bag and they set off again along the track to Broxton. It seemed to Idris that they walked as companions now, and when they came to a stream that crossed the track, she did not flinch as he held her hand to help her across. After a while, they came to the edge of a hamlet when she turned to him and smiled as she held out her hand. 'This is Broxton, Idris, I'll be safe now.'

Feeling strangely regretful, Idris offered her the bag but she waved it aside, her hand now inviting his embrace. His arm around her, she kissed him then and as she did he felt the warm breath of the child on his face, the warmth of the mother's lips on his before, drawing back from him, she said softly, 'Thank you, Welsh Idris, for both of us. I will long remember you.'

Taking her bag from him, she turned and hurried away along the road into the shadowy village. He stood there for a moment watching, wondering what had taken him so far from the safety of Owain's camp. Shrugging his shoulders and vowing to keep his own counsel when he got to the cottage again, he turned to start the long walk back.

Dawn was breaking as he carefully opened the door to the cottage anxious not to disturb his two companions there, but as he pushed it slowly open, it was suddenly pulled from his hand and there was an arm tight around his neck, a knife at his throat.

The pressure on his throat relaxed, the knife was taken from his throat, as Dafydd snorted.

'Oh, it's you! You put the fear of death into a man, coming in all furtive like that!'

'Me! Put the fear of death in you!' said Idris angrily. 'It's me who had a knife stuck in his throat, Dafydd!'

Dafydd stood there, the knife held loosely in his hand now, with Rhys also holding a murderous looking knife, standing beside him.

'No! No, Idris! Not stuck in your throat it was. Pointed at it, yes, but never stuck in it!' He held the knife up now, as if to examine it closely. 'There, see? Not a drop of blood on it!' He held up a warning finger. 'Now if you'd moved, there would have been a different tale to tell, but you're getting wiser due to good training, see!'

Idris was massaging his neck, pausing the while to look at his hand to see if Dafydd's knife had drawn blood. Satisfied at last, he turned on Dafydd, pointing to the floor in exasperation. 'Few thanks to you I've not spent my life's blood there! I could not sleep and went out from the stink of cattle here but minutes since to find fresh air: and would you slit my throat for that?'

Dafydd raised his eyebrows. 'Minutes?' he asked, the disbelief evident in his voice. 'Minutes? Four hours ago it was, before I slept, that you crept out for your assignation with who I know not.'

Rhys chimed in then as he looked doubtfully at Idris, ''Tis so, Idris, more than four hours! And you would have us trust you, then you would tell us what kept you out as long in these silent hours. It was not to empty your bladder 'gainst the wall!'

'Trust me?' asked Idris incredulously. 'Must I tell you all I do, for you to trust me?'

There was no suspicion in Dafydd's voice or eyes as he replied. Somehow though, it seemed all the more menacing that he asked in a flat voice, his eyes blank, 'Where have you been Idris? A man, a soldier, leaves an armed camp at dead of night in the land of his enemies and there must be an explanation. Tell me and Rhys here and maybe it need go no further than us three. Tell us not, and you'll tell Prince Owain or he'll hang you else!'

Idris hesitated and looked from Dafydd to Rhys, but finding no comfort there either, he shrugged and told them all. Told them all in the only way they would understand the telling. Of how he had found her, how she had cried and how he had taken her.

Chapter Fourteen

Others beside Idris had had little sleep that night, for Prince Owain and his lordly kin feasted and drank long into the night, rejoicing at the havoc they had caused amongst the English towns. There was no sign of the irritation that Prince Owain had displayed on hearing from Maredudd of Tudor's plans for pursuing the campaign, nor was there any talk of a council of war, only obvious pleasure at the reunion. When Tudor at last broached the subject, Prince Owain merely smiled and said with a sweeping gesture of his hand, 'Such serious talk demands clear heads and the cold light of day, brother. Tonight we revel in our enemy's discomfort,' he raised his pot of ale, 'and at his expense! Tomorrow we can give thought as to how best we may savage England before winter stays our hand. Take stock of our exchequer too and count our gains, so we shall know with certainty how long we may yet campaign unless we further rob the English purse.'

His cousin, Rhys, laughed. 'Quite right, cousin Owain, such heavy talk calls for lighter heads than those around this table now . . . '

He paused as Gruffydd, frowning into his pot of ale, muttered loudly, '*Prince* Owain!'

Owain turned his head quickly and almost spat, 'Gruffydd!'

Rhys though, was nodding as he waved his hand dismissively to say in quick agreement, 'Quite right again!' But smiling now, he added, 'My prince indeed! Yet cousin too and so he was long ere you were born, young Gruffydd. Tonight we feast and all here are kin, by blood or marriage. Tomorrow we talk of war and then, hand on sword, I'll call my cousin Prince, as I shall call no other!'

With a warning glance at Gruffydd, Prince Owain shook his

head and there was silence for a moment as he paused, an almost audible sigh of relief when, smiling, he spoke:

'Nay Rhys, not cousins are any here, but brothers! Blood brothers in a bloody enterprise that shall succeed only as we all remember that!'

The messenger from Ruthin had ridden hard for days, with only brief stops along the way to feed and water his horse. To rest his own weary bones and dry his clothes too, for it was a wet October and crossing the Pennines, shrouded in blustery rain as they were, had not been pleasurable. A day's ride now though, should bring him to Knottingley, where if all he'd heard was true he should meet up with King Henry's army as it drove south from warring with the Scots and there deliver his letter to Lord Grey of Ruthin.

The messenger frowned, pray god Lord Grey would not blame him for the news he bore, for whilst he did not know what the letter said, he knew his lord would not welcome tales of the sacking of Ruthin. Nor yet of how his lord's captain there had viewed it all from Ruthin Castle walls and had not ventured out to the townsmen's aid.

Perhaps it was the hesitation caused by such doubt of his lord's reaction to the news that slowed his pace, so that when he arrived at Knottingley he found that King Henry's army had left on their southward march a full day since. Even more fearful now, he rode south in hot pursuit, but it was not until he reached Doncaster that he came up with the King's army, only to spend hours seeking out Lord Grey. He need not have feared his lord's reaction however, for it seemed that Lord Grey was pleased rather than angry and had given him five marks for bringing the news, before hurrying off to seek audience with the King.

It was with some reluctance that the King, still in bad humour after the indecisive campaign in Scotland, was persuaded to see Lord Grey. He was still in some doubt over Ruthin's part in that business over Owain whatever his name was. One could never get one's tongue around those Welsh names, even when the men who bore them were supposed to be a sort of nobility, one's own esquire even!

He favoured Lord Grey of Ruthin with a sour look as the marcher lord entered.

'What is it now, Ruthin?' he asked, 'not yet another argument over some land you've filched, I trust!'

Lord Grey flushed, his anger rising at the King's remark, but diplomatically he bit back his angry retort, instead saying softly, 'No land have I ever "filched" that was not ever mine, or should have been by right of conquest, your Majesty. Nor do I bring to your ears any dispute of mine. I do but come to warn you of such treason that I blush to give it name.'

With raised eyebrows King Henry turned to Essex who, standing at his side together with the Percies, the old Earl and his son Hotspur, was frowning at Ruthin's ominous words.

'What devilry can it be, my lords, that causes such as Ruthin here to blush? I've never seen him blush before!' Getting only a shake of the head from Essex, the King turned back to Ruthin. 'Well, speak on, no doubt your tale of treason arises from our troublesome Welsh marches!'

'Treason it is indeed, your Majesty!' replied Ruthin, 'by Owain Glyn Dŵr, your own esquire, who refused his feudal duty to march on Scotland at your array.'

King Henry glanced at Essex and raised his eyes ceilingwards, before turning back to Ruthin, and saying with a touch of irony in his voice, 'No doubt he's stolen sheep or cattle from your lands at Ruthin, or fired woods on that disputed common land of yours?'

Ruthin sensed victory in this war of words now and shaking his head, paused before saying quietly, 'No your Majesty, much worse than that, although I must confess that he has sacked the town of Ruthin and laid it waste.'

King Henry turned to the others and, although saying nothing, his look could have been interpreted as 'I told you so!' Turning back to Ruthin, he looked concerned as he stroked his chin, before saying, 'Drastic I grant you, Ruthin and action which we, on due examination, must justly punish. At this first sight though I would, I fear, call it revenge against you, rather than treason!'

Ruthin bowed his head in apparent humility or perhaps sadness for a moment, before he replied:

'Were I to tell your Majesty, that this Owain Glyn Dŵr, who I dare call traitor, rebel, has assumed and is by his adherents hailed as Prince of Wales, I do believe that that is treason indeed! Were that all, you might in charity say that it was but madness, the workings of a distempered mind. This it cannot be, your majesty!

117

Not when his army now exceeds three thousand men and daily grows. Not when the towns of Denbigh, Flint, Rhuddlan, Oswestry, Holt . . . ' He threw his hands up before continuing, 'I lose track of all the names, your Majesty, but they all are pillaged, burnt to the very ground, their citizens murdered, ravished. Even while we rest here, he marches on to I know not where next, but march he will until he's stopped by main force!'

The King's face had progressively darkened as Lord Grey listed the crimes of Owain Glyn Dŵr and now, banging his fist on the arm of his chair, he shouted, 'Enough! Doubts I had over your quarrel with this Glendourdy, Ruthin! Aye, and questioned in my mind that he had truly received from you my array for our Scottish campaign. For these my doubts I treated him with due leniency, forgave him much where others would have paid full penalty and now this is how such mercy is repaid. If it is true and not mere malice, then treason it is indeed!'

The King paused and frowning, looked to Essex then back at Lord Grey. 'All this is true, beyond all doubt, Ruthin?'

Ruthin waved the letter he had received. 'It is all listed here your Majesty. My captain left at Ruthin witnessed with his own eyes the rape of Ruthin town and heard from men of good repute the ravages that Glyn Dŵr has caused elsewhere.' He shook his head, as though sorrowing to be the bearer of such bad news. 'All true indeed, your Majesty and still the rebel rampages through the marches, like a wolf amongst the flock!'

King Henry looked at him thoughtfully for a moment, before saying decisively, 'Well then, you'd better go and tend your sheep, Ruthin! If in so doing you seize upon this rebel Glendourdy, then mark my words and harm him not, for I would mete justice upon him myself!'

'I disagree!' said Tudor emphatically. 'Shrewsbury would be a fat prize for us to take and a few day's chevauchee on the march there would let all know that Prince Owain rules the marches now! Then quickly back into Wales along the Vyrnwy or the Severn valleys.'

Owain, the older image of his brother sighed. 'When we set out I would have agreed with that and more, even felt it bordered on timidity, but the weather, once our friend, has turned its spite

118

against us!' He smiled. 'Do you hear that, brother,' he paused and they all listened to the rain beating a thunderous tattoo on the roof of the farmhouse he had made his headquarters. 'That's no drummer boy calling us to battle, 'tis our other enemy, the weather! No, brother Tudor, we shelter here a day or so and keep our forces dry as they may be, lest their temper and their ardour cools. Then we march for home, taking what we may gain upon the way.'

Owain's cousin, Ednyfyd, nodded his head in agreement. 'Aye, no torch will set Shrewsbury alight in this, cousin Tudor, and with winter nigh upon us, it's time, I think, for me to take my men back to the safety of our island 'til spring shall bring us firmer ground to march upon!'

Burly Rhys scratched his ginger beard thoughtfully before saying gruffly, 'I'd side with that, Tudor, for I know not what this chevauchee of yours might be, but in this weather, I doubt I like it much!'

Prince Owain smiled. 'Chevauchee, Rhys, is laying waste as you march through a land, taking what you can and denying its sustenance to your enemy.'

Rhys grunted. 'I thought 'twould be fancy French for something similar, but little enough there is to waste along the road to Shrewsbury from here!'

When the Hanmers joined the Tudurs of Mon in favour of discontinuing the campaign for the winter, it seemed to Prince Owain that he had gained a consensus. Looking around the table, he smiled, saying, 'So, we are agreed then . . . '

His brother Tudor though, was unsmiling as he interrupted harshly, 'No! We've put our hand to the plough and must continue 'til the seed is sown, the harvest reaped, or what is the point of it all? Shall we melt at a drop of rain, like frost before the sun? No! I'll not turn back, I'll march on Shrewsbury if I march alone, yet any man amongst you all will march with me!'

As Tudor pushed his chair back and stood up, so did Prince Owain, to say angrily, 'All men we are here, Tudor, from Maredudd there to Ednyfed, from Rhys to Philip! We are all agreed, it's only a futile gesture to march on Shrewsbury. Our forces are not great enough to spend on such futility. I command here and have decided 'tis time to save our resources 'til they can strike most usefully.'

Tudor smiled thinly. 'It is agreed, brother, that you command all here. But since from here we shall to our separate manors go, I'll go to mine by way of Shrewsbury town and garner what I may upon the way.'

He looked around the table, but all eyes seemed cast down, as though reluctant to look upon this first breach of their brotherhood, all that is except those of Gruffydd ab Owain, whose bright eyes watched him intently as he continued, 'Any amongst you here who'd taste the hospitality of my manor are welcome to join me on my journey . . . or chevauchee!'

Gruffydd stood up and, his fist clenched, he punched towards Tudor. 'I'll ride with you, Uncle Tudor!'

Owain shook his head as though despairing of such foolishness, but glancing around the table he saw only faces unresponsive to Tudor's invitation. All other than his brother in law, Gruffydd Hanmer, who was watching Tudor appraisingly, as though weighing the risks against the gain. Owain turned to Tudor.

'I'll not attempt to dissuade you from this foolishness brother, though Shrewsbury lies far from your road to home and thus you deny, at least in spirit, obedience to my leadership.' He smiled and shook his head. 'Instead I'll let our third enemy, the weather, show you in time the wisdom of our decision here today!' With an ironic smile he added, 'Nought in all that is 'gainst us wreaking what havoc we may upon the English as we make our separate ways. Let them remember we passed their way, and tremble lest we pass again!' Glancing at Gruffydd, he added firmly, 'You will accompany me to Sycharth, what you have seen already is enough for your first campaign!'

Looking around he saw his brother smiling good-naturedly from across the table.

'More than enough I would have thought,' said Tudor. 'It is time you were back at Sycharth Gruffydd, lest Grey of Ruthin returns from Scotland and strikes at the manor where none but your sisters hold the fort!'

He caught Owain's eye then and Owain gave a slight nod in appreciation of the words that would discourage Gruffydd going against his father's wishes. Then they were all leaving the farm to go to their men and organise the departure from Holt. Prince Owain noticed though that his brother in law, Gruffydd Hanmer left with Tudor, their heads bent against the rain. Perhaps it is better so, he thought, that would give Tudor five perhaps six hundred men on his march to Shrewsbury town. Standing at the farmhouse door, he nodded, if all went well that would be enough.

The rain that had made torrents of little streams and turned fields into quagmires eased by the next morning and all around the devastated town of Holt there was the bustling activity of an army breaking camp. By mid-morning the first contingents were already on the march as the men from Ynys Mon set off on the long march back to their island home. Not long afterwards, Tudor's men joined up with Gruffydd Hanmer's force near Owain's encampment and set off southwards to Shrewsbury.

Idris, standing with Dafydd and Rhys near Prince Owain, watched them depart. Their attire, be it leather jerkin or mail already glistening wetly, horses' hooves squelching in the muddy track. Looking at the grim faces of the men, he pitied the townsfolk of Shrewsbury if this was the temper of their assailants as they set out! Somehow he felt relieved that they were marching southwards and not to the East, the girl Rose and her baby would be safe for now, after all. Dafydd interrupted his thoughts.

'What are you thinking, Idris?' he asked. 'Thankful you're not marching on Shrewsbury with Lord Tudor, are you?'

Idris nodded. 'Aye, I'd rather march on Sycharth than have us sweep so far south before returning to the manor!'

Dafydd turned to Rhys. 'What makes our young archer yearn for idleness and his thruppence a day, do you think Rhys, when a march to Shrewsbury could bring him a year's pay or more? Is it perhaps a maid that lures him back to Sycharth?'

Leering, Rhys nodded. 'Oh aye, I'm sure of that Dafydd! Just as I'm sure he'll buy us ale all winter through for our silence! '

Frowning, Dafydd shook his head.

'Our silence, Rhys? Why nay, Idris here is a friendly fellow, he'd not want our silence!' Turning to Idris, he reached out and grinning, patted him on the shoulder. 'Unless, of course, it is about the filly he found wandering in the woods at Holt and how he brought her to the bridle!'

Flushing now, Idris opened his mouth to deny that anything

121

f

had happened at Holt, but realised that to do so would raise again the question of how he'd spent that night. Not relishing that idea, he gave them a shamefaced smile, saying, 'Is there not more honour then, amongst friends than thieves? Or are you thieves as well, who'd rob me of my ale to buy your doubtful silence?'

Dafydd frowning, thought for a moment before saying at last, 'You've lost me there, Idris bach! If you buy something from us, how can we then be robbing you? As to honour, well, we all are soldiers of a sort, whose honour is bound tightly by the rules of war . . . ' and smiling now, he added, 'which gives us all much latitude. Fear not though Idris, our silence is assured for a little while. Tomorrow we shall march again not westwards as at first I thought, but eastwards, where doubtless we shall find sufficient coin for you to buy our ale the winter through.'

Idris thought of Rose at Broxton, of Prince Owain's train marching through it, trampling it down with hardly a pause and looked at him askance.

'You said Prince Owain had abandoned the campaign because of this baleful weather and we'd return to Sycharth!'

Dafydd laughed. 'If you could but see your face, Idris! No harm will come to the Lady Catrin because you're delayed a day or two! Tomorrow, should the weather favour us, we march on Whitchurch some ten miles distant and then, our pockets full, we turn our faces west. We'll be on the march to Sycharth before Lord Tudor sights Shrewsbury town!'

Idris breathed a sigh of relief, Whitchurch was not only a mere ten or twelve miles away, but it was to the south east so they would not march through Broxton. Rose and her baby would be safe after all, for now at least.

Rhys turned to Dafydd. 'There, you've made him happy now, Dafydd, he'll be back to his Lady Catrin in a few days . . . and buying us ale too!'

Chapter Fifteen

A few days later, with the sacked town of Whitchurch behind them, its once white Norman church from which it got its name blackened with the smoke from the burning town, Owain's now relatively small force returned to Sycharth. As Dafydd had promised, Idris's pouch was heavy with the profit from their short but turbulent visit to the English town. More than enough to buy Dafydd and Rhys ale for the winter, although they both assured him they had only been jesting.

Looking at them both now as they rode towards Sycharth's drawbridge behind Prince Owain and his two sons, Idris could not help but feel some misgivings. It would be ironic he felt if an unjust accusation of rape should turn Catrin's face against him, when all he had done in charity for her sake, was to take the girl to safety. His heart sank as he thought how he'd be damned as traitor if he told the truth, damned too if Dafydd and Rhys turned his own lie against him! Shaking his head, he thought his only hope lay in their strange sense of soldierly honour keeping them silent. His eyes closed for a moment as he thought of all they had done in the last few months and knew that if that were so he had but little hope indeed!

Minutes later as they clattered over the drawbridge and into the courtyard Idris felt a great sense of relief as he looked at the familiar surroundings. Lady Marged, Catrin, Alice and all the Prince's other children were there smiling happily as they waited to greet them, the younger ones jumping up and down in their excitement. Idris thought how much older the Lady Marged seemed now as she stood there, hands clasped together in front of her, a tinge of grey in her hair, a smile on her lips but relief in her eyes.

As Prince Owain dismounted and went over to hold the Lady

Marged in his arms, Idris envied him. Whilst he yearned to follow his lord's example and hold Catrin, all he could do was to look at her out of the corner of his eye, for it seemed that Gruffydd was watching them both like a hawk. As ostlers took Gruffydd's and Maredudd's horses away, Catrin walked over not to him, but to her brothers.

'It is good to see you all safely home, brothers,' she said as she was joined by her sister Alice. 'We have feared for your safety in this war and Sycharth has seemed defenceless with you all away!'

Whilst Maredudd went over and hugged his sisters, Gruffydd merely stood apart as he said sourly, 'Aye, no doubt! But I would rather be with our Uncle Tudor, who at this very hour will be at the sack of Shrewsbury town and thereby gain much honour for my father's banner!'

The two girls seemed taken aback that he showed such little joy at being home, but Maredudd turned on him, to say sharply, 'Necessity of war leads us to pillage the English towns, Gruffydd, but little joy or honour do I find in doing so! As little as if they should repay us in like coin and raze Sycharth or Glyndyfrdwy. For repay us they surely will when the winter ends. Pray God that our lady mother and our sisters here are not present when they do! Think on that when next you storm an English town.'

With that Maredudd turned on his heel and marched over to the great hall and disappeared indoors. Watching them both Idris smiled to himself as he thought that there was at least one other who, like him, had mixed feelings about the necessities of war.

Idris had no opportunity to talk with Catrin though, for she was already following her father and mother towards the great hall along with Gruffydd who was surrounded by his admiring younger brothers and sisters. With a sigh, he started leading his horse towards the stables wishing that it were he who would be telling Catrin of their adventures rather than Maredudd or Gruffydd.

Turning his head he looked towards the great hall just as Catrin looked over her shoulder at him. Stopped in his tracks, his heart gave a little leap as she smiled at him and made a strange little fluttering gesture with her hand before disappearing into the hall. He heard the laughter then, not Catrin's girlish laughter that he remembered so well, but the coarse, rude laughter of Dafydd and Rhys and he flushed as they jeered, 'Remember Holt, young Idris, for we've not forgotten!' Then, breaking into a bawdy song they followed him all the way to the stables.

That evening there was feasting in the great hall and rejoicing at the return of the menfolk to Sycharth for the winter. Wine and ale flowed, minstrels played and sang their lays and Iolo at his harp, sang in praise of Owain: of how his sword would bring the light of freedom once again to Wales. Sitting below the salt, at the bottom of the table with Rhys, Idris looked morosely towards the head of the table where a relaxed Prince Owain sat by the Lady Marged, with his family around him. All Idris saw though was the beautiful, unattainable, Catrin.

Whilst all were quiet except for the minstrels, Idris began to wonder what Catrin had intended by that gesture as she had gone into the hall earlier. Perhaps it was the ale he had drunk, or his physical remoteness from Catrin up there at the head of the table, but he was sure that it could only have meant farewell. Suddenly, being back at Sycharth meant little other than serving another lord in another castle. Reaching out for the jug of ale on the table he poured himself another pot and he and Rhys drank to each other until all he could see at the top of the table was a blur of faces.

In the courtyard the next morning, Rhys smiled mockingly. 'What, off to practise your archery again, Idris?' he asked. 'I doubt you'll see the target butt nor yet have strength enough to bend your bow, the way you supped your ale last night!'

Idris put a hand to his forehead and glared malevolently at Rhys as he replied, 'Strong enough to whip you with my bowstring if you do not cease your noise!'

Rhys laughed. 'You were sorry enough for yourself last night, Idris, but ale it seems is not the cure for your sorrow.' With a sly look he added, 'Though from your ale talk last night it seems whatever is the cause, 'tis lost!'

His stomach churning, Idris looked at him blankly for a moment then, as hazy memories of last nights feasting returned, he scowled at Rhys before turning on his heel and walking off without a word. You're right though, Rhys, he thought bitterly as he remembered Catrin sitting at the top of the table last night and of himself below the salt, at the bottom. As he crossed the drawbridge he sighed, thinking, whatever profit I may gain from campaigning it will never bridge that gap!

An hour later he shook his head and grinned ruefully, realising Rhys was right again, a churning stomach and a bleary eye were no twin aids to archery. He knew really though that he had only come down there to get away from the bustle around the manor and in some quiet activity regain his own peace of mind. Plucking his last shaft from the target, he replaced it in his quiver and despondently started back towards the manor.

As he got to the church he paused and raised a hand in salute to Talwyn, Prince Owain's captain from Cardigan, who was setting out with his men on the long march back home for the winter. As the last of them went past, Idris wondered what had become of Lord Tudor's men who had gone on to storm Shrewsbury. Gloomy again now he walked on slowly, thinking as he did so that it might have been better had he gone with them rather than return to Sycharth.

A few minutes later he stopped in his tracks by the dovecote as he saw a smiling Catrin walking towards him lightly, eagerly. His heart began beating quickly, but pursing his lips he breathed deeply, calming himself, before saying respectfully, 'Goodmorrow, Lady Catrin!'

Frowning, open mouthed, she just stood there for a moment with eyebrows raised, before exclaiming, 'Have you been gone so long that you forget that I'm your Catrin? That on your return I asked you to meet me here?'

It was Idris's turn to look amazed now as, wondering what had happened at the last night's feasting he might have missed, he asked, 'Asked me to meet you here, my lady?'

'Aye,' she said somewhat petulantly now as she made that fluttering gesture again with her hand, 'the dovecote!'

Careless of who might see him, Idris took her by the arm and shaking his head said, 'Dovecote, my lady? I thought you bade me farewell!'

By then though, they were inside the dovecote, Catrin was in his arms her body pressed to his and with her lips on his, it was some time before she could answer him.

It was some days later that Prince Owain's brother Tudor and Gruffydd Hanmer returned with their men to Sycharth. The few fit men led the way wearily, but there were many wounded too:

126

the halt and the lame who trailed behind, hobbling back on crutches or borne like sacks on pack horses. These were the lucky ones though, for many did not come back at all.

The alarm had been sounded as soon as Lord Tudor's force was sighted, but all who manned the parapets at Sycharth quickly realised that it was a beaten rather than an attacking force who approached. Minutes later Idris was riding out with the quickly assembled sally force led by Dafydd that Prince Owain sent out to meet Lord Tudor: to aid and protect him if he were pursued, to help the halt and lame if he were not. Whilst the women bustled around the manor preparing to care for the sick or wounded, the remaining men stayed watchfully on the parapets: clearly this was no time to relax the guard.

Nor was there time for any to relax after that, for it was hours before some order was achieved from the the seeming chaos of getting Lord Tudor's beaten force safely within Sycharth's palisade and the drawbridge raised. So busy were they all that it was some time before the saga of Lord Tudor's attack on Shrewsbury town and its aftermath could be told. At least, told where Idris might hear.

He was keeping watch on the gate-house tower, pleased to be alone after the activity of the late afternoon, pleased to be on his own, above the crowded manor and away from the cries of wounded men. It was a cloudy night but although the moon only appeared fleetingly, there were a few stars and he breathed a great sigh. It was one of contentment however, for he was thinking how lucky he was not to have been sent to Shrewsbury, thinking of meeting Catrin at the dovecote and . . .

His brief moment of contentment was shattered by heavy footsteps on the staircase to the tower and moments later a head appeared, then a burly body and Dafydd, who never seemed to rest or sleep, was saying gruffly, 'Not asleep are you, young Idris? Men keeping their watch have been hanged for less!'

Exasperated, Idris snorted, 'No, I'm not asleep, Dafydd! And were I dead, you tiptoeing up those stairs would be enough to waken me!'

Dafydd nodded, smiling. 'Aye, that's my charity! If you're asleep, my feet will waken you and if you're dead already, it matters not!'

He stood there for a moment, rubbing his chin as he gazed around, then turned to Idris.

'No, we'll have no visitors tonight, I'm thinking, Idris. If they

127

were following Lord Tudor, they'd have been closer on his tail than this!' Raising a warning finger he added, 'But many a man has died from thinking his enemy slept, so keep awake!'

Idris nodded soberly. 'Have no fear, Dafydd, I relish an English dagger at my throat no more than yours!' He frowned. 'What happened to Lord Tudor's force? One of his archers told me they'd sacked Shrewsbury town and, laden with the booty gained, they marched on to Welshpool,' Idris shook his head, 'but pale-faced already from his wound, he fainted then, I do not know not if he still lives.'

Dafydd scratched his beard. 'Nor I, a few have died since they made it safe back to Sycharth. Many more died beside the River Vyrnwy though, I'm told.' Leaning on the parapet and looking down towards the church he said quietly, 'Leaving Shrewsbury burning, they made their way by Garreg Bank, with Mynydd Hir to the south of them, to Welshpool which they sacked as readily. They met no trouble there it seems, so then they headed north, to ford the River Vyrnwy, but burdened now as they were with their gain from the two towns, they made slow progress.

'Their attack on Shrewsbury and on Welshpool would not go unnoticed and it seems, whilst they were busy at Welshpool, an English squire called Burnell or some such name gathered forces to wait in ambuscade for them. Whether he knew his business well, or they were too content with their success, he fell on them by the Vyrnwy where they lost nigh on half their men and most of the treasure gained, before they could escape his clutch. Therein lies a lesson for you Idris!

'If you would go raiding, do not burden your main force with the profit you have gained! Keep your profit light or send it off, burn what you cannot take, but keep your main force mobile, tight knit, lest you are overwhelmed!'

With a positive nod at Idris, as if at instruction well delivered, Dafydd turned away and stomped off down the staircase. Idris grinned at the retreating figure, thinking as he did so, Dafydd tries to teach me the science of warfare as though he would have me a captain too! The grin faded as he wondered whether that would make Catrin any the less unattainable.

Whilst Idris continued to keep his watch on the gate-house tower,

Prince Owain sat at the table in the great hall, with his brother Tudor on one side of him and Gruffydd Hanmer on the other. Frowning now, he asked, 'Why, Tudor?' Shaking his head in exasperation, he asked again, 'Why, after Shrewsbury, did you not return to your manor, why go on to attack Welshpool? Why take all with you, burdening yourself so you could hardly fight for all the candlesticks and other trinkets your soldiers bore?'

As Tudor remained silent, his face brooding, fingers beating an almost silent tattoo on the table, Gruffydd Hanmer spoke hesitantly, his English voice strangely at odds with the Welsh Christian name his mother had given him.

'Once safely across the Vyrnwy . . . '

Prince Owain interrupted him sharply. 'What better place for their ambuscade? A weary force, burdened with its spoils would be most vulnerable at a river crossing! Did your scouts not warn you of their presence, that the English came upon you unawares?'

A stubborn look now in his brown eyes, Tudor answered truculently, 'We sent no scouts, there seemed such little need. Shrewsbury town and Welshpool both fell into our hands like over ripe fruit, nor was there any resistance to our march. Another half an hour or so, a few wet feet and you'd have toasted us for the treasure we brought for your war chest, instead of taking us to task like naughty children! We've lost a few men in a skirmish, not lost a war! Come spring I'll take me back to Welshpool and teach Squire Burnell how to dance on air!'

Prince Owain looked at his brother for a moment then shook his head and tapped his own chest. 'The blame lies here! I should not let you go across the drawbridge here alone, much less with men that you should lead, protect. No! I should send a maid with you, to take you by the hand and lead you safely home! How many were the "few" you left behind on Vyrnwy's bloody banks, a hundred? Two hundred? We shall lose more, I grant you, before this strife ends, but let it not be because we did not care, or that we did not know our trade!'

Tudor opened his mouth as though about to make an angry retort, but Prince Owain held up his hand. 'Enough of this! I doubt either of you will forget Vyrnwy or reconnaissance when we campaign again. Let us all remember though, the English have many more men than we and can thus afford a war of attrition that would quickly bleed us to death!'

Chapter Sixteen

King Henry was at Northampton when the news of the attack on Shrewsbury by Owain Glyn Dŵr reached his ears. He was outraged, both at the temerity of this Welsh upstart and, because he could ill afford another campaign, was reluctant to be diverted from his return to London after his Scottish campaign. As he listened to the Percies, father and son, counsel an immediate attack on Owain Glyn Dŵr's stronghold, he was counting the cost of his Scottish campaign. Wondering too, whether it was more important to deal with this rebel from the Welsh marches, or nurse his resources against attack by Charles of France who, as he knew to his cost, eyed with envy Aquitaine and Calais. It was the old Earl who swayed him in the end.

'Put him down now, sire,' he counselled, 'else this Welsh magician will conjure up a platform from which Charles of France can assault the very heart of England's oak. If the tree dies, the branches will surely wither. Without England's crown you'll not be Duke of Aquitaine or Lord of Calais port! March on Shrewsbury now, sire! Then strike at the viper's nesting place whilst he believes bleak winter keeps retribution for his crimes at bay!'

Not only was King Henry affronted by Owain Glyn Dŵr's rebellion but it was nearly a month now since he had sent Lord Grey of Ruthin to deal with the rebel. He was livid that Ruthin had failed to capture Owain Glyn Dŵr and even more so that the Welshman's depredations had continued.

He nodded now and smiled at the Earl of Northumberland.

'Wise counsel as always!' He almost purred as he added, 'And who better to aid me in this task than you, when lesser men have failed me!'

The old Earl visibly winced, seemingly he had no wish to campaign in Wales at this time of year, however strategically important it might be to do so.

'I would that I could your Majesty,' he said with a sigh. 'My old bones have been sorely tried in this foray 'gainst Robert the Scot and I would crave your indulgence that I be saved the hills of Wales!' He nodded towards his son. 'If it pleases your Majesty, young Hotspur here will accompany you in my stead!'

'Young Hotspur' who, like both the King and Owain Glyn Dŵr was in his mid forties, seemed less than honoured by his father's proposal, but had the grace to mutter a grudging, 'An' it pleases your Majesty!'

Smiling, King Henry nodded. 'Aye, that pleases me indeed! Other then your noble father, there's no one I would rather have show me the path to Wales or how to hang a rebel high! From Shrewsbury we'll march through Wales and show the rebels there how ill advised it is to succour such as wild Glendourdy!'

The decision once made, King Henry now embraced it enthusiastically and the council of war that followed lasted late into the night. Throughout that night orders went out to his captains that would change their leisurely return to London into a forced march on Shrewsbury. Early the next morning the King led his army on its long march, too late to go to the aid of a town already pillaged and torched, his mission now was to exact a bloody revenge.

The roads that led to the north west from Northampton to Shrewsbury were little better than tracks and were no great aid to progress for Henry's army. Nor did the October weather, which turned the tracks into quagmires, help either its progress or his temper. When he eventually reached Shrewsbury the sight of the ravaged town roused him to fury and later he harangued Hotspur over the effrontery of the wild Glendourdy as he persisted in calling the Welshman. Seizing his opportunity when the King paused for breath, Hotspur tried to placate Henry.

'I'm told sire, that a local squire taught him a lesson he'll not forget a few miles north of Welshpool.'

Henry turned on him quickly. 'What's this? Glendourdy taught a lesson by a country squire?' Eyebrows raised he began to smile. 'Are you sure of this, Hotspur?'

Hotspur nodded. 'It was told me on oath sire! This Burnell ambuscaded Glyn Dŵr, if indeed it was he, as he prepared to ford a river a few miles north of Welshpool where the Welshman lost some two hundred men or more . . . '

Henry interrupted him, asking eagerly, 'Yes! but was it indeed Glendourdy, did he take him? I'll knight him this very day if he holds Glendourdy!'

Hotspur shook his head. 'No sire, Glyn Dŵr or perhaps his brother Tudor with over half his force escaped across the river and Burnell's men, after acquitting themselves so well 'gainst the rebel's superior force, had not enough strength left to pursue him northwards.'

Henry scowled. 'Not pursue him? God's blood, why not? Had I the devil on the run I'd follow him to the gates of hell if needs be!' He shrugged. 'Well, no doubt this squire will have gained reward enough from what Glendourdy dropped!'

Hotspur coughed and said dryly, 'Certainly Glyn Dŵr was well laden when the fight began sire and no doubt this encumbrance led to his failure there. With ten score rebel Welsh left dead on Vyrnwy's eastern bank, I wager there'd be a trinket or two for Burnell to garner before he left the field.'

Henry snorted. 'Aye, and he'd spent less time "garnering" and more time pursuing, I'd have Glendourdy hanging from a gibbet now! This news though greatly alters our intent! If Glendourdy can be taught such a lesson by one country squire, I doubt the need to pursue the wretch ourselves. I shall send word to Lord Grey of Ruthin to apprehend the rebel and send his head to me: I care little if the body be attached!'

Hotspur looked askance at the King. 'Do you think that wise, sire? Glyn Dŵr's losses at the Vyrnwy's banks were small indeed, and like a snake unless you crush the head, he'll grow another tail and strike again!'

Smiling, Henry shook his head. 'If one country squire can deliver such defeat upon his force, I warrant now his bolt is shot. I do not doubt that Ruthin, with some local aid, can put an end to Glendourdy's pranks!'

The King had barely finished his announcement when a rider, spattered with mud from hard riding, reigned up in the town square in which they stood. As the rider dismounted, the King and his retinue stared in surprise at being so unceremoniously interrupted and Henry, frowning, turned to Hotspur to say sharply with an imperious wave of his hand, 'See to it that the fellow learns better manners than to ride roughshod into our royal presence!'

As Hotspur stepped forward, the man brushed past him and rushed towards the King, to drop on one knee before him, saying, 'I crave pardon your Majesty for my rude approach, but I bring urgent news from your royal castle at Beaumaris!'

With that he thrust a sealed letter towards the King, who hesitated a moment, looking at Hotspur who stood behind the man now with drawn sword. Then, with a nod at Hotspur, the king took the letter and breaking the seal began to read, his face reddening with anger as he did so. The hand holding the letter dropped to his side and glaring at Hotspur he stood there apparently speechless, before almost screaming in his rage, 'I'll have Glendourdy's head myself, for there is no end to his treachery, his . . . his rebellion!'

As he could know nothing of what the letter contained, Hotspur was just standing there, obviously nonplussed. The king waved the letter in his face. 'Glendourdy's cousins!' he raved. 'They've seized the whole of Anglesey, even laid siege to my castle there!' Pointing to the messenger who had risen from his knee and now, bareheaded, stood somewhat uncertainly before him, the King continued, 'This valiant man, at risk of his own neck, escaped to bring us news of their perfidy.'

Frowning, Hotspur hesitated before asking, 'Who are these cousins of the rebel, sire?'

Henry shook his head angrily, as if their names were irrelevant. 'Welshmen both, part of his evil tribe!' Then as Hotspur seemed to be none the wiser, Henry glanced impatiently at the letter again. 'Gwilym and Rhys ap Tudur, but it matters not, too soon for their liking their names will be but history along with that of that damned Glendourdy!'

He stood there, tapping his chin with the folded letter and then, as though coming to a decision, he said to Hotspur, 'Give this man a purse and be not ungenerous on my behalf, then pass the word we ride on Anglesey today!'

As the King set out on the long march through hostile Wales to Anglesey, Prince Owain was drinking a toast with his cousin Ednyfed Tudur to the success of his other cousins on Ynys Mon,

133

Gwilym and Rhys. Putting his goblet down, Prince Owain smiled at his cousin.

'It is good to see you so soon cousin and all the better for bringing such good news! Yet what stirred you all to such activity in Ynys Mon? I thought you sought a quiet winter there, hopefully to campaign the better against the English come the spring!'

Ednyfed grinned. 'Opportunity, cousin, knows no season. Since you are Prince perhaps my brothers sought to be the Dukes of Mon, or just take profit from its fertile land!' More seriously he continued, 'Beaumaris is a rich prize, Owain, which if we can take and hold, it will be long indeed before the English set foot in Ynys Mon again. What better time to lay siege there than now? It is not we who have to traverse long wintry trails to sustain our soldiery, nor we who have to cross the Menai Straits against opposition.'

Prince Owain stroked his beard then nodded thoughtfully. 'All true, Ednyfed, but I've just had news that even whilst we talk, Henry storms through Wales from Shrewsbury, much angered by my brother's sacking of the town. With him too, I'm told, rides Hotspur, the younger Percy, nor do I doubt now where their journey's end might be! Have you sufficient forces in Ynys Mon to hold them off until we can gather aid?'

Apparently unconcerned Ednyfed shrugged. 'His men will be weary Owain, from their campaign against the Scots and marching south again. If you and yours can harass their supply trains and so prevent them gaining further aid, I have no doubt that we can fend them off all winter through and meantime starve Beaumaris out as well!

Prince Owain pursed his lips and frowned. 'My force here is now limited to my own retinue and brother Tudor licks his wounds after being mauled at Vyrnwy, but we'll send what men we can to harass Henry's flanks. I shall send messengers to both Cardigan and Marged's brothers, the Hanmers: given some little time we'll have a force that can attack his rear whilst he views Beaumaris fall to you!

Whilst Prince Owain was marshalling his forces again, King Henry's army reached Bangor where he expressed his resentment

of the Franciscan Order's support for the deposed Richard by
sacking the abbey there. It was easy for him to vent his spite on
such a soft target but facing him now was the harder task of
retaking Anglesey from the Tudur brothers. As he stood with
Hotspur looking across the narrow straits towards Beaumaris, he
knew that the end of October was not the best time for him to
attempt an opposed crossing. He turned grim-faced to Hotspur.
'We must cross! I cannot suffer Glendourdy taking a Royal
Castle, we must raise the siege if it costs a thousand in the
crossing!'

The look of determination on Henry's face as he made the
pronouncement stifled the protest on Hotspur's lips before it was
uttered and he too was grim faced as he nodded in agreement.
'Aye, sire,' he said quietly, 'the pity is, it will be no surprise to
them I fear. News of our approach will have reached them long
before this. They'll be on the shore there, waiting for us!'

It was barely light and a cold rain swept the straits the next
morning when Henry's army attempted the crossing to find, as
Hotspur had predicted, that the Welsh were not asleep.

Rain and the Tudur brothers' archers combined to ensure that
it was only a small force led by Henry himself that eventually
succeeded in making the crossing. Even then they only escaped
the bitter hand to hand fighting that ensued on the shore of Ynys
Mon to seek refuge in beleaguered Beaumaris Castle.

A virtual prisoner now in one of his own castles, King Henry
was furious as he stood on an uncompleted tower at Beaumaris
looking towards the mainland. Vainly he tried to see where
Hotspur mustered the remainder of the army, where he would
make his assault to free his King. At last, seeing nothing that
would lead to hope, he turned a scowling face on the Constable
of the castle, to say sourly, 'Before we came, Oldcastle, were you
sure you could hold out against these rebels?'

Grey-haired, ruddy cheeked, the Constable stepped forward
ponderously, his blue eyes reflecting the concern evidenced by
his frown.

'With so few men to guard the walls sire, we had stores enough
to last the winter through and every man we lost to their archers,
stretched our rations further. But before the winter ended they
could well overwhelm us by sheer numbers. With an apologetic
smile, he shook his head. 'Your coming has changed our

circumstance, Sire. Now we have men enough to last the winter through, if we could but feed them. Unless young Hotspur over there can raise the siege, then before November's end I fear we shall have to sally out and take our chance with cut and thrust!'

Henry looked at him in silence for a moment, then his eyes glittered as though he had glimpsed hope, smiling now he raised a finger. 'Much better to do both together, Oldcastle! We must so arrange a sally whilst Hotspur engages their attentions at the shore. Not only shall we lift the siege, we'll line the shore with gibbets for these rebels! Can you send out a messenger to Hotspur tonight?'

The Constable smiled. 'Aye, sire, but the messenger must not know the plan, for if he's caught, the Welsh will toy with him all night and by the dawn would know the essence of our plan!'

Hotspur frowned at first when next day a bewildered messenger delivered the King's message to him, having succeeded in evading the Tudurs' vigilance. All the messenger could tell him was that the king had said, "At an ungodly hour you first gave cry!" From that though he quickly determined that it was to do with the time of his own birth, seven in the morning of the second of November, nor was it difficult for him to understand that "give cry" meant give chase, or in his present circumstances, attack. At least, he was fairly sure that was what it all meant.

Looking around him at the depleted forces of the King's army he was a little less certain of the outcome of another attack on the Isle of Anglesey, for surely, the Tudurs would be expecting an attempt to rescue the King? At least, thought Hotspur, he now knew that the King was alive and that he was safe in Beaumaris. Knew too that the King expected him to attack and when. Dismissing the messenger, Hotspur shrugged and called his captains around him, liking the idea no more now than when he had first attempted storming Anglesey with Henry.

Whether this second attack was unexpected or because the Tudurs' forces were deployed around the castle, Hotspur landed more successfully and with fewer casualties than he had expected. Having done so he struck out towards Beaumaris, where the besiegers suddenly found themselves defending themselves on both sides as King Henry and the Constable sallied out with all their men. Soon the two English forces were united and fighting their way back to the Menai Straits.

Once on the mainland again Henry's march became more of a retreat than a punitive expedition. Pursued by the Tudurs he took his weary army south to Caernarvon, then eastwards through mist and driving rain across the mountains south of Cader Idris, harried by Owain Glyn Dŵr along the way. Although, like many another beaten general, he told Hotspur that it was but a battle lost, he vowed to make the Welsh pay in blood for the loss of Beaumaris and was grateful when at last he passed through the Welsh marches into England.

He knew now that his revenge would have to wait until the spring, but barely was he on English soil again before he announced that all of Owain Glyn Dŵr's lands and manors in North Wales and Cardigan were forfeit to the Crown. Hotspur smiled secretly as he heard the King's announcement and wished the Earl of Somerset, the King's bastard half brother and the new lord of those manors, good fortune should he seek to claim his new manors this wintertime.

Chapter Seventeen

It seemed a long winter to Idris for, despite the wintry weather, all at Sycharth daily expected an attack by John Beaufort, Earl of Somerset, come to claim his new possession. Prepared for siege, Prince Owain's armed retinue was ever kept on guard and Idris had few opportunities for stolen moments with Catrin and never outside the manor. Except for Gruffydd and Maredudd, who joined the soldiery in keeping watch, the Prince's children were seldom allowed outside the manor unescorted.

Seeing Catrin inside the manor, in the courtyard or from a distance at table in the great hall, but unable to speak to her or touch her was more frustrating for Idris than if he were away on campaign. The gate-house where they had sometimes met in more relaxed times was only a thoroughfare now for sentries going to or from their watch on the towers and the dovecote or the meadows by the church were forbidden to such as Catrin. The only place they seemed able to meet, however briefly, was at Emrys the fletcher's workshop beneath the parapet. Apparently no longer surprised at the lady Catrin's interest in his wares, the old craftsman busied himself at the front of his workplace whilst Catrin and Idris talked quietly in the shadowy rear.

It was nigh on Christmas and the two were standing close together there in the shadows when she looked up to him with appeal in her eyes. Her lips pouted as, with a quick glance at Emrys, she put her hand on Idris's arm and, her voice dropping to a whisper as if reluctant to utter the words, she told him that her father was sending her away. Idris looked at her in dismay for a moment, caught in a whirlpool of mixed emotions: relief that she would be somewhere safe, afraid that she would be lost to him. He smiled sadly then and took her by the shoulders. 'I'm glad,

Catrin,' he said. 'I'm so glad! Sycharth is no place for you now.'

Tears came to her eyes and she shook her head in desperation as she replied, 'But I don't want to go, Idris, I want to stay here with you! Even Father says that Lord Beaufort will not attack us here before the spring! Why do I have to leave here now?'

Idris looked away for a moment and blinked before turning back to her and saying softly, 'It is better so, Catrin. Better you leave now when it is safe to do so.'

'Take your hands off my lady sister, archer, or I'll run you through!'

There was no mistaking the voice or the intent and, as Idris felt the sword at his back, he turned his head sharply to see Gruffydd standing there menacingly. Idris raised his hands, palms open, then stood stock still not to give Gruffydd the excuse to do that which his hatred filled eyes showed he so obviously desired. Out of the corner of his eye, Idris saw Emrys watching all open-mouthed, an arrow shaft clutched in his hand as though it were a dagger.

Standing alongside Gruffydd, his face a mask, was his younger brother, Maredudd and it was he who spoke next. Putting his hand on Gruffydd's sword arm, he said quietly, 'Put up your sword, brother, we'll have no bloodshed amongst ourselves at Sycharth. I saw no malice in the archer's hand or look.' He paused and glancing at Catrin, added with raised eyebrows, 'Our lady sister can tell me if I err?'

Gruffydd hesitated, then slowly his sword point dropped away from Idris and he stood there, scowling, legs astride, the sword held across his body, point in one hand, hilt in the right. The appeal was there again now in Catrin's eyes as she looked at Maredudd and said urgently, 'No, Maredudd, the archer did me no harm! I was upset at leaving Sycharth and he only told me that it was safer so!'

Maredudd said dryly, 'Too close was he as he told you it seems, sister, for our brother Gruffydd's taste. Perhaps you'd better seek our mother's solace than this rough archer's!'

Blushing now, Catrin glanced at Idris briefly before, with a defiant look at Gruffydd, she walked away from them towards the great hall, her head held high. Idris watched the two brothers warily now, his hands on the fletcher's bench, where arrows in various stages of the making lay. Suddenly, like a flash of light,

Gruffydd's sword flicked up to draw a bead of blood from under Idris's chin. His head held back now to ease the pressure of the sword, Idris grasped uselessly at an arrow, glaring at Gruffydd the while. The lordling held him there helpless as he gazed at Idris with brown, malevolent eyes for a moment before saying, his voice a sibilant menace, 'I've warned you before, archer! Next time, no soft words will save you!'

With a flick of the wrist, Gruffydd whipped the sword away, the razor sharp point cutting the soft skin under Idris's chin as he did so and, turning on his heel, strode off to follow his sister. With lips compressed, angry eyes watching Gruffydd, Idris put the back of a hand to his chin to stem the blood. Emrys was by his side now, his old eyes concerned as he handed Idris a rag. Taking it from him, Idris held it to his chin, his eyes still following Gruffydd's progress to the great hall.

Maredudd's dry voice broke into Idris's thoughts, 'It seems, archer that my brother does not care for you comforting our sister in her distress!'

Idris could tell from the amusement in Maredudd's eyes, the half smile on his lips, that he did not entirely share Gruffydd's resentment and was about to reply when Maredudd held up a warning finger. 'No! Say not a word, lest you betray yourself! Your temper is too like my brother's for you, in your station, to always say what you may think.' Maredudd paused, hand to his chin and frowned before continuing, 'As well becomes a soldier, you doubtless fear losing that which in all truth you can never have, greater than the reality of my brother's wrath! Yet, if for nothing else than to save her blushes, it would be best that you stay away from my lady sister.'

He was about to turn away when he hesitated and looked intently at Idris as though seeing him for the first time. Shaking his head he said softly, as if to himself, 'Aye, alike you are in temper . . . and in looks!'

Lady Marged glared at Prince Owain.

'I knew no good would come of all this talk of independence,' she said in a voice shrill with indignation. 'Independence enough we had here at Sycharth, Glyndyfrdwy and your manors south in Cardigan! Wealth and dignity you had too, for chief amongst the

140

Welsh gentry you were. Now all that is lost! Christmastide and every stick and stone forfeit to the Crown! I ask you, Owain, where will our children lay their heads this Christmastide?'

Standing there in the great hall, Owain raised his eyes to the rafters and asked innocently, 'In a manger, Marged?'

It was as if she had only partly heard him, for apart from correcting him by saying, 'I've told you often enough, Owain, my name is Margaret.' She ignored his interjection and continued, tight lipped, with her tirade: 'I never greatly liked your cousin Ednyfed and kind though it might be for him to offer shelter to your poor children in his place on Ynys Mon, it breaks my heart to think we have to flee over the ocean because of your impetuous . . . '

Losing patience, Owain interrupted her sharply, 'Marged! Not once before this have you ever said that you disliked cousin Ednyfed, who has ever been gracious to you in both word and deed! Nor do you fall off the end of the world when you go to Ynys Mon! The Menai Straits are no great ocean, I've seen young maids, aye and stout men too, jump as far when you snap at them! Nor is my only quarrel with the usurper, Henry, that Wales should be an independent Principality. 'Tis about unjust governance, the crown he wears unlawfully and that I swore allegiance to Richard. Aye, all that and more, for do you not recall the trap he set for me in that array? Our lands were forfeit then as surely as they are this day! Wales, resurgent now, will rally to our side and though we lose our manors, Beaufort shall not hold them long . . . nor Henry, Wales!'

Marged reached out to him and put her hand on his, soft-eyed now, she said in quiet resignation, 'It is just that I've been so happy here these many years, Owain, it grieves me so to leave Sycharth now and I only wonder when we shall find such happiness again.'

Owain smiled at her and, taking her in his arms, looked in her eyes to say with conviction, 'Oh we shall, my love, we shall! Our court we'll hold in Aberystwyth, but here at Sycharth will be our home!'

Her eyes brimming, she nodded slowly. 'If that pleases you Owain,' she said quietly. 'If it pleases you!'

'Oh that does, my love, that will please me greatly!' Stroking her cheek, he smiled and said in encouragement, 'You'll like

Mon, Marged, a place of great magic is Mon, for there, in ancient days, Gwydion ap Don worked his magic with the stars at Bryn Celli Ddu.'

Alarm in her eyes now, Marged stepped back from him. 'Magic? I like not magic, magic places, nor yet wizards like this Gwydion ap Don of yours, Owain!' She shook her head and said with determination in her voice, 'I'll not go to Mon, nor take the children there! Ednyfed, is he related to this wizard, Gwydion ap Don?'

Owain shook his head in exasperation. 'No, Marged! More time has passed than man can tell, since Gwydion, a bard of great learning, practised his science there. From there he studied the heavens with great care, foretold the seasons' change, the ocean's wrath, when comets came, what they foretold and much other learning which time has stolen from us. Would I that I had such a man to advise me now in the conduct of this war!'

Marged snorted, 'Would I you'd had such a man to teach you what folly it was to embark upon such an enterprise!'

Owain sighed. 'Folly or not, Marged, we ride for Ynys Mon the morrow and we'll celebrate mass there at Christmastide!'

Idris watched Prince Owain's departure with a certain amount of apprehension, for the Prince was taking with him only Maredudd and a few men at arms as escort for the relatively safe journey to Ynys Mon. Gruffydd was left in command at Sycharth with the old campaigner, Dafydd, there to temper the impetuosity of youth.

Whether it was the absence of Catrin however, or that command weighed heavily on Gruffydd's shoulders, Idris saw little of him during the Prince's absence. After Owain's return Idris seemed to spend all his time on the parapets or the gatehouse towers, watching, waiting for Lord Beaufort and the assault that surely would come soon now.

Prince Owain was not however idly awaiting attack, for there were frequent toings and froings of messengers who sought, or brought offers of, support. Every day too, seemed to bring its trickle of labourers and students who had been working in England or studying in the colleges at Oxford. All said they were returning to Wales to join Owain Glyn Dŵr's banner for the Great

Rebellion.

At the end of January, Idris was by the gate, the drawbridge down, when one such student, appeared and sought entrance. His eyes burning with the fierce light of the zealot, he said his name was Geraint and that he had news for Prince Owain of a Parliament the King had called.

A few minutes later Idris led Geraint towards Prince Owain who was sitting in a tall oaken chair beside the blazing fire in the hearth in the great hall, quietly talking with an older man. The other man's silver grey hair contrasted sharply with his dark cloak, adorned solely with a silver cross and his austere countenance bespoke a man of learning rather than of good humour.

Prince Owain turned as Idris approached and half frowning asked, 'Who do you bring to us and with what news that needs such immediacy, Idris?'

His back unbending, Idris waved a hand at his forehead in salute. 'If it please your honour,' he said unabashed. 'This is Geraint, who has come from Oxford to join your banner. His news of Parliaments and such the King has held, I judged you'd want to hear.'

Prince Owain glanced at the man sitting by the hearth with him, who remained sober-faced, silent, then back at Idris and smiling, nodded. 'You judged aright, Idris, for such news we'll stop our talk and listen whilst Geraint here tells us his news of Parliaments . . . and such!' Prince Owain turned to the young student and, smiling now, asked, 'What is this news you bring so urgently from Oxford, Geraint?'

Interested in what Geraint had to say and not being dismissed, Idris stood there whilst Geraint began his tale.

'Ten days ago, your honour, the King held Parliament and with the lords assembled there debated only Wales and the turmoil your just campaign has caused therein.' He paused as Prince Owain glanced at the cleric with raised eyebrows to receive a cautious nod in reply to his unspoken question. 'There was much talk of pillaged towns along the marches, of Anglesey and Beaumaris seized. My Lord Bishop Trefor of St. Asaph spoke, it seems your honour, of unrest throughout all Wales and of the need for the Welsh to be treated with clemency lest their over heated tempers break all bonds of fealty.'

Prince Owain held up a hand and smiling as though in satisfaction, turned to the other man. 'Young Geraint here, brings confirmation of your report, Hywel, on the advice Bishop Trefor gave to Parliament.'

Hywel favoured the Prince with a wry smile, as though he had not realised that any report of his required confirmation.

Prince Owain turned to Geraint again. 'We thank you for your news, young Geraint, but this much we learnt from Dean Cyffin here. Have you ought else of which we should be advised?'

Geraint nodded but hesitated a moment before replying, 'More recent news I fear, your honour,' he began, before pausing again, as though reluctant to be the bearer of bad news, 'but three days since the King, by royal proclamation, pardoned all who'd risen with you against the crown . . . all, that is, except your princely self, your brother Tudor and your cousins in Anglesey.'

Prince Owain stroked his beard whilst looking at Geraint steadily for a moment, then turning to the cleric, smiled as he said quietly, 'Now that is news indeed, is it not, Hywel?'

Fleetingly, Dean Cyffin looked discomforted, but quickly regaining his composure, he pursed his lips and nodded sagely. 'As I feared, my Lord Prince,' he said, 'King Henry seeks to disaffect your subjects and thus isolate you and your immediate kin. Some few will, no doubt, be tempted by such seeming leniency. Across the Principality though your cause gains strength each day, men are selling cattle, sheep to buy their armour and warlike weapons. The weak will fall by the wayside, but the strong will flock to your banner. For your sword, which seeks to free your people, is the sword of the Lord and of Gideon.'

It did not seem to Idris that Prince Owain was impressed with the idea of his sword belonging to Gideon, whoever that was, for he turned abruptly to Geraint again. 'What other good news do you bring to us from England, young man?'

'Nought else your honour,' replied Geraint, 'except that it is said the King marches on Wales and that the Earl of Somerset marches north with Sir Edmund Mortimer to seize, the gossip says, your manors here.'

Prince Owain grinned and shook his head. 'That "nought else" was quite enough for one mouthful, Geraint! Now you'd best get yourself away with Idris there, for food and drink, before you find much else to say!' Turning to Idris, he added, 'See that Geraint is well fed, for he has given us valuable service, but meanwhile send Dafydd and my sons to me here, for I would take counsel with them.'

Barely an hour later, Idris met Dafydd bustling out of the great hall, grim faced, hand on sword, as though about to storm a battlement. Dafydd waved to Idris, his very stance expressing urgency, to say as Idris walked up to him, 'Gather the archers together, Idris, prepare to march, for we leave Sycharth at dawn tomorrow!'

Surprised, Idris asked, 'Where do we march then, Dafydd?'

Unusually, Dafydd snapped, 'We march where Prince Owain tells us and at his behest!' As he looked at Idris, the worried frown softened into obvious concern. 'We leave Sycharth for the mountains to the west, Idris, nor shall we see it again as it stands now! Take all with you that you can safely bear . . . and fight!'

With that he hurried away, leaving an amazed Idris staring after him. Then, gathering his wits, Idris rushed away to spread the startling news.

It was a cold morning when they left Sycharth and a dusting of snow lay on the parapets as Idris took a last look around the familiar landscape before joining the others in the courtyard. He was all ready, all his few possessions either on his person or in his horse's saddlebags. Prince Owain and his two sons were in the courtyard now too, ready to lead the Prince's retinue over the drawbridge and to the safety of the mountains.

Idris was prepared, but somehow it still seemed a betrayal to him, that they should leave Sycharth in this way. Dafydd had told him about it the previous evening over a pot of mead, one of the last they were to have at Sycharth.

'It's no good, Idris,' Dafydd had said, 'had we a thousand men here, Sycharth could not be defended against an army such as Beaufort and Mortimer bring against us. They'd starve us out in a few days did they but sit and wait! And if they brought a catapult, they'd breach the palisade in hours! Sycharth's no Caernarvon Castle built to withstand a siege of months, it is a manor built for comfort. No, Idris bach, we must go and bide the time when we can strike back, regain that which the Prince rightly owns.'

g

Looking around him now, Idris had a strange lump in his throat as he realised how little there would be to regain. It was then that Prince Owain waved his drawn sword in the air and, with a bitter smile on his lips, led his soldiery off across the drawbridge. Already there was the pungent smell of smoke in the air, a wisp of smoke around the entrance to the great hall. As Idris passed the gate-house, he was sure that it was only the smoke and not the memory of holding Catrin there, that caused the pricking sensation in his eyes. Then they were away from the manor and going down the gentle slope that led to the meadows by the church, the same meadows where he had walked with Catrin.

Idris noticed that Prince Owain looked not once behind, but could not help but look back himself to see the smoke billowing from Sycharth manor. As he did so he could hear the crackle of the flames already licking around the roof of the great hall and the palisade, as they reflected redly on the low clouds. Little enough there would be left of Sycharth he thought sadly, for John Beaufort to claim. Then, turning away, he followed Prince Owain towards the distant mountains.

Chapter Eighteen

The first hints of spring were welcome to the small band who had wintered with Prince Owain amongst the foothills of Snowdon. From their hiding places there they had made occasional sallies to harass the King's army, commanded now by Hotspur, who sought to capture Prince Owain. Never in one place for more than a night or two Prince Owain proved to be an elusive target, his small force mobile, irritating as the midges on a summer's night, as it struck at the flanks of Hotspur's ponderous army before quickly disappearing again into the night.

Sitting in the makeshift shelter of their fireless camp one night at the end of March, Idris shivered and pulled his cloak tighter around him. He looked up at the stars glittering in the clear sky, at the near full moon which shed its cold, ghostly light over all, then turning to Dafydd, said with an edge to his voice, 'There'll be a frost on our blankets again this night Dafydd, it was in Sycharth's hall I last felt warm! When, do you think our Prince will array his forces and give battle to Hotspur? These two month's past we've done little but annoy him with our pinpricks.'

'Do you think campaigning is all warm beds and cosy nights of drinking ale? This winter has been mild, a joy indeed, to when I campaigned with the Prince against the Scots!'

With a sigh, Idris raised his eyes to the moon again, then quickly, before Dafydd could enlarge upon his favourite theme, asked again, 'Aye, hard indeed it must have been there, Dafydd, but when do you think we shall attack Hotspur's force in earnest?'

Dafydd pursed his lips as though in deep thought for a moment, then nodded towards Geraint who, pinch faced, lay huddled in his blanket. 'If the Prince arrayed two thousand eager

147

lads like that, he'd only lead them to their graves against Hotspur's seasoned force! No, Idris, nip and tuck's the order of the day, to sap the temper of men who fight in hostile land so that, in due season, we can indeed bring them to combat as an equal force and that will bring you warmth enough!' Pulling his blanket around him, Dafydd grinned. 'Now let me sleep and don't keep me awake with your chattering teeth!'

Minutes later Dafydd, the old campaigner, was indeed asleep and already snoring. Idris smiled as he thought, Dafydd's dreaming of Scotland. Whether because of the cold, the moonlight or Dafydd's snoring though, Idris was wakeful, his thoughts going around in circles. At the centre of every circle was Catrin, smiling, laughing or tearful, or her eyes pleading as they were that day before she left Sycharth. Despondently he thought of her now on Ynys Mon, a lady in her silks and satins, of himself, lying unshaven in this fireless camp, his clothes still damp from yesterday's showers. He sighed as he thought that it was not mere distance that separated them, not even rank: Catrin was unattainable to him because they dwelt in worlds apart.

It seemed only a few minutes later that he awoke to find his blanket, stiff with frost and an irritatingly cheerful Dafydd rousing him.

'You were right, young Idris, there's a thick frost this morning!'

Idris sat up, readily containing his pleasure at being proved right and looked around him with bleary eyes as the camp began to come to life.

'Come on, Idris, did you not sleep last night? It's not like you to be laggard,' scolded Dafydd. 'But rise you must, for we are on the march as soon as we break our fast!'

As Idris glowered at him, Dafydd, still smiling, eyebrows raised, asked, 'Was this not what you sought last night? No mere pinprick this, we ride full blooded to assault Hotspur's camp.'

Throwing the stiff blanket from him, Idris hurriedly arose, fumbling around him to seek his bow, his quiver and where his sword might lie.

'Assault, this day, Hotspur's camp?' he asked his words still slurred with sleep. 'There are but fifty of us here!'

Lips pouting, Dafydd nodded. 'Aye, that's so! But as I told Prince Owain, there's only ten or so of them to each of us, we need not fear the day!'

Idris, mouth opened in dismay, stood there speechless, his sword now hanging uselessly by his side. At last he spoke, incredulity in each word, 'Five hundred? More like a thousand Hotspur has in his force and we . . . we ride to assault his camp? If we do so, then we are mad, each one of us!'

His face serious now, his voice cajoling, Dafydd spoke softly, 'Come now Idris, what better day than this to take on such odds? That shooting star you saw last night was but a pointer to where our destiny lay today! Bestir and arm yourself, today's dawn saw April's first sunrise!

Suddenly it seemed as if all the camp was awake and, raucous laughter all around him, Idris scowled as he flung his sword where he had lain. A grinning Dafydd put an arm around his shoulder.

'What, put out we do not raid Hotspur in his encampment, Idris? Last night I could have sworn that you'd attack it by yourself if no one followed!'

Shamefacedly, Idris muttered, 'Aye, that was last night Dafydd, my courage ebbs with dawn!'

A few days later a messenger arrived at Prince Owain's camp and Idris's heart lifted, hoping to glean word of Catrin if the messenger came from Ynys Mon. Although the man came from Gwilym and Rhys Tudur however, he had not come from Ynys Mon, but Conwy and the news he brought quickly spread around the camp.

It seemed that it was whilst Dafydd had been tweaking Idris about attacking Hotspur that it had all started. It was Good Friday and the garrison of Conwy Castle, led by its pious constable, John de Massy, were at church with but a few men keeping watch. It was then that a craftsman who daily worked at his craft within the castle gained admittance, a canvas bag with the tools of his trade over his shoulder.

Apparently the watchmen who gave the craftsman entry saw what they expected to see and afterwards saw little else, for he was a man who followed more trades than one and they lay dead. Soon Gwilym and Rhys had forty men inside the castle and the Constable with over a hundred of his disarmed, disgruntled, men trooped out of it to make their way to wherever they might find safety.

Although Prince Owain was delighted at the news of Conwy Castle being taken, Dafydd was less impressed for, as he told Idris later: 'That de Massy man's a pious fool! In war you keep one eye open even whilst you pray, lest Satan comes upon you unawares! Small though his garrison might be, the Tudurs never should have taken Conwy had he stayed but half awake. I doubt King Henry's thanks to him will take the form of gold! Doubtless though, Hotspur will now lay siege to Conwy and we will shift our camp to lend our arm to aid the Tudurs.'

'True the Tudors took the castle by artifice, not force of arms, Dafydd, but can they hold it with so few men?'

Dafydd grimaced. 'The king will not relish that it was lost at all, he'll move heaven and earth to ensure it is regained. Our trouble is it's spring, when men are loath to leave their farms to fight, and we are too few to more than harass Hotspur as he lays siege. Were I in Hotspur's place, I'd say a month at most before the garrison sought quarter.'

April passed however and still the Tudurs kept Owain's banner triumphant on the battlements and as May wore on Hotspur sent emissaries to the Tudurs to negotiate their surrender. Each week of siege though, reduced the numbers of defenders within the castle and, unable to get supplies through the English lines, hunger began to take its toll on those who remained. Towards the end of June, Prince Henry, who had been in London reporting to his father on the siege, returned to Conwy with reinforcements under the command of Sir Hugh Despenser.

Hotspur's forces it seemed were now deployed to pursue Prince Owain, whilst Sir Hugh Despenser took over the siege of Conwy Castle. Fully occupied in defending themselves against Hotspur's superior force, Prince Owain's band were unable to prevent the fall of Conwy to Sir Hugh Despenser's forces at the end of June.

Idris heard the news as they made camp for the night in the hills above Conwy. He was standing with Dafydd when the man approached them, a spearman by his look and dress, thought Idris. Gaunt and bitter faced as though he'd only supped on gall, he addressed Dafydd sullenly: 'Does Owain Glyn Dŵr camp here this night?'

Dafydd braced his shoulder's back and took a deep breath

before answering sharply, 'Who is it asks for Prince Owain?'

The man turned his head and spat, 'One who's had enough of Lords and Princes to last a lifetime! A spearman I, who fought and starved nigh on three months in Conwy with the Tudurs.' He spat again as though trying to rid himself of a foul taste. 'Aye and for what? For them to surrender to Despenser nine of my comrades to be hanged, drawn and quartered as rebels so the Tudurs could walk free!'

Idris's mouth opened in horror but could not bring himself to speak whilst Dafydd frowned and replied quietly, 'How many walked out of Conwy with you?'

'Of the score of us there, but ten men at arms . . . and my lords the Tudurs, of course.'

Dafydd sighed and shook his head. ' 'Twas the best they could do perhaps, to save what they could!'

The spearman sneered, 'The best they could do, when we had fought alongside them for months? We said Despenser could do his worst, we'd fight to the last! No, just prisoners they'd be, the Tudurs said! Well, I've given my message and now, if you had sense, you'd do what I'm doing!'

With that, he turned and started to walk away into the night, but Dafydd raised an arm and called after him, 'Stay, have a bite to eat, a pot of ale, a bed for the night . . . '

The man did not falter in his stride, just turned his head to the side and spat again, before he was lost in the shadows as quickly as he had appeared.

Pursued by Hotspur, Prince Owain's small force headed south through Powys to Cardigan where he would be able to strengthen his force from his manors and other adherents there. It was no easy journey though, for shortly after escaping into the mountains of Powys after a brush with a company of Hotspur's soldiery at Cader Idris, they were forced to retreat into the mountains again after nearly falling into an ambuscade.

It seemed that Lord Charlton, the English Lord of Powys was lying in wait for them, no doubt having been warned of their progress by Hotspur. All that long night they were pursued before they eventually managed to evade their pursuers and even then not without some loss. As dawn broke the next morning they were able to draw rein and rest their horses, whose breath rose like smoke in the cool mountain air.

Idris turned to Dafydd. 'What will they do to him, Dafydd?'

Dafydd's face was expressionless as he he shook his head.

'Rhys is just a man at arms, Idris. Doubtless Lord Charlton will persuade him to join his retinue,' he grinned. 'Rhys is not learned, yet wise enough to know that alive, mayhap he'll have the chance to turn again!'

Idris thought of his last fleeting image of Rhys, dismounted in the confusion of the ambuscade, his arm outstretched as he sought help when none could pause . . . none except Lord Charlton's men. He thought too of the spearman from Conwy and his tale of what had happened to his comrades and shuddered.

Dafydd clapped him on the back and laughed. 'Why so solemn, Idris? Grieve not for Rhys, he'll be drinking ale with Lord Charlton's men by now. Aye, and trying to sell those boots he gained at Ruthin market to one of them! He sells his sword to survive, so who the buyer is matters little so long as he survives to turn his coat again, eh?'

Thankful to have escaped so lightly from brushes with such powerful forces Prince Owain's men made their way to Plynlimon, near the head-waters of the River Severn. There they were to make their base for the summer campaign, to lick their wounds and gather forces for forays into Cardigan and the south.

All the next month raiding parties went out pillaging the English held towns, but gaining supporters as well. So effective were they in creating havoc that others beside Lord Charlton were now seeking Prince Owain and his marauding forces. It was on the eighth of August when Prince Owain's personal retinue, now some one hundred and thirty strong were returning to Plynlimon that the rider caught up with them. So lacking in stealth was his approach that all had turned to see who it was that so furiously rode his horse in his effort to overtake them. Ignoring all others he rode past the column until he came abreast with Prince Owain but, panting nearly as much as his steed, it was a moment before he could speak, meanwhile pointing behind, as though in warning.

At last he spoke, the words tumbling out in their urgency,

'They're coming, my lord, over a thousand of them, not more than an hour behind me!'

Idris looked from the messenger to Prince Owain, who merely nodded and asked calmly, 'Aye, no doubt lad, but do you know who they are and what is their business?'

The messenger had seemingly caught his breath now, or was calmed by the Prince's manner.

'Aye, my lord, Flemings they are mostly, some fourteen hundred of them gathered from as far as Pembroke, Rhos and Cardigan. Come to bring you to battle so they say, my lord.'

Prince Owain stroked his beard as he looked evenly at the man. 'Fourteen hundred of them, you say?' he asked quietly. Then, as the man nodded, he smiled and added in a voice loud enough for all to hear, 'Well then men, there'll be enough to go around!'

To Idris's surprise, instead of leading his force off at a gallop, Prince Owain called over his captains, Dafydd and Talwyn from Cardigan, together with his sons Gruffydd and Maredudd and talked quietly with them for a few minutes before setting out at a canter obviously to the mountains, but not it seemed for Plynlimon.

As they rode on Idris frowned as he turned to Dafydd to ask, 'Should we not make more haste, Dafydd, with so many close behind?'

'With our mounts already weary we durst not force the pace.' He shrugged. 'The mountains lie ahead where the chase will be the harder, our defence the easier, for those that follow are not mountain fighters.'

Idris looked at him doubtfully. 'Yet there are ten and more of them to each one of us . . . '

Dafydd grinned. 'So? Would you live forever? Before night falls it will be time to earn our pay, we are so few that not one must shrink or Talwyn here and I will make him pay his due!'

It was not long before they were making their way along a valley, high in the mountains, its rough ground strewn with rocks where heather grew amongst small peat bogs, treacherous footing for those who did not know the way. Idris, keeping a wary eye behind him as often as seeking the way, saw movement in the distance as though a swarm of midges hovered there, and called to Dafydd,

'I see their van now, Dafydd!'

Dafydd smiled knowingly. 'Aye, they follow where we lead them to their disadvantage!'

Idris with a doubtful glance at Dafydd, muttered, 'Would that our advantage were as great as theirs!'

Looking around him as though anxious to see beauty in the stark hills whilst he might, he saw a small river glinting in the sun as it wound its way along the valley, a stone cairn atop the nearest hill and asked Dafydd, 'A dreary place this, where are we?'

With a wry grin, Dafydd replied, 'Nant Hyddgen, where many a man will make his home this day!'

Dafydd paused as Prince Owain, at the head of their small column, raised his sword and turned to them as they all reined up. His reins held loosely in hand, his sword now resting on his shoulder, Prince Owain waited a moment for silence and then, as they all looked at him expectantly, he spoke, his voice not loud, but rich and clear in the still mountain air:

'Men, this is our chosen place for battle! Of our choosing,' and here he pointed at the advancing enemy with his sword, 'not theirs! We'll let our weary nags rest awhile whilst we assail the enemy on foot as they stumble amidst these bogs and rocks. When,' he paused then continued, his voice louder in emphasis, 'when we prevail, we'll mount and chase them back to hell again! And we all do our part, all Wales will long remember our victory here today! Now I commend our cause to God as each man takes his allotted station!'

Idris joined in the cry of 'Prince Owain am Cymru!' but to his ears it was somewhat more subdued than usual, the faces around him serious rather than exultant. Hurriedly, the horses were taken to the rear as Idris took his twenty archers to the right flank of the men at arms who were in a thin extended line facing the enemy. On the other flank were Talwyn's archers, who, like Idris's archers, were spread out diagonally from the main force as though two arms waited to embrace the advancing Flemings.

As Idris stood there, his own bow readied, it seemed as if there were thousands, not hundreds, of the enemy relentlessly approaching in an irresistible wave and he gritted his teeth as he waited for the signal. So close were they now it was not an army, but a sea of faces and still no signal came from Dafydd. Suddenly Dafydd's sword fell in a hacking motion, Idris screamed, 'Now!'

154

and from each flank of Prince Owain's force arrows flew to find their targets amongst the enemy. Barely was an arrow in flight before another was notched and fast and furious they flew to cause havoc amongst the front ranks of the Flemings. Horses reared and men fell screaming as those behind pressed on and heedlessly trampled over them.

In the midst of this confusion, Idris heard a wild cry rise from Prince Owain's main force, though whether a cry of rage or despair he could not tell. Then, out of the corner of his eye, he saw them hurl themselves at the foe. With an urgent call to his archers, Idris now directed their arrows to the enemy's flank away from their van, trying to prevent them encircling Owain.

For there it was Prince Owain fought, his sons alongside him, as desperately as all his men. For them there could be no retreat nor yet surrender, for such was the rage of battle that those who cried for quarter would die before the call left their lips.

As Idris let fly his last arrow and, with as little hope left, drew his sword to lead his few men to close combat on the enemy's flank, he glimpsed the impossible. Their serried ranks wavered for a moment as a man might shiver in the cold. Even as they did so, the archers on both flanks raced screaming to join the frenzied attack of Owain's main force and incredibly, the wavering turned to flight. Leaving their dead and wounded littering the field, they fled pursued by Owain's men who, crazed by impossible relief and blood lust, pursued them, baying like hounds on the chase.

The sky over Hyddgen that evening was red, reflecting as much perhaps the bloody field of battle as the sun's dying rays, as Prince Owain called halt to the chase of the vanquished army. Laughing now, as much in their surprise at seeing the setting sun as in disbelief at their victory, they stumbled their way wearily back up Nant Hyddgen. Looking around them they totted up the butcher's bill: an arm lost here, a bloody head there and ten who would not see the setting sun. They shook their heads in wonder though as they tallied the enemy who lay fallen there.

Dafydd was telling Idris there were over two hundred of them when Prince Owain strode over, his face begrimed with blood and sweat. Unsmiling, as though weary from the fray, he nodded at Idris. 'You did well, this day, Idris the Archer.' He paused, looking at Idris steadily the while, then, nodding again, he added, 'Indeed, I would expect no less from you.' Half smiling he turned away, to say over his shoulder, 'Henceforth, you are my captain of archers.'

As Idris, gaping in amazement now, stared at the retreating figure of Prince Owain, a grinning Dafydd slapped him on the back. 'More than one pot of ale that will cost you Idris,' he said gleefully, 'all down to my good advice it is, see!'

Chapter Nineteen

It seemed that the fame of Prince Owain's victory at the battle of Hyddgen had spread far and wide, for daily now, men came to Plynlimon to join his banner. His brother Tudor also came with a large following to join him there and their armed bands roved freely across Mid Wales terrorising the English towns. As August drew to a close, a force led by Tudor and Prince Owain's son, Gruffydd, set out to raid Radnor and, if fortune favoured them, to take its castle. As the days passed with no sign of their return, Dafydd and Idris speculated that Tudor had either laid siege to Radnor Castle or was raiding even further abroad.

On the last day of August, Ednyfed Tudur came with a small band to Plynlimon bringing news from Ynys Mon and there was great feasting in the Prince's headquarters in his honour. Safe in the knowledge that such was their strength now that few would dare assail them, or indeed approach them unawares the Prince, his kin and all his captains, made merry late into the night.

It was late too, when Maredudd came to where Idris, drinking with Talwyn and Dafydd, was seated. Of an age with Prince Hal, the English Prince of Wales, Maredudd was fifteen now and though slighter than his brother, just as tall and more amiable than Gruffydd, with a ready smile that endeared him to his men. Bright eyed, a goblet of wine in his hand, he was smiling now at Idris and said with a slight slurring of his words, 'I would have words with you, Idris!'

Standing, Idris smiled too and with arched eyebrows, replied, 'Aye, my lord?'

Maredudd shook his head. 'Not here man. Privily!'

So saying he took Idris by the elbow and, with a surprised Dafydd and Talwyn staring after them, led Idris away to a corner out of earshot from the table. There, leaning confidentially towards Idris, he said in a voice almost a whisper, 'I have news from Ynys Mon, Idris.'

Pausing, he smiled again and nodded, whilst Idris stood there wondering whether he was going to keep his news a secret. At last Idris asked impatiently, 'What news, my lord?'

'My sister Catrin!' replied Maredudd. 'She sends her f . . . felicitations on your captaincy!'

Then, swaying slightly, he started to walk back to the head of the table but, looking over his shoulder, he positively winked at Idris before turning away again.

Idris gazed at him, his head in a whirl. He wasn't sure what felicitations were but it all sounded very grand. Smiling now, he tried to repeat the word, stumbling over the syllables as he did so. He was still muttering the word aloud as he got back to the table but his companions must have misheard him for Talwyn, nodding, seemed to be agreeing with him, saying, 'Quite right, Idris, a fig for all lords!'

Dafydd though, just looked thoughtfully at Idris for a moment before asking quietly, 'Good news then, Idris?'

Idris, hugging his little secret to his heart now, just mumbled. 'No news, Dafydd, it was just about tomorrow!'

He could see from Dafydd's raised eyebrows that the old captain didn't believe him, but he wasn't about to share Maredudd's message with anyone. As he sat there, now quietly sipping his pot of ale, he wondered how Catrin could have found out about him being made a captain of archers. Prince Owain would not have mentioned it in any letter to the Lady Marged and Gruffydd certainly would not have done so. Pursing his lips Idris nodded thoughtfully, it could only have been Maredudd. He smiled to himself as he thought, I have an ally there! His thoughts were interrupted as Dafydd said irritably, 'Fine companions I have here! Talwyn snoring away there and you nursing your no news to yourself!'

Idris smiled apologetically. 'I'm sorry, Dafydd, I was lost in thought!' And so saying he turned to Talwyn to shake him roughly by the shoulder. 'Come on Tal, you can't sleep here! The English are at the door!'

Jumping up, his hand on sword, a wide-eyed Talwyn cried out, 'The English? Where?'

Others were standing now, echoing his cry and for a moment pandemonium reigned until Dafydd, glaring at Idris, took Talwyn by the shoulder and sat him down saying, 'Just a joke it was, Tal, just a joke. Have another pot of ale!'

Talwyn glared around him muttering, 'No humour in a jest like that. A cry of wolf it was!'

Idris, abashed at the evident truth of Talwyn's remark and seeing all around scowling at him took refuge in his pot of ale. A moment later he looked up, to see Maredudd grinning at him and thought of Catrin and felt a warm glow again as he thought of the message the young lord had given him.

Idris's warm glow seemed to be shared by many that night for wine and ale flowed freely. It was in the midst of these festivities that a messenger entered the hall whose message sent a chill around the room, for what he had to say to Prince Owain left the Prince in an icy rage. His brother Tudor, it seemed, had taken Radnor Castle and laid waste the town, that of itself could only be good news, another triumph over the English. It was the aftermath of this victory though, that caused the Prince such anger and indeed chilled all who heard the news. Furious that his early call on the castle's garrison to surrender had been rejected, Tudor had put all sixty of the survivors to the sword when at last he took the castle. He said it was in revenge for Despenser's execution of the men at Conwy, but that did not lessen Prince Owain's fury.

Idris heard Prince Owain snarl at Ednyfed, 'What quarter can my men expect now when a battle's lost to the English?' he demanded. 'Where does such revenge stop?'

Ednyfed was more phlegmatic as he shrugged Prince Owain's remark aside: 'It's but a spur Owain,' he said almost nonchalantly. 'In this rebel game of ours we can but win or lose and if we lose, we die, for there can be no surrender now.'

As autumn yellowed the leaves Prince Owain's enlarged force left Plynlimon and went raiding through Llanidloes and Newtown and on to Montgomery intending to lay siege to the castle there. It was so well defended on its spur of land jutting out into the River Severn, however, that Prince Owain, lacking siege weapons, gave it best and contented himself with ravaging the town. With his laden baggage train following on behind, his force then marched on Welshpool where he hoped to find the castle there less well defended.

He found that Welshpool was no Conwy, nor was it held by a John de Massy, to be easily conjured out of his castle. John Charlton, Lord of Powys, whose ambuscade had so nearly entrapped Prince Owain on his way to Plynlimon, held Welshpool. Confident, even arrogant, he was an experienced soldier who had led many a campaign, had laid siege and been besieged often enough before. His large garrison fought off all Prince Owain's attacks, toppled every ladder laid against its walls and made confident sallies out of the castle, regardless it seemed, of the likely cost.

It was after one of these sallies that Idris thought he saw one of the fallen stir and, alert, sword drawn, approached warily. Nearer now, he could see that it was one of Lord Powys' men at arms who, strangely after the fury of the affray, was not bloodied as any decent corpse should be. Calling over one of his archers, he addressed the fallen man at arms sternly in English, 'Stand! And rise carefully, unless you wish to fall again!'

Slowly, his face still buried in the grass, the erstwhile 'corpse' stretched out his arms to show his hands were empty then, turning his head, glanced up at Idris.

'Prince Owain am Cymru!' said a grinning Rhys, adding, 'Can I get up now? I've been lying here afraid to move until I half believed I was indeed dead!' Standing now, he grasped an amazed Idris by the shoulders, to ask, 'What's up, Idris, do you yet think you've seen a ghost? It's just a change of coat that makes me different.'

Then they were both laughing, slapping each other on the back and hastening to find Dafydd so Rhys could tell all he knew of the castle's defences. Such was the intelligence Rhys brought that Prince Owain, unwilling to become involved in a lengthy, futile, siege determined to continue northward on his chevauchee. They did not leave Welshpool, however, before completing its devastation commenced by his brother Tudor earlier in the year.

As they made their way to the north, Idris half hoped that perhaps Prince Owain would visit Ynys Mon and, in his more optimistic moments, imagined going there too and seeing Catrin again. It was not to be, for all autumn they raided town after town, burning, looting wherever they went, not only towns but churches too, for generally Owain had more faith in bards than the church, something of which priests and monks were well aware.

If such activity was rewarding for Prince Owain's war chest and incidentally making his captains wealthy men, it seemed King Henry felt that it should not go unpunished. For, at the beginning of October, King Henry assembled an army at Worcester and proceeded to march into Wales to seek out the rebels. His march took him through Hereford and Llandovery, at both of which he paused to execute rebels, then on into Carmarthen. Perhaps he had news there that Prince Owain was at Plynlimon, for he headed north, pillaging the abbey of Strata Florida on his way, apparently believing the Cistercian monks there supported Prince Owain's cause.

His information on Prince Owain's movements was out of date however, for when he arrived at Plynlimon the bird had flown. Venting his spleen on the people there for, willingly or unwillingly, supporting Prince Owain during his stay, King Henry, weary of his futile expedition, made his way back to England. Even as he did so his son was also suffering embarrassment for, far to the north, Prince Owain was profitably looting Prince Henry's baggage train.

Idris and Dafydd stood in the November drizzle watching their men leading off the pack-horses, whilst the former drovers of the baggage train looked on disconsolately. A few of the train's escort, disarmed, stood under guard nearby whilst others lay as they had fallen. Laughing, Idris turned to Dafydd. 'What do we do with these then, Dafydd?'

'None here are worth their keep for ransom Idris,' Dafydd replied with an evil grin, 'so we take none prisoner . . . '

With the recent tales of Lord Tudor taking Radnor Castle fresh in his mind, Idris looked in horror at Dafydd. 'I'll have nought to do with that, Dafydd,' he interrupted sharply, 'even though the Prince himself commands me so!'

Still grinning, Dafydd held up his hand pacifically. 'We take no prisoners here, Idris, but bootless send them to their master,' nodding now at the departing baggage train, he added, 'so he might know who took his supplies and trinkets there!'

Idris laughed in his relief and brushing the back of his hand across his wet lips, shook his head. 'You do but provoke me in the manner of your telling, Dafydd!' Pausing, he frowned, then asked, 'Do we follow on their heels to Harlech to besiege their master there?'

Dafydd shook his head. 'No! Despenser and young Prince Hal have too great a hold on Harlech for us to wrench it from their grasp, instead we march on Caernarvon.'

'Caernarvon?' gasped Idris. 'Can we assail that vast pile with any hope?'

'Big enough it is, I grant you,' conceded Dafydd, 'but weakly held, or so our spies would have us know.'

A week later Idris's friend Rhys lay dead outside Caernarvon Castle. He had enough company, for over three hundred of his comrades in arms were killed in their attempts to storm the castle.

Dafydd shook his head in sorrow. 'Not lucky was Rhys see, Idris!' he commented. 'A good soldier he was, but no, not lucky.'

Idris looked at him blank faced for a moment, then said with bitterness in his voice, 'You can't be more unlucky than that, can you, Dafydd?' Despondently, he turned away and joined his archers, to lead them on the long march north to where Prince Owain intended to establish his winter base.

All winter through Idris, frustrated with inactivity, yearned to visit Ynys Mon to see Catrin but could not escape the bonds of duty. Although much of Prince Owain's main force had dispersed for the winter he tenaciously held on to his personal retainers. Even the occasional message that Maredudd passed on to Idris was small comfort and only tended to make his frustration the greater.

If Idris was bored by the forced inactivity, Prince Owain had few such problems, for there was much toing and froing from his winter camp. He sent missives to King Robert III of Scotland and Charles VI of France and was gratified when Charles responded by sending an emissary, one Dafydd ap Jevan, to Robert on his behalf. The emissary never reached Scotland for, shipwrecked, he was taken by the English. Languishing in the Tower of London he had failed in eliciting the foreign support that Prince Owain had hoped to gain.

Came the spring, however, and there was a sign: a sign more potent than any written word or spoken promise. A sign that made all at Owain's Snowdonian winter camp gaze at the sky in awe. The comet that blazed its golden trail across the night sky left all wondering what great event, what dread happening, it might presage, but there was no one there to explain the mystery, yet all knew it was a star of history.

As the comet made its stately way across the heavens, some priests said it foretold the second coming of the Messiah. Other men prophesied the end of the world whilst each night of its presence there, Iolo Goch sang in Prince Owain's hall of great victories and of a star rising in Wales to match the one in heaven. It was dusk on the third night of the comet's appearance that the aged seer came, his lined face weary from long travel, but his eyes bright with the fervour of a prophet with a clear vision of things to come. Frailer than ever now, Crach Finnant leant on his staff, a young acolyte supporting him by the other elbow and paused as Prince Owain hurried to greet him, hand outstretched.

'My old friend Crach! Never more timely was a visit from a friend than this! These few nights past I've yearned to speak with you, that I might learn what message this bright new star writes in its passage across the heavens. But first, you must eat and drink and rest you after your long journey!'

Crach shook his head and freeing his elbow waved his hand dismissively as he said urgently in an old man's treble, 'No, Owain, there is no time!' Putting his hand to his chest now he pressed it there then, breathing heavily, continued, 'The star . . . '

Seeing Crach was in pain, Owain took him by the arm and frowning in concern now, said persuasively, 'Come rest now, Crach, you are not well, it will wait an hour whilst you recover from your journey!'

The young man beside Crach raised his eyebrows and shook his head in exasperation. 'It's no use my lord,' he said, as though he had himself tried persuasion. 'He'll not rest 'til he's spoken with you!'

There was a stubborn light in the old man's eyes too as, pointing heavenwards, he said angrily in that high pitched treble, 'There is no time, I must tell you now! That comet tells of great happenings here in Wales! In its journey past the lesser stars it writes of great victories for you, Owain, as you in your like

163

journey pass many lesser men.' He grimaced as though catching his breath in pain and clasped his hand to his heart but, as Owain reached out to him, brushed his hand aside and continued, 'Yes, great victories it presages and great . . .'

It was a sentence he was never to complete, for with his face ashen, his lips purple, he gave a great groan and collapsed there as Prince Owain and the young man started forward to support him.

They carried him inside then, but it was an all but lifeless Crach Finnant they lay on the couch inside. Prince Owain sent a messenger in all haste for a physician but somehow knew that long before one came Crach would have made his last journey.

Sullenly the young man Prince Owain now knew as Emlyn turned to him. 'I told him he was not strong enough to make the journey,' he said belligerently, as though blaming Owain. 'I told him that I could bring his message to you. He could have written if he felt I should not know, but he would not heed!'

Frowning, his eyebrows arched, Prince Owain looked at Emlyn in disbelief as he asked, 'He told you nothing?'

Emlyn shook his head. 'He told me nought, except that it meant different things to different men dependent on the day and hour of their birth and where they came into this world.'

Prince Owain looked sadly at Crach whose last breath had now been spent and nodded as he said quietly, 'Aye and of their departure therefrom as well, no doubt!'

Chapter Twenty

The appearance of the comet and Crach Finnant's dying prediction of great victories seemed to add new impetus to Prince Owain's campaign. Either that or the coming of spring and better weather had raised the morale of his soldiery, and so it was with a light heart that Idris set out with Prince Owain's force a week later to raid the lands of Lord Grey of Ruthin. The Prince was in high good humour, but Idris knew not whether this was because of the prophecy, of which all now had heard, or at the prospect of crossing swords with Lord Grey.

Riding behind the Prince and young Maredudd, Idris turned to Dafydd to ask, 'Do you think the old man was right and the star foretold victory for the Prince's arms, Dafydd?'

Dafydd, not a great believer in ought but the power of the sword it seemed, favoured him with a sardonic smile and answered tersely, 'He'll as likely prove to be right as wrong!'

Idris bit his lip and frowned. 'But the comet in its travel, Dafydd, truly seemed to point a finger to Ruthin Castle and old Crach Finnant is renowned for prophecy!'

'Aye,' Dafydd replied dryly, 'and Lord Grey, as he watched from Ruthin's battlements, no doubt saw the comet blaze a path to Westminster palace and a golden throne. I fear though that we shall find him safe at home and, if his spies are not all asleep, accoutred in his armour waiting to greet us there!'

It was a small band which rode into Ruthin town the next day with Prince Owain. Maredudd, his proud standard bearer at his side ensured all knew who it was had come again to Ruthin town on market day. Idris, his mouth dry, his palms moist, looked around him at the scattering market folk and at the sturdy men, who still seemed to stand idly by the shelter of the market stalls.

Swallowing, he looked up to Ruthin Castle as the drawbridge fell, the great gates opened and out of the castle poured a band of men at arms.

No small sally this, for the banner at its head proclaimed Lord Grey himself came to do battle with Prince Owain's puny force. With thundering hooves they rode arrogantly into Ruthin town determined, it seemed, to make Prince Owain pay in full for his last visit there.

They were not the only forces riding into town though, for at full gallop, Dafydd now brought the power of his men at arms from where they had been waiting in the copse outside the town.

As Lord Grey rode into the market square, those idle men who skulked by stalls were no longer idle, as Idris put his archers to work. At such short range they took a bloody toll of Lord Grey's force and it was a smaller band that finally extricated itself from the chaos in the market square and fled back to the safety of Ruthin Castle.

They left behind alive few of their number and it was only one of those that Prince Owain took prisoner, for the rest, mainly wounded, he left there littering the streets like garbage. Of his sullen prisoner, trussed like a chicken for the oven, he took great care, for this was a prize indeed. This prisoner offered not only personal satisfaction but the promise of rich reward by way of ransom. For as he sojourned in Snowdonia, waiting to be ransomed by King Henry, Lord Grey would remember and bitterly regret, Prince Owain's third visit to Ruthin town. They tarried little on their journey to Snowdonia, so anxious was Prince Owain to be out of reach of Lord Grey's men and to have his hostage securely held in a mountain fastness there. It was not until they crossed the Afon Corris at Pont yr Alwen that they paused to rest the horses.

Idris stood by his steaming horse, hand on saddle, a flask of water raised to his lips, weary after the stress and turmoil of the day, when Prince Owain strode over to him, smiling broadly as he approached. Clapping Idris on the arm, he said enthusiastically:

'Your plan to infiltrate your archers into Ruthin before I entered and have them mingle with the townsfolk, worked well, Idris. Grey's sally force was much diminished long before they came within sword's reach of us.' Turning now to Dafydd, he added, 'Even so, I was not displeased to see you bring your men to our aid so readily.'

'Aye, my lord, it all worked well, though I confess my blood ran cold to see you ride into Ruthin town, your standard borne, with but a score of men at arms.' Dafydd shrugged. 'Yet I know full well had we gone in with our main force at first, Idris there would still be letting fly at Ruthin Castle's walls, for Lord Grey would not have sallied out.'

Still smiling, Prince Owain nodded. 'Aye, our stratagem worked well thanks to the parts you both played therein.' He turned away, then pausing, looked back at them, to say. 'I promised you we'd return to Ruthin town. Twice we have now and each time you both were central to my enterprise, I am only sorry that your comrade, Rhys, was not there to share our victory today.'

Striding over to his own horse, he mounted and, as they all followed suit, he led them off along the track that led to safety amongst the mountains. Not for all however: for one of their number it led only to a place of imprisonment and chains.

During the weeks that followed the capture of Lord Grey, Prince Owain was in ebullient mood and, even amidst the spartan conditions of his mountain fastness, there was great merrymaking. None of this was shared by Lord Grey who, shackled in his cell, rarely glimpsed the light of day, for Prince Owain felt little charity for his long time enemy. Often Grey was brought in chains, however, to the Prince's presence, to remind him who his captor was perhaps or, yet more likely, that the Prince might be assured the stock he held would live for ransom.

After a week or so in which he kept his prisoner in some uncertainty, Prince Owain allowed him to write to the King pleading to be ransomed, for the sum that Prince Owain sought was much beyond Lord Grey's means. April passed with no word from King Henry, May came and went and Lord Grey grew so listless and despondent that Prince Owain even allowed him a little wine, though not enough to bring forgetfulness to the unhappy lord.

Rumours came to Owain now of plots against the King by those amongst the English lords, and Friars Minor too, who held that King Richard lived. Torn between hopes for ransom and desire to see King Henry toppled, Prince Owain fretted now and, fearing an assault on his stronghold by the King's forces to recapture Lord Grey, the sounds of merriment in his stronghold became muted. To forestall any such enterprise by the King, Prince Owain had Lord Grey write again to him, pleading once more to be ransomed and urging that no attempt be made to seize him, for he feared for his life in such event.

Towards the end of May, Prince Owain, hearing that Hotspur had been sent to Chester by the King, sent word to him suggesting that they might meet under a truce to discuss the terms under which Lord Grey might obtain his freedom. As they had at sometime met before and in that meeting had some regard for one another, Prince Owain was not surprised to receive Hotspur's agreement. So, at the beginning of June, when Hotspur was at Ruthin to all intents to see for himself what havoc Owain had inflicted there, the two lords met.

Some twenty miles from Ruthin at a place called Cyffilliog, where many roads met amongst low hills, they met privily. Only Dafydd and Idris accompanied Prince Owain for the last mile to Cyffilliog for such had been the agreement and, despite Dafydd's loud protests, Prince Owain trusted the lord from the North. What passed between them Idris never knew for when the two lords came out of the small cottage, nothing was mentioned that revealed an inkling of what had been said inside. Idris saw however that as Prince Owain came out Hotspur glanced at him with a face that spoke of friendship rather than enmity.

Nor did the Prince confide in either of his captains, on their long ride back to Snowdonia, what had transpired between him and Hotspur. He was silent on the return journey, as though deep in thought on some matter of great import and both knew him well enough not to disturb him with idle chatter at such times.

Whatever had so engrossed him on their return to Snowdonia did not prevent Prince Owain from planning a great summer campaign, planning that involved the comings and goings of his kin from all parts of North Wales. Long into the night they discussed and argued the pros and cons of this plan or that, of the path their campaign should take and what their main targets should be.

At last in mid June they all set out to converge in Radnorshire, for there lay the castles of the Earl of March and there were many who had ancient enmities to settle with the Mortimers. Even though the young earl was still a King's ward, his fiefdom there was held for him by Sir Edmund Mortimer, a knight who Hotspur, his brother in law, held in high regard for his skill at arms.

It was not that skill at arms that caused the frown on Prince Owain's brow now as they set out, but the fact that he had courted alliance with Hotspur during his talks with him rather than hostility which an attack on Mortimer would surely bring. Yet, if he ruled at all amongst his unruly Welsh lords, it was by consent, his overlordship a fragile thing unless he brought them victory.

Their long march led them through Llanidloes and thence across hilly country to the valley of Afon Ithon and the lordship of Maelienydd where they separated, with bands led by their own lords going off to raid the towns and castles there. The main force of his army though, some thousand men, Owain kept under his own command as it marched on Knighton, his kinsmen promising they would meet him there in but a few days time. It was a promise Prince Owain hoped they would keep, for he was sure that news of their ravages would quickly reach Sir Edmund Mortimer at Ludlow Castle.

Sir Edmund Mortimer, his confidence belying his twenty-six years, stood on the battlements of Ludlow Castle looking at the church of St Laurence in the town below as he talked with his constable of this latest threat. News had reached him of attacks on castles and churches alike in Maelienydd lordship by the rebel Owain Glyn Dŵr. Whilst Sir Edmund had a sneaking admiration for the man's seeming ability to strike as and where he wished, that admiration diminished drastically when he struck so close to home.

Already Sir Edmund's call had gone out to the four knights who owed allegiance to his nephew, the young earl, to pay their knightly due of military service together with their men. Now he was ordering his constable to send out an array to the earl's tenants both in Wales and Herefordshire to come at once to their lord's aid. He had considered calling on the Sheriff of Herefordshire to order an array but after much thought, he felt the urgency of the situation demanded he rely on those forces he could muster more quickly.

h

Within a few days, the forces Sir Edmund had called upon began to arrive, the first being led by the white haired Sir Robert Whitney from Wye, Knight Marshall to King Henry. Close upon his heels came Sir Thomas Clanvowe, who like Sir Robert was a former sheriff and no longer young. His family, of Welsh descent, held four castles for the Earl and he had no love for the Welsh rebel, Glyn Dŵr. With the arrival of the other two knights, Walter Devereaux and Kinaird de la Bere with their retinues shortly afterwards, Sir Edmund's main force was complete.

With little fear of the outcome, his army set out from Ludlow to Wigmore, where he was joined by the remainder of his muster of tenants. His force now some two thousand strong and having had news that Owain Glyn Dŵr was rampaging to the westwards between the Teme and the River Lugg he marched northwards to the south bank of the Teme and thence to Brampton Bryan Castle. Being told there that Glyn Dŵr was pillaging Knighton, he marched on in all haste but, inevitably, on reaching Knighton he found only a town in flames.

Even so he was jubilant now, for he knew that he was close on the heels of the rebel Welshman, knew too, from what the Knighton townsmen said, that his own force was far superior to Glyn Dŵr's. Pausing hardly for breath at Knighton, he hurried southwards, hot on the trail of his enemy, then on through Witton town he marched to cross old Offa's Dyke south of Lanmore hill.

It was there his van first caught sight of Glyn Dŵr's men, a band of rebels perhaps some fifty strong. They must have known they had been sighted too, for they galloped away like fury on their small Welsh ponies.

Sir Edmund gave a satisfied smile and, turning to old Sir Thomas Clanvowe, said confidently, 'We have them now, I think, Sir Thomas. That will be his rear-guard, or perhaps a laggard group. In either case they'll lead us to our prey!'

His lined face unsmiling, Sir Thomas replied thoughtfully, 'We should beware of false trails Sir Edmund, no bird leads you to its young nor does Glyn Dŵr whistle to his pursuers. I would advise we send out scouts to seek the strength of the rebel band and what lays beyond.'

Sir Edmund shook his head obstinately.

'I think not, Sir Thomas!' he said sharply. 'Should those rebels be but a lure and Glyn Dŵr's main force lay beyond, my only fear is that he'll not stay and fight! We march on!'

All that day they pursued their quarry and not until dusk, late on that summer's day, did they stop to make camp on the north bank of the River Lugg near Witton. The town must have feared a visit from Glyn Dŵr, for shortly after the camp fires had been lit, three archers came strolling from the town seeking Sir Edmund's captain of archers.

That same night, the twenty-first of June in the year of our Lord 1402, not far away, in Prince Owain's encampment near the village and church of Pilleth, Dafydd was fruitlessly seeking Idris. Nowhere was the archer to be found, however, and at last, with much reluctance, Dafydd reported to the Prince the fact that Idris was missing. Prince Owain's face fell when he heard the news and looked even grimmer as Dafydd reminded him, 'If you recall, my lord,' the war-wise captain said, 'he joined your retinue from Ludlow Castle where he served the Earl of March. Today, like us he heard the strength of Mortimer's force. Mayhap he had no stomach to fight his one time friends against such odds!'

Prince Owain seemed taken aback at this suggestion that Idris had deliberately deserted not only from cowardice but to turn coat.

'But I made Idris captain of my archers and he was your friend, Dafydd!'

Dafydd smiled cynically. 'Aye, and I trust my friends, do they but stay by my side, but archers less than most for theirs is a callous trade: they kill a man beyond the reach of his good blade.'

Prince Owain sighed and shook his head. 'I sorrow for a good man lost, Dafydd, for yet I doubt that Idris will face us in tomorrow's strife.' Briskly now he dismissed the subject. 'Are all our men advised of our strategy for when Mortimer comes to do battle?'

Dafydd nodded. 'Aye my lord and, praise God, it is one well known to them from previous use, the better that it may serve us now.'

Stroking his beard, Prince Owain nodded slowly and turned to walk away, but looking over his shoulder at Dafydd, he muttered, 'I would never have believed that of Idris!'

*   *   *   *

171

Early on the morning of the twenty-second of June, Sir Edmund Mortimer, at last heeding Sir Thomas Clanvowe's advice, sent out scouts to learn of Glyn Dŵr's movements. The sun was still low in a near cloudless sky on that mild summer's morning when they returned to inform him that Owain Glyn Dŵr, together with a few hundred men, were in a valley below the mountain of Bryn Glas by Pilleth church.

His confidence reinforced with the news they brought, Sir Edmund turned to the four knights gathered around him. 'As I thought,' he said briskly. 'We have little to fear from Glyn Dŵr, his force is fragmented and, no doubt, wearied from his chevauchee: our biggest problem here is bringing him to battle. We do that and take his head to the King and there'll be reward for all in our company!'

Sir Thomas Clanvowe, shook his grey head, to say quietly, 'Let us but take the Welsh magician, Sir Edmund, before we sell his head to any man!'

The smile left Sir Edmund's lips as, with an exasperated air, he muttered, 'Well named are you, Sir Thomas, though I have no doubt that we shall take the rebel!'

They broke camp then and it was not yet mid-morning when they approached the little village of Pilleth nestling in the valley below Bryn Glas. Above the village they could now see too the white walled church with its tower, prominent against the background of green hillside beyond.

Marching familiarly amongst Sir Edmund's archers was Idris with his two companions who, it seemed, had deserted with him from Prince Owain's force. They had found many old friends amongst Mortimer's Welsh archers, with some of whom Idris had served at Ludlow. Late into the previous night they had talked of times long gone, of the morrow and of times yet to be. How some they'd known had long since fallen, of others who might march on Pilleth and not march away again.

Now though, the time for such talk was long since gone for as they marched they could see the enemy: There, thinly spread across the valley were Prince Owain's men and Sir Edmund Mortimer turned to Sir Thomas riding beside him.

'Great magic will your Welsh magician have to perform to bring him victory over power such as ours, Sir Thomas!' He shook his head. 'I fear though that he will but turn and run!'

172

Hardly had the words left his mouth before the Welsh began slowly retreating up the hillside.

'I told you so!' cried Sir Edmund and, drawing his sword and pointing it at the retreating Welsh, roared, 'Forward!'

Led by experienced knights, Mortimer's army turned into line to begin their advance up the valley in pursuit although, unusually, some hundred of the archers lagged behind Mortimer's main force.

Perhaps it was the excitement of the chase, the imminence of victory over the King's arch enemy or the prospect of rich reward, that led Sir Edmund and his knights not to notice this. Perhaps too the archers were unfit after years of soft living at Ludlow Castle, unaccustomed to chasing rebels used to mountain warfare.

The rebels were almost half way up the mountain when, with Mortimer's men still out of bowshot, they turned to face their pursuers, as though despairing of reaching the woods above. Even as Mortimer cried 'Charge!' hundreds of rebels appeared out of those same woods who, with fearsome yells, came racing down the hill to their countrymen's aid.

Seeing his force still outnumbered the rebels, Mortimer charged on undismayed only to find men falling all around him from volley after volley of arrows that flew at them at short range. He was not the only one to look over his shoulder in horror to find the attack came not from the Welsh ahead but from the bows of some hundred archers to his rear.

The havoc caused by that attack from the rear by erstwhile comrades, together with the fury of the assault from above led to a desperate battle, the outcome of which had been determined when the first arrow flew. The sun was high in the summer sky when those of Mortimer's army who were still able, fled the field.

Of the knights who accompanied Sir Edmund to Pilleth only one escaped, for Sir Richard de la Bere and Sir Robert Whitney were amongst over a thousand of his army killed that day, whilst both Sir Edmund and Sir Thomas were led away to join Lord Grey in captivity.

As the two knights were led downhill towards Pilleth, Sir Edmund paused in his stride by a group of his turncoat archers, where Prince Owain stood with a great ox of a man with a drooping moustache who scowled fearsomely at the archers. Sir Edmund's guards urged him on, but Prince Owain, smiling, made them desist, saying, 'Do not hasten him, no man hurries to his prison willingly!' Glancing at Sir Edmund he said civilly, as one speaks to an equal, 'What, would you pause in your dire hour to commend your archers, Sir Edmund?'

Sir Edmund glared at him. 'Had these archers been truly mine, not traitors, this in truth would have been your dire hour, Glyn Dŵr, not mine!' Stabbing a finger towards Idris, he almost spat, 'And it must be he who suborned my men, for he left my service two years since!'

With a glance at Dafydd, that seemed to shout 'I told you so!' Prince Owain said quietly, 'I fear he did but bring them late to their duty, Sir Edmund, for these are Welshmen all!

Chapter Twenty-one

'Blame, if blame there be, lies with yourself,' Dafydd said somewhat truculently. 'Am I a seer, that I can peer into men's minds and foretell their actions? I could not even see your body here, much less your mind. It was that I told Prince Owain, as was my bounden duty!'

Idris looked at him scornfully and with a toss of his head replied angrily, 'My foot was hardly outside the camp when you went running to him hotfoot!'

Dafydd looked horror-struck. 'What, me run? I am not built for speed and running is against my very nature!'

Idris stood there for a moment just staring at the burly man at arms, then slowly, his face broke into a grin. 'In that at least you speak the truth,' he said but, frowning now, added, 'yet did you not know me better than to think I'd shrink from such hazard?'

A shrewd look in his eyes, Dafydd shook his head. 'No, not that and there's the rub: I remembered well a tale that you once told when we were on campaign. All night you left our camp and on return told me and Rhys of some adventure you'd had with an English maid. Now that I never did believe of you and long it left me wondering what mischief you'd been up to that night that did not bear the telling.' He paused before, holding up a warning finger, he continued, 'Now once I might hold back and keep a watchful eye, but not twice and even less when we were in such danger! Why did you not tell me what madcap enterprise you were intent upon?'

All this time, thought Idris, and he never believed me about that girl at Holt, yet never let that show, just watched and waited! Realising at last that there was much more to Dafydd than the big man at arms' bluff exterior revealed, he shook his head. 'How could I tell you, when even now you think it was a madcap scheme! Yet it succeeded better than I ever hoped!'

Dafydd's lip curled. 'Aye, hope without reason is the lure that leads many a good man to his death in war! You put yourself in jeopardy twice over, Idris. If but one of Mortimer's archers had run to his lord, and told a tale, then you'd have died most painfully. If battle's surge had overtaken you, without me knowing of your plot, I would have cheerfully felled you where you stood!' He turned his head and, raising his hand warningly, said, 'But hush, here comes our Prince, no doubt he would have words with you!'

Prince Owain must have heard Dafydd, for smiling, he nodded. 'Aye, I would indeed! Your sudden leaving without word caused some to think it showed a change of heart, Idris! Much as your secret plan tipped the balance in our favour here this day, I would advise that in future you should show such courage in sharing your plans with us!'

Pouting his lips and tugging at his drooping moustache, Dafydd nodded vigorously but raised his eyes disbelievingly as Prince Owain, tossing a purse to Idris, added, 'Yet this time only, for the grain or two you added to our balance pan there's a grain or two for you to wet your palate!'

Sending messengers to his kin still raiding in Maelienydd to warn them of his departure, Prince Owain headed north, anxious now to ensure that his two valuable prisoners were soon safely secured in Snowdonia with Lord Grey. On his arrival there, however, perhaps because of his personal animosity to Lord Grey, he treated his new captives more leniently than Grey, according them almost the status of guests. So much so that Sir Edmund occasionally interceded, without great effect, on Lord Grey's behalf.

Although negotiations over the subject of ransom for the captives continued through intermediaries, this did not prevent Prince Owain from continuing his struggle. Indeed, the victories at Hyddgen and Pilleth, achieved as they were against great odds, only served to intensify his efforts. Whilst continuing to seek support from potential allies such as Robert of Scotland and Charles of France, he also maintained his military assault, aided as he was by growing support across Wales.

Six weeks after the defeat of Mortimer at Pilleth, Idris, wealthy now beyond all hope and greatly in Prince Owain's favour, was at the sack of Abergavenny and Cardiff. All Glamorgan had risen in Prince Owain's support, for these, as all such towns, were English held. His host, now swollen to many thousands, swept on through east Glamorgan and into Gwent, where castle after castle was overwhelmed by his power. Castles at Usk, Caerleon and Newport all fell and flew his banner from their battlements. Across all Gwent his name became a word to frighten the children to their beds, for the Welsh there favoured him no more than did the English.

Persuaded of the urgency of the situation there, King Henry marshalled his forces for another assault on Wales, sending out an array to all sheriffs whose counties bordered Wales. Warned of Prince Owain's growing power, he also ordered Lancaster and Derby to send men to join those from Shropshire, at Chester.

At the end of August, in torrential rain, the King, his forces led by the Earls of Stafford and Arundel together with Lord Codnor, began his assault traditionally by entering Wales along the valleys running West. Prince Owain, aided no little by foul weather as hail and snow impeded the royal forces, turned the assault into a rout. Insult was added to injury when a falling tent pole struck King Henry as he lay sleeping and once again he was as grateful to return to England as Prince Owain was to see him go.

Prince Owain, already exultant over the King's ignominious retreat, received news almost as pleasing shortly after his return to North Wales. Surprisingly, after his expensive and ignominious foray into Wales, the King was at last prepared to pay the ten thousand marks Prince Owain had demanded as ransom for Lord Grey. Apparently the king also arranged for the Earl of March, Sir Edmund's nephew, to pay a more modest ransom for Sir Thomas Clanvowe. It was not without some pleasure Prince Owain gave Lord Grey the news of his release for he knew that, impoverished by this vast debt to the King, the baron had paid dearly for the common at Croesau.

Having taken a liking to the personable young Sir Edmund, however, Prince Owain was sorry to impart the news that the King had adamantly refused to ransom him. Owain's unwillingness though to retail the explanation he had been given was pre-empted by a letter Sir Edmund received from Hotspur.

From this the young knight learned that when his brother in law, Hotspur, approached the King for a contribution to the ransom, the King replied he would not ransom those who conspired against him!

Over a meal that night, Sir Edmund, loquacious in his cups, told Prince Owain, 'It's you and I the King believes conspired! Pilleth, though I can never sober say the word without obscenity, the king believes was the result of such conspiracy!' He shook his head despondently. 'That I should be deemed traitor there, when I arrayed against you all the power at my command, aye and at great expense to us Mortimers. Not only ransom, but repayment for my array I should receive in justice.' Peering at the far end of the table to where Idris sat, he scowled and muttered, 'Sitting there is the maker of my misfortune, that archer fellow scant honour takes to any field of battle.' Sipping his wine now he stared at Gruffydd then back at Idris before turning to Prince Owain, and waving his hand as though to dismiss his remark, 'If he is kin to you, Prince Owain, I meant no offence it was after all but the fortune of war.'

Before Prince Owain said a word, a grim faced Gruffydd said abruptly, 'No kin of ours, Sir Edmund, the fellow's but a peasant archer, with ambitions beyond his reach!'

Prince Owain smiled and neither agreeing with nor yet denying Gruffydd's remark, said quietly, 'He served you as an indentured archer some time since, Sir Edmund, but is captain of my archers now and has a feel for warlike tactics.'

Seeming to sense a dissension he was unwilling to aggravate, Sir Edmund looked thoughtfully into his goblet for a moment, then changed the subject abruptly. 'This ransom that you seek, Prince Owain, is one beyond my scant means. The King, as you now know, favours me not and will not contribute nor yet allow his ward, my nephew the Earl, to fund my freedom. Hotspur would, even though it brought the King's displeasure,' he shrugged, 'but his resources have been stretched by campaigns both here in Wales and now in Scotland once again! I fear that, unless in charity you were to set me free, I must be your captive for some time hence.'

Prince Owain smiled again, this time perhaps because, by the repeated use of his title, Sir Edmund apparently acknowledged his station. He shook his head deprecatingly. 'Freedom,' he said, 'is a somewhat transient thing, for were I to let you free and you returned to Ludlow, do you think that it would it be long before you changed your pillow there for one in London's Tower? For if the King truly believes you conspired with me, right quickly would he make his displeasure tangible! No, rather I think that we should wait awhile, for it may be your king will come to better humour, when we both will profit from such change of heart. Meantime, let us not talk of captive and captor here, but you the welcome guest and me the host!'

If Sir Edmund noticed Prince Owain's reference to Henry as 'your king', he made no comment, merely saying, 'I could not wish for a host more generous than you have already been, Prince Owain! Now in return I give all that I can in my present circumstances, something which I could not have vouchsafed before this: my parole.' He smiled. 'I shall not try to escape your "hospitality" until you tire of my presence here!'

Smiling in acknowledgement Prince Owain nodded. 'So be it then,' he said, 'and in a few day's time there will be some gentler presence here than us poor soldiery, for my wife Marged and some of my older children arrive to bring some civility to our harsh ways!'

Although Idris had heard that Prince Owain's wife and children were arriving, he was not there to greet them, for, along with Dafydd, he was away raiding in the Welsh marches with Gruffydd and Lord Tudor. Whilst anxious to return to Snowdonia to see Catrin, there was no escape for him and all through September and into October they campaigned without any talk of return. At the end of September news reached them of a victory in Scotland for King Henry's arms, something more of interest to Dafydd perhaps than of any immediate importance to them, or so Idris thought at the time.

It had all happened in mid September, so Dafydd told him as they were seated sharing a pot of ale by their temporary camp.

'It was young Harry Hotspur who o'erwhelmed the Scots at Homildon Hill,' said Dafydd enthusiastically and, getting carried away now, added, 'he left nigh on half of their force dead in the field and took many prisoners.' He shook his head in apparent disbelief . . . or envy. 'A wealth of prisoners! For there were many of note, including their commander, Earl Douglas and a score or more of Frenchies too!

Idris, amused at Dafydd's enthusiasm, stabbed a finger towards him. 'It's treason that you speak here, Dafydd! For those you praise so loudly are our enemies, and those whose defeat you now take pleasure in, could be our allies. Are not those who fight our enemies, our friends? And were not Hotspur warring with the Scots, he could as well be fighting us!'

Dafydd, looking a little chagrined, tugged at his moustache and muttered uncomfortably, 'Well . . . it's just that I've fought the Scots as oft I've fought the English and little enough love have I for the French.' He shook his head, as though even he were now confused. 'When fighting for the English, I've fought the French. Later they were allied to the Scots when I fought them!'

Idris laughed. 'The tally will be the shorter, Dafydd, if you just tell me who it is you've not fought, than listing all your foes!' Smiling, he added, 'And you held grudge 'gainst me for I was once Lord Mortimer's man!'

'Never for that! It was . . . ' He began, but hesitating, changed the subject. 'Hotspur's victory there is no ill wind for us, for there's no doubt the Scots will the weaker be for this chastisement and thus perhaps more eager to join with us against the English.'

Idris looked at him with raised eyebrows. 'Little advantage there would be in that,' he said scornfully. 'Beaten thus, they'll not march the length of England to succour us! But if they fight the English, they aid us as much as any ally would!'

Dafydd winked and waved an admonitory finger. 'It's not the same!' he said. 'Long have the Scots and French been allied and were we allied to the Scots then were we also allied, or nearly so, to the French who can, unresisted, land forces to aid us here in Wales!'

Idris grinned. 'And with your little love for these French, Dafydd, who you would now have as allies, will you then fight with, or against them?'

He was still grinning as he heard Gruffydd say almost pleasantly, 'Archer, I would have words with you!'

Idris stood and, unsmiling, replied, 'Aye, my lord?'

Dafydd rose to stand by Idris's side now, as a smiling Gruffydd said amiably, 'I have some news for you, archer, of my sister,

Catrin!'

Idris's eyes opened in astonishment, not only at this promise of news but at the tone in which it was delivered. Except for addressing him as 'archer' and not captain as was his right, Gruffydd had never been so gracious. Before he could say a word however, Gruffydd continued, 'Yes, I thought since she has spoken kindly to you at times, you would be pleased to learn my sister is betrothed to Sir Edmund Mortimer!'

Idris opened his mouth but, speechless, looked from Gruffydd to Dafydd and back again, his eyes pleading, before at last saying, the anguish now in his voice as well, 'No, my lord, this cannot be . . . not Catrin!'

Gruffydd, smiling with evident pleasure, nodded in affirmation. 'Oh, aye, 'tis so, archer! She is to wed Sir Edmund in but a little while, no peasant he but true knight indeed!'

His face white with fury now, Idris lunged forward intent upon smashing the smile off Gruffydd's face, only to find his arm held in Dafydd's iron grasp. Gruffydd though had hardly flinched, instead, hand on his sword, he said softly, his voice now a sibilant threat, 'Restrain him not, Captain! Let him see how a gentleman deals with such peasant manners!'

Dafydd looked bleak faced at Gruffydd. 'Restrain him, my lord? Not I, I do but support my fellow captain, who's supped more ale than wisdom would have him partake!' His grip even tighter now as he almost dragged Idris away, he added, 'Come Idris, it's sleep you need, not ale!'

Then, with a terse, 'Good night my, lord!' he led Idris into the tent they shared.

'He lies!' Idris said vehemently. 'He only says it to provoke me to anger!'

Dafydd looked at him askance. 'He took pleasure in the telling and that I grant!' Shaking his head now, he added, 'and if it was only said to goad, then he accomplished all he sought! Had I not held you in restraint, you'd now be hanging from a gibbet for striking your lord's son . . . had he not first skewered you with his blade!'

He looked at Idris, now sitting shoulders slumped, hands hanging loosely in his lap, the light of the oil lamp etching sharp the misery in his downcast face. Dafydd smiled in sympathy as he said quietly, 'Come now Idris, she's but a young lass who's done as she was bid . . . as she was bound to do! Can you not see advantage for Prince Owain in this match? With young Catrin married to Sir Edmund, in law she will be sister to Harry Hotspur and aunt to the Earl of March. Now there's alliance for you!'

Idris looked at him aghast. 'Speak you to me of "advantage", of "alliances"? How can she marry him? She loves me!'

Chin tucked in, eyebrows raised, Dafydd glanced sideways at him, to say, 'Only the poor can afford love, Idris! The nobility sacrifice all on the altar of advantage and alliance!'

Idris stared at him without comprehension for a moment before saying indignantly, 'But I'm not poor, Dafydd! Two years and more of campaigning have filled my purse o'er full!'

Dafydd, on safer ground now, grinned. 'Aye, you are a wealthy archer,' he said, 'but if you were a knight, a poor knight you'd be! Come, have another pot of ale before we seek our bed!'

Chapter Twenty-two

The sense of desolation, of bereavement almost, felt by Idris was something he had never known before. The nearest he had come to it was his mother's death when he was twelve years old. Not that he knew then how old he was, other than he was old enough to fetch and carry at Montgomery Castle where his mother had been a lady's maid, until she died of that racking cough.

The Mortimers held Montgomery then as now and their constable there, with little ceremony, had her buried there, whilst a wondering Idris looked on . . . wondering, mainly, how he would survive now that she'd gone. He had survived cuffs and kicks until, at last, few there were who dared to kick or cuff. By pestering and badgering he'd learnt the archer's trade so well in time the constable indentured him. As an archer he'd gone from one Mortimer castle to another until at last his skill took him to Ludlow Castle, where Sir Edmund Mortimer dwelt.

Happy enough he'd been then even though he'd sometimes wondered what manner of man that it might be who'd brought his mother to child. Now she was long since gone, his father still unknown and the girl he loved about to marry that same Sir Edmund. Standing on the high ridge, he looked at Harlech Castle and the shadowy grey mountains that lay beyond, the drizzle that slanted in the wind pecking at his face like hungry birds.

The cold, driven rain with its depressing persistence and promise of a bleak winter coloured his whole mood. All he could think of was Catrin's impending marriage and of how, but for his own part in the battle at Pilleth, the two might never have met. Now there was little hope of seeing her himself: indeed, with her marrying Sir Edmund, he might never see her again! As part of Prince Owain's forces besieging the redoubtable Harlech Castle, desertion would be his only means of getting to see her. Nor was it the thought of inevitable capture and the equally inevitable penalty that had deterred him. It was his feeling of complete helplessness and bitterness at the knowledge that, for whatever reason and under whatever compulsion, Catrin must have agreed to marry Sir Edmund.

Brushing the rain off his face, his lips compressed in bitterness, he finally realised that Catrin was not for him. She never had been, all there was for such as he, all there had ever been, was his bow and his sword, for in these a man could place his trust. Standing there looking at the windswept castle, he turned and said sourly to one of his archers standing nearby, 'Why stand you there idle, man, whilst men at arms stride boldly on their battlements?'

The grizzled archer looked at him in surprise. 'In this wind, Captain?' he asked incredulously. 'I might as well break a shaft on my knee, as loose it in this wind, for little use it would be to me and even less harm to them!'

Idris's mouth opened to make sharp rejoinder when a familiar voice interrupted him and he turned his head, to see a smiling Dafydd standing there.

'Goodmorrow, Idris,' said the man at arms taking him by the arm. 'I fear you must leave your lone assault, for the rest of us take shelter on this inclement day and Prince Owain would now take counsel with both you and me!'

With a sour glance at the old archer, who still seemed surprised at his ill humour, Idris gave a sullen look at Dafydd and the two captains walked off towards Prince Owain's camp, leaving the archer shaking his head at their departure.

Idris, the dark shadows beneath his eyes seeming to emphasise his sullenness, turned to Dafydd to ask, 'What does Prince Owain want with us?'

With a sideways glance, Dafydd, unsmiling now, replied, 'Nothing that I know of, Idris! It's just that I would take counsel with you myself! You and I are both captains and, though in age I have the advantage, as equals we lead our men in siege or war.'

Idris scowled and, with a touch of irony, asked, 'Will this sermon last overlong, Father Dafydd?'

Dafydd shook his head and answered quietly, 'No, not overlong, yet you'd do well to hear me out! That man we left behind us there, is old enough to be your father and from what you've said could well enough be so! Campaigns he fought when you were at your mother's breast and yet you speak to him as you'd not have Lord Gruffydd speak to you! Do not vent your spleen on him because a wench, for whatever cause, has changed her mind! Before this siege is out his life could well depend on you . . . and yours on him. Be sure you're fit to care for his and that he'll wish to care for yours! If you can be sure of neither, then get you far enough away from here, for there's men's work to be done here, that's not fit for love sick boys!'

Idris, flushed with anger, started back from Dafydd to ask, 'Have you done?'

'Aye,' said Dafydd quietly, his hand on Idris's arm now, 'I've finished my sermon and it's only as a friend can speak have I delivered it, for I'd not lose you, but you must shake this sickness off or it will kill as surely as the plague!'

Idris shook Dafydd's arm off, to say with anguish in his voice, 'I am not sick! I love Catrin, Dafydd!'

'Aye,' said Dafydd nodding soberly, 'and she's marrying another and on the morrow, you'll love another, for such is the nature of these things! Mean times, we have a war to wage and we must give it all our heart! So think on that an' treat your archers civilly if you and they would live and win!'

With that the burly man of war strode heavily away, leaving Idris looking thoughtfully after him. Sighing, he was about to walk on when Prince Owain walked out of his nearby tent and catching sight of Idris, came over to him.

'Well met, Idris,' he said smiling. 'I would speak with you!'

Idris restrained another sigh, thinking, yes, everyone would have words with me, as I would have words with none but one! Then, eyes downcast, he answered dutifully, 'Aye, my lord?'

'Aye,' replied the Prince as he stroked his beard. 'Your face grows longer by the day and melancholia seems to have you in its grip. Why so sad, when your campaigning in my cause has rightly turned that wandering archer you once were into a bird of richer plumage?' Glancing shrewdly at Idris now, he added quietly, 'This, of course, has nothing to do with my daughter's wedding!'

Idris, looking down, said nothing, but Prince Owain smiled as though in understanding and touching him familiarly on the arm said, 'Come, share a goblet of wine with me, for I must needs lose

185

a daughter and would not readily lose my captain of archers too!'

As they got inside the tent, the Prince said to his man, 'Some wine!' and, as he and Idris were both given a goblet of wine, nodded to the man who left as silently as he had appeared. A quiet smile on his lips, Prince Owain raised his goblet, saying, 'To Harlech's speedy surrender, eh?'

Dull-eyed, Idris followed suit, saying, 'Aye, my lord!'

They sipped their wine, then with a shrewd look at Idris, Prince Owain asked, 'And would you drink as loyally a toast to my daughter's marriage to Sir Edmund Mortimer?'

Unsmiling, Idris hesitated as he looked at his goblet then, looking up at Prince Owain, asked, 'Should I fight a man one day and drink to his health and happiness the next, my lord?'

Prince Owain, his face grim now, his voice as stern, said sharply, 'Aye, if that my enemies of yesterday are my friends today! '

His face expressionless and still looking Prince Owain eye to eye, Idris replied, 'It sticks in my craw, my lord, to drink to turncoats today, lest they turn their coat again the morrow.'

Prince Owain nodded slowly, before asking, 'And would you not drink to my daughter's happiness?'

Idris nodded but said icily, 'Oh aye, my lord, cheerfully I'd drink to that and I knew but where it lie, though I doubt it would be in forced marriage to an Englishman!'

His face taut with anger now, Prince Owain pointed a stiff finger at Idris. 'You go too far! I bring you here to softly bring you back to reason when many others would find harsher means! Gruffydd has advised me of how you and Catrin have passed the idle hour in each other's company. How you were enamoured and she confined in my small manor house, with little choice of company. Little wrong I found in that, despite your disparate stations, for I looked with favour upon your valour in the field. Now let me tell you this, though I had hoped to find a kinder way. Two years since, Catrin was in truth but a child and now, full grown woman, she has made her choice, with no command of mine for sake of politics!' Prince Owain shook his head. 'I make no apology, Idris, when I say you're not the first to find that distant battlefields, from which there may be no return, are little aid to memory of a love new born. And you choose to be a soldier, then that's a fact, just like an untimely end, which you must realise!'

Reaching for the pitcher, he smiled. 'Come, Idris,' he said as he refilled the goblets, 'let us not fall out over this, for we have work to do that will change the lives of those in Wales for years to come. And we would succeed, it is a cause which we must love more than we love any other!' Offering a goblet to Idris, he asked, 'Would you drink to that?'

Taking the goblet, Idris stared into it for a moment before, raising it, he shrugged and said grimly, 'Aye my lord, I will!'

Prince Owain chuckled and slapped him on the back. 'Well said, Idris! I was beginning to doubt you'd even drink to that!'

Idris gave a reluctant grin. 'Oh, aye, my lord, if you call the right toast, I'll drink to them all!'

Prince Owain grinned in return. 'Only 'til that pitcher's dry,' he said, 'for I have work to do!' Looking at Idris speculatively now, he asked, 'Where did you serve, Idris, before Ludlow Castle?'

Frowning, surprise evident in his eyes, Idris replied slowly, 'Why, mainly at Montgomery Castle, my lord, for I was reared there.'

Prince Owain, stroking his beard, gazed steadily at Idris now as he said, 'Your father, he served there then?'

It was a statement rather than a question, but Idris shook his head. 'No, my lord, I knew not who my father was!'

Prince Owain smiled in understanding. 'It's a wise man who ever did, Idris!' Then, perplexed it seemed at the response, Prince Owain frowned. 'Your mother then, she dwelt within the castle walls?'

Smiling, Idris nodded. 'Oh, aye sir, she was a ladies maid.'

Prince Owain sipped his wine thoughtfully then, sighing, put it down.

'Well, you must to your duty, Idris,' he said, 'and I to mine!'

'Idris emptied his goblet in one draught and carefully put it alongside the Prince's, saying as he did so, 'Ay, my lord, to my duty!'

Lifting the flap of the tent, he was about to leave when, glancing behind him, he saw the Prince standing there stroking his beard and gazing at him. Embarrassed, Idris turned quickly and hurried out of the tent.

*   *   *   *

Idris's heart lifted at the news. 'When do we march then, Dafydd?'

All winter through Prince Owain had laid siege to Harlech Castle and that of Aberystwyth further south and, though neither fell, he stubbornly refused to lift his interdict. Now, as the first signs of spring began to ease the lot of the besiegers, Dafydd had brought news that Prince Owain was gathering his forces for his spring campaign.

'A week hence,' replied Dafydd rubbing his unshaven chin, 'and glad enough I'll be to go, for I have no love of these long sieges, even in summer. In winter they play the very havoc with my bones! Give me a storming of a castle any day before squatting in the rain at its gate, like a bedraggled hound at a rabbit's burrow.'

Idris grinned as he replied, 'It's not the wintry chill that aches your bones, Dafydd, 'tis but great age that stiffens up your joints. If we storm Harlech, I'd best lend you my bow, that you may lean upon it to aid your progress through the breach!'

His massive hand raised, Dafydd stepped forward with surprising agility for such a heavily built man, but as Idris had already moved well outside reach, Dafydd, hand dropping to his side, paused in his advance. Shaking his head, he smiled. 'Well, it's better I suppose to bear such insolence than that grim countenance you wore all winter through!' Head on one side now, eyebrows arched, he asked, 'Do I see an Idris recovered from his fever now?'

Unsmiling, Idris nodded. 'Aye, well enough Dafydd!' Changing the subject quickly, he asked, 'Do you know where we march?'

Dafydd looked at him steadily without answering for a moment, as if aware of the evasion, then, 'Aye, we march south, but to what end, I do not know.'

Idris, with a toss of his head, said bitterly, 'And we just march away, your joints will have ached to no purpose outside those castle walls, Dafydd!'

The man at arms shook his head. 'It will not be so,' he said firmly. 'Lord Tudor maintains the siege of Harlech here, whilst your young friend Gruffydd keeps Aberystwyth tight ringed!'

Idris glanced at Dafydd grim faced as he replied, 'No friend of mine and never was!'

Eyebrows raised, Dafydd smiled. 'What, because he told tales of your dalliance to Prince Owain?'

Idris scowled. 'That was in malice told, malice held since we first met and for no reason!'

Dafydd smiled and held his hand up palm outwards. 'Enough! 'Tis an old quarrel that will only more angry grow with its retelling! He's good enough at the soldier's trade to maintain the siege there, though I fear it would be no balm to your ancient wound were he to take the castle!'

Idris snorted. 'Him, take the castle?' he said with derision in his voice. 'He'd not know how to take it were it offered as a gift! At least it saves me from his company on campaign!'

King Henry was not a happy man that spring of 1403, nor was he any happier when in the beginning of June he received a letter from Prince Henry. Owain Glyn Dŵr's siege of Harlech and Aberystwyth castles was still being maintained it advised, but Prince Henry's soldiers were restive through lack of pay! His plea for money to pay their wages that he might relieve these sieges had not come at an opportune moment. There was treachery in the air in the North and the King was now more worried about the Scottish marches than Wales.

With Sir Edmund Mortimer now allied with the rebel Glyn Dŵr, Hotspur's loyalty was to be questioned and if Hotspur's, then the older Percy's too! There was no doubt that in the face of such treachery he needed to secure the northern borders himself! His resources already stretched, he was furious that Hotspur still refused to surrender the captive Earl Douglas to him. Douglas would be a valuable hostage, worth more from the Scots by way of ransom than even that which he had paid for Lord Grey and now this was being denied him.

Nor was his humour much improved at news of Owain Glyn Dŵr rampaging almost at will throughout Carmarthen with some nine thousand men, and irritably he sent out a commission of array to the Earl of Worcester and Lord Derby to raise troops to guard Carmarthen and Pembroke. Concerned about his northern borders and the dubious loyalty of the Percies, he headed north, leaving Wales to the care of the nobles and fifteen year old Prince Hal.

189

The news that reached him on his royal progress was no more encouraging. In June, aroused no doubt by the presence of Owain Glyn Dŵr in South Wales, the people of Brecon and Builth rose in rebellion. Whilst the Sheriff of Herefordshire lifted the siege at Brecon with much loss to the rebels, he did not pursue his advantage and withdrew to Hereford. Whilst some questioned his courage, none could doubt his prudence.

Despite the King's commission of array, it seemed that neither the Earl of Worcester nor Lord Derby had much stomach for entering the fray, for they did not respond with great enthusiasm. All through June the tales of Owain Glyn Dŵr's successes multiplied. Rebel gentry of Carmarthen led by the Dwnns of Kidwelly besieged Dinefwr Castle. Llandeilo and Newton were put to the torch by Owain and his retinue, who then went on to lay siege to Llandovery Castle held by Ralph Monnington for Lord Audley.

Nearby, Carreg Cennen Castle, dominating the surrounding area from the great crag on which it stood above the River Cennen was in danger. Its constable, John Scudamore, in fear for the safety of his wife and daughter, sought safe conduct for them of Owain Glyn Dŵr, to be told it would only be given on surrender of the castle. Everywhere it seemed Owain Glyn Dŵr's name was on all lips, for some it was a spur to rise against the English in their midst, to others a dread sound that made brave men tremble.

Idris watched as the constable of Carmarthen Castle, shoulders stiff, his head unbent, walked out of the castle flanked on either side by a man at arms. Bareheaded, although still in his warlike armour, the tall figure was erect, but his face was pale and drawn, as though he walked to the execution block. Standing behind Prince Owain, Idris turned to Dafydd to say quietly, 'Here comes a worried man, Dafydd!'

With a sideways glance, Dafydd nodded. 'Aye, and well he might be!' he replied. 'Those who stubbornly reject calls to surrender, cannot expect a sweet response when at last, under dire compulsion, they bend the knee. Too much blood has been spent needlessly by then for their own to be valued highly.'

Robert Wigmore, the constable, was approaching now and the

two captains, hands on sword hilts, watched closely as he carefully drew his sword whilst well apart from Prince Owain. Offering it now, hilt first, to the Prince, Wigmore with a touch of resignation in his voice, said quietly, 'Owain Glyn Dŵr, with this sword I surrender the castle I held for His Royal Highness the Prince of Wales.'

Idris could not see Prince Owain's face but could sense the smile in his voice as he replied, 'Ah yes, young Hal, the Prince in absentia! Well Robert Wigmore, is it not appropriate that you give custody of the castle to the de facto Prince?' A touch of irony in his voice now, he continued, 'Yet I would counsel that you, who beyond all reason have resisted my just claim to its possession, should take especial care upon whom you bestow such title! Now, have one of your men here lead out your garrison, well spaced and disarmed, for if any one of them brings out a single knife, then he shall pay for it with his head!

With an air of resignation, both men at arms were now unbuckling their sword belts and turning to one of them, the constable quietly gave the order before, shoulders drooping, turning back to Prince Owain. The shadows under his eyes accentuating the pallor of his cheeks he said, bowing his head as though in emphasis of his submission, 'Few men have I who have survived the siege and most bear the mark of wounds unhealed, but all have valiantly done their duty as you would expect of yours. For that I ask that you, in charity, grant them the courtesies of war.'

Idris, at Prince Owain's side now, glanced anxiously at the Prince, his breath held as he waited for the reply.

Grim faced, the Prince gazed steadily at the constable for a moment before, nodding towards the castle, he answered, 'More thought you have it seems for their well being than when you barred yon gate to me, for then you made them hostage to your fortune, whilst now you plead my charity! And for yourself, what "courtesy of war" do you expect?'

There seemed little hope in the blank eyes that held Prince Owain's gaze, but Wigmore stood erect as he replied defiantly, 'Only that which you would expect of me, Owain Glyn Dŵr!'

Head on one side, Prince Owain asked softly, 'No "Prince" before my name to temper my severity?'

Steadily Wigmore held the Prince's gaze as he replied coldly,

'I held a castle for my Prince and though I am a captive, he is still that to me!'

Prince Owain shook his head in exasperation. 'You're yet a stubborn man, Wigmore and that, which could well have cost your head, will cost your Prince a greater ransom than, his castle lost, he may think that you deserve!'

Idris breathed a sigh of relief, as with a nod to Dafydd, Prince Owain said tersely, 'Take him away!'

Later that day, after the castle had been secured and Prince Owain's banner flew proudly from its battlements, Idris stood gazing at the town below and turned to Dafydd to say with something approaching wonder, 'Prince Owain was amazingly lenient today! When the constable denied our Prince just acknowledgement I thought for sure he'd lose his head and yet he lives! Was it but the hope of ransom that spared his neck?'

The look of surprise in Dafydd's eyes seemed genuine enough. 'Have you not heard?' he asked. 'Prince Owain is in high good humour, for Harry Hotspur and the Earl of Worcester march to our aid. They too have raised rebellion against King Henry.' He hesitated a moment but then, as though unable to resist voicing the thought, added, 'Now that he is indeed allied to our cause who knows what English nobles will call Henry the usurper and Richard, if he is yet alive, the king!'

Chapter Twenty-three

Idris gazed at Dafydd wide-eyed.

'Hotspur joins us in rebellion?' he asked incredulously. 'And the Earl of Worcester, too?'

'Aye, 'tis all in the family, you see Idris, for Worcester is uncle to Hotspur and Hotspur's brother in law to Sir Edmund Mortimer who's son in law to our own Prince! With his ten children, given time Prince Owain will be in law to half of England's peerage.' With a mischievous grin he added, 'Now, if we could only make young Prince Hal prisoner perhaps he'd be persuaded to marry Catrin's sister, Alice, for the Prince's daughters have captivating ways!'

Scowling, Idris said bitterly, 'Aye, truly captivating, if not faithful, ways!'

Grinning now, Dafydd persuaded, 'Come now, Idris, is not love well lost if it brings such a host as the Percy's to our aid? Why with such succour, we'll live to make old bones yet!'

With a derisory glance, Idris replied quickly, 'So old are yours already, Dafydd, I hear them creak with every step you take, or would but for your malicious tongue!'

Bright eyed, Dafydd nodded. 'Aye, my bones give yours a score or more of years, but my ears are yet sharper than yours, for already I hear the whisper that we leave Carmarthen town on the morrow!'

Idris snorted, 'That news is almost as ancient as your bones! A band of spearmen left at break of day, no doubt to see the path we take is clear. Do we march to join forces with our one time adversary, Harry Hotspur, do you think?'

Frowning, Dafydd shook his head. 'Truly, I do not know, Idris. Yet I doubt that our Prince would take his main force deep into

j

England, even to join force with Hotspur. Pitched battle does not favour our strength or cause, and if we join up with Hotspur such a battle must we face in time.' He rubbed his chin thoughtfully and pointed at the castle behind them. 'Each castle that we take both strengthens us and weakens us. Strengthens, because an English garrison no longer dominates the land around. Weakens, because we have to garrison and hold it and thus immobilise that force. Each one we take is then a drain on our resource, each man we leave behind here when we march has to be fed, paid and supported if besieged. Only when our borders with England are secure, each Welsh castle held by a Welsh lord and the land productive once again should Prince Owain consider such adventure.'

Idris, frowning, scratched his head. 'Where then, Dafydd, eastwards to Glamorgan, Gwent?'

With a quick nod, Dafydd replied, 'Aye, North Wales is held well enough for Prince Owain by his kin. Eastwards I'd go and gather friends about me there, though those of Gwent I fear would need persuasion more than Glamorgan's men!'

With a clasp of hands the two friends parted company, going their separate ways to prepare their men for departure on the morrow. When that day dawned, however, all eyed their weapons carefully as they wondered if the edge on their weapons was keen enough and the archers checked their quivers full, each arrow true. Before dawn a trickle of survivors from the seven hundred who had set out the previous day had returned to tell of their defeat north of Carmarthen at the hands of Lord Carew.

The very real threat posed by Lord Carew's powerful force was supported by a prophecy made to Prince Owain by a seer only days earlier. Prince Owain, who ever held the bards in great esteem, had sought the advice of Thomas ap Hopkin, a learned bard from Gower, who he invited to his camp in Carmarthen. Perhaps with a touch of self interest, the bard told the Prince that harm would befall him near Gower.

In a siege camp few secrets can be kept and soon it was being whispered abroad that danger lay on the road to Gower. Those whispers and the defeat of Prince Owain's scouting force, took the edge off the euphoria over the capture of Carmarthen Castle and each man in Prince Owain's army was alert for ambuscade by Lord Carew's men as they marched eastwards. Perhaps because of Thomas ap Hopkin's warning, or maybe just out of regard for the bard, Prince Owain gave Gower a wide berth as he headed towards the Black Mountains.

Far to the North, Harry Hotspur and his uncle the Earl of Worcester were marching towards Shrewsbury, hoping to join forces with Prince Owain there or, failing that, in the marches of North Wales. His intelligence of the Prince's movements, however, were not as accurate as King Henry's. The King, learning of Hotspur's insurrection whilst at Nottingham on his way north on the twelfth of July, set off with his army on a forced march towards Shrewsbury where he hoped to intercept Hotspur.

As both armies hurried to a fateful meeting, Prince Owain, now east of the Black Mountains was harrying Lord Abergavenny, some of whose soldiers were captured by the Prince. King Henry though, had more to worry about than a pitiful plea from Lord Abergavenny, his whole kingdom was at stake lest he reached Shrewsbury in time!

Racing towards Shrewsbury, Hotspur, hearing that the King's army was also advancing there, was anxious to get there first, to assail rather than be assailed. Each hour he expected to have word from Prince Owain that he, too, was marching to join battle with the King, but it never came.

On the twenty-first of July Hotspur finally learned both that he was to fight unsupported and that the King, having arrived at Shrewsbury before him, had chosen the field of battle. Not that he or the Earl of Worcester shrank from battle, nor indeed could they, for the die was cast and they were denounced traitors. With cries of 'Richard, Richard for King!' bravely they hurled themselves against the King's forces.

Never had Henry Percy's courage been denied, but this was a forlorn hope, a charge of desperation, one to be rewarded with neither victory nor honour, for the day went to the King. In victory he showed no magnanimity, the body of Hotspur, killed in the battle, was mutilated, Worcester and other prisoners of rank were executed whilst others were killed where they stood.

Leaving the bloody field, where Prince Owain had lost a powerful ally in the making, King Henry marched on to Scotland. In the far north, the old Earl of Northumberland, seething with anger, was no longer one upon whose support the King could rely. At Shrewsbury, both King and Prince Owain had lost an ally.

That other Prince, the English Prince of Wales, faced Hotspur's charge alongside his father, the King, at Shrewsbury but did not march from there. Wounded by an arrow in the face, he bore his injury bravely for so young a lad, or so it was said. So sorely was he wounded that, since he would not again govern Wales for some time, the King appointed a council of lords to govern the Principality in his stead.

Their governance of Wales was held by a slender thread however, for with many of the castles now held for Prince Owain and every English lordship there impoverished by war, only the marches were indeed secure. Even those were not entirely safe, for by September Hereford was under attack from Prince Owain's forces, causing the chronicler Adam of Usk to record:

> Owain and his manikins marched through Wales with a great power as far as Severn sea and brought into subjection with fire and sword all those who made resistance and also those beyond the same sea, sparing not even churches. Then with vast spoil he retired for safety to the northern parts of Wales, whence are spread all the ills of Wales.

Idris took little pleasure at the thought of returning to North Wales, for there was nothing there for him now. Nor was the long march there without its hazards, for they ever risked ambuscade on the way. It was rumoured too that the King was gathering at Worcester men from every English shire.

Looking around him at the ponderous progress of Prince Owain's army, hindered as it was by the baggage train laden with the spoils of war from Gwent and Hereford, Idris frowned and turned to Dafydd.

'I do not like this,' he muttered, 'it is against all sense to burden our main force with booty in this way! Often enough you've said our main force must be unencumbered and mobile, and here we march like snails, our house about our backs!'

Dafydd nodded and smiled as he replied, 'Truly said, Idris bach! You'll yet learn the art of war! Now though, we are in

196

friendly country and with such a force as ours, can safely march through Glamorgan before marshalling our forces in more warlike fashion.'

The worried frown still on his brow, Idris grimaced. 'So long as it is soon enough! This talk of all England on the march against us, makes me look over my shoulder anxiously!'

Dafydd grinned. 'The fox that takes the chicken forever anxious looks,' he answered, 'and it is prudent in our trade to follow suit, lest we are taken unawares! Fear not though, Camarthen and Pembroke both will remember our last visit there well enough to still fear the power of our main force.' With a sly glance at Idris he added, 'Nor need we fear too greatly the garrisons of the castles on the western coast, for aid is coming to our besiegers there!'

Not relishing the thought of another winter besieging nigh on impregnable fortresses, Idris, eyebrows raised, asked incredulously, 'We march to their support?'

Dafydd shook his head. 'No!' he replied. 'Though Hotspur failed, greater power comes to our succour now! The French, in answer to Prince Owain's call, are sending ships of war to aid our power there!'

Knowing little of such warfare, Idris shrugged and asked dubiously, 'I doubt such ships can take a castle when months of siege have failed!'

Sighing, Dafydd explained patiently, 'If they are to hold out, the garrisons need food, weapons and men besides. To provide all this across Wales, despite our harassment, is perilous work for Henry's men and so it's sent by sea. We have few ships to interdict such trade and thus the French now come to spite their ancient enemy!'

'I pray it may be so,' said Idris, adding doubtfully, 'though I fear this aid may come at such price that we can ill afford. France is as powerful as England, I grant, and therein lies great danger. The Frenchies came before, from Normandy, to leave harsh memories of their rule here. I have as little stomach for their governance as that of Henry Bolingbroke!'

Dafydd looked askance at him. 'It is not governance of which I speak,' he replied, 'but alliance and if we are to succeed, then we need allies. Nor can we look too closely who they may be, so long as our enemy's enemy is our friend!'

*   *   *   *

Whilst the two captains marched westwards with the Prince's army, the King, with the forces he had gathered at Worcester, was also hastening westwards. He marched with all speed through the Usk and Towy valleys, hoping to repeat his earlier victory over Hotspur with another over Prince Owain at Carmarthen. Unlike his previous invasion the weather was kinder to him this time and it was in good spirit that his forces arrived at Carmarthen. That, however, proved to be the only solace he was to take from his third venture into Wales.

When he reached the town on the twenty-fourth of September, he found the bird had flown. Prince Owain, as ever refusing to be drawn into a set piece battle with superior forces, had withdrawn into the hills to the north, to leave Henry seeking the small elusive groups into which the Welsh army had fragmented.

Finding no resistance and unable or unwilling to pursue such will o' the wisps, King Henry left the Earl of Somerset to deal with the intransigent rebels and, retracing his steps, marched back to England's more certain ground. No sooner was he clear of Carmarthenshire, though, than the rebels resumed their domination of the countryside. Even as the King left Wales he received a letter from his constable at Kidwelly that was to emphasise the ineffectiveness of his campaign.

The constable reported that Kidwelly Castle had been attacked, the town and surrounding countryside pillaged by one Henry Dwnn, a formidable supporter of Owain Glyn Dŵr. More worrying perhaps for Henry, should have been the fact that Dwnn was supported by 'men of France and Brittany with ordnance'.

The King seemed not to be unduly concerned, for if the constable's pious hope was that the King's forces might come to his aid it was not to materialise. The King, it seemed, had savoured enough Welsh hospitality for one year.

Idris's hopes of a winter free of a castle siege were disappointed, for in November he stood with Dafydd gazing at the seemingly invincible walls of Caernarvon Castle. As ever, when he looked at an enemy held castle, he stood under a lowering sky, the castle dark and brooding. Feeling that they were less of a threat to the

198

castle than it was to them, he turned to Dafydd. 'Your bones will relish a winter here, Dafydd!' he said, his own disenchantment at the thought evident in his voice. He snorted and added bitterly, 'One look at that vast citadel tells me it will withstand our siege all winter through!'

Dafydd, tugging thoughtfully at his moustache, paused before replying, 'Mayhap they'll not hold out that long, for all the gossip tells the garrison there is much reduced. Of the hundred there two years since, it seems there are only two score there now, so they'll be spread thinly enough along those walls.' He turned to point seawards. 'Look, there comes the aid Prince Owain promised!'

Idris turned to look out into Caernarvon Bay but all he could see was a few sails and, no sailor, he knew not whether they made for Menai Straits or had sailed from there. With a scornful glance at Dafydd, he asked. 'Those few sails, aid? As like as not they bring succour to the garrison there!'

Dafydd smiled knowingly. 'They're not English ships!' he said, 'Jean d'Espagne out there, with his French ships, brings men to aid us in our siege.'

'This John of Spain is French?' Idris asked, grimacing. 'His very name tells he does not come from France!' Laughing now, he shook his head. 'A Spaniard fighting for the French, he now comes to make war upon the English in Wales!'

Exasperated, Dafydd snapped, 'D'Espagne is but his name! I care not where he comes from so long as he fights alongside us as we storm those walls!'

The arrival of the French did not signal the surrender of the castle for, despite its depleted garrison, Idris and Dafydd were still outside its walls as a flurry of snow heralded the new year of 1404. Their cloaks wrapped well around them, they were at the harbourside watching material being unloaded from two French ships that had arrived the previous day.

Idris stroked his stubbled chin, as he exclaimed.

'Timber to build a palisade or mayhap a bridge they've brought, not engines of war, Dafydd!'

Dafydd nodded. 'Aye, 'twill take the craftsmen a week or more to turn those beams into siege engines. The ladders will be ready sooner, this time long enough to reach the battlements I trust.' He laughed. 'As you are younger far than me and, as you so often say, more agile too, then you can mount the ladder first, whilst I take shelter here below!'

Idris grinned, safe in the knowledge that when the castle was stormed he would be busy with his archers keeping the battlements clear of the enemy whilst Dafydd led his men at arms in the assault.

The next few days there was great activity amongst the besiegers as ballistas and mangonels were ranged against the castle. These were engines of which Idris had often heard but seldom seen and he watched with interest as three ballistas, huge crossbow machines, then two mangonels were put to action.

Whilst the French crews readied their machines of war, Dafydd's men were bringing up long ladders in readiness to fling them against the walls and make their hazardous ascent. Idris had little time to watch these preparations, his archers were kept busy at their trade, for the castle's archers were loosing clouds of arrows at the French crews whilst others of the garrison launched red hot bolts at them.

On the fifth day following the arrival of the war machines the mangonels hurled their first heavy rocks against the castle. For a moment there was silence amongst the besiegers as they watched the missiles fly in a high arc towards the castle. Straight and true they went and still that silence held as though all there held their breath. The silence was followed by a great sigh as they watched the huge rocks bury themselves in the earth well short of the castle walls.

Idris turned to one of his oldest archers, who was standing close by. 'If there are many more like that, Morgan, we shall build another curtain wall for them!'

Morgan grinned as he notched another arrow in his bow. 'They do but find the range, Captain, I'd yet rather stand behind that thing than afore it!'

Even as he spoke, both mangonel crews were reloading their catapults and furiously winding on their winches. The ballistas were firing now too, their missiles aimed at the battlements. Prince Owain standing by the war machines with young Maredudd, pointed towards a section of the castle wall and called to Dafydd, 'Get ready to place your ladders there, but wait upon my command!' Then, turning to Idris, he said urgently, 'Do not let up, Idris. Clear those battlements!'

Idris nodded, little more could be done, there were few enough on the battlements and his men were husbanding their arrows for when the assault began. After so long a siege the fletchers were hard put to keep his men supplied. With so much activity around the castle, there could be little doubt the garrison were expecting an assault and would not expose themselves until it began.

He looked over towards Dafydd, but the man at arms was busy readying his men for the assault, upon whom the castle archers from their slits now directed their shafts. In the background there was the swishing sound of the missiles from the ballistas and mangonels, the creaking sound of straining timber as they were reloaded, hoarse foreign shouts as their crews were urged to their work.

Dafydd, all ready now it seemed, was watching Prince Owain, waiting for the word. Then, with a fierce punch aimed at the castle, the Prince cried 'Now!' and all hell broke around Idris's ears. Dafydd, his great sword drawn, with one wild yell led the race to the castle walls, a screaming Welsh wave following upon which the ladders seemed to float like flotsam. Yelling, shouting, they rushed headlong at the castle walls, as a foaming sea upon the rocks.

Not all were there when the ladders were finally flung against the walls, for as the wave advanced it had left debris behind, a bloody debris, brought down as they ran by the castle's defenders who were there in numbers now, numbers far greater than Dafydd's gossip had him believe. As Idris's archers notched their arrows and bent their bows ever steadily against the toy-like figures on the battlements, ladders were being put against the walls. He could see Dafydd now too, first on a ladder, his sword blade glinting in the weak wintry sun as he quickly made his ascent, others followed and ladders either side of Dafydd were now being manned.

As men on the battlements raced to dislodge the ladders, Idris's archers worked furiously to hold them back for Dafydd and his men to gain a foothold. Despite the cloud of arrows that enshrouded the battlements there, two men reached one of the ladders to push at it with staves. The climbing men now clung on as it shivered, first of all upright and then beyond until, screaming, some men fell whilst others still clinging grimly to the

201

ladder, fell as certainly to their death.

Other defenders were on the battlements above the ladders now, hurling rocks down upon their assailants and however many fell to the archers' shafts, others took their place. It seemed to Idris that it took Dafydd an eternity to reach the battlements and having reached them, fight his way onto the parapet, but of the four ladders placed against the walls, only his remained.

Now that Dafydd, followed by a few men, had reached the battlements, Idris's archers could help them little other than in an attempt to stop others of the garrison reaching them. All Idris could see now, as he anxiously looked for sight of Dafydd and his men, was a scuffling there and he was so far away, that he could hear but little sound of the fray. Others were still ascending that last ladder when suddenly it too began to shake, the climbers' yells changing to ones of fear as it slowly toppled backwards, taking most to their death.

Idris's heart sank, for there could be no aid to Dafydd now. However many ladders were placed against the walls, they would not be scaled in time to bring him succour. Desperately he urged his archers on to greater effort, though in his heart he knew it was of no avail. However many of the garrison he might bring down, Dafydd had made his last assault. Sickened, Idris looked over at Prince Owain who just slowly shook his head.

Leaning despondently on his bow, Idris watched weary men carrying broken ladders well away from the castle, whilst others helped wounded and broken men back to relative safety. The assault was over, the surprising strength of the castle's garrison had beaten them. This time. There would be other assaults and sometime, one would succeed, but it would not be led by Dafydd. His face grim, Idris knew that whatever happened, he would be there to take his revenge.

Chapter Twenty-four

Their high hopes dashed by the defender's repulse of the January assault, the besiegers gloomily settled in for the siege continuing through the winter. As he listened to the rhythmic sound of the missiles from the ballistas and mangonels being hurled at the castle, Idris thought bitterly that there would be other assaults, but none led by Dafydd. Looking at the spot where Dafydd had reached the battlements with a few men at arms, he imagined the furious struggle that had taken place there. He shook his head sorrowfully, there is no hope, he thought, for they would not have taken Dafydd, not alive! Turning away he saw a smiling Maredudd coming towards him and he started walking towards the Prince's son. As they drew near, Idris could see that the young lord's smile was one of sympathy rather than amusement. It was there in his voice too as he said quietly, 'I share your sorrow over Dafydd, Idris! My father lost a good captain in that assault and you a good friend.' As Idris replied only with a bleak nod, Maredudd continued, enthusiastically now, 'But I bring great news! Harlech has been taken by my good Uncle Tudor who holds it now until he may be relieved!'

Idris, failing to see how this news greatly affected him, was not enthused and his voice was devoid of emotion as he replied, 'Good news my lord, I would we had as much success here at Caernarvon!'

Head on one side, Maredudd looked at him appraisingly for a moment, before saying, 'All those who aid my Father's cause are rebels, lest we gain victory. A man at arms was Dafydd, who full well knew the penalty for such as we and would have died in battle thrice over rather than be taken to slaughter like a haltered bullock.'

Idris sighing, nodded. 'Aye, so he would, my lord!'

A grin on his face now, Maredudd said cheerfully, 'But I brought news to you I thought would lift your spirits, Idris! My mother comes to Caernarvon ere noon to be escorted to Harlech Castle with its new lord.'

Idris, hearing nothing that could lift his spirits, just gazed at him blankly until he continued: 'My father asked me to tell you that you are to be the captain of the escort to Harlech! That will take you away from this siege for a week or so!'

Idris smiled, the thought of a safe journey to Harlech, hearing there of its taking and no lords or ladies to burden the quiet ride back to Caernarvon, did indeed lift his spirits. Smiling for the first time since the approach of the young lord, he asked, 'Who is to hold Harlech for the Prince, my lord?'

Straight-faced, Maredudd replied, 'Sir Edmund Mortimer, the one we took at Pilleth!'

Idris flushed. 'So I escort a turncoat now! Why does he need an escort at all, my lord? If taken he can always turn again!'

Maredudd raised a finger in warning, but with an artful smile on his lips, amusement in his eyes answered, 'I fear it's not the turning that raises such choler in you, but who he takes to bride! Yet my father places much faith in you in that he entrusts you with their escort.'

Idris favoured him with a baleful glance. 'I am honoured to guard your lady mother, my lord,' he replied, before adding with evident distaste, 'and will escort this . . . this knight as my Prince commands!'

Nodding, as if the matter were settled, Maredudd turned and started to walk away. He had only taken a couple of paces however before, pausing, he looked over his shoulder to remark, 'Oh, Idris! That knight, he takes his lady wife with him to Harlech!'

As Idris gazed at him speechless, Maredudd, chuckling now, hurried away.

Idris gazed after Maredudd, his enthusiasm for the journey to Harlech ebbing as quickly as the young lord was hurrying away. The thought of spending two days or so escorting Sir Edmund was bad enough, but spending them watching Catrin at the knight's side was . . . intolerable, that was the word! With a sigh he shook his head again, no, not intolerable, for if the Prince commanded, then it would indeed, have to be tolerated.

Rubbing his chin, his brow was furrowed in anguish: not that he cared for Catrin any more, she meant nothing to him now, it was but the thought of her fawning over that turncoat! Knowing how he felt, or had felt about the both of them, it was unfair of Prince Owain to have given him this task. Lips compressed, chin thrust forward, he braced his shoulders, determined to seek out the Prince and ask to be excused this insufferable duty.

The sentry at the Prince's tent called out, 'Captain Idris, my lord!' and allowed him past. As he entered the tent, the Prince looked up, to say with a smile, 'Ah, Idris, I was expecting you!'

Eyebrows arched, Idris asked, 'Indeed, my lord?'

Prince Owain was still smiling as he replied, 'Aye! Maredudd must have given you my message full two minutes before you came to be excused the Harlech escort duty!'

Flushing redly, Idris stammered, 'I . . . er . . . I think a man at arms would be better suited for such an escort, my lord.'

Prince Owain held his hand up. 'It's not like you, Idris, to take the serpent's path in answer to your lord, nor yet to deny your own ability!'

As Idris, shuffling his feet, avoided the Prince's gaze, Owain continued, 'Yet it is not you, but I, who must decide with whom to place my trust on such a mission. I send you not to entertain Sir Edmund with your social chatter for, so distracted, your eye may not observe the path you travelled on! Nor dalliance will you have upon the way with Catrin, for she has eyes only for Sir Edmund now.'

As Idris flushed, Prince Owain continued quickly, 'All this I know and yet I know this too: you have a care for Catrin and for that you'll watch her as you would your own sister and see her safe to Harlech gate. When you return, if God so wills, we may have taken the castle here, with Dafydd standing at its gate to greet you!'

Idris's eyes clouded as, with a wry smile, he replied, 'I fear not, my lord! I have no hope there either! Yet if it so pleases you, I'll see Sir Edmund and his bride safe to Harlech.'

Standing there looking at Idris with a steady gaze, Prince

Owain nodded. 'Aye,' he said quietly, 'I thought no less of you, Idris!'

Mounted, Idris surveyed his escort of six men at arms and spearmen and, satisfied at last that they were all equipped for the journey, looked towards Prince Owain's camp. Sir Edmund and the ladies were already mounted there and he watched sober faced as they said their farewells to Prince Owain and Maredudd. Sitting there he was confident now that this would be a safe journey, one that would give him no cause for concern, sure too that, as Prince Owain said, he could escort Catrin as though she were his sister. He watched without emotion, as smiling demurely, she sat on her palfrey alongside Sir Edmund and bade goodbye to her father.

Raising his hand in a last salute to Prince Owain, Sir Edmund, accoutred in the armour he had worn at Pilleth, led Catrin and her mother over to where Idris waited with the escort. His face cold as a winter wind, he greeted Idris tersely, 'Ready, Captain?'

As Idris, touching his helmet, replied, 'Aye, Sir Edmund!' the knight said shortly:

'Well, don't just sit there, man! To your duty, lead on!'

His anger rising, eyes blazing, Idris bit his tongue to stifle a retort and instead turned to the oldest of his men at arms, to order, 'Lead on, Maldwyn!'

Normally he would have led the way himself, but the turncoat's order rankling, Idris decided he would bring up the rear. As he watched the party ride past he saw Catrin glance at him for a moment, in her eyes that old provocative look they'd held when she was teasing him. His heart leapt to his throat but then she was past and he almost choked as he watched her go by. Despite Prince Owain's trust in him he found it amazingly difficult to see Catrin, riding there beside her lord, as he would a sister.

It was not long before Idris decided that with Catrin ahead of him, he was not watching where the hazard might be as they journeyed, but only saw her talking, laughing with Sir Edmund. Spurring his horse he galloped past them to the head of the column and curtly ordered Maldwyn to the rear. Anxious to hasten the end of the journey and the enforced company of Sir

Edmund and his bride he set off at a canter, only to have the knight call sharply to him, 'Hold up there, Captain, this is no chevauchee! The ladies are not used to rough, warlike ways. Ease your pace! We halt for the night near Beddgelert!'

Slowing his horse to a walk, Idris glanced behind him and held up a hand in acknowledgement of the order. His visor up, a scowl on his pink face, Sir Edmund waved his hand negligently in reply but Idris had eyes only for Catrin who was obviously amused at the exchange as if aware of the reason for his haste. Flushing, he turned quickly away lest danger lay ahead, or mayhap to shut out the memories that came rushing back.

It was a long ride before they came to Beddgelert's few cottages by a cross roads and it was nigh on dusk when, shortly afterwards, they reached the small manor where they were to pass the night. Signalling to a man at arms to assist Sir Edmund dismount, Idris strode over to aid the Lady Marged, but found Maldwyn already at her horse's side. He stood there irresolutely for a moment before Catrin, her voice all honey, said plaintively as she held out her hand, 'Will you help me dismount, please, Captain?'

Idris thought how often he had seen her running light-foot along the meadow or by Afon Cynllaith's banks and sighed, knowing well that Catrin needed no aid. His face reddening, he walked over to her to take her hand. Slipping off her palfrey, she almost fell into his arms, her body pressed to his, her warm breath on his face. She was still smiling up at him as he quickly drew back and tearing his eyes away from her, he saw Sir Edmund standing there scowling.

'Have a care, Captain! Would'st let my lady fall?'

Idris frowned, for the look in the knight's eyes held warning rather than concern. The lord and lady of the manor were there now though, to greet their guests and, with a dismissive glare at Idris, Sir Edmund went to meet his hosts.

The lord of the manor was obviously a supporter of Prince Owain for there was much laughter and jollity as he and his lady ushered Sir Edmund and the ladies indoors. Catrin had held back and was last to enter and, as Idris watched, she glanced over her shoulder to smile at him, then she was gone and the studded oak door closed behind her.

He stood there, oblivious to all, as an old yearning came back to haunt him, yet knowing well there was no hope. Miserable now, he turned away to become aware of his surroundings again as he heard someone speak. It was Maldwyn who, looking at him strangely, pointed to a large barn to the side of the manor.

'I said it's the barn for us, Captain!' Grinning, he added, 'And a bed of straw no doubt!'

His mind elsewhere, Idris nodded and said quietly, 'Aye, no doubt, but it will do for me, Maldwyn, I've had my fill of lords and ladies for the day!'

Maldwyn grinned. 'Aye and more on the morrow, eh, Captain? But the servant said there's ale and meat set out for us in the barn and I'm as dry as a tinder's kept!'

Idris stepped back in surprise as, eyebrows raised, he asked, 'Ale, Maldwyn, when you keep the first sentry's watch about the manor?'

Surprised, Maldwyn's face fell. 'Me, sentry keep, here in this safe manor, Captain?' Almost in despair now, he added, 'If I must, then a pot of ale first, for mercy's sake!'

Laughing now, Idris slapped him on the shoulder. 'Come, Maldwyn,' he said jovially, 'I do but jest! No need for sentries here, a round or two around the manor will suffice tonight and you and I will take it turn about to do the rounds!'

'Thanks be to God for that,' Maldwyn said with gratitude, 'for one dread moment, I thought it was said in all seriousness!' Grinning now, he added conspiratorially, 'Did you see how the lady Catrin looked at you, Captain? Were she not already wed, I'd have thought she had designs upon your honour!'

Idris's face paled as he said angrily, 'Speak not ill of your Prince's daughter, Maldwyn, and think upon that as you walk about the manor the next hour before you sup your ale!'

Grim-faced now, he turned quickly away and strode off to the barn, leaving Maldwyn standing there, mouth agape.

It was a cold, clear night when Idris left the barn to walk around the manor and see that all was well. A pale moon hung low in the night sky casting its eerie light over all, a bat flitted around the chimneys of the manor, the only sound was an owl hooting mournfully and a sense of mystery pervaded the night air. Pulling his cloak tighter around him, Idris walked towards the manor where the yellow light of lanterns lit a few of the windows.

Seeing light in some windows of the upper storey Idris swallowed as he thought of Catrin standing there in Sir Edmund's arms and looking up at him with that mischievous smile of hers. Suddenly there was the taste of bile in Idris's throat and he turned away, wanting to flee from there, but there was nowhere for him to go, so he just stood there for a moment dejectedly, arms loose at his side, loneliness enveloping him like a shroud.

The sound broke slowly into his despair insidiously like the sound of dripping water, hardly noticeable at first then permeating into his awareness, until at last he became conscious of someone whispering his name. He peered around and, seeing a flutter of movement in the shadows of the manor's doorway, took a few tentative steps forward, hand on sword. He saw her then. It was Catrin, her pale face hovering above the dark dress hidden in the shadows, her hand reaching out towards him as she whispered again, 'Oh, Idris!'

He held back now, for there was more danger there than any he faced on the road to Harlech. Held back but, his heart urging him forward, he walked slowly towards her. Even as he told himself it was madness, he was holding her, Catrin's arms were around his neck and it was as though they were at Sycharth once more, that they had never left there. She leaned back from him, her mouth open as if about to speak, when there was a call from within. It was Sir Edmund who sounded anxious, perhaps angry, as he called her, 'Catrin! Where are you?'

Catrin was whispering again, urgently now, 'Go!' she was saying, 'Oh Idris, go quickly!'

He hesitated a moment, then stepped sideways and, back pressed against the wall to the side of the doorway, held his breath as hand on sword, he waited there, eyes half closed. He heard the door slowly opening then and a shaft of yellow light lit up the area by the door.

There was a note of suspicion in Sir Edmund's voice as he asked, 'Why are you standing there in the dark, Catrin, it is cold in the night air?'

Idris heard Catrin reply softly, 'It was noisy in the hall, my lord and the lady of the manor befuddled my head with constant chatter so I crept out for a moment's peace.' Idris imagined her smile as she added, 'But my head is clear now, I was about to

209

return.'

Hearing the sound of running feet, Idris saw men coming towards him from the barn, and closed his eyes, wishing that Maldwyn had been more concerned with his pot of ale than noises around the manor. Maldwyn, puffing, was nearing the doorway now, his face caught in the shaft of light from the doorway. Idris signalled to him urgently, but the man at arms could not or would not see, for he spoke only to Sir Edmund.

'Is ought wrong, my lord?'

The petulant voice now of Sir Edmund: 'No! Nothing wrong!' There was a shuffling of feet, then Sir Edmund's voice again, quieter this time, 'Come, my dear it's cold for you out here!'

Idris was glaring at Maldwyn, praying he would hold his tongue, when Sir Edmund spoke again, obviously to Maldwyn, 'It pleases me you keep alert even though we seem safe enough at this manor!' Then, as if it were an afterthought, he asked sharply, 'Where is your captain, I would have thought he'd lead you here!'

Idris raised his eyes to the stars as he waited for Maldwyn to reply. Touching his helmet, the man at arms gazed stolidly at the knight as he replied, 'The captain skirmishes around the manor with three men at arms, my lord and sent me here to guard the manor.'

There was silence for a moment as though Sir Edmund was giving thought to Maldwyn's reply, then, 'Good! It will do no harm for him to skirmish yet awhile, but you may return to the barn!'

Maldwyn touched his helmet again then, turning, marched off in the direction of the barn, looking neither to the right or left. Idris knew the manor door was still open, for the shaft of light lit Maldwyn on his way. Then, as Idris leant back against the wall, waiting with bated breath to make his escape, he heard Catrin say, 'Come, Edmund, there's no one there!'

Sir Edmund then: 'No?' But it seemed as if there was suspicion rather than agreement in his voice and there was a pause before, reluctantly, the door finally shut. Idris waited there a moment before carefully making his way to the side of the manor then gratefully into the shadows and back to the barn. Opening its door, he casually entered the barn to be met by the grinning faces of the men at arms and Maldwyn offering him a pot of ale.

'Right worried you had me there, Captain!' he said. 'Each

210

moment I stood there at the manor's gate I thought Sir Edmund would take a step outside and discover his worst thoughts were truth indeed!'

Taking the pot of ale from the man at arms, Idris drunk deeply, looking straight faced at Maldwyn the while, at last he put the pot down on the trestle table to say coolly, 'I did but pause in my rounds to bid good night to the Lady Catrin!'

Pouting his lips, Maldwyn nodded. 'Aye. It's just as I thought, cap'n!' He smiled as he added, 'But it is as well I star gazed as I supped my ale!'

Chapter Twenty-five

It could only be his imagination, of course, but Idris felt all eyes were on him as they prepared to set out the next morning. Not all were watching him though, for Catrin seemed to be studiously avoiding his eye and if Sir Edmund saw him at all it was only by way of the occasional glare. At last Catrin and the Lady Marged were mounted and Sir Edmund, seemingly impatient to be off, said curtly to Lady Catrin, 'Are you ready then, madam?' And as, palefaced, she merely nodded in reply, he turned to Idris. 'What are you waiting for, man?' he asked, his blue eyes cold as ice. 'A long ride and a short day brooks no laggard escort!'

His ill humour suffered no reply, so Idris, his face expressionless, just touched a finger to his helmet and, a man at arms at his side, led off, leaving Maldwyn to bring up the rear. The knight's ill temper cast a cloud over the small party as they made their way south with little chatter and less laughter. It was a mood shared by the weather, for by mid-morning a drizzle commenced that soon became heavy rain that forced even the bad tempered knight to seek shelter for the ladies. Pointing at one of the few cottages by the side of the track at Penmorfa he said arrogantly to Idris, 'Get the villeins out of there . . . and see it's fit for the ladies to enter!'

The Lady Marged held up a hand. 'No, Sir Edmund!' And turning to Idris, she smiled as she said, 'Captain, ask if we may share the shelter of their home!'

Cold eyed at the rebuke, Sir Edmund nodded at Idris. 'Aye, and make sure, *Captain*, they know better than to refuse!'

With a touch of a finger to his helmet, Idris smiled at the Lady Marged to say, 'Aye, as it pleases you, my Lady,'

Sir Edmund's pink face paled with anger at his reply, which so obviously ignored the knight's command, but Idris, dismounting quickly, was already at the door of the nearest cottage where a man quickly appeared. Hardly had the ladies dismounted before they were ushered inside with Sir Edmund following on their heels, whilst the men at arms took shelter in a byre adjoining the cottage. Idris, desiring little company, stood at its entrance, preferring its meagre protection to the less fragrant shelter of the interior.

As he watched the rain turning the track into a rivulet he wondered what had transpired between Catrin and Sir Edmund the night before. Whatever it might have been it seemed to him that it had left the knight not only bad tempered but suspicious. Suddenly he was aware of Maldwyn standing at his elbow and turned to him. 'The rain seems to be easing, Maldwyn,' he said quietly, 'best get the men prepared to mount!'

The man at arms nodded. 'Aye,' then added thoughtfully, 'best leave well alone Captain, there's nothing but trouble there!'

Idris, knowing well that Maldwyn spoke of the previous night, gazed at him steadily for a moment before saying tersely, 'Trouble is what we're paid for Maldwyn. Let us hope that is the only trouble we find on this journey!'

Pursing his lips, Maldwyn turned away and, as Idris walked over to the cottage door he heard Maldwyn issuing his orders to the men at arms. Banging on the door of the cottage, Idris opened it and put his head inside to say, ' 'Tis but a drizzle now, my lord.'

His eyes took in the bare interior of the cottage, its few sticks of furniture offering little by way of comfort, the flames flickering desultorily in its small hearth. Sir Edmund and the ladies were seated around a bare wooden table, the knight's head bare, his fair hair newly brushed. Catrin and her mother were sitting there silently, hands resting on the table; the Lady Marged looked up as Idris spoke, but Catrin, head bowed, stared at the white knuckles of her clenched hands as if avoiding his eyes.

Sir Edmund, leaning back in the only armed chair in the room, his arm resting on the table, fingers drumming, glowered as he replied, 'Well then, mount up, man, mount up!'

It was two days before the keep and towers of Harlech Castle came in view, a sight that left Idris with mixed emotions. Sir Edmund's ill tempered arrogance had often tested his patience, the more so since Catrin had not been spared the knight's moody humour on the journey. Nor had Catrin spoken to Idris again, for it seemed that Sir Edmund never left her side. Now, the castle in sight, Idris thought that he would at least lose the knight's ungracious company. The cost, however, was almost more than he could bear, for after that night at Beddgelert when he had held Catrin in his arms again, he was sure that she still loved him and the thought had tormented him ever since.

If Sir Edmund never left Catrin's side, Maldwyn was ever at Idris's elbow and when taxed with it, would only give a quiet smile and say, 'There's safety in numbers, Captain!'

They were approaching the drawbridge now and there was much toing and froing as men repaired the ravages of the siege. With Maldwyn bearing Prince Owain's banner there was but a desultory hail of 'Who goes?' from the tower and a wave as Maldwyn roared back, 'Sir Edmund Mortimer!'

With the knight leading now, followed by Idris and Maldwyn, there was a hollow clatter of their horses hooves as they rode over the drawbridge and into the castle. Looking around Idris saw little sign inside the castle of the fighting that must have taken place before it fell to Lord Tudor. Smiling, Prince Owain's brother stood there, legs astride, hands on hips, the undoubted victor, waiting to greet his kin. Idris shook his head, thinking that it could be the Prince himself who stood there, they were so alike.

'Marged! It is good to see you safely here,' Lord Tudor was saying gruffly as he came forward to help her dismount. He had a smile for Catrin too, as he greeted her. 'And Catrin! Prettier than ever you are, my love!' Holding the Lady Marged's hand as she dismounted, he glanced at Sir Edmund, but his cool gaze belied his words as he said formally, 'You are welcome here, Sir Edmund!'

As Idris stood holding his horse's reins he noticed there was no offered handshake and gave a quiet smile, it seemed Lord Tudor had little liking for turncoats either!

Unsmiling, Sir Edmund nodded. 'My thanks, Tudor,' he said condescendingly. 'You have the castle secure, I trust? Little challenge there was, I thought, to our entry here!'

Lord Tudor bridled and his reply held no familiarity, 'Challenge enough you would have found had you not Lady Marged and Catrin here, by your side, Sir Knight!'

With a bleak smile Sir Edmund nodded in acknowledgement. 'Well said, Tudor! But I am well used to such challenges!'

Lord Tudor, a dour expression on his face, raised his eyebrows. 'Aye? Well I trust you'll hold Harlech, hard won by me, better than you held the day at Pilleth!'

Idris nearly choked as Sir Edmund, his face white with anger, put his hand to his sword.

'It was treachery that won the day at Pilleth, such that I'll not suffer here!'

Amused, Lord Tudor stood there solid, immovable as an oak, a touch of irony in his voice. 'Unhand your sword, *nephew*, we are all kin here and oft enough you'll blood your weapon an' you side with Owain Glyn Dŵr!' Smiling now, he added softly, 'But raise your sword against him or his and such as Maldwyn there will have your head!'

Idris shared Lord Tudor's amusement as Sir Edmund glanced around to find Maldwyn and another man at arms, standing there grim faced, their swords drawn. Slowly, the knight withdrew his hand from his sword.

'Ah, better prepared than I gave you credit for, Tudor,' then, with a sideways glance at Idris, Sir Edmund added, 'such men as these your brother had at Pilleth!'

Smiling, Lord Tudor nodded. 'Aye, strategy was ever Prince Owain's ally.' A note of caution in his voice now, he continued, 'If you are with us long, you'll find that we must mimic the fox and not rush headlong into contention like the bull!' He stroked his beard thoughtfully for a moment, then wagged a finger. 'But holding Harlech for Prince Owain you'll not have cause for such plot or scheming and King Henry will need long arms if he would reach you here!'

Idris's eyes widened, so that was why Prince Owain had given Sir Edmund the charge of Harlech Castle! Not only did it make him beyond all doubt the Prince's adherent, but its position combined with his marriage to Catrin ensured that he was far removed from any temptation to change allegiance. For a fleeting moment he had some sympathy with the English knight: beaten in battle, his plea for ransom rejected, ensnared into alliance with his erstwhile enemy and now given guard over this rock bound fortress in an alien land.

One look at Catrin though and the sympathy quickly

evaporated, the thought of her married to this arrogant upstart as a political ploy brought the taste of bile to his mouth, and he wished the man had really drawn his sword a moment ago.

Sir Edmund was removing his helmet now, his fair hair blowing in the breeze and for what must have been the first time in days, he was actually smiling. 'Should King Henry seek me here, then I must keep him waiting at the gate, for he'll not come to see I keep a tidy house!' Holding out a hand he said, 'Come Tudor, this castle was hard won and upon my life, I'll not give it up easily!'

The brief confrontation seemed to be over and Maldwyn's men were already readying their horses for the stables whilst talking to some of the garrison who were eager for news from the outside world. Idris looked on listlessly, eager to get away from Harlech yet knowing that on his departure he would be reluctant to leave.

Lord Tudor was leading the family into the keep now, all good humour, perhaps at having achieved ascendancy over Sir Edmund. As they went in, Catrin glanced over her shoulder at Idris and involuntarily he took a step forward as he saw the look of pleading in her eyes. Then, with a slight shake of her head, she turned quickly away and she was gone, leaving Idris standing there despairing at the widening gulf between them.

That night Lord Tudor, with the Lady Marged beside him, sat at the head of the lavish table, where wine and ale flowed freely for all according to their station. Sir Edmund and Catrin were on his right, with the knight more amiable it appeared to Idris, than he had been throughout the journey to Harlech. Sitting morosely at the foot of the table with Maldwyn, Idris saw that Catrin, her eyes downcast, ate barely a morsel and he thought with anguish of the long gone days at Sycharth and of how changed she was.

There was a touch on his arm and Idris glanced around: it was Maldwyn.

'A pot of ale, Captain!' he said, grinning. 'It's a wonderful remedy for that which cannot be: if you gaze into it, the eyes you see there tear not at your heart!'

With a sour look at Maldwyn, Idris took the offered pot, saying bitterly as he did so, 'Such wisdom harks of the tavern and does not suit my mood tonight . . . ' He paused, for Catrin, with a whispered word to Sir Edmund, had risen to leave the table and putting the pot of ale back on the table, he also started to rise, only to find his arm held in an iron grip that kept him there. He turned quickly on Maldwyn. 'Hold off!' he said angrily. 'No affair is this of yours!'

With a good humoured smile, Maldwyn nodded. 'Oh aye, it is, Captain!' he said quietly. 'I had strict orders from Prince Owain to see no harm came to you upon the journey and where you would go now, lies ambuscade! Why risk such hazard when there's ale a'plenty here and good fellowship to boot!' As Idris still strained at his grasp, Maldwyn grinned. 'If you go, Captain, then must I follow and I would make but dolorous company!'

His eyes still on Catrin, Idris sighed and relaxed back onto his stool, to say irritably, as Maldwyn let go the grip on his arm, 'Dolorous company yet better suits you than wet nurse!'

Smiling, Maldwyn replied, 'If I were a wet nurse, no joy would you find there either, Captain!'

The next morning a bleary eyed Idris was at the stables saddling up his horse, ready for the return journey to Caernarvon, when she came to him. She had come soft footed and it was not until she put a hand on his forearm that he was aware of her presence. Her touch startled him and he turned quickly, to see her standing there gazing at him, her blue eyes moist. His voice charged with emotion, he said, 'Oh Catrin . . . ' and reached out to take her in his arms but she stepped back quickly before saying, her voice low, as though the words were wrung from her:

'Oh no, Idris, I can't . . . we must not! I only came to bid farewell.' Lips parted, she hesitated a moment before saying, her voice a whisper, 'I must go, Idris! I doubt we'll meet again, my love.'

Frowning, he opened his mouth to speak and reached out to her but, biting her lip as though to stem her tears, she turned away suddenly, to run quickly towards the keep. She ran, not tripping gaily as she had so often by the banks of Afon Cynllaith, but head forward, her hand to her face as though she were fleeing.

As he stood there gazing after her, heart sinking, his own eyes moist, he heard Maldwyn say cheerfully, 'It's better so, Captain, a long hard ride on this crisp day will chase away the devils that would hold a man in thrall!'

Realising that Maldwyn must have been nearby when Catrin

came, Idris's eyes blazed, and he snapped, 'Your mouth will be the death of you one day, Maldwyn!'

The man at arms grinned. 'As well that, Captain, as be turned deaf to hazard by a woman's soft words, for then it would be my ownself, eyes wide open, that took me into hazard!'

Mounting, Idris gazed at him balefully for a moment before, spurring his horse, he led the way across the bailey and out of the castle on the long road that would lead him away from Catrin for ever. Sick at heart, he knew that it would be so and could not bear to spare even a backward glance, for he knew were he to do so, it would be the death of him, for he would not leave Harlech Castle again . . . not alive.

Morosely he rode on, caring not where they went, or the company in which he rode. Mercifully, Maldwyn kept his own counsel and the other men at arms, warned perhaps by him, were subdued as they journeyed on. No longer hampered by the ladies, they travelled at a brisk pace and, with only brief halts along the way, they reached the manor at Beddgelert as night fell.

No lord of the manor was there to greet them this time, but a servant who wearily pointed them towards the barn before, with much mumbling, eventually bringing them ale and bread and cheese. Nor did Idris care: he supped his ale and ate his bread and cheese standing alone by the barn door heedless of the jesting of the men at arms, but thinking only of holding Catrin, there by the manor door, those short few days ago.

The spell was broken, for Maldwyn was at his side again now, saying, 'With no lords or ladies there'll be no need of rounds this night, then, Captain!'

As Idris just shook his head and took another draught of ale, Maldwyn touched him on the arm almost consolingly, as he said quietly, ' "Might have been" is just an epitaph, Captain, and you and I . . . well, we live to fight again the morrow!'

Idris nodded slowly.

'Aye, true enough, Maldwyn,' he paused, then, 'but to what purpose, eh?

Chapter Twenty-six

Arriving back at Caernarvon, Idris found Prince Owain standing looking out over the Menai Strait where some men o' war were making sail. The Prince turned as Idris approached.

'Ah, Idris!' he exclaimed, then, his smile reflected in his brown eyes, 'I trust Sir Edmund and the ladies dwell safe in Harlech?'

As Idris touched a knuckle to his helmet and replied, 'Aye, my lord!' The Prince, still smiling, turned to Maldwyn, who was as ever, by Idris's side.

'Nor mischance did you find upon the way, Maldwyn?'

Touching his helmet, Maldwyn replied, 'We met nothing, my lord, other than rain and mud and our arrival there was timely.'

Eyebrows raised, Prince Owain turned back to Idris, to ask, 'Timely?'

Idris nodded. 'Aye my lord, as we left Harlech, Lord Tudor marched to Aberystwyth to reinforce its siege!'

Prince Owain smiled and pointed to the men o' war. 'Good! That French squadron, makes sail for Aberystwyth. I have no doubt that, invested by such power on land and sea, the constable there will quickly yield!' He nodded towards Caernarvon Castle. 'It's somewhat different here, for I have work to do elsewhere. Go tell your men we march eastwards tomorrow to raid in Shropshire!'

Idris smiled, for the prospect was more to his liking than gazing at the walls of Caernarvon Castle for months on end: not only might it be more profitable but such action was more suited to his present mood. He and Maldwyn began to walk away but paused as Prince Owain called after them, 'Before you do, Idris, seek out Lord Maredudd, for he has news that will be much to your liking!'

Surprised, Idris turned towards the Prince, but Owain was gazing seawards again, intent it seemed at the manoeuvring of the French ships. Turning away he walked on with Maldwyn but they had not gone far before meeting a smiling Lord Maredudd, who asked, 'Still all of one piece then, Idris?'

Idris tossed his head. 'Aye, my lord, thanks only to Maldwyn here!'

A finger raised in caution, Maredudd replied, 'Such angry visage well becomes a soldier setting out on chevauchee. Yet save your ire for the English, Idris, there are enough of them to sate an anger even greater than yours! Long before summer's out, the marches north to south will be alight from a vengeance such as the English never suffered yet! My uncles, the Hanmers, have already put Ardenfield in Hereford to the torch and their visit will be long remembered by the nuns of Aconbury.'

With a nod as if in emphasis of his warning, he turned and seemed about to hurry off; so Idris held out a hand as if to detain him saying, 'The Prince, your father, said you had some news for me, my lord!'

Maredudd waved a hand negligently and said with a mischievous glint in his eye, 'I thought I had already detained you overlong with my counselling, Idris! Yet I have no news for you, but rather someone I would have you meet!'

With that, taking Idris by the arm he led the way to a nearby tent. Idris stood there mystified as, holding a finger to his lips, Maredudd lifted the flap before signalling for Idris to enter.

In the tent's dim interior a figure lay on a straw palliasse, a leg in bandages. There was a broad grin under the familiar drooping moustache as Dafydd said in his gruff voice, 'A friend I thought you were, Idris the Archer, and you did not come to my rescue!'

Idris knelt by the palliasse, clasping hands with the old man at arms, speechless for a moment, then, shaking his head, said, 'Oh, Dafydd if only I could have.'

Dafydd, a hand the size of a ham on Idris's shoulder, smiled understandingly.

'Aye, lad, I know!'

Frowning, Idris gazed at Dafydd wide-eyed, open-mouthed, without understanding, then asked quietly, 'But what happened, Dafydd how did you escape?'

'Escape, lad, with my leg like this? No escape, but an

exchange of prisoners! A knight's son I was worth,' with a proud toss of his head, Dafydd added, 'but when he saw me lying here, Prince Owain told me he'd had best of the bargain!'

Looking on, a smiling Maldwyn interrupted him, 'It's good to see you back, Captain and that's no error, though it's a fair wind that blows no ill, for I hankered after captaincy myself!'

Dafydd grinned. 'Aye, and that is why you'll ever march in front of me and not behind!'

Long after Maldwyn had left on his errand to have the men prepare to march the morrow, Idris stayed on in the tent listening to Dafydd tell of his furious battle on Caernarvon Castle's parapet when only he and one other survived. Of his imprisonment too, and his amazement at his release.

At last, frowning, Idris pointed to the bandaged leg and asked, 'And what of your leg, Dafydd?'

'Prince Owain had his own physician tend to it,' Dafydd replied, 'for it was festering from lack of care. A mite shorter will it be, it seems, than 'tother but on the morrow I shall ride, though I will pick my way carefully beside the baggage train, but a week hence I'll run as fast as you, albeit in lopsided fashion!'

As spring turned into summer, Prince Owain's forces rampaged along the marches. They were advancing through Shropshire, when the news reached them of the surrender of Aberystwyth Castle to the combined forces of Lord Tudor, Lord Gruffydd and the French squadron to seaward. With no prospect of relief from either land or sea, the constable had yielded to force majeure and Prince Owain's banner flew proudly over yet another of King Henry's strongholds in Wales.

The surrender of Harlech and Aberystwyth castles to Prince Owain's forces brought comfort to his supporters in South Wales and heralded a resurgence of their activity there. Once again they swept eastwards overcoming all who opposed them, whilst Prince Owain marched relentlessly southwards through Shropshire, his path marked by the smoke from burning towns and churches alike.

Idris coughed as they rode out of Buildwas for the air was full of smoke from the burning town and its abbey. Except for the Friars Minor, Prince Owain had no great love for the Church and the Cistercian monks of Buildwas could now vouch for this. Glancing across at Maldwyn, Idris asked, 'Does Dafydd still ride with the baggage train?'

Sober faced, Maldwyn replied, 'Aye, his leg still bothers him sorely but, as ever, he says he'll ride with us the morrow!'

Idris nodded. 'Aye, I'd hoped his wound would have healed by now, but I fear it pains him yet.'

So it was as they went southwards on their chevauchee through Shropshire and into Herefordshire, burning and pillaging as they went and taking few prisoner other than those whose station offered prospect of ransom. It was in Archenfield in Herefordshire that Idris saw Dafydd in the centre of the fray again, his huge sword wielded with deadly efficiency as he limped from one victim to another. Sword held aloft, teeth bared in a fierce grin, Dafydd paused momentarily, before the sword slashed again and another hapless victim fell to the ground. No baggage train guard was Dafydd now but a man at arms again.

It was almost midsummer when they joined forces with the rebels from South Wales to sack Cardiff and take its castle. Such was Prince Owain's power, there was no long siege and the castle, weakly held, quickly yielded. It was there before the castle keep on its motte, that Prince Owain received a deputation from the Friars Minor of the city, whose friary he had left standing in its city street for the sake of their loyalty to King Richard. Grimy from battle, his sword still unsheathed, he stood there smiling at the three friars, his legs astride, arms akimbo, to ask with raised eyebrows, 'Why come you to this scene of battle, brothers, when you could still safely pray in your friary?'

The oldest of the three friars bowed his head in humility.

'We pray you, Lord Prince, that you may return our books and silver that we placed for safety here.'

Prince Owain laughed. 'You placed them here? I thought the Friars Minor were loyal to King Richard! Oh ye of little faith, if you had kept them at your friary your chattels would still be safe, for does not your friary still stand amongst the smoking ruins of the town?'

The friars stood there sheepishly silent for a moment before one, with a wry smile answered, 'Aye, Lord Prince, much faith

222

have we, but the good book tells us of the foolish virgin who was caught unawares. So we have, perforce, learned prudence in these troubled times, even though it might sometimes go awry!'

Prince Owain threw his head back and roared with laughter.

'Foolish virgins I might find in a nunnery, brother,' he replied, 'but prudent ones never amongst the Friars Minor!' The merriment still there in his eyes, he paused before he sighed and added, 'I fear me you've come too late, but go with my captain there who'll seek out for you anything that might yet be saved.'

As Idris came striding up to the group, Prince Owain addressed him now, 'Idris, take these holy brothers and with them seek out all that might pertain to their holy order and let it be known that any man who covertly keeps anything of theirs will answer for it with his head!'

As Idris walked off with the friars, one said to him, 'We would not wish any man to suffer such penalty, for any chattel of ours, Captain!'

Weary after the battle for the town Idris answered him curtly, 'I answer to my lord, the Prince, Brother, and I'll not answer with my neck for such as thieve a candlestick of thine!'

In the midsummer of the year of our Lord fourteen hundred and four Prince Owain's writ ran across the whole of Wales, save for those few castles on the north coast which still held out despite siege and assault. Only Time itself, it seemed, now stood in his path to victory over Henry Bolingbroke, for those castles in the north were isolated: whilst the Prince's forces deprived them of support by land the French squadron maintained their blockade at sea.

This hard won achievement had taken four long years of war: years which had hardened Idris both physically and emotionally. He seldom thought of Catrin these days and then it was only when, late at night and the better for a few pots of ale, he'd start dreaming of those days at Sycharth. Even then he'd quickly brush the thought aside, for Dafydd always seemed to read the signs aright, as he did now.

On their march from Cardiff to Monmouth they camped for the night on the outskirts of Abergavenny and Dafydd had quickly discovered an alehouse there. Weary from the day's long march,

Idris sat there gazing into his ale, his thoughts drifting back over the years to when he had first met Dafydd at Sycharth. It wasn't Dafydd's face he saw in his pot of ale though, but Catrin's. As he sat there, almost half asleep after the day's march, he saw her clearly in his imagination walking by the church meadow, heard her laughing . . .

Dafydd slapped him on the back and, with a wink at Maldwyn, called for another pot of ale, saying, 'There's no return to Sycharth, Idris bach, there never was! Old Rhys put the torch to it e're we left and I well remember Prince Owain saying then, "There'll be no turning now!" '

Idris gave a wry smile. 'There never was, Dafydd,' he said quietly. 'And no bad thing at that! Little enough taste I had for Prince Owain's dungeon there and it seemed that you and Rhys took great pleasure in seeing me there!'

Waving his hand dismissively Dafydd replied, 'A taste was all you had of lodging there and that only to let your temper cool! But sup your ale for we march north tomorrow and it's rumoured the Earl of Warwick's force is thereabouts!'

The sun was still low in the east when they broke camp the next morning and warily they made their way on the long road to Hereford. A powerful force, they were some six thousand strong and spread along over half a mile of track, with the mounted men keeping to the brisk pace of the spearmen on foot. Pausing only to rest the spearmen and water the horses, they were making good progress when, at Camstwn near the town of Grosmont, Prince Owain's scouts reported that a large force was approaching the town from the north.

With much pushing, shoving and shouted orders Prince Owain's army were soon arrayed across the nearby fields in order of battle. Idris, with his archers, was in the centre van, the men at arms and spearman on either flank. Ahead of all, Prince Owain sat astride his horse, the sun shining on the princely helmet given him by Charles of France. Ellis, his banner bearer, was at his side with young Lord Maredudd mounted at his right, the light breeze riffling his tabard and the matching trappings of his mount.

It was not a field of their choosing, for with the enemy so close there was little time for manoeuvring but, not caught entirely unawares, they were ready, prepared for battle. Idris glanced to his right to see Dafydd, both hands resting casually on his great

224

sword, its point in the earth soon to be painted red. Dafydd turned his head and waved a hand in salute, but turned quickly to his front as they heard the first murmurings of an approaching army. The sound rose quickly until they could hear the thunder of hooves, the jingle of accoutrements and shouted orders in the alien English tongue.

Over the crest of a small rise they could see the banners of the enemy now, the sun glinting on armour, the crested helmets of the knights who led the field. Remorselessly, without pause, the English came on for they would have no parley with rebels, nor would they give any quarter. Defiantly, Prince Owain's army moved forward now, to encompass the Prince as it did so, Idris gave an order and his archers notched their shafts, pointed their bows skywards. Idris ran his tongue over his lips, a moment now and it would all begin: the moment when some would see no other.

Then, as the enemy knights and mounted men at arms spurred their chargers, Idris, his head back, bawled an order and some six hundred arrows darkened the sky in their short flight to their targets. Barely had they reached their mark before another volley was on its way. Horses fell, hooves threshing, men struck by arrows fell to their knees to be trodden down by the press behind, knights struggled from under their horses, only to be felled again, but still the English tide surged on. It seemed it was only seconds before Welsh and English were at each other's throats like snarling dogs.

Casting his bow aside, Idris drew his sword and with a wild yell led his men forward into the fray. Time meant nothing there, all that mattered was to strike and survive to strike again . . . and again. Face bloodied, arm weary when there could not be both life and rest, Idris fought on until he saw Dafydd, sword pointing, his face contorted, calling urgently, 'The Prince! The Prince!'

Turning, Idris could see that Prince Owain, with Maredudd and Ellis beside him, were almost surrounded by the Earl of Warwick's knights and men at arms. All were intent, it seemed, upon taking the Prince at whatever cost. Already they had paid dearly for their attempt, for dead of both sides lay all around. Rising above the sounds of battle, Idris could hear the cry from all sides now of 'The Prince! The Prince!' and they were all rallying to the banner. Idris and his drinking companions, Dafydd and Maldwyn were amongst the first to reach the beleaguered Prince. As they all fought to rescue him, Dafydd was bawling his battle cry, 'Prince Owain am Cymru!' and hacking away impartially with his great sword, caring little whether it be lord, knight or man at arms who fell, so long as he beat a path to his Prince.

Gradually the tide of battle turned and late in the afternoon the English left the field to the weary Welshmen of Prince Owain's army.

Breathing in great gulps of air as he surveyed the battle field from his seat on a dry-stone wall, Idris turned to Dafydd who stood there drinking from a flask of water, to ask, 'Do you think we won the battle, then Dafydd?'

Wiping his mouth with the back of his hand, Dafydd handed the flask to Idris, and with a wry grin replied, 'Oh aye, no doubt of that, the English left the field to the victors!' Waving a hand at the corpse littered battlefield, he shook his head. 'But we can afford few such victories! We lost six hundred men or more out there, the English perhaps that and a score more, which they can better bear than us!'

Nodding soberly, Idris offered him back the water flask and head on one side asked, 'Is it true that we shall give chase to Warwick's men tonight?'

With a look of distaste Dafydd nodded towards the the the battlefield, where men and women alike were hovering over the corpses.

'Aye, once the crows have finished with the carrion no doubt we'll give chase.'

Idris smiled, whilst he never thought of Dafydd as a sensitive man, the man at arms always appeared to be disgusted by the scavengings of the camp followers after a battle.

'I must join the scavengers,' Idris said wryly, 'for I must seek out my bow before they rob me of my weapon.'

'Dropped your bow, Idris?' asked Dafydd, looking surprised, 'it's not like you to lose your weapon!'

Idris grinned. 'The English were almost upon me in their mad charge, I had barely time to draw my sword!'

Dafydd scowled. 'I always say that if a man looks after his weapon it will look after him! Bad enough that Ellis lost the Prince's banner to the English, but for an archer to lose his bow . . . '

With a sheepish grin, Idris walked wearily away, leaving Dafydd, lost for words, shaking his head despairingly.

Chapter Twenty-seven

There was little rest for Idris after the battle at Camstwn, for soon Prince Owain's army was in pursuit of Richard Beaumont, the Earl of Warwick. Some miles from Camstwn, near the town of Grosmont, the Earl was brought to battle and, once more, the opposing armies fought furiously throughout the whole long day. At its close, as the remnants of the English army fled the field, the sun tinged the western sky ominously red, reflecting the carnage of the battlefield. The Earl of Warwick's force that had so imperiously charged at Camstwn was defeated yet again, its power broken, despite Prince Owain's reluctance to engage the enemy in such set piece engagements.

Idris was gathering his surviving archers together after the battle when Prince Owain and Dafydd, returning after pursuing the defeated English army, reined up alongside him. Wide-eyed their horses stood there, flanks steaming, breath like smoke in the cool evening air, exhausted after the furious chase. In contrast the Prince sat there soberly, not elated it seemed at their victory but dull-eyed, frowning, as he asked, 'How many of your archers paid their due this day, Idris?'

Idris wiped his mouth with the back of his hand then glanced around at his assembled archers before, shaking his head, he replied, 'The muster is not yet complete, my lord, so I do not know, but I would hazard nigh on two hundred will not bend a bow again.'

Prince Owain gave a weary smile. 'So many, Idris?' He shook his head and sighed, 'Yet every one amongst them full earned his pay today and stood his ground to break the English charge before it even began!'

'Aye my lord,' replied Idris grimly, 'earned their pay, albeit paid in so much ground!'

Prince Owain paused before saying sharply, 'If man lived forever it would be a crowded place in which we dwell!'

Idris nodded at the battlefield. 'Oh aye, my lord, but if we win many battles such as this, there'll be no fear of that!'

With one stern glance, his mouth set, eyes blazing, Prince Owain turned his head and, spurring his horse, rode off at a gallop.

Dafydd glared at Idris. 'If you speak to our Prince like that again, it's me you'll answer to!'

Idris jerked a thumb towards the battlefield. 'I speak like that, for my archers lying there must lie silent! We cannot win the field against the English yet lose one for every one of theirs, it's victory at too great a price, as you've said often enough. Is the butcher's bill today one that we can really afford, Dafydd?'

Dafydd gave a great sigh. 'No, Idris, it was a Pyrrhic victory I fear.'

Idris snapped, 'I do not know who this Pyrrhic is, but I do not like the way he wins his wars!'

Dafydd it seemed wished to change the subject for with a wry smile he said, 'We camp here tonight, Idris and together on the morrow, escort the Prince to Machynlleth.'

Perplexed, Idris frowned as he asked, 'Machynlleth, is that far?'

Dafydd smiled. 'It's near Aberystwyth, so it will get us far enough from here, but you will need to guard your tongue if you would wish to reach it whole!'

As they made their way through Wales by way of Hay on Wye, north of the Black Mountains, then Llandridnod Wells and Rhayader, Idris asked Dafydd dryly, 'Why do we ride to Machynlleth, Dafydd, should not we chase Beaumont back to his stronghold at Warwick and beard him there?'

Dafydd glanced at him scornfully. 'Your tongue will yet take you to a dungeon, if you keep on, Idris! We go to Machynlleth for the Prince to hold parliament with lords who even now assemble there from all of Wales.'

'Parliament?' asked Idris, frowning, 'I thought it was held by Henry in his Westminster Palace.'

Dafydd sighed before answering patiently, 'Aye, and few Welsh may have their say there, as Prince Owain knows to his cost! Prince Owain calls his parliament for it is the very evidence of his governance over all Wales!'

Idris scratched his head. 'Why does he need this parliament when all know that, by the power of his sword, Prince Owain's writ runs over all Wales?'

'Do you think,' asked Dafydd, 'that if we run the last Englishman from Wales peace would reign here, with every man hearkening to Prince Owain's each word?' He shook his head. 'We Welsh were ever warring tribes, not one family content within its home!'

Still not satisfied, Idris persisted, 'Will this parliament then cure all such ills?'

Grinning, Dafydd replied, 'Never, did it hold a dozen such as you who questioned every word!'

With that he spurred his horse away to the head of the column, leaving Idris still frowning in puzzlement.

The brownstone house in Machynlleth was no Westminster Palace. It was there, however, that some fifty of the uchelwyr — the gentry — from all over Wales assembled for the first parliament that had been convened in Wales for nearly a hundred and thirty years. There was an air of expectancy amongst those who gathered there as Prince Owain entered, but none could doubt that he was their acknowledged Prince.

From princely coronet to gold buckled, fur trimmed robe and scarlet cloak held by a golden brooch, to the regal golden sceptre in his right hand, he was indeed every inch a prince. A prince who had won his right to such title not merely by inheritance, not even by his undoubted royal lineage, but by his success in battle against a more powerful foe.

A sober faced Hywel Cyffin, the Dean of St Asaph, dressed in his clerical regalia was at the Prince's elbow, as if giving the church's blessing on the parliament, and followed sedately as the Prince walked to the throne-like chair at the head of the table. After calling on the Dean to pray, the Prince, through lowered eyes, looked around the room assessing the support he might receive and where opposition or jealousy might lie. He smiled,

229

Dafydd Gam at least had not answered the call, for which the Prince had little regret. All knew that one-eyed Dafydd had that eye only for himself, at least when he was not fawning upon Henry Bolingbroke!

Dean Cyffin was never short winded and his prayer echoed the importance of the occasion in length if not in substance. At last he was finished and Prince Owain, raising his head and glancing around the crowded table, smiled as he addressed them:

'Welcome my lords, to this first parliament to be held on Welsh soil since Llewellyn the Great held such assembly. It is to our nation's shame that over a hundred and thirty years has passed before we gather in such governance of our ancient Principality.' He paused before adding, 'Nor will such time pass before we assemble here again!'

There were murmers of approval from around the table, though some few remained ominously silent. Prince Owain's cousin, the ginger haired, bluff, Ednyfed Tudur was the first to respond and he rose to glare around the table as if daring any to contradict.

'We all have heard, Prince Owain,' he said in his gruff voice, 'news of your victories over Warwick's power in Monmouth. This welcome news is evidence, if such was needed, that Bolingbroke's feeble hold on Wales grows weaker by the day!'

Hywel ab Evan, portly and pallid of face whose manor sat appropriately on the fence, or borders, of Pembroke glanced slyly at Ednyfed.

'Victories they were indeed . . . from what we hear,' he said in qualified agreement, 'but at great cost,' he shrugged, as if disclaiming responsibility, before adding, 'if what I'm told is true!'

Others, stolid faced, were looking at Prince Owain, waiting for his reply, and he sat for a moment just gazing steadily at Hywel ab Evan before saying quietly, 'It is four years or more since first I set out from Sycharth to unsheath my sword against England's power. Even then I knew it would not be without cost and cost indeed there's been to get thus far, as much for me as any here! Nor were our victories at Camstwn and Grosmont without their cost in blood, but I and mine stood wager for that cost that some might only talk about!'

He smiled placatingly. 'Such talk, however, has its rightful place in our debate and, conscious of England's greater power, when the fighting lulled, my hand has never idle been in seeking allies. My envoy, Gruffydd Young, has been graciously received by Charles of France, who has furnished arms for the pursuance of our struggle. Even as we talk French ships of war do battle with the English and raid the southern English ports. French squadrons too, have aided in the capture of the castles on our western coast and soon now their promised soldiery will arrive to aid our cause.'

There were cries of 'When?' 'Where?' 'How many?' and as he sat there smiling, he wondered how much of this talk would reach the ears of Henry Bolingbroke, so would only answer 'Soon . . .' and 'Enough . . . ' Such was enough to worry Henry, he thought and yet too little for him to act upon!

The following three days spent at Machynlleth were not idle ones for Prince Owain, involved as he was in establishing the structures of statehood. There was little to occupy Idris and Dafydd other than to keep a watchful eye on those who sought the Prince's company. Whilst none there were overt enemies of the Prince, there were some whose friendship or support might yet be questioned. Ever mindful too was Dafydd of that earlier Owain, Owain Lawgoch, murdered in France by a spy in England's pay.

The two captains were not sorry therefore, when at last all the talking was over and, with the last of the lords departing from Machynlleth, they also gratefully rode away with Prince Owain to renew the summer campaign.

One of the problems of state that exercised Prince Owain's mind at Machynlleth and was foremost in his discussions with Hywel Cyffin, was the Great Schism. This was the rift caused in the Church by the election in Rome of a rival pope to that of Avignon, where, controlled by the French kings, popes had dwelt for the greater part of the previous century. It was a problem for Prince Owain largely arising from his alliance with Charles of France. Charles, like Robert of Scotland, supported the Avignon pope, whilst Henry Bolingbroke, as all other English kings, supported the pope of Rome. So too, until now, had Prince Owain. It was apparent though, that his alliance with France was dependent upon him changing this allegiance and acknowledging the Avignon pope. Moreover Gruffydd Young, recently returned from

231

his negotiations in France on Owain's behalf, had been promised the see of Bangor . . . by the pope of Avignon!

As he rode along with Dafydd and Idris by his side he thought regretfully that on balance he preferred such seers as Crach Finnant to either popes. Smiling he turned to Dafydd, to ask in jest, 'Which pope do you support then Dafydd, Rome or Avignon?'

Eyes widening, Dafydd did not answer for a moment, before replying, 'Why, my lord, it's not a question that I often ponder on, but where I go when I pay my due I fear I'll meet them both and preaching at me yet!'

Prince Owain laughed. 'No greater aid in battle would I seek than yours, Dafydd,' he said, 'but to help me choose a pope, then I will need further counsel!'

Two days after leaving Machynlleth, Prince Owain and his escort approached Harlech. Idris dreaded the thought of meeting Catrin again and as they drew near the castle hoped their stay there would be brief. However much he told himself that she mattered little to him now, he knew that nearness to her would bring him hazard greater than any he faced in battle.

Nor did he find any comfort at the sight of Sir Edmund Mortimer waiting in the bailey to greet Prince Owain as they rode into the castle. As the Prince dismounted, Sir Edmund stepped forward, his hand held out as he greeted the Prince, 'Welcome to Harlech, Prince Owain!'

Idris had no eyes though for the English lord for there, standing beside her lady mother, was Catrin, her blue eyes holding his in a steady gaze. Tearing his eyes away from her, Idris dismounted and, handing his reins to a waiting ostler, turned to Dafydd. 'You go on, Dafydd,' he said abruptly. 'I'll see the men and horses settled and join you later.'

There was a ghost of a smile on Dafydd's lips as, nodding, he replied, 'Aye, and Maldwyn will be at your side should you need help!'

Snorting, Idris turned away, to see as he did so a man standing to one side of the Lady Marged and Catrin. No Welshman he, thought Idris, as he glanced at the tall stranger. Fair haired, the man had the alertness of a bird of prey as he stood there gazing in blue eyed condescension at those around him.

Following the escort now as they walked their horses to the stables, Idris heard Sir Edmund say to Prince Owain:

'This courier arrived from the Lady Despenser, scant hours before you rode in, Prince Owain, with news of great import to your cause . . . '

Idris heard no more for, averting his eyes from Catrin, he followed the escort, anxious to reach the safety of the stables.

Prince Owain leaned back in his chair in the great hall of Harlech Castle, toying with a goblet of wine as he stared at Sir Edmund.

'And you say your uncle, the Duke of York is involved in all this?' he asked. Then shaking his head in disbelief continued, 'Why does he so need to aid our cause, when these few years past he has fought against us here in Wales?'

Sir Edmund smiled knowingly. 'Therein, my lord, lies the very cause of his disaffection! His warring here in Wales and in Scotland too, has been at great expense to his own chancellery. He has received no payment from King Henry, nor yet is he likely to!'

Prince Owain smiled. 'Bolingbroke was ever thrifty!' Then pursing his lips, he nodded slowly before adding, 'There lies our greatest hope. Plagued as he is by campaigns in Scotland, Ireland and here in Wales, his southern ports raided too by Bretons and the Spanish, his coffers will have claims even more demanding than the Duke's!'

He gazed thoughtfully into his goblet for a moment, stroking his beard, then looking up at Sir Edmund asked, 'So the Lady Despenser has intrigued with her brother and the Earl Marshal to free your uncle, the young Earl of March, from Henry's guardianship!' He paused before, stroking his beard he frowned and asked, 'But why does she seek our aid?'

Sir Edmund smiled confidently. 'Where else but Wales can Earl Edmund find refuge safe from Henry's clutch, my Lord Prince? They plan to bring Earl Edmund straight across England to Ross on Wye and would have us meet them there to take the Earl into our safe custody! Would not that be to great advantage of your cause? Since Earl Edmund takes precedence to Henry Bolingbroke in his claim to England's throne, his presence here

233

could bring the support of those English lords who even now waver in their allegiance to Henry!'

Smiling now, Prince Owain nodded. 'It would indeed! Send Lady Despenser's messenger back to her hot foot with safe conduct for his ride through Wales! Tell her that we shall gladly meet at Ross on Wye and accept into our safe custody her son, the Earl!' He grinned as he added, 'We shall meet her there! Such will be our force that if Henry Bolingbroke is there with all his power, he'll hesitate before treading on our Welsh soil again!'

Idris was standing disconsolately by the stables when she came to him. Anxiously looking over her shoulder, Catrin laid a hand on his arm.

'Oh Idris,' she whispered, her soft voice echoing the tender look in her blue eyes, 'it's good to see you again, I thought you'd never come again to Harlech!'

His heart in his throat, he stepped back from her hurriedly, his harsh voice shielding his yearning as he muttered sullenly, 'It was not of my choosing, my lady!'

Frowning now, eyes pleading, she came closer, whispering, 'Did you truly not wish to see me, Idris?'

She stood there, vulnerable, looking into his eyes and Idris, softening now, hesitated as she put her hand on his arm again, saying, 'please, Idris . . . ' then he was holding her in his arms again as though they had never been apart. They were still standing there in each other's arms when a gruff voice startled Idris and he turned quickly to find Maldwyn standing beside him.

'Prince Owain would have words with you and Captain Dafydd in the great hall, Captain,' he said gruffly, 'and he said it was urgent, so he will bide no waiting on your pleasure!'

As Catrin stood there abashed at the interruption, Idris let his arms drop to his side quickly, as if they had held nothing warmer than a tankard and, obviously irritated with Maldwyn, replied, 'Aye, tell Dafydd I will meet him in the hall!' Then, turning to Catrin, he said quietly, 'I thank you, lady Catrin, for your good wishes, I trust we may meet again before I depart.'

Eyes downcast, Catrin replied softly, 'I'll walk with you to the hall, Captain.'

Maldwyn, who still stood there, alert, taking all in, interrupted,

'Sir Edmund waits upon Prince Owain there my lady, and Prince Owain is impatiently awaiting Captain Idris!'

With that, he grabbed Idris by the arm and started walking towards the keep, leaving Catrin standing irresolutely by the stable door. As he was reluctantly led away, Idris turned on the man at arms, to ask bitterly, 'Do you ever skulk in my shadow, Maldwyn?'

Smiling, Maldwyn shook his head as he replied, 'No, Captain, it's only when danger lurks in your footsteps that I follow!'

Arriving at the door to the great hall they met Dafydd who asked straight-faced, 'I trust that Maldwyn broke not upon your resting, Idris?'

Before a scowling Idris could reply, Maldwyn said soberly, 'No, tending the horses was our captain here, better than any ostler might. Why, when I got there he had his arms around a filly's neck and so ardent was his care for her, he heard nothing of my approach!'

Dafydd replied dryly, 'It was as well that Maldwyn dragged you from your labours, Idris, or before we left Harlech you'd be fortunate indeed to clean those stables out!'

With that he turned and led the way into the great hall, where Prince Owain, with Sir Edmund beside him, sat waiting for them.

Dafydd turned to Idris, and said in a voice tinged with disappointment, 'These last few months, I thought you'd cast the shadow of m'lady Catrin off your shoulder. Now, after only a few days at Harlech and you're like a cow lowing after its calf again!'

As Idris only glared at him in reply, Dafydd snapped, 'Aye, an' it would be better that you looked like that at m'lady Catrin than me, for I care more for your neck than your arms about mine!'

Looking at the burly man at arms who made the Welsh horse he sat astride look diminutive, Idris's face broke into a reluctant smile until, laughing, he replied, 'God save me from that, Dafydd! If I had your great head on my shoulder, it's weight would bring me to my knees!'

Still serious though, Dafydd wagged a finger at him, to say sternly, 'Nothing good will come of it, Idris! Following the Prince's banner brings hazard enough, but you'll follow his daughter's petticoats only to your certain death!'

His sermon delivered he turned away, his face having the stubborn look of a man who knew equally that he had given sound advice and that it would be ignored.

Idris smiled quietly to himself, little chance there'd be of him even seeing Catrin again. On the morrow, they'd be on their way to Ross on Wye to meet those English lords the Prince had told them about. He snorted, more turncoats, for they were kin of Sir Edmund Mortimer or so Prince Owain said.

Dafydd glanced sharply at him and snapped again, 'Grunt as you like, it's sound advice I give and you take it not at your peril!'

Idris smiled. 'It is not that, Dafydd! It's that I have such little pleasure in being nursemaid to these English lords!'

Pouting, Dafydd nodded. 'Nor yet do I, yet every one that turns his coat is one less we face in battle!'

Chapter Twenty-eight

Idris need not have concerned himself either at the prospect of escorting another English lord, or of meeting Catrin again on returning to Harlech. After waiting anxiously for days at Ross on Wye, Prince Owain received news that almost within reach of safety, the fugitives had been captured again by Henry outside Cheltenham. His disappointment at the news was somewhat assuaged on learning that the Duke of York, an erstwhile champion of the King's cause in Wales, was now safely housed in the Tower of London at the King's pleasure.

It was not only Prince Owain who had mixed emotions over not returning to Harlech with the young earl. Idris was quietly thoughtful as they rode out of Ross on Wye and Dafydd turned to him with a sly smile.

'The rest of summer we can safely spend campaigning, Idris,' he said, 'with no return to Harlech with the English lords for us!'

Idris scowled. 'Aye, and Maldwyn no longer to be my nursemaid!'

Dafydd grinned as he replied, 'In battle or in boudoir, he'll watch your back as well as mine!'

There were no great battles, however, for Idris that summer for it was spent, more profitably for him, in raiding along the marches, raiding which continued sporadically throughout both autumn and winter. The end of the year found Prince Owain, with Idris and Dafydd in his retinue, in the northern marches of Wales with much coming and going of messengers. It seemed to Idris, that the Prince's presence there was no mere coincidence. These messengers, who always came to the Prince's camp covertly and at night, always departed eastwards whence they came long before break of dawn.

February of the year fourteen hundred and five was a cold month in a chill winter and a dusting of snow lay all around the archdeacon's house in the town of Bangor. Idris stamped his feet and, pulling his cloak closer around him, frowned as he asked Dafydd, 'Who are these English lords who gather here with our prince, Dafydd?'

Dafydd shrugged. 'I do not know, Idris,' he muttered as he clapped his hands together, 'nor do I greatly care so long as they leave as quickly as they came, for the longer they stay in there, the longer we freeze out here!'

In the warmth of the archdeacon's house Prince Owain was less anxious for the English lords to depart, for their presence there was the culmination of months if not years of intrigue that some might call diplomacy. Seated beside the Prince was his cousin Ednyfed whilst either side of the two cousins were Bishop Trefor and Bishop Byford. Foremost amongst the English lords present was the Earl of Northumberland, accompanied by the royal councillor Lord Bardolf and Thomas Mowbray, the Earl Marshal.

The Earl Marshal was no stranger to such intrigue for he had also been involved in the abortive attempt to release the Earl of March from Henry's 'guardianship'. Now he was involved in the most overt threat yet to Henry's claim to sovereignty over England and Wales. The treaty, the Tripartite Indenture, to which they were all to put their hand, divided Henry's realm into three. The Earl of Northumberland was to have the north of England and Edmund the Earl of March, presently held prisoner by Henry again, southern England. Prince Owain, content that his powerful neighbour was to be so divided, was to have the whole of Wales including the area west of Severn, for him and his heirs.

With the departure of the rebel English lords, Prince Owain was well satisfied with the result of the long and secret negotiations culminating in this Indenture. Not only with the indenture itself, but the fact that such powerful English lords were prepared to so openly declare themselves against King Henry.

Idris dusted the snow off his cloak as he watched the Englishmen ride away. He too was pleased at their departure and grinned at Dafydd as he said, 'The promise of a pot of ale and a good fire to roast my toes before, offers greater pleasure than stamping about out here, Dafydd!'

'Aye,' agreed Dafydd, 'but I fear it will not last! Those English lords did not come to pass the time of day, I warrant we'll not wait for spring before we are on the march again!'

Dafydd was proved right, for by the beginning of March he and Idris were campaigning again with Prince Owain in the northern marches, whilst some of Prince Owain's other forces in the south were marching into Monmouthshire again. The Prince was determined that, on his part, the Tripartite Indenture was to mean more than mere words and whatever happened in England, Wales would be his!

The Ides of March, however, were to prove as ominous to his cause as they had proved to Caesar. On Wednesday, the eleventh of March, the town of Grosmont, near the scene of Prince Owain's victory of the previous year, was plundered and burnt by some eight thousand of his forces from South Wales led by Lord Gruffydd ab Owain. Caught in disarray in the midst of their pillaging, the Welsh were brought to battle by Lord Talbot and the knights William Newport and John Greyndor. Unprepared for battle as the Welsh were, the outcome was inevitable, with over a thousand of them being killed in the fighting around the town and the pursuit that followed. Bad as the news of this defeat was for Prince Owain, the following month was to herald an even more serious and personal loss.

It was a fine spring day when Idris saw the man riding furiously towards the camp as though pursued by Lucifer himself. Reigning up alongside Idris, he leapt off his horse and frowned as he said, urgency in both mien and voice, 'I have news from Usk for Prince Owain!'

Idris stood there for a moment, silently staring at the man, but he was so obviously a messenger that Idris did not demur and, though on the alert, took the man to the Prince. Idris stood there, hand on sword, as the man knelt before the Prince before, rising, to say, 'I bring news from Usk, my lord!'

Smiling, Prince Owain stroked his beard, before replying quietly, 'Indeed? Why are you so reluctant to impart this great news?'

The man hesitated a moment then blurted out, 'It is ill news I bring, my lord and I would not have you blame me.'

The smile gone and irritated now, Prince Owain said sharply, 'Come, speak man, I am no child and often enough before have heard bad news!'

Idris, seeing that the man still hesitated, nudged his elbow in encouragement and, gulping, the messenger began hesitantly, 'It was at Usk, my lord, on the fifth day of May.'

Prince Owain frowning, said impatiently, 'Go on man!'

'Lord Gruffydd led his power against the castle there,' continued the messenger, 'but it was powerfully held by Lord Grey of Codnor who sallied out in great strength and put Lord Gruffydd's men to flight.'

He hesitated again and Prince Owain smiled patiently as though he had indeed heard worse news before. Still smiling he asked quietly, 'And where is Lord Gruffydd now?'

The man looked down, before continuing as though ignoring the Prince's question.

'Lord Grey pursued us through the hills of Higher Gwent, my lord and brought us to battle by Pwll Melin mountain. Furiously Lord Gruffydd and Lord Tudor fought, my lord, as too did every Welshman there, nor did any leave the field until the English took our lord prisoner.' His face sombre now, he paused and added, 'Soon after, Lord Tudor fell and we knew then there was no hope left for us!'

Idris saw Prince Owain's face blanch and his voice was almost a whisper as he asked, 'Lord Gruffydd taken, Lord Tudor dead?'

The messenger nodded slowly as he apprehensively replied, 'Aye, my lord!'

Prince Owain shook his head as though in disbelief, before saying quietly, 'Ill news you brought, indeed!'

Then turning to Idris, he almost whispered, 'Give him ale and food, I will question him further later.'

Turning abruptly, he went into his tent and Idris stood there for a moment looking after him, not knowing what to do, yet believing in his heart that the Prince needed support as he had never needed it before. Turning to the sentry who stood by Prince Owain's tent, he said quietly, 'Go tell Captain Dafydd the Prince needs him now!'

Then, with a nod, he led the messenger away. Later, as the man

240

sat drinking his ale and munching his bread and meat, Idris asked him what had happened after Lord Gruffydd had been taken prisoner.

'Chaos is what happened then, Captain! Each man looked for his own safety as best he could and there was nothing for us but flight. Even so we left hundreds for dead, and they were better served than those who were captured. From peasant folk who dwelt at Ponfald we heard Lord Grey put to the sword all prisoners he had taken there, excepting only those of rank!' He paused for a moment as he chewed his bread, before adding bitterly, 'We left the abbot of Llantarnam, John ap Hywel, amongst the dead, he was a pious man, who earlier had taken our confessions and swore that all who fought against the English would be greatly blessed, alive or dead. I trust that those who were butchered by Lord Grey found much comfort at the thought!'

With a pat on the shoulder, Idris left him sitting there looking at his ale with the haunted look of a man who had seen more than he could comprehend. Seeking out Dafydd, he found him standing tugging at his moustache outside Prince Owain's tent.

'You saw the Prince?' asked Idris.

Dafydd nodded. 'Aye,' he said, 'I saw him! His face grey, he told me of Lord Gruffydd taken and Lord Tudor dead then said that high or low, it was a price all soldiers paid.' Dafydd shook his head. 'Then he would speak no more, but sat there silently no matter what I said and so I left. Nor is it any wonder that he grieves so for his eldest son, for there's no ransom that will free Lord Gruffydd from Henry's imprisonment. Nor will it last long I fear, for there is no doubt that Henry will exact rebellion's dread penalty from Lord Gruffydd!'

Despite the old enmity between them, Idris could not help but shudder at the thought of Gruffydd's plight, knowing that to which Dafydd referred was not mere beheading. The awful death of being hanged, drawn and quartered was a penalty that he, like Dafydd, had little doubt that Henry would exact.

Close on the heels of these setbacks came other bad news, when they heard that the men of Glamorgan, who had long been staunch supporters of Prince Owain, had finally submitted to Prince Henry, who still styled himself the Prince of Wales. Together with Lords Cobham and Grey of Cadnor, he had taken

l

a great army into South Wales and, putting to the sword all those who defied him, forced the Southern Welsh to submit. It was no great surprise to Prince Owain that riding with the English Prince was the one-eyed Dafydd Gam, as ever seeking preferment from his countrymen's blood.

Nor was that to be the end of Prince Owain's misfortunes that summer. Beaumaris Castle on Ynys Mon, one of Owain's prized captures from the English, was retaken for King Henry by Lord Scrope, the King's deputy Lieutenant in Ireland. This was indeed a calamity, for in taking Beaumaris, Lord Scrope had also pillaged the island, destroying an essential source of food supplies for Owain's armies.

With South Wales in submission to Henry and Ynys Mon ravaged and held in submission by the English garrison of Beaumaris Castle, Prince Owain urgently needed the active support of those English rebel lords party to the Tripartite Indenture. Not only them, but if the French were to be of help at all, their aid too was needed now! Urgently he sent his emissaries abroad urging these allies to act before time ran out for both them and him.

Some such help was not long in coming and although short lived it was welcome news to Prince Owain. For the second time in Henry's short reign, the Earl of Northumberland rose in rebellion again actively to pursue his own interest in the Tripartite Indenture. With him on his march south were Lord Bardolf, Thomas Mowbray and Archbishop Scrope of York together with Prince Owain's envoys the Bishops Byford and Trefor.

The King, at Derby, acted firmly and for him, with unusual decision. Marching north, he quickly brought the northern rebels to battle. With the battle lost, the Earl of Northumberland fled to Scotland with Lord Bardolf and the Welsh bishops, leaving the Archbishop and Thomas Mowbray to be executed by the King.

Joined now by his Tudur cousins from Ynys Mon, Prince Owain sat in council with them and his brothers in law, the Hanmers, in Harlech Castle. With the recent Welsh defeats, together with the news of the speedy suppression of Northumberland's rebellion by the King, it was a grave faced group who sat around the table in the great hall.

Ednyfed had already related the story of the loss of Beaumaris and Lord Scrope's chevauchee through all of Ynys Mon that followed. They all sat there quietly then as Prince Owain told them of the defeats in South Wales, the death of his brother Tudor and capture of Gruffydd, and lastly the news he had just received of the failure of the rebellion in the north.

When Prince Owain finished, Rhys Tudor sat there for a moment, frowning, blue eyes thoughtful as he rubbed his beard. Then, looking as a man might who had wagered all on a throw of the dice and lost, at last asked Prince Owain bluntly, 'Do you think then, Owain, that it is ended?'

Prince Owain leant back in his chair and stared at him, eyebrows arched, as though he had not understood the question. 'Ended?' he asked in surprise. 'Why, Rhys, it has but begun! All this is but fortune's reverse, which we have met before and overcome. We were never as strong when we first marched on Ruthin town as we are now! And soon we'll be stronger yet, for before we met I had news which should give heart to any doubting Thomas. Before next month is out thousands of French soldiery will land at Milford Haven where we will meet them in strength, then march East to show Prince Hal his grasp on South Wales is only feebly held!'

Dafydd turned to Idris with a knowing smile. 'It's strange Idris,' he said dryly, 'that three whole days have passed since we arrived at Harlech and Maldwyn has not chanced upon you with my Lady Catrin in some quiet corner. She must keep close to her boudoir or perhaps Sir Edmund is more watchful of his stock than ever he was of his archers at Pilleth!'

With a sour glance at Dafydd, Idris muttered, 'It were stranger had the constable's lady wife had assignation with an archer here in her lord's castle!'

It was not a subject that he was anxious to pursue for it was only on the previous evening that he had stood there, atop the western tower, gazing at the empty sea. Suddenly the silence of the still night was broken by a rustling, a whispering of soft footsteps on the stone staircase and he had turned to find her there beside him. A few stars peering between the clouds offered the only light and he could not see her face but he knew that it was

Catrin, for no other would come upon him light-footed there.

Surprised, his heart beating faster now, he had asked huskily, 'What do you seek here, my lady?'

His eyes accustomed to the dark now, he could see her standing there, pale hands clutched together in front of her dark dress, shoulders drooping, dejected it seemed at his curt greeting.

She just stood there for a moment before saying hesitantly, 'I . . . I sometimes come here to be alone and think of more pleasant days before this . . . this war, Idris.'

With a wry smile he asked quietly, 'And did you come you here tonight to think, my lady?'

He saw her shake her head.

'No,' she admitted, 'I came because I am frightened, Idris, and saw you go to the tower. I wanted so to see you again before you ride tomorrow.'

He remembered then when she had come to him at Sycharth, frightened at the thought of her father rising in rebellion. He smiled at how Gruffydd and Maredudd had come upon them and at the thought of Gruffydd's anger then. He softened at the thought and said quietly, 'You came to me once before when you were frightened, Catrin. It brought us trouble then, as it would now!'

She shook her head again, in sorrow it seemed now. 'Poor Gruffydd,' she said, 'I grieve for him, Idris, even now I wish I heard his footsteps on those stairs!' There had been a note of resolution in her voice as she had continued, 'I was frightened for myself then, Idris, and sought your comfort. It is for you that I am frightened now . . . for all of you! Sir Edmund has told me of all the fearful things that have befallen my father's cause.' He heard her sob now before, hopelessly, she asked, 'With Gruffydd and Lord Tudor gone, for there is little hope for Gruffydd now, who next will live only in my memory?'

Reaching out, he had put a hand on her shoulder consolingly and as she put her hand on his, she had said softly, tearfully, 'I came to tell you that I still care for you, Idris, my archer, and pray that you may safely dwell in peace someday.

He had been about to reply but she had gone, the sound of her light footsteps fading 'til there was only silence on the tower once again and, looking hopelessly to the sea, he had wondered whether it had all been only a dream.

Suddenly he heard Dafydd ask petulantly, 'Do you sleep there, Idris? Twice have I said the ostlers bring our horses and you have not answered! I trust you are more wakeful on our march than this, for there will be no ransom for us if we are taken.'

Minutes later Prince Owain was leading them out of Harlech Castle on the long march to that Little England – Pembrokeshire. As he rode out of the gate, Idris turned his head to see the womenfolk standing in the courtyard to bid them farewell. Etched forever in his memory would be the sight of Catrin standing forlornly at her mother's side.

Dafydd favoured him with a sly grin. 'You rode out the storm safely at Harlech this time, Idris, I yet may have some hope for you!'

Tongue in cheek, Idris smiled as he replied, 'Aye, more than I shall ever have for you, Dafydd.'

Chapter Twenty-nine

Prince Owain encamped around the town of Milfordhaven with all west Pembrokeshire ravaged by his raiding, for he was anxious that the French who he awaited there had safe landing. Such was the power of the host that he had gathered, there was no fear of any attempt to repel the landing even though the men of Pembroke had little love for him. For over two weeks he had been waiting there with growing impatience, watchmen scanning the sea anxiously for sight of sail.

Standing on the hillside overlooking the small harbour with Dafydd, Idris turned to ask, 'Do you think they'll ever come, Dafydd? I have little faith in aid from France!'

Dafydd nodded his agreement. 'Nor I, Idris, but if it suits them, no doubt they'll come and every man who lifts a sword against Henry will be a loving friend of mine!'

He had hardly finished speaking before a nearby watchman hailed excitedly, 'A sail, Captain, a sail!'

His excitement was not without some self interest, for Prince Owain had promised a mark to the man who first sighted the French.

With a quick glance in the direction to which the man pointed, Dafydd said dryly, 'Don't fret for your mark, man, for that's an English sail!'

With a wink to Idris though, he nevertheless set off with Idris for the Prince's tent. On hearing the news, Prince Owain beamed. 'At last!' he cried. 'We've dallied here long enough eh, Dafydd? Tomorrow we'll start our march through South Wales and gather forces as we go. With such power will we march that all South Wales will rise again and shed the meek, submissive face Prince Hal's overweening power forced it to show.'

246

It was late that afternoon though before the first French ship entered harbour. There were some thirty small transports altogether and as they entered harbour, two large men o' war lay off, to guard in case prowling English warships fell upon them unawares.

Idris had never seen so many ships and gazed bemused by all the activity as men came pouring off the ships eager, it seemed, to put their feet on dry land again. There was a great bustling around the harbour as the foot soldiers formed up into their companies and, shepherded by guides, marched off to make their camp. Screeching derricks unloaded stores of arms and strange machines, that Idris could only guess might be siege engines, were unladed and piled up on the wharfside. French sailors bawled orders in their strange tongue and boats plied to the ships that waited in the outer harbour, yet amongst all this activity Idris thought how strange it was that there was no sign that the French had brought a single horse with them.

Prince Owain stood in his canopied tent, the summer sun enlivening its red and yellow stripes. With him were the commanders of the French army, all noblemen of rank, of whom he knew from hearsay as experienced soldiers. Marshal of France de Rieux, Sieur de Hugueville, the Grand master of cross bows and the one-eyed Seigneur des Ventes.

'Ah, yes, Prince Owain,' Marshal de Rieux was saying now, his neatly trimmed pointed beard bristling in his irritation, 'You will provide the horses, eh? The winds, they did not favour us, the sea was rough, our horses,' he shrugged dismissively, 'they all died!'

Hiding his own irritation at what sounded more like a command than a request, Prince Owain frowned. 'Horses, Marshal?' he asked. 'I fear such as we may provide will be few enough . . . and those we can will not be chargers as your men at arms are used to mount. Nimble though they might be, our small Welsh horses are unused to bearing fully armoured men at arms!'

The Marshal's smile was one of condescension now.

'These Welsh horses, I have seen! They are what you call in English, ponies, are they not?' He shook his head, 'Non, Prince Owain, they will not do! My *hommes d'elite*, their feet would touch the ground, eh!'

Prince Owain bit his tongue, holding back a sharp retort, the *hommes d'elite* he knew were full armoured men of rank and he smiled at the thought of them astride the sturdy little Welsh horses. Frowning now, he shook his head doubtfully as he asked, 'How many *hommes d'elite* have you in your company, Marshal?'

With a stony stare, de Rieux replied, 'In my *army*, Prince Owain,' he shrugged expressively, 'I 'ave eight hundred *hommes d'elite*, who must 'ave destriers and your little . . . ponies, they will not do, eh?'

Prince Owain, with hopes of a quick advance through South Wales fading rapidly, nodded in agreement. It would take weeks of scouring the countryside to provide sufficient mounts for such a force of heavy cavalry. Thinking that the French had brought more problems with them than hopes of immediate aid, he sighed, the delay would rob him of any element of surprise he might otherwise have had. Bowing to the inevitable, he smiled again.

'We shall camp here, Marshal,' he said. 'And whilst we try to find horses for your force we shall make this English . . . ' he hesitated, seeking a word for Pembrokeshire the French would understand, ' . . . province, pay dearly for our stay!'

Smiling at what he seemed to feel a little victory, de Rieux, replied, 'Bon! The castles here, they will have destriers, eh?' he asked and, as Prince Owain nodded, he added confidently, 'Then we shall 'ave their horses and their castles too!'

Prince Owain grinned, such talk was more to his liking.

De Rieux had brought with him, as well as the eight hundred *hommes d'elite*, nearly two thousand crossbowmen and foot soldiers who together with Prince Owain's army of ten thousand Welshmen savagely treated Pembrokeshire as enemy territory for the next few weeks.

Laying siege to Haverfordwest Castle they defeated a determined sally by the Earl of Arundel and, in a fierce battle resulting in heavy losses to the English, gained a few much needed mounts for the French cavalry. Despite their success however, they found the castle too strongly held for it to be taken and after many assaults, the allies abandoned the siege and marched eastwards.

Nearby Picot Castle however quickly succumbed to a large force of French and Welsh men at arms. Their baggage train laden with booty from their raiding, the allies pressed on to surround Tenby, envisaging an early conquest. Hardly were they entrenched around the town, however, before a fleet of English men of war was sighted coming to the aid of the town. The delays caused by the French lack of horses were coming home to roost! Fearful for the safety of their own fleet, the French hastily abandoned the siege to rejoin Prince Owain's main force.

Idris watched with Dafydd as the French sappers cut trenches towards St. Clears Castle walls. For days now, they had been laying siege there with no sign of surrender by the defenders of the strongly held castle.

'The French are nearly at the walls now, Dafydd,' he said admiringly. 'The English bowmen have not held them back!'

His respect was not undeserved, for whilst the sappers were hacking away at the hard ground they were under constant assault by arrows from the castle walls and the nearer they approached the castle the heavier were their losses.

Dafydd fingered his moustache. 'Aye,' he responded, 'such grubbing is no work for true soldiery, give me an assault with sword in hand any day, but courage enough they have, it's true!'

Idris nodded silently, the bodies of sappers who would never reach the end of the zig-zagging trench the French had dug were evidence enough of the truth of Dafydd's remark. The sappers were attacking the walls of the castle with their pickaxes now, whilst others were erecting a hide covered shelter to save them from the oil and other missiles the English were hurling down. Idris winced, for such work was not for him either and he pitied the men who beavered there. Frowning he turned to Dafydd to ask, 'Can they indeed breach the wall by such burrowing, Dafydd?'

A voice beside him, not Dafydd's, gave him his reply, 'Oh aye, Idris, they'll breach it well enough!' It was Prince Owain, who had approached unheard by Idris, so engrossed was he at the labours of the sappers. 'For they have brought powder more powerful than any burning branches might be!'

Traditionally it had been the practice to undermine a castle's

249

walls and burn wood to crack the foundations. It was a slow, but effective enough method given time: gunpowder was not only more effective, but quicker too.

After much toing and froing of men carrying small barrels, Idris saw the sappers scurrying away from the walls along the trench, followed by flights of arrows from the defending bowmen. Not all the sappers outran the reach of arrows to arrive in safety, and panting, lean on their pickaxes, their grimy faces bathed in sweat.

The one-eyed Frenchman, known as Le Borgue was there to greet them now. He asked the sapper's leader curtly, 'Is the mine set, mon brave?'

Still panting from his rapid flight, the man nodded as he touched his helmet, the sweat running down his face.

'Oui, monsieur.'

Le Borgue turned away abruptly as he muttered, 'Bon!' Then, turning to Prince Owain, 'One moment Monsieur and you will see how we French bring down the castle's walls, eh?'

Irritated, it seemed, at the familiar form of address, Prince Owain said brusquely, 'I trust your hope becomes fact indeed, *Monsieur!* We yet need horses for your *hommes d'elite!*'

Turning again, he watched intently, as did they all, the castle walls. For minutes it seemed to Idris they watched with nothing happening, before he turned to Dafydd to mutter, 'Their magic powder avails them as much here as their crossbow men at Tenby did, Dafydd.'

With a malicious glint in his one eye, Le Borgue turned on him, to snap, 'This is no Jericho, capitaine! Have patience and you will hear a blast louder than any trumpets and the wall will surely fall!'

Stung by the rebuke, Idris sniffed, but turned nevertheless to watch the wall again. Suddenly there was a thunderous roar and a cloud of smoke and earth billowed from the base of the castle wall. Eyes widening, Idris stared at the castle expecting the whole curtain wall to crumble, for surely nothing could withstand such a powerful blast! Nothing happened though, nothing! Then slowly a whole section of the curtain wall crumbled, to come crashing down in a cloud of dust. For minutes, it seemed to Idris, there was the roaring sound of falling masonry, but all he could see was a pall of dust that hid the curtain wall. As the dust slowly cleared and he stood there gaping at the tremendous breach in the curtain wall, he heard Le Borgue say smugly to Prince Owain, 'There, monsieur, your army can . . . ' he shrugged, 'if you wish, of course, march through there well enough, eh!'

Prince Owain was silent as he stroked his beard for a moment before answering, then, grinning, replied, 'An army, monsieur? Why, I think my two captains here will take the castle now!' Turning to Dafydd and Idris, he said, 'Under a flag of truce, take my compliments to St. Clear's captain, and let this be the burden of your errand there . . . '

A few minutes later, bearing the white flag of truce, Idris accompanied Dafydd on the long, lonely walk to the breach, to stand waiting amongst the rubble there. They had not long to wait before the castle's captain appeared on the other side of the breach, his armour covered in dust, his face black with filth. Evidently he had been on the castle's parapet directing the defenders at the time of the breach. Scowling, he asked angrily, 'What seek you here after such devil's work?'

Dafydd grinned. 'Devil's work, Captain? Why, we did but bring some good Welsh air into your English stronghold and now we seek to make it cleaner yet! Prince Owain commands me to tell you that we shall shortly enter castle and town. And if you still defy, none shall be spared the sword. In his great mercy though, if you prudently submit and all your people render up their arms, all shall have safe conduct to any English town.' He paused. 'But do not dwell too long upon your thought of this, for though his mercy is great, his patience is short lived.'

The English captain stood there for a moment looking beyond Dafydd to the great army of French and Welsh poised, it seemed, for the assault. His shoulders sagged and beneath the dirt his face looked grey. Taking a great breath he hesitated, then said in a voice husky in its resignation, 'Tell Owain Glyn Dŵr that we submit.'

'Ah, Captain, I would that I could,' replied Dafydd sorrowfully. 'No submission can I receive, for that must be to Owain, Prince of Wales!' He smiled now. 'If you would walk out of here, then you must hand your sword to him and bend your knee.'

Seeing the English captain hesitate, Dafydd said quietly, almost sympathetically, 'Come, Captain, it's no disgrace to surrender to force majeure! Your castle walls are down and we, both soldiers, know you can hold out no longer. Do not sacrifice your people here to false pride but bend your knee and, by your submission, save their lives!'

All arrogance gone now, the captain, his eyes shadowed by defeat, nodded slowly as he reluctantly said, 'If you must, Captain, take me to Prince Owain.'

It was but a day's march to Carmarthen, whose defenders having already heard of the fate of St. Clears, offered but little resistance. Jubilant after such early success, the allies continued their eastward progress without opposition through Glamorgan and on into Monmouthshire. Despoiling towns and countryside alike in their passing, they turned northwards, their march taking them through Ross on Wye and Ledbury until at last their advance brought them to the outskirts of Worcester. There they paused after their long march to set up camp on the hill fort to the north west of the town. Never in its long history had the fort at Woodbury Hill seen such power gathered there nor yet such unwelcome guests, but their stay there was not to remain undisturbed for long.

Whilst raiding parties sacked the outskirts of nearby Worcester and foraging parties sought sustenance for Prince Owain's army, King Henry was already on the march from Leicester determined to bring the allies to battle and finally quell the Welsh rebellion.

They had been at Woodbury Hill for three days now and Idris scratched his unshaven chin. 'There's little profit in sitting here atop this hill, Dafydd,' he said at last. 'Scant provision do our foragers find nor is there any profit in raiding cottagers on Worcester's edge. Why do we not sack the town and march on?'

Dafydd favoured him with a knowing smile.

'Do you think that Henry has not yet heard of our march from Carmarthen and sits idly at home?' he asked. 'Even now he's on the march, and we must wait, our power undivided, to meet in strength such force he brings.' His lips pursed and brow furrowed thoughtfully, he paused before he continued quietly, 'This will be our final test I fear, Idris! If we but vanquish Henry here, then all

252

Wales will be Owain's. Yet should we fail, it will be a long march home for those of us who leave the field . . . if there is a home to find!'

The two friends had not long to wait, for looking across the valley towards Abberley Hill later that day they saw the banners of a great army as it encamped to the west of the hill. King Henry had arrived and there could be no doubt that his host was as great as theirs.

For over a week the two armies faced each other across the valley, each day drawing up in line of battle, each ready to meet the other's challenge yet neither prepared to risk all and commence the contest. Each day there were skirmishes that sapped at both army's strength, forays in which the French shortage of horses placed them at disadvantage. Prince Owain was disadvantaged too, for King Henry had far less difficulty in securing supplies for his army from the surrounding countryside than did Prince Owain. The longer the stalemate lasted, the hungrier grew the allies' army.

On the morning of the ninth day of this impasse King Henry's army broke camp and by midday, as Idris looked across the valley, there was no sign that the King's army had ever been there. Smiling he turned to Dafydd.

'Henry had no stomach to do battle after all, then Dafydd! The day is ours without battle!'

'Do you think so, Idris?' asked Dafydd quietly, as he nodded towards a grim faced Prince Owain standing nearby with the French nobleman de Rieux. 'Look you there at Prince Owain. Do you see victory writ on his face?'

Turning, Idris heard Prince Owain say to de Rieux, 'You return to Milford Haven then, monsieur?'

The Frenchman shrugged. 'Oui, mon ami, without the battle, which I fear we may 'ave lost, I must save my men, do you not agree, eh?'

Prince Owain nodded and, sighing, said with resignation, 'To Milfordhaven then!'

Prince Owain took little comfort from King Henry's retreat, and the capture of a baggage train by a raiding party did little to assuage his sense of frustration. Nor did he receive great comfort from de Rieux, whose only interest now was so obviously to reach the French ships at Milfordhaven. As they morosely made their way into Wales by way of the Teme valley, their progress had an air of retreat now rather than the return home of a victorious army.

The further their march took them into Wales, the more relations between the French and Welsh leaders seemed to deteriorate, with a sullen de Rieux desperate to reach the French ships. Less concerned with French transport arrangements, Prince Owain, dismayed that there had been no support from dissident English lords at Woodbury Hill, was already receiving reports of Henry marshalling his forces at Hereford. This news led him to fear a fresh incursion by Henry into Wales, and concern lest their retreat into Wales should be turned into a rout.

Neither he nor de Rieux had time to reflect that this first invasion of England by French forces since 1216, when they had invaded to support King John's rebels, might cause Henry to fear a war with France that he could ill afford.

When at last the allies reached Milfordhaven, there was little dignity in the French embarkation. With scant courtesy in their farewell, de Rieux and his *hommes d'elite* boarded the six of their vessels remaining there and hastily made sail, leaving seventeen hundred foot soldiers and crossbowmen in Wales under the leadership of an esquire, one le Begue de Belay.

Idris and Dafydd stood on the harbourside watching the French ships leaving harbour and, sour-faced, Dafydd glanced at Idris. 'It's a long time, if ever, since I've seen such cowardice in captains, Idris,' he said, emphasising his disgust by spitting in the harbour. 'What captain runs and leaves his men to face the hazard? One, in dire fear for his life, might flee to his disgrace, but nearly six hundred of them? Why, it's a country's dishonour they take with them to France and well rid are their soldiery of such poltroons!'

Idris nodded. 'Little faith had I in their arrival here and less sorrow at their leaving! But what now for us? We marched the breadth of Wales and eight whole days we stood there face to face with Henry's men and all for nothing!'

Dafydd clapped a hand on his shoulder and, turning led him

away from the harbour. As they walked slowly towards their encampment he said quietly, 'That, Idris was the greatest battle we never fought and our greatest defeat!'

Idris turned on him, frowning. 'Our greatest defeat, Dafydd, how can that be, when we did not even fight?'

Dafydd smiled sadly. 'Therein lies our defeat, Idris, which Henry knows as well as I! Well might we stand on the brink for one day before we go into battle, but for eight whole days Henry dared us to challenge his might and, strong as we were, we did not dare to take up his challenge.' He shook his head. 'No! Henry must have laughed as he broke camp that day, for we shall rue the bloodless victory he won there more than any he has had yet.' He was silent for a moment but Idris, sensing Dafydd had more to say, looked at him expectantly. When at last Dafydd spoke again it was with a note of resignation in his voice, 'It were better, Idris, had we fought and lost with honour!'

He did not speak again and suddenly Idris was afraid of what might befall him for the first time since that day outside the dovecote at Sycharth when he had determined to leave Prince Owain's service. But now, as then, he knew he could not leave, nor ever would, even though it meant he paid his archer's due.

Chapter Thirty

A cold March wind ruffled Idris's hair as in solemn mood he stood watching the rushing waters tearing at the river bank in their haste to reach the sea. The long wet winter had not only filled the rivers but caused both sides to pause in their hostilities, inactivity which, broken only by sporadic raiding, had sapped the morale of Prince Owain's forces. As he looked at the fast flowing Afon Dyfi, Idris gave a wry smile, his thoughts of another world and those spring days when he had walked with Catrin by Afon Cynllaith. A lot had happened since then, he thought, battles won and lost, friendships made . . . and friends like Rhys and Iestyn lost. He sighed, Catrin lost too, but at least she was safe in Harlech.

Turning, he walked in contemplative mood back towards their camp at Pennal thinking, even hoping, that the coming of spring would augur the start of new campaigns. He was nearly at the camp when he met Dafydd striding towards him, with only a hint now of the limp caused by that wound he had suffered at Caernarvon.

Dafydd smiled as he approached. 'Have you some maid hid down there by the Dyfi, Idris?' he asked before adding slyly, 'It's not the Cynllaith, where you might find a lord's daughter there in wait!'

Idris smiled as he replied without irritation, 'Nor yet a Gruffydd or a Maldwyn to fright her away!

Dafydd sobered quickly as he said quietly, 'No fright will Gruffydd give but to himself which each morning he will face anew!'

Grim faced, Idris nodded, Gruffydd they both knew, was still imprisoned in the Tower and Idris, the old enmity forgotten, could feel only pity for him now.

'What brings you here, Dafydd,' he asked, quickly changing the subject, 'when you could sup your ale by the fireside?'

Dafydd grinned. 'Me, sup ale, when there's work for us? It's bad enough that one of us should be mooning by the river, dreaming dreams of past conquests!'

Irritated now, Idris asked curtly, 'What work?'

'Why, a messenger from France has come and Prince Owain has called council here at Pennal!' He winked. 'That bodes work for us if nothing else!'

Eyebrows arched in surprise, Idris turned his head and spat, before saying curtly, 'Work such as the French brought when they last came, I would not see again!'

In the house at Pennal, not far from Machynlleth where he had held his parliament, Prince Owain sat reading again the letter from Charles VI of France. When he came to the end, he sat for a moment sipping his wine, gazing thoughtfully at the fire. The letter brought renewed hope for the alliance with the French. Hope that despite the failure of their last incursion into England, could bring renewed impetus to the rebellion which for the better part of a year now had lost its momentum.

Nor was the cost one that he could not bear, although the support of others would be essential if Charles' proposal were to be accepted. For what Charles implicitly required if the alliance was to continue was that Prince Owain should change allegiance from the Pope of Rome to the Pope of Avignon. Prince Owain smiled, he'd make Crach Finnant posthumous Pope of Wales, if that would suffice and Rome or Avignon, what did it matter? Yet he could only govern by consent and others cared for such matters far more deeply then he. He pursed his lips, he must persuade both the clergy and magnates in Wales if the war against Henry was yet to succeed. What did it matter, he thought, Rome or Avignon, if Wales were sovereign once again!

Others did care more deeply than Prince Owain and for days the Council debated whether they should accede to Charles' proposal, with Gruffydd Young, lately Owain's envoy to France, arguing

257

strongly in favour of Avignon. Bishop Trefor, who held the see of Bangor, argued equally strongly for maintaining the allegiance to Rome. Each day it seemed the tide of support changed from one cleric to the other and with it Prince Owain's hopes for the alliance rose or diminished.

On the fourth day, both factions were at last silent, their arguments exhausted. Prince Owain, weary of the indecision and determined that the alliance be saved, addressed the Council.

'My Lords,' he said sternly, 'the schism in the church between the Popes of Rome and Avignon, reflected as it is in our debate here, has continued for many years.' He spread his hands. 'Both popes, I have no doubt, are men of God and it is not doctrine that separates them any more than it does any here. They are divided but by politics of state. I pray, as surely as all do here, that in time they will be united once again. If they both safeguard the faith, is it not to the faith that we owe our allegiance rather than to any man, however spiritual he may be? If that is so, whilst we all pray they may be reunited in God's fellowship and they both keep the faith, it matters little whom we regard as earthly holder of St. Peter's keys. I say to you therefore that we lords temporal in Wales, guided ever by our reverend clergy, must have regard for matters both temporal and spiritual in our decisions of state. I therefore lean to the arguments of Gruffydd here and pray you all agree.'

He looked around the room, hoping for assent but there was silence for a moment before one or two heads gravely nodded, then more, until at last it was only Bishop Byford who sat there stony faced.

During the days that followed the Council, Prince Owain spent days with Gruffydd Young formulating the response to Charles' letter. After great deliberation, the cleric finally penned a letter which in its first part formally acknowledged Prince Owain's allegiance to Pope Benedict of Avignon. The second, which set out in detail the considerations on which that allegiance was offered, began:

Most serene Prince, you have deemed it worthy on the humble recommendations sent, to learn how my nation, for many years

258

now elapsed, has been oppressed by the fury of the barbarous Saxons; whence because they had governance over us and indeed on account of that fact itself, it seemed reasonable with them to trample upon us . . .

In acknowledging the primacy of the Pope of Avignon the letter went on to stipulate the conditions under which the allegiance was given . . .

Again that the same Lord Benedict shall provide the metropolitan church of St. David's and other cathedral churches of our Principality, prelates, dignitaries and beneficed clergy and curates who know our language . . . and that as a metropolitan church it (sic, St. David's) had and ought to have, suffragan churches, namely, Exeter, Bath, Hereford, Worcester and Leicester.

Again, that the same Lord Benedict shall grant unto us, our heirs and subjects and adherents, of whatever nation they may be, who wage war against the aforesaid intruders and usurper, as long as they hold the orthodox faith, full remission of our sins, and that such remission shall continue as long as the wars between us, our heirs and our subjects, and the aforesaid Henry, his heirs and subjects, shall continue.

Prince Owain put his seal to the letter with an ironic smile. Even though Henry acknowledged only the Pope of Rome, the granting of the suffragan sees of the English cities to St. Davids by Pope Benedict would rouse Henry to fury. That and the confirmation of the French alliance would be reward enough for his own change of papal allegiance!

Barely was the letter to Charles on its way before news reached Prince Owain that the King had publicly given Prince Hal discretion to grant the royal grace and pardon to all rebels who submitted, all that is excepting 'the rebel Owen Glendower'!

Idris dispiritedly tossed a stone into the placid Afon Dyfi, he had spent the winter at Pennal with Prince Owain and a small retinue, waiting for news from France, but there had been none. With the war against England now seemingly almost at a standstill, even Idris had begun to hope for news of a fresh invasion by the

French. He threw another pebble into the river, then turned at the sound of heavy footsteps. It was Dafydd, who waved a hand in greeting.

'Why stand you there playing a child's game, Idris,' he asked with a sardonic smile. 'Do you, too, contemplate seeking the King's pardon?'

'Nay, Dafydd,' replied Idris with a grin. 'If I did, I promise you would be the last to know if I place any value on my neck!'

Serious now, Dafydd shook his head as he said quietly, 'I never doubted, Idris! Yet there are others, less staunch of faith and loyalty, who've disavowed Prince Owain and bent the knee to Henry!'

Idris raised his eyebrows inquiringly, to ask, 'More, then Dafydd?'

His face grim, Dafydd nodded. 'Aye, more than we can afford, Idris! 'Tis not good news, for all of Ynys Mon have now submitted at Beaumaris.' He shrugged. 'Yet all is not lost, we still hold Harlech and Aberystwyth. It was Woodbury hill,' he added bitterly, 'we walked away, when we should have fought and damned be the cost! The raiding of the last summer has done nothing to arm the spirit of our men nor yet the coffers of the Prince. If we yet put our hope in aid from France we'll spend the winter yet again cowering in mountain cave not caring where dwells the pope!'

'I never did,' Idris answered dryly.

Whilst Dafydd had been speaking, he had thought fleetingly of Catrin, she was safe enough at Harlech, but for how long now, he wondered. Brushing the thought aside, he added more cheerfully than he felt, 'All is not yet lost, Dafydd, we've held Henry at bay for nearly six years, often with less forces than we still have. Glamorgan submitted once before, yet rose again against Henry, so too might Ynys Mon!'

Nor was the rest of the year to bring more cheerful news. Appropriately enough for the English, on St. George's Day an army, led by Ednyfed Tudor and Prince Owain's son Emlyn, was defeated in the marches of North Wales. Ednyfed escaped with the remnants of the Welsh army, to bring Owain worse news than of his defeat by the English.

Quietly, as though knowing what the answer might be, Prince Owain asked, 'How great the butcher's bill, Ednyfed?'

Bluff Ednyfed, the evidence of his defeat there in his blue eyes, hesitated as though he could not bring himself to utter the words, nor yet look his cousin in the eye. Then, his voice a whisper, 'Greater than I can tell, Owain,' he murmured. Then, taking a deep breath, he continued, 'I am sorry, Owain, for we left young Emlyn there. He was but a boy but bravely he fought until he was o'erwhelmed before we could reach him. Nor could we ever press the English back so we might bring his body home.'

Prince Owain's eyes shadowed, Emlyn was his youngest son and for a moment he just stood there looking at Ednyfed, then with a sad smile he said softly, 'No boy was Emlyn, Ednyfed. A man he was and a Prince's son at that! He died as many might if Wales shall ever be free of the English yoke!'

Ednyfed looked at him steadily for a moment, then shook his head. 'No, Owain,' he said firmly, 'only a boy he was, who should yet be with his mother!'

Then, turning on his heel, he walked slowly away.

That defeat was quickly followed by another. In June the Earl of Northumberland and Lord Balford, having made their way South from Scotland, were defeated by the English Prince of Wales in Herefordshire. Fleeing after the battle to France, they left behind them not only a beaten army but all hope of the Tripartite Indenture ever coming to fruition. With their defeat following upon Hotspur's failed rebellion, Prince Owain was left with little hope of support from English magnates.

Prince Owain could now find allies only in France and Scotland, but Robert of Scotland was dying, his son, James, captured by Henry on the way to France for safety. Scotland as an ally was rapidly becoming a forlorn hope. Only France remained and there was no sign yet of Prince Owain's Pennal letter to Charles bearing fruit.

Idris's earlier optimism was not to be lent substance, for with the approach of autumn it became obvious there would be no aid from France, not that year. Despite the heavy fines imposed on those submitting, the number of submissions to Henry's offer of pardon also grew steadily as the months passed. The question now was whether, if the French came next year, it would be possible for them to land unopposed: if not, would they come at all!

261

* * * *

The spring and summer of 1407 passed by with no sign of the long awaited French landing and the murder of the Duke of Orleans, a supporter of Prince Owain there, dimmed even further hopes of such aid. In September of that year, Idris and Dafydd stood gazing at mist shrouded Snowdon bemoaning their empty purses. The summer had been a profitless one for them, with scant booty from the little raiding in which they were involved.

'Our sixpence a day barely buys our ale, Idris,' Dafydd was muttering. 'It's a campaign we need and I see little enough prospect of campaigning now with autumn upon us!'

Idris nodded his agreement, then, hearing the clatter of hooves he turned to see a group of horsemen approaching the camp.

'Do you think they bring news?' he asked Dafydd.

'Aye, yet none good I fear,' replied Dafydd sourly. 'That's Rhys Ddu who leads and he held Aberystwyth for the Prince!'

Idris frowned, Aberystwyth had been under siege for weeks now by Prince Hal, and Rhys Ddu's presence here could be but bad news indeed. They watched Rhys Ddu greet the Prince and be led into his tent, then nosily sauntered over to the group to glean what news they might. Smiling, Dafydd asked their captain, 'Will you have a pot of ale with us, Captain, whilst you wait upon Lord Rhys?'

Grim-faced, the captain shook his head as he answered tersely, 'I thank ye, but I dare not. We ride back straight to Aberystwyth if Prince Owain gives us leave!'

Dafydd countered with a smile, 'Come Captain, a pot of ale, while I have your horses fed and watered, will not delay you!'

The captain ran his tongue over his lips as he dismounted, then hesitantly handed his reins over to a man Dafydd had called over. Minutes later the three stood supping their ale as the captain told them of the siege.

'The English Prince has nigh on a thousand men at arms and archers there,' he told them, and loyal though our men are to Rhys Ddu, starving, they say they'll hold no longer unless we are relieved. Rhys Ddu has made truce with Prince Hal and comes to Prince Owain for leave to yield and save his men!'

Eyebrows raised, Dafydd gaped for a moment before he asked in amazement, 'Is that the burden of Rhys Ddu's errand here?'

Draining his pot, he did not wait for reply, but said curtly, 'The Prince will not have Rhys Ddu yield Aber, not for all the men therein! It's key to our hold on all West Wales! Nor shall you return alone!' He turned to Idris. 'Come, Idris, we must ready our men for the march!'

They did not ride immediately to Aberystwyth, for a few days were to elapse whilst Prince Owain gathered his forces. After a forced march they eventually arrived there the day before the truce was to end, with such a show of force that brooked no attack from Prince Hal. To stiffen the resistance of the garrison, Prince Owain sent the captain to assure them Rhys Ddu would hang if the castle were not held. The eleven others in the castle who, together with Rhys Ddu, had signed the truce indenture had been given notice of their fate!

With the truce at an end and Prince Owain's forces outnumbering his, Prince Hal declined battle preferring to depart whence he came, harried constantly by the Welsh along his way. Aberystwyth was yet held for Prince Owain, but not by Rhys Ddu and for how long?

With Aberystwyth Castle secure again, a smiling Idris turned to Dafydd, to say, 'A victory at last Dafydd!'

But Dafydd turned on him to say bitterly, 'A victory, Idris? That was a victory we should never have needed! Whilst we in Gwynedd stood idly by we all knew that Aberystwyth was under siege, hard pressed, yet we did not march to bring them succour. Too many victories like this will yet cost the Prince his coronet!'

Chapter Thirty-one

'Will this snow ever stop falling?'

Idris's question was not without cause, for the first snow had fallen in December. It was now March and the little settlement in Gwyneth where they were camped was still covered in its white blanket. Dafydd pulled his heavy cloak around him and shivered.

'It will not last forever, Idris. We are fortunate to have the shelter of this cottage. Scant comfort would a tent have offered this last winter, but soon a thaw will augur spring's campaign.'

'Good fortune indeed for us,' agreed Idris. Then added wryly, 'Ill fortune for the cottagers here who did not live through the winter!'

Dafydd shrugged. 'Good fortune never comes alone! It was Ynys Mon's loss to the English that starved the people here and you should yet bless this snow that's held us here, for it has kept the English at bay all winter through!'

Idris nodded, for the harsh winter of 1407, which had added to the misery caused by the general shortage of food, had also called a halt to any fighting between the warring sides in the conflict. Now though there were the first signs of a thaw as the icicles hanging from the eaves of the cottage began to melt. Soon there would be hope of new campaigns which brought, if not victory, at least the prospects perhaps of food in plenty. He salivated at the thought of roast meat, with ale to wash it down.

Whilst the elements had called a halt to any campaigning in Wales by the two captains, the winter had not passed without a further reverse to Prince Owain's fortunes. Returning to the North of England from France, the Earl of Northumberland and Lord Bardolf had mustered their forces yet again to renew their own rebellion against Henry. Any hopes they may have had as they marched south, that Henry's forces were dormant that cheerless winter were soon dispelled. Towards the end of February they were brought to battle by the Sheriff of Yorkshire on bleak Bramham moor.

In the fierce fighting which ensued the two rebel lords were killed and with them finally died the last vestige of any hope Prince Owain might yet have had for the Tripartite Indenture.

Although the coming of spring alleviated the hardships they had endured through the winter, it brought no great campaigning for Idris and Dafydd. With Prince Owain's forces fragmented now, they spent the spring and summer of the year 1408 in sporadic raiding in the marches of North Wales. With Harlech and Aberystwyth castles still held for Prince Owain, his writ still ran in West Wales. Pembrokeshire, however, ever English, had long since welcomed back Henry's governance whilst Carmarthenshire and Glamorgan had perforce submitted to the king. Ynys Mon too was under the English yoke, dominated by English held Beaumaris Castle once again. Prince Owain's claim to the Principality now depended on holding the two Western fortresses of Harlech and Aberystwyth against all odds.

The two castles faced great odds as autumn approached that year. Besieged by the powerful forces of Prince Hal the garrisons held out determinedly. After weeks of being assailed by cross bow bolts, arrows and cannon balls they still held out despite heavy losses. With no French ships now to interdict the English seaborne supplies, nor yet supply the defenders, it was not constant bombardment but hunger that eventually forced them to yield. At the end of September, weakened by hunger, the few defenders remaining reluctantly conceded defeat and sought the King's mercy.

Idris was camped near Prince Owain's old manor of Glyndyfrdwy, where the first sparks of the rebellion were ignited, when he heard the news from a subdued Dafydd:

'Both Harlech and Aberystwyth lost,' Idris asked incredulously and, as Dafydd just nodded sombrely. 'What news of Catrin . . . and Lady Marged?'

If Dafydd knew that it was news of Catrin that Idris sought, it seemed that he had little heart to make jest of Idris's concern.

265

m

Grave-eyed he only shook his head.

'I learned nothing of them, Idris,' he said quietly, 'the messenger was in haste to tell his tale to the Prince.'

Heart pumping, Idris looked at him aghast. 'No news of Catrin?' His voice desperate now, he added, 'There must be news! Prince Owain will know . . .'

With that he turned and, leaving Dafydd standing there, hurried off to seek the Prince. The messenger was already leaving as Idris reached the cottage where Prince Owain now dwelt. Idris brushed past him to burst in upon the Prince.

Prince Owain grey of face and beard, was standing by a bare wooden table, a hand resting on it as though for support and looked up as Idris entered. There seemed little recognition though, in his brown eyes as he asked irritably, 'What brings you here, man, at this time?'

Frowning in his anguish, Idris replied, 'It is this time that brings me here, my lord!' Then urgently, 'What news from Harlech, my lord?'

Prince Owain's eyes softened, his voice less harsh and there was a trace of a smile now as he asked, 'Ah, is it news of Catrin that you seek, Idris?' As Idris nodded, he continued, 'Harlech is lost . . !'

He fell silent then as though he had no heart to say more and Idris nodded impatiently. 'I heard my lord . . . but what of Catrin?'

Prince Owain looked at him for a moment as though he did not understand the question, then his eyes clearing, he nodded.

'Ah yes, Catrin . . . she is safe Idris, as safe as any there.' The eyes clouded again and he was lost to Idris as he retreated into his own private world. When he spoke again, it was as if it were to a stranger that he spoke, 'She is a widow now, you know? Sir Edmund Mortimer, her husband, was killed there at Harlech and she so young to be widowed!'

This was a Prince Owain that Idris had never known and he stood there irresolutely, wondering what to say. At last he asked again, 'Aye, praise be that Catrin is safe my lord, but where is she now?'

Prince Owain braced himself; as though the question had brought him back to face reality. 'Safe enough, Idris,' he said, his voice firm, assured. 'Safe enough, all the womenfolk are prisoners and King Henry will not harm them . . . will he?'

Idris shook his head. 'No, my lord, the King will not harm them!'

Though his heart sank, he said it confidently, for he felt the Prince sought, as much as offered, such assurance.

Prince Owain gazed at him thoughtfully for a moment before saying quietly, 'You yearn for Catrin yet then Idris?' And, as Idris nodded, the Prince sighed and shook his head. ' 'Tis no use you know Idris . . . it never was!'

Frowning Idris asked, 'No use, my lord?' But his question was rhetorical and he continued without waiting for reply, 'Why, she needs me now! I'll find her, free her!'

He stopped there for, shaking his head, the Prince smiled, a sad smile.

'Ah, faint hope there is of that now, Idris!' Then pausing, before seemingly changing the subject. 'Your mother, she was a serving maid with the Mortimer's at Montgomery?'

Surprised at the abrupt change, Idris, nodded and eyebrows raised, replied, 'Aye, my lord?'

Prince Owain's eyes had a distant look about them now as, in a voice without inflection, he said quietly, 'Yes, her name was Eunice. I knew her once . . . a long time ago. He paused and looking Idris in the eye, added, 'Nigh on twenty-nine years ago!'

Idris frowned again. 'You knew her, my lord?'

Prince Owain nodded. 'Aye, but briefly, I knew her well!' He drew a deep breath, as though steeling himself, before he spoke again, whilst Idris stared at him in amazement, then continued, 'I once told Gruffydd the friction between you and he rose from your likeness to each other. For like enough you are in temper . . . and in looks!'

Idris's eyes widened. 'No!' he whispered, 'it cannot be!'

Prince Owain, a half smile on his lips, nodded slowly. 'Aye, Idris, it is so! I have long felt affinity between us stronger than any bond between Prince and brave captain can ever be. Now am I certain . . . as sure as man can be, that though two sons have I lost to Henry, I've gained another, the eldest of my brood!'

As Idris still stood there speechless, Prince Owain, with raised eyebrows, asked, 'Come Idris, have you nothing to say to your new found father?'

Bemused, his head in a whirl of mixed emotions, Idris shook his head, in disbelief rather than denial. Prince Owain reached out to put a hand on his shoulder.

'You shall free Catrin . . . your sister Catrin,' he said reassuringly, 'but do not strive alone to set her free, Lord Idris, for we'll yet free her . . . and with her, Wales!'

Bewildered, Idris murmured, 'Aye, we shall indeed, my lord!' and turning left the cottage less certain of himself than when he had entered there. Returning to Dafydd, still hardly able to believe Prince Owain's amazing statement, he blurted out his news.

Dafydd grinned. 'Then it's Lord Idris now! Prince Owain may well have gained another son, yet after all the learning of the art of war that you have gained from me, I have but lost a friend.'

Idris stepped back in surprise, to say, 'I, Lord Idris? You have lost a friend, Dafydd? Why it's just make believe! An archer am I yet and in what realm am I a lord? It was yesteryear the Prince's writ ran over all Wales but now, half Wales has submitted to the King. There'll be many a skirmish, raid or battle before the Prince gains ascendancy again and we may well pay our due before the warring ends.' He shook his head. 'Never fear, Dafydd we'll yet sup our ale together!'

Dafydd grinned as he touched his cap. 'Aye, my lord!'

There were to be no great battles for the two captains that year, however, and their only skirmishes were with aggressive marcher lords. Their confidence restored after Henry's successes, these lords were ever vigilant and even the occasional raiding of Prince Owain's scattered forces, met with little success. Nor were the marcher lords the only threat to Prince Owain's men. Prince Hal, spurred on by his father's exhortations, pursued them relentlessly throughout the length of the marches all summer through.

Idris and Dafydd were grateful to see winter come that year and bring an end to Prince Hal's pursuit, even though it meant cold beds and lean rations for the winter. There was no town or settlement now where they might winter, for the King's spies, it seemed, were everywhere. At last, with a small band led by the Prince they sought safety in the mountains of Mid Wales, with little promise of safety even there.

A cold harsh winter kept them secure but with scant comfort. When spring came and with it Prince Owain spoke of gathering his forces again, even Dafydd wore a sceptical frown.

'From where?' he asked Idris. 'Now spring is here, Prince Hal's forces will scour all Wales to prevent such muster, his spies whispering to him at first sign of men taking up their arms! And arms! Have we some magic store? Will France send ships to bring us more?' He shook his head. 'No Idris, it's a forlorn hope! It's raiding now for us, and poor pickings even in that!'

Despite Dafydd's pessimism though, by May Prince Owain had gathered a small army together, Rhys Ddu and Rhys Tudur having brought their men from West and North Wales to join him. At the end of May, with hopes of any further reinforcements fading, the Prince set out with some three thousand men to march on Shrewsbury town. Banners fluttering in the spring breeze, proudly they went, hopes of a resurgent Wales in their hearts.

They were not the only ones on the march near Shrewsbury though, for Prince Hal's spies were indeed active and news of their approach had reached his ears. As the spires of the town came in sight, Idris heard the tramp of marching feet, the clatter of heavy cavalry and the jingle of their accoutrements. Ahead of them in battle array was a powerful force that had not waited for them to besiege the castle but was confidently challenging them on the field of battle. Nor were the time or field of Prince Owain's choosing.

There were horses galloping, men running, orders bawled, as Prince Owain hurriedly tried to prepare his small army to meet the English in battle array. Many there were who were still out of breath as the English fell upon them and many more who had not time to draw another. Idris's archers plied their weapons furiously in their endeavour to break the English charge. Yet, so little time had they and so numerous were the enemy, it was not broken.

Though enemy men and horses alike fell, slaughtered by the cloud of arrows falling on them, others trampled over them in their haste to reach Prince Owain's ranks. Soon there was no further use for bow, for the English were upon them face to face and hand to hand. All that could be heard was the clash of steel on steel, shouts of triumph and screams of pain. Nor could Idris see how the battle went for there was no time to look, only to hack and hack again at the contorted face in front of him and there were many such faces, each one that fell replaced by another. Once in the middle of the nightmare he heard Dafydd's battle cry,

269

'Prince Owain am Cymru!' Briefly it was taken up by others, to rally or give heart, then the cry faded for all breath was needed for the deadly work at hand.

To and fro the battle surged and all sense of time or place was lost for Idris, only aware now of the desperate need to survive. Suddenly he was aware that comrades were faltering as, slowly but surely the English tide advanced. No longer faltering, some were turning, others running, not towards the enemy any longer, but away. Even as they ran some were hacked down by their pursuers. What had started as one man turning, another running, was becoming a general flight from the battlefield and glancing around he saw Prince Owain's banner fall. As he frowned in anguish, he saw Prince Owain on his charger, then saw the white flash of the prince's tabard. Saw it and knew that all was lost, for it meant that Prince Owain too had turned!

A riderless horse was running towards him, wild eyed and, with one last slash at the enemy in front of him, Idris made a desperate lunge to grab the horse's reins. The horse checked momentarily in its mad gallop, then Idris, feet flying, was running beside it. At last he managed to haul himself onto the saddle and gasping in his exhaustion, he too was fleeing.

It was dusk before the scattered remnants of Prince Owain's army; pausing in their headlong flight, began gathering in small groups. They gathered so, more to learn news of comrades and seek safety from pursuers than in any hope of becoming a strong fighting force again. Not yet, perhaps not ever. Finding one such band, Idris sought news from them of Prince Owain. Their leader, a man at arms who from his voice was one of Rhys Tudur's men, replied with more bitterness than respect:

'Is it your father you seek, my lord?' and, as Idris nodded, 'I know not where he may be, but when you find him, say Lord Rhys is dead and with him lies Rhys Ddu as well. Tell him too, I take those of Lord Tudur's men that I may find away from here to seek the King's pardon, for we'll not fight again for a lost cause!'

Idris only nodded, for he had little heart and fewer words, with which to reply. It was after a sleepless night that he found Prince Owain the next day. There were only a few men at arms and

270

archers gathered there with the Prince beside a small stream. The Prince, bareheaded, was seated on a fallen tree trunk, his horse tethered beside him and he looked up as Idris approached.

Dismounting, Idris was greeted by Prince Owain with the weary smile of a man drained of all resources. His voice strained, he asked, 'You brought none with you, Idris?'

Idris shook his head. 'No, my lord,' he said quietly. 'Alone I left the battlefield, those of my archers who were able, already left. Since then I've met only one band of Rhys Tudur's men who said both he and Rhys Ddu are dead.'

Prince Owain sighed and nodded slowly. 'Aye,' he said, 'I have been told that it was so, though I was too closely engaged to witness it.' He paused, before asking, 'This band, they came not with you then?' And, as Idris shook his head, the Prince added, 'No . . . they'll go North and seek the pardon now, no doubt.'

Standing up carefully he braced his shoulders and gazed at Idris for a moment. 'These men here, they seek the safety of the hills with me,' he said quietly, 'what of you, Idris?'

Idris frowned, his eyes questioning. 'Why, my lord, I go with you!'

Prince Owain smiled as he said softly, 'I never doubted it, Lord Idris!'

Chapter Thirty-two

There were only two of them now. For seven years they had been hunted in the hills where they had sought a transient safety. When at first their small band attracted a few stragglers from that last battle, Prince Owain had spoken optimistically of gathering his forces once again. But the days of glory were past and with King Henry's subjugation of Wales now complete there were few new recruits to Prince Owain's cause. Their early raiding gradually became not a way of regaining support, but their only means of survival. Their ranks thinned by desertion and death, even raids and hopes of another victory had gradually deteriorated into a desperate search for food, for survival.

Idris looked at Prince Owain lying huddled there, wrapped in a blanket on the floor of the cave, face pinched, his white hair and beard matted. Idris shivered and threw a few more sticks on the fire he had lit, they flared briefly, but gave little warmth.

'Father,' he said quietly, 'it's morning and I must go to find some food.' Try to find some food, he thought, as he saw his father's figure stir.

Prince Owain, bleary eyed, lay there for a moment gazing at him sleepily, then, shaking his head, muttered, 'I slept not, Idris!'

Idris smiled. 'No, of course not Father!'

Even now one of them always kept watch lest they be discovered. More often though now it was Idris who sat there at the cave's mouth, cloak pulled close around him, often nodding, but alert again at any sound.

Prince Owain nodded firmly. 'No,' he said again, 'I lay not asleep, but planning, Idris!'

Idris sighed quietly, his father was always planning these days, but it was he, Idris, who had to plan that they might eat!

Slowly, Prince Owain put the blanket aside and stiffly rose. He stood there for a moment, hand against the dank wall of the cave as though to steady himself, then shook his head. 'We must go to Monnington again, Idris,' he said reprovingly, as though Idris had thus far resisted the idea, 'and seek shelter there for a few days. It is not good for you to lie on this cold floor in winter time!'

Idris suppressed a grin, little chance there'd be for him to lie there, for one of them needed to keep awake. He looked at his father, thinking sadly how the years of privation had aged Prince Owain. No longer was he the sturdy, powerful man that Idris had first met that day at Sycharth, but emaciated, frail. The fire was still there in the eyes though, and Idris smiled as he thought, even the arrogance!

'Yes,' Prince Owain was saying firmly now, 'we must go to Monnington!'

Idris thought of the manor there, the comfort, the food it offered and he salivated at the thought. They had been to Monnington a couple of times before, hidden there by its lord, Sir John Scudamore, the one they had fought often enough. Kin he was now though, married to Prince Owain's daughter, Alice. Smiling, Idris nodded.

'As it pleases you, Father.'

It was days later that, weary after their long journey, they arrived in the courtyard of the rambling manor house at Monnington. Little food and less shelter they had found along the way, for few there were now who welcomed Prince Owain at their door. Too great were the penalties for harbouring such fugitives from King Henry's justice . . . or his wrath.

As Idris helped Prince Owain dismount, a man appeared at the manor doorway, a serving man by his attire, for his neat grey clothing was unadorned with any frippery. He smiled not as, nose uptipped, he came reluctantly towards them and drawing near said to Idris, as though to some passing vagrant, 'You here again!'

Idris stood there, legs astride, hand on sword as with steady gaze he looked deep into the man's pale blue watery eyes. When he spoke at last it was with chin out-thrust and an arrogance he remembered well from his brother Gruffydd.

'Aye,' he said, 'here again, and you had better be civil when

273

you speak to your lord's kin! Go tell your lord and the Lady Alice too, that Prince Owain has arrived.'

The man hesitated and, those watery eyes lowered now, he turned away, mumbling as he did so, 'Yes, my lord,' as though it were wrung from him with his last breath.

He had taken but a pace though before Idris said imperiously, 'What! Would you keep Prince Owain waiting here in the courtyard like some beggar?'

Turning again the servant drew a deep breath, but lacking courage, just nodded and led the way into the manor's entrance hall. Taking the Prince's arm, Idris led him gently to a settle there and fussed to see him seated comfortably until at last Prince Owain said irritably:

'Cease man! If you would a nursemaid be, a poor one would you make.' He smiled then though as, looking at Idris, he added, 'Nor yet a very pretty one!'

Tired as he was, Idris could not help but smile, neither of them could be said to be that, he thought. Grimy of face, matted hair, their clothes in rags, it was little wonder the serving man had looked on them as he would beggarmen. Idris's face sobered at the thought, what else are we he asked himself, are we not beggars seeking a night's shelter, a bite to eat? Pray God they turn us not away and the very thought was indeed a prayer. Looking at the Prince slumped there on the settle Idris knew that, were their fugitive existence to continue, it would not be long before . . .

His thoughts were interrupted by the sound of hurrying footsteps and a moment later the Lady Alice came briskly into the entrance hall. Looking at her, his heart gave a little leap, as it always did, for she was alike his Catrin as two peas in a pod. He pulled himself together, not my Catrin, he told himself, my sister Catrin.

'Oh, Father!' Alice was saying, her face agonised, her hands reaching out to Prince Owain but hesitating to touch. 'Where have you been, what are you doing to yourself?"

Prince Owain was standing unsteadily by the settle, a hand resting on one of its arms for support and he smiled apologetically before saying, 'It's good to see you again, Alice!' He hesitated then, as though seeking words he found too hard to say. 'Idris and I were nearby and thought to see you my dear . . . ' he paused again before adding lamely, 'but no, we cannot . . . we

274

must not, stay.'

'Oh, Father,' Alice said again, striving unsuccessfully it seemed to keep the pity from her voice, 'of course you must stay, Sir John would have you stay! Why only yesterday a messenger from the King arrived . . . ' and here she glanced at Idris, 'to offer both of you his pardon. Do you but agree, here you can always stay and safely so!'

Prince Owain drew himself up, eyes blazing with an age old fire and spluttered, 'Seek pardon from a usurper's son?' he asked angrily. 'From Henry? When he and his father both have trampled o'er all my Principality? Never! My pardon should he seek for all the wrongs of his usurped governance!' Proudly he pulled his rags around him and turned to Idris. 'Come, Idris,' he said sharply. 'It is time we made our way, there is much for us to do this day!'

He faltered then and grey faced, his hand slipped from the settle's arm. Even as he fell, Idris was there to support him and gently lower him to the settle again. Idris turned to Alice, and eyes pleading, shook his head. 'No talk of pardon, Alice,' he said quietly. 'But if you have pity in your soul, some food for him, perhaps some wine!'

Mouth open, she looked at him for a moment then, silent now, she hurried away. A few minutes later Prince Owain was lying on the first soft bed he had seen for months, his rags discarded, his body bathed, servants scurrying around bringing steaming broth, bread and wine.

Seeing the Prince lying there, Idris smiled, thinking there was yet hope. Turning he walked away to see the horses settled, for it was all they had left now, their mounts and their swords. He was crossing the courtyard when he met her. Mary was Sir John's eldest daughter by his first marriage and she smiled as she greeted him. 'Idris! You're back!'

Different to the way the servant had greeted them he thought, even though the words were much the same. Not just her words, but the way her blues eyes matched her smile made him feel welcome there. He smiled too.

'Aye, but for a little while, Mary,' he replied, 'then we must be on our way again.'

Her face fell and she frowned as she brushed her fair hair back with a soft white hand.

'But the King's pardon . . . ' she began.

Lips pursed, Idris shook his head and said quietly, 'Though the old king is dead, the Prince will seek no pardon from King Henry, not now or ever.'

Mary frowned. 'And you, Idris, what of you, will you not seek pardon? Maredudd has and you are . . . you are both welcome here.'

He stood there looking at her for a moment, thinking of being no longer hunted, of a peaceful life there at Monnington, perhaps even . . . he brushed the thought aside.

'No, I'll not seek pardon, Mary,' he said at last. 'The Prince has only me now and I'll not leave him.'

Her face crumpled and there was a touch of pleading in her voice as she asked, 'Can't you persuade him, Idris . . . '

He smiled as he interrupted her. 'No, Mary not even though the old king, the usurper, is dead, for were the Prince an easy man to persuade, Mary, these last few years would have lent force to any pleading!' He laughed then continued, 'It would be easier perhaps for you to persuade young King Henry to seek the Prince's pardon!'

She smiled wistfully. 'But you'll come back to Monnington?'

He shrugged. 'Aye, if it is safe, Mary, we'll come back, if it so pleases the Prince.'

With a toss of her head, she turned and hurried back into the manor. Idris watched her go for a moment then, with a sigh, he too turned, to see the horses settled for the night.

Going back to the manor Idris found that Sir John was away on the King's business and thought that it were better so. Bad enough for the knight that he was married to Prince Owain's daughter without being found harbouring fugitives who even now rejected the King's offer of pardon!

As the days passed there, with the luxury for him of food in plenty and a warm dry bed in the loft above the stables, he sometimes thought how easy it would be for him to succumb and take up the King's offer. He knew in his heart though that he could never look Prince Owain in the eye and tell him so. Restless too, were the nights he spent on his straw bed thinking of Catrin, of Dafydd and of the long, long years with Prince Owain, their victories and defeats. Lying there now he wondered whether Dafydd had ever left the field at Shrewsbury. He smiled, Dafydd, perhaps a man at arms in some English castle now, was probably

276

even at this moment, drinking ale and telling tales of his battles with the Scots!

He turned his face to the straw, for Catrin he knew was not sipping wine at some lord's table. At their last visit to Monnington, Sir John had told the Prince that both she and the Lady Marged had died. Poor Catrin, he thought, dead and buried now in alien soil at St Swithins in London. Gruffydd too. Never was he freed, for he died a prisoner and was still a prisoner in a way, for it was in the Tower's grounds he lay.

Face after face jostled each other in his mind's eye, memories too of their laughter, their fears and hopes. It was Mary's face though that was there as at last he fell asleep and he smiled as he remembered her saying, 'But you'll come back, to Monnington . . . '

A pale light filtered into the stables of Monnington Manor and Idris stirred into alertness on his bed of straw at the creaking of an opening door. His breath held and hand on the sword beside him, he rose silently and stooping, crept to the ladder. He smiled and relaxed as he saw it was Prince Owain, then frowned, wondering what his father might be doing there. Clambering hastily down the ladder, he turned his head to ask, 'Is ought wrong, my lord?'

The stooped figure turned towards Idris, not quickly as one alarmed, but with the weary movement of a sick man. Even in the dim light of the stables, the Prince's face looked pale and lined, his eyes lack lustre.

'Nothing wrong, Idris,' he said quietly. 'Go back to sleep, it's early.'

Turning he walked over to the stalls where they always kept their two horses saddled, ready for flight, and opening the gate to his own horse, began leading it out. Idris was beside him now, a hand on the horse's bridle, frowning, eyes peering in his surprise.

'Why, my lord,' he asked, 'where would you ride, the sun not yet risen?'

Prince Owain smiled and there was a glimmer of the old fire in his eyes now as he said firmly, 'I would ride by way of Sycharth, Idris, where I shall rest and dream awhile, then on across the Menai to Ynys Mon and Bryn Celli Ddu. In but a little while it will be the solstice when the Venus gate will open there.'

As Idris stood there without understanding, Prince Owain frowned in irritation. 'Do you not see, Idris? My time is nigh and I would stand in Venus' light within Bryn Celli Ddu, for Crach Finnant oft told me great magic is worked there!'

Idris shook his head. 'No, my lord it is too great a journey for you to undertake! If indeed you must go, then I ride too!'

Prince Owain smiled sadly and patted him on the shoulder.

'No Prince or lord am I, Idris! I am but a rebel fugitive, which matters little now, for my time is due and on this last journey I must ride alone.'

Idris looked at him for a moment, as though looking into a mirror in which he saw the image of his own future. His eyes moist, he said softly, 'E're I knew you as Prince or Father, I served you, my lord and I'll serve you yet awhile.'

So saying he led his own horse out of its stall and together they led their horses out into the courtyard and mounted. With a last look at the manor, the Prince and Idris ab Owain walked their horses quietly out of the courtyard and set off on their long journey.

They stood there together in the dark, father and son, beside the stone pillar at the innermost end of the tunnel in Bryn Celli Ddu waiting for what Idris knew not. Prince Owain was relaxed now though, assured, as though knowing what was to come and he put a hand on Idris's arm. 'Patience, Idris,' he said quietly, ' 'twill not be long now! Watch the Venus gate and soon you'll know the purpose of our visit here.'

Idris turned towards him, eyes questioning, but could only see the Prince as a shadowy figure. He was about to speak when the Prince gripped his arm as though urging him to silence and Idris held his tongue. Suddenly Idris saw a bright star appear in the Venus gate, and there was a sharp intake of breath beside him as Prince Owain's hand held his arm in a vice-like grip. As the star slowly moved towards the centre of the gate, Idris held his breath, caught up in the air of mystery that enveloped him. The star was at the centre-point of the opening now and suddenly the interior of the tomb was bathed in a bright, warm light that for a brief moment almost blinded him.

There was a gasp beside him and the years seemed to fall away, leaving a young Prince standing there, hand on sword, firm, resolute, all doubts of what the future might hold gone. Looking down, the Prince saw the frail form of Prince Owain lying there, face relaxed in the smile of the peace he had found at last. Bending down Prince Idris ab Owain tenderly picked up the slight figure of his father and gently carried him along the stone walled tunnel and away from Bryn Celli Ddu.

Author's Note

More than half a millennium has passed since Owain Glyn Dŵr, larger than life then as now, strode through victory and defeat into the pages of history. This, together with the fact that the sources from which historical facts have been gleaned are often contradictory, can inevitably give rise to argument as to who did what to whom and when.

It will never really be known now whether Owain raised his rebellion for purely idealistic reasons of national sovereignty or personal aggrandisement, from pique or lust of power. What is undoubted is that he nearly succeeded against immense odds, if for that reason alone he is justifiably a figure of legend.

Whilst I have endeavoured to reflect fairly the events of the rebellion as well as the brutality of the time, from which neither side were immune, this novel is really the story of Idris the Archer. Idris might well have been one of Owain Glyn Dŵr's real life illegitimate offspring and as such doubtless could have met Catrin.

Catrin did indeed marry Sir Edmund Mortimer after his capture by Owain Glyn Dŵr. I think it unlikely that this marriage was the love match represented by William Shakespeare, but rather think it far more likely to be one of political expediency, something not unknown then or later. Poor Catrin, like her mother and brother Gruffydd, died a prisoner in London, after her husband Sir Edmund was killed when Harlech Castle fell to the English.

It is ironic that, whilst Owain Glyn Dŵr's rebellion failed, his kin were eventually to gain the English throne. Henry Tudor, a direct descendant of Owain Glyn Dŵr's cousin Rhys Tudur of Anglesey who had supported Owain ably during his rebellion, landed at Dale in Pembrokeshire in 1485 to seize the throne from Richard III and become Henry VII. Even more ironic is the fact that it took nearly six hundred years after Owain Glyn Dŵr called his Parliament together at Machynlleth before another such Assembly was held in Cardiff.

It is appropriate enough for such a legendary figure as Owain Glyn Dŵr that, like King Arthur before him, nothing is known of his death or burial place. Some believe that it was in 1415 near the Manor of Monnington where his daughter Alice lived after she married Sir John Scudamore. Perhaps, though, he is just waiting beyond the veils of time, with Idris and Dafydd, to raise his banner once again – when the time is right!